Praise for Donna Keel Armer

"Donna Keel Armer hits another home run with Moringa-The Tree of Life. An electrifying second novel in the Cat Gabbiano Mystery Series."
–Dana Ridenour, author of the award-winning *Lexie Montgomery FBI series.*

"Donna Keel Armer's second novel in her Cat Gabbiano Mystery Series continues the spine-tingling page-turning allure of The Red Starfish. After fleeing Italy, Cat returns to her South Carolina Lowcountry home. While struggling to rebuild her business, she stumbles into a covert FBI operation on an abandoned plantation on the cusp of a wedding reception, a setting interwoven with ties to a Spanish count, a state senator, and an undercover federal agent. Once again, fate calls on Cat to solve a seemingly impossible mystery as she struggles to find her footing against the backdrop of corruption, human trafficking , and dangerous liaisons. Armer has gifted new and returning readers with a resolute and emphatic heroine, one who fails and falls, and nevertheless rises again. Cat's appeal is universal; she is on a journey, as are we all."
–Jonathan Haupt, coeditor of *Our Prince of Scribes: Writers Remember Pat Conroy*

Praise for Donna Keel Armer

"Set against the backdrop of marshes and Oaks draped with Spanish Moss in South Carolina, Moringa – Tree of Life is book #2 in the Cat Gabbiano mystery series. It's a page turner of a mystery that addresses real life and difficult societal issues. Like Armer's other novels, readers are drawn into the lives of her characters and their stories and are pulling for them all the way. Moringa – Tree of Life is yet another beautifully crafted masterpiece destined for an award."

—Author of seven books, Niles Reddick's latest collection is Who's Going to Pray for Me Now? and his latest novella is Forgiven.

"Moringa, Tree of Life – the second of the much-anticipated Cat Gabbiano mystery series - is a compelling tale that intertwines the alluring landscape of South Carolina's Lowcountry with the mysterious dark side of human nature. At the center of the story, we find our hero, Cat, a local caterer whose strongest desire is to lead an uncomplicated life while recovering from recent trauma and the stunning loss of her life-long friend. Still, at the start of this narrative, Cat unwittingly stumbles upon a dark web of intrigue and danger. As she weaves in and out of suspicion, secrets, and shadows., readers are drawn into themes both intimate and global –from resilience and personal growth to the sinister grip of human trafficking.

Donna Keel Armer is a rich storyteller in the Southern tradition. Her voice is at once literary and down-to-earth. Moringa, Tree of Life is the page-turner you are longing for, combining mystery, magic, a touch of romance, and the timeless question of what it means to find 'home.'"

—Karen Warner Schueler, author of The Sudden Caregiver: A Roadmap for Resilient Caregiving and president of the coaching firm, Tangible Group

Praise for Donna Keel Armer

"Set in the beautiful and mysterious Lowcountry of South Carolina, Moringa-The Tree of Life is a first class crime story with just the right touch of romance to make it appealing to fans of both genres. Donna Keel Armer is a master story teller, and her intrepid and complex character Cat Gabbiano is a wonderful addition to the lore of the modern crime novel and not to be missed. I highly recommend this terrific book!!"

–Michael Vecchione, First Deputy District Attorney and Chief of Rackets (ret.), Brooklyn District Attorney's office; author of *Fallen Angel-True Crime Fantasy series*; *Homicide is My Business-Luigi the Zip, A Hitman's Quest for Honor*; *Crooked Brooklyn-Taking Down Corrupt Judges, Dirty Politicians, Killers , and Body Snatchers.*

MORINGA

TREE OF LIFE

CAT GABBIANO MYSTERY SERIES
BOOK 2

DONNA KEEL ARMER

For Carol
Thanks for coming along on Cat's
Lowcountry Adventures—

Grande Gioia
Great Joy!
Donna

RedPenguin
BOOKS

Also by Donna Keel Armer

Fiction
The Red Starfish

Nonfiction
Solo in Salento: A Memoir
Un'americana in Salento (Italian Translation)

Anthologies
London: Smokes, Blokes and Jokes of Foggy Town
Darkness Before Dawn
Paris: Love, Loss, and Longing in the City of Lights
If It Waddles and Quacks, Is It a Duck?
Centuries of Stories of the Internal City Rome:
The Gritty City

Red Penguin Books

Bellerose Village, New York

ISBN

Print 978-1-63777-579-0 | 978-1-63777-580-6

Digital 978-1-63777-578-3

For All The Voices That Are Not Being Heard
&
Sempre Ray

Contents

Prologue   1

Moringa∼Tree of Life   3 - 324

Acknowledgements   325

"You Have Become a Forest" by Nikita Gill   329

Author Notes   330

Preview of *One Note Murders*   335

About the Author   340

Maybe You Are Searching Among the Branches
For What Only Appears in the Roots
—Rumi

Prologue

The predator wants your silence. It feeds their power, entitlement and they want it to feed your shame ∼ Viola Davis

South Carolina has over a half-million acres of salt marshes, more than any other state.

The coastline teems with life. Species range from the sublime to the dangerous. A good day is full of blue herons, nesting ospreys, snowy egrets, rusty sandpipers, marsh wrens, clapper rails, and a Broadway production performed by a pod of dolphins dancing in the Beaufort River.

On a bad day, spiders, mosquitos, and no-see-ums wait to attack. A marsh snake may slither out of the spartina, or a gator might open its jaws to a foot straying off the path. Pluff mud, if disregarded, can suck a body into its sulfurous thickness and will it to suffocate.

But it is not nature that is without a moral compass. It is the human predator, the one who has a choice and chooses evil.

Carrington Point Plantation was built on the salt marshes before the Civil War. Early on, it had been an indigo plantation. As climate, erosion and populations changed, crops shifted from indigo to cotton. Tumbled-down structures, skeletal remains of old cotton sheds, still languished on the property. The once fertile land lay barren for years until nature reclaimed it.

Kids, notoriously mindless beings, had been warned to stay away. But in a small town, where else would they go but to the place they've been told to avoid? Picnics, campfires, sing-alongs, lost virginity, and drunken brawls were regularly scheduled events known only to kids who could keep their mouths shut. That is until one of their own went missing and was never found. In this small, safe town, it was assumed that it would never happen again. Until it did.

After the disappearance of the first young girl, the plantation was shuttered, boarded up, and abandoned for years. The locals couldn't remember a time before. If asked when someone last lived there, they'd mutter, *nobody in my lifetime.* Sometimes, they'd say, *Don't be going out there. It ain't safe.* If questioned further, they'd avert their eyes and swiftly walk away.

Sheriff Blackwell inspected his leather-clad feet. His favorite boots were ankle deep in the murky river. The worst kind. Salt. It would eat away at the leather if he didn't get out of the water soon. In his mind, he was already back home with his shoeshine kit, carefully wiping off the salt with a clean, damp cloth, then blotting and drying before beginning the polishing ritual. He liked polishing his boots. It was one of those soothing tasks—the kind that set the world right again.

He watched as the forensic officers poked and prodded the body —a young girl. From the looks of her, she was barely in her teens. Sad thing to see those once bright blue eyes filming over with a milky glaze.

"Any ID?"

The heads shook in unison. No shoes, no shirt or blouse, just a pair of cut-off jeans and a bright red barrette in her muddy hair and 'Hannah' tattooed inside her right arm. Shame, he thought. Close to his youngest daughter's age. Why was this girl in the river instead of home on a Saturday morning? Why wasn't she still in bed like he knew his daughter was? Teenagers slept til noon.

He searched his memory but couldn't recall a time when he'd had that luxury. Growing up, he'd had a paper route, then a job as a bagger at the local market. After high school, there was the military, and now this—a small-town sheriff thinking nothing too bad could happen here. Yet, here he is looking at another child lost. At this rate, he'd never have time to sleep in.

He looked down at the girl and figured it was time to retire. This was the second time in the past six months they'd found a body discarded in the river. Like so much trash, as if they had no value. No thought had been given to this young life dumped and left to rot in the salt marshes.

In my imagination, this life has been a path with many, many forks, each one a choice to be made... No destination is really known until you arrive, and then it becomes merely a point along the way—a vague place rarely planned for, simply the start of another adventure. People sometimes get frozen and unable to decide which path to take; others instantly regret their choices. What could have been has never been and never will be. This is the Tree of Life where each branch grows and bears fruit and, ultimately, ends in a bud. There are no rules, and nothing planned by humans is ever planned that way again. The way is vague and unknowable.

— Marc Hamer, *Seed to Dust: A Gardener's Story*

1

An avenue of oaks half a mile long leads to the *For Sale* sign. Faint markings of a former dirt driveway blur beside the realtor's forlorn sign. It swings on one rusted hook. A melancholy moan squeaks out an off-tune melody in the pre-storm breeze. The letters *e* and *r* are missing from the realtor's name. It creates a whimsical 'Sand land' instead of the intended Sanderland. The neglected sign, the overgrown driveway, and the fading façade of Carrington Point Plantation are all indications of abandonment. Of course, the realtor said she was retired and no longer had oversight of the property. Said she hadn't visited the place in years.

"Catherine Maria Lucia Gabbiano, why do you even bother?" I admonish myself. I consider turning around, as no sensible person could possibly choose this forlorn site for a celebratory event. But then Mary Elizabeth Cunningham Berkley didn't have a reputation for being sensible, and her upcoming marriage to Jackson Scarborough Callaway had scattered her even further into la-la-land. She had informed me at our first meeting that this dilapidated structure was at the top of her list as a venue for her wedding reception. It's difficult for me to envision the no-dirt-on-her-hands Mary Elizabeth in this down-at-the-heels place.

The entire town considers this old plantation haunted. I grumble under my breath. It's another wasted day for me. But I'm here. I might as well make an effort to investigate its potential for my client. I need some facts to back me up when I tell her it's not suitable.

I'm early. Punctuality was drilled into me at a young age. I have an extra hour before my clients arrive—plenty of time to document all the reasons why Carrington isn't an ideal setting for the wedding reception of the year.

A cursory glance around the property signals it's a caterer's nightmare—my nightmare. If I were in the right frame of mind, these people wouldn't be on my client list. As a South Carolina Lowcountry caterer, I'm passionate about my work. I love creating memorable food events, or I did until I'm hired by people like Mary Elizabeth. She is surely punishment for some crime I didn't commit.

Being able to pick and choose my clients ceased the day I had a falling out with the number one social setter in the Lowcountry, Mrs. Randolph Augustus Harrington. Even the months I spent in Italy did not soften our exchange of words or the sordid scandal that grew out of proportion in my absence. While I was away, Mrs. Harrington made it her mission to destroy my business reputation.

When I was new to the Lowcountry, Mrs. H had gone out on a limb to hire me. When she did, it catapulted my small catering company to the top of everyone's list. Before our disagreement, I'd often questioned why I continued to cater events for her. She made impossible demands, and her snarly personality made it difficult work. I'd put up with her until the day she pulled a stunt so vile I couldn't forgive her. Without revealing the reason for a grand event at her home, she knowingly hired me to cater the engagement party for my recent ex-fiancé and his newly minted bride-to-be, who just happened to be Mrs. Harrington's daughter. What kind of low-life would do that?

I didn't discover her deceit until the day of the engagement party when I was on my way to deliver the food. If my friend Cassie hadn't found out and called me, I'd have been the joke of the town. The exchange of less-than-nice words had me storming off after telling Mrs. Harrington I would never work for her again. She, in turn, yelled back that she would ruin my business. In a town as small as this one, that threat changed the course of my life.

Since my return from Italy six months ago, I've worked round the clock to restore my reputation and my business. I've had to accept clients who, in the past, I wouldn't have considered. The Berkley family is one of those. While they are a well-established name in the area, the daughter is spoiled rotten. During a fleeting moment of insanity, I assured myself that if I catered the wedding reception for this family, more business would come my way.

Mary Elizabeth's mother, Mrs. Julius Barnwell Berkley, aka Margaret, is Mrs. Harrington's adversary in the Lowcountry's world of social know-how. Margaret isn't the one who is my nemesis. She's nice enough. It's her overindulged daughter, Mary Elizabeth, who is a first-class royal pain in the butt. Every aspect of this grand reception must pass whatever image Mary Elizabeth conjures up.

Her whining is why I'm at Carrington Point this afternoon. She declared in her shrill little girl voice that this pre-civil war plantation was too, too, too romantic and absolutely perfect for her special day. In my eyes, it's one of those end-of-the-world places, and the logistical problems abound.

It's too far from town. There's no access to the house, and even if there were, according to the information I received, there's no electricity or running water. These factors alone determine what kind of food can be served. Nope, this is not shaping up to be an enticing venue.

Maneuvering the almost extinguished pothole-pitted driveway, I guide the van onto the weed-filled lawn and park. At least there's ample parking. I take out my iPad and make notes to add parking attendants and port-a-potties along with a landscaping company to whip the place into shape. The dollar signs rack up.

Last night, Google gave me an overview of the plantation. It was built circa 1800. There are approximately five thousand acres. History documents Carrington Point Plantation as having been home to two hundred-plus slaves prior to the Civil War.

I shudder, wondering why Mary Elizabeth would possibly want

to celebrate the beginning of her life with Jackson on land that had previously enslaved people. The word tasteless comes to mind as I reach into the back seat and grab my rain jacket.

Once out of the car, I inhale the salt-laden air as I view the desolation. Years ago, it must have been magnificent. My sigh fills the emptiness of the place. With my measuring tape, I walk off space for tents, food tables, and a dance floor, plus room for tables and chairs for the guests. I tramp through knee-high weeds and locate a reasonably distanced spot for the VIP port-a-potties. Today's weather reminds me the wedding month is October, so I jot down hurricane season to my growing list of disadvantages.

There's a great spot a little off-center of the grand staircase leading to the front entrance that could easily accommodate a band or DJ. As the day darkens and storm clouds congregate, I automatically pick up speed. The wind whips around the corner of the house and tears at loose-hanging shutters, kicking up a racket.

Since there's ample time before the bride-to-be arrives, I wade across the lawn through knee-high sand-spur weeds. I'm thankful I wore boots, as they prevent the nasty, prickly bits from sticking to my jeans. At the bottom of the staircase, I pause. My eyes follow the flow of the Greek Revival mansion. For the first time, I glimpse the possibilities of the place.

Even with boards across the windows, the structure is splendid. The massive columns sag, yet they radiate strength and grandeur from a long-ago past. The double front doors have lost the original luster, but the transom above retains soft rose-infused stained glass. The unusual wrap-around porch creates images of leisurely afternoon soirées. It's easy to envision beautiful ladies with silk fans and dresses that swish and gentlemen in full formal regalia.

My imagination gallops away as faint strains of music float in the air. The current rotting porch becomes a fairyland of intimately arranged tables draped in fine white linens with vases of red roses and warm candle glow. Crinoline-gowned women rest their hands lightly on the arms of men clad in deep burgundy waistcoats overlaid with elegant royal blue tailcoats.

Violins whisper a Viennese waltz. Dance partners lock gazes and sway in time with the rise and fall of Johann Strauss's magical notes. The majestic rotation of step, slide, step in three-quarter time has the dancers gliding across the surface. I hold my breath, transfixed—lost in the mystery of the music, the dancers and the glory of another age. Then they vanish.

Sorrow hangs side-by-side with the Spanish moss in the branches of the massive oaks as I stride toward the porch. I want to touch the dancers. I want to hear the music. I want to dance. Since my best friend Stella was murdered less than a year ago, I've been unbearably sad. Her dying and my close call with death left me no option but to end my stay in Italy far earlier than I had planned. Today is the first time since I returned home that the desire to dance, sing, or even hum has wrapped its golden threads around my heart and beckoned me back into life.

I marvel at my own transformation—one minute, I'm grumbling because of all the inconveniences of this place, and the next moment, I've fallen under its spell. I shake off my reverie and march up the old brick steps. My feet slide into the worn grooves—the ones made by previous generations as they marked their place in history. I count ten steps to the landing. It dog-legs and leads up to the entrance. I count another ten steps. Counting is one of those quirky habits I've had as long as I can remember. When all the complexities of life overwhelm me, it's the simple act of counting that brings me back to center.

At the top of the stairs, I pause to examine the porch which is a wasteland of rotten and missing boards. Another reason to not choose this place is added to the growing list. All the staircases would have to be roped off with large 'No Admittance' signs. Even then, some adventuresome fool would ignore them, sneak up the steps, and be hurt. I add an asterisk to indicate another liability.

Ahhhh, I mutter under my breath. Even with all the drawbacks, this place is magical. However, I won't let its charm sway me to reconsider catering an event here. It's my job to convince Mary Elizabeth that Carrington Point isn't the best choice for her grand wedding reception. She won't be happy when I tell her it's a sweet mess and would require far more work than I'm interested in doing. I'd have to hire more staff than usual, and who knows if the place is available? No one seems to know who owns it.

There's no doubt the Berkleys will pay whatever I ask, but this plantation is nothing but a money pit, not to mention an injury lawsuit waiting to happen. Yet, it's necessary to check out every detail, including the rotten porch.

My foot hovers over a board. I pray it's solid. I step lightly, then pause like a frozen-in-place statue. The old boards creak and pop before settling. As I check out where to step next, the same strains of music I thought were in my head continue to play.

Thinking something is wrong with my hearing, I close my eyes and focus on the sound. Musical notes seem to flow from the back of the house. A strong gust of wind grabs at my jacket. My hands are hampered by the iPad and measuring tape, so I place them on the railing before taking the next step. The old boards accept my weight. I continue with great caution as I let my feet follow the music.

Counting each board keeps me focused and closes my ears to the creaking and moaning of the shifting porch. With each step, the music swirls in the stormy breeze. As I creep forward, I notice all the windows are boarded over with plywood.

Reaching the back of the house is slow, not to mention nerve-wracking. Once there, the porch opens into a massive and recently repaired deck. Vestiges of sawdust and a stray nail or two rotate in the ever-increasing high wind gusts—strong enough to topple over a wobbly workbench. The new boards have been sloppily nailed into place over the old rotten ones. Only the frail porch railing appears to be original. The few spindles still in place sway in the wind like fragile toothpicks easily snapped.

The music that I'm sure is in my head stops. I turn from the cursorily repaired porch to the turrets and alcoves. There are three large windows across the back of the house. They appear not to be boarded over. Being curious, I pivot and tiptoe across the newly repaired deck. Chills charge up and down my spine. The hair on the back of my neck tingles. My imagination takes flight as I wonder if some vagrant is inside waiting to pounce on me.

Knocking away the cobwebs, I press my forehead against the glass. What I expect to see are blank walls, vacant rooms, and rotting infrastructure. Instead, my eyes feast on a room out of *Architectural Digest* designed for a well-heeled bachelor. I back away from the window, rub my eyes and step forward to take another look.

A mahogany leather sofa centers the room, paired with two matching side chairs. A coffee table is layered with books and magazines. It sets on a deep brown and white checkered rug. My heart rate increases. I pull away, expecting the door to swing open and someone appear to yell at me for trespassing or offer me a sweet tea. The wind whispers and moans. The isolation of the place reminds me that only the Berkleys know I'm here. Leaning toward the window, I press my forehead against the glass.

A small gas blaze in the fireplace flickers with comforting flames of red and gold. The heart pine floors are burnished to a high gloss. A fully stocked bar and a state-of-the-art work area are across the opposite wall along with a big-screen TV. All of these electronics defy the former realtor's notion that this place doesn't have electricity.

As my eyes sweep to the outer edges of the room, I see the corner of a bed poking out from behind a screen of some sort. Someone is definitely living on the premises.

More chills zip up the back of my neck as the porch creaks and pops behind me. A faint vibration moves through my feet. Jerking away from the window, I silently pray it's my clients and not some mass murderer. There's nothing but the whoosh of wind as it passes through the grand live oaks.

Glancing over my shoulder, all I see are the turrets with their rounded shapes and recessed alcoves. They create a perfect curvature to hide anyone wishing to observe without being seen. Counting slowly, I breathe in and out, forcing my rapidly beating heart to slow down. When I turn back to the window, I'm stunned. My face, distorted by the antique glass, is pale and washed out. In the reflection, another body joins me with an arm-wielding hammer aimed at my head. Scrambling to save my skull from being split open like a ripe melon, I nosedive across the porch.

2

My head slams into the railing. Footsteps thunder closer as I struggle to throw my body off the deck. Heavy puffs of breathing and a sinister chuckle hover over my head. With all my strength, I push against the rotten spindles and pitch head-first into weeds.

Mary Elizabeth's squeaky, excited voice rounds the corner, "Cat, Cat, where are you? Oh, don't you love this place? Mommie, Mommie, keep up with me. We have to find Cat."

The same heavy footsteps thud away from me. I keep my face buried in the sandy soil. A door slams. Strange scraping noises reach my ears. I uncoil and push to my feet just as Mary Elizabeth turns the corner and comes to a dead halt.

She looks me up and down and says, "Why whatever are you doing, Cat? Did you lose something? Oh God, there's blood on your face? Did you fall? Mommie, Mommie come quickly. Cat needs help."

With that, she begins a high-pitched wail. Smacking her would give me great pleasure. Instead, I wipe my forehead with the sleeve of my jacket and yelp when a sharp stab of pain accompanies the wipe. Sand spurs are stuck to my sleeve.

Margaret Berkley, who is infinitely more capable than her daughter, arrives on the scene, pulls out her phone, and starts to dial 911.

"No, please, Mrs. Berkley. I'm fine," I protest. "I tripped on one of the loose boards and hit my head on the rotten spindles. It's nothing. I have some water in the car. I'll just clean up, and we can get started."

"Lordy, Cat. You look a mess," Margaret Berkley mutters as her eyes roam over my body. "Your jeans are torn, and your knees are scraped. We don't have to do this today. It's going to pour any minute. I'll call 911, or drive you to a clinic. We can reschedule."

"No, really, I'm fine. If I'm still bleeding or if I have a headache when we finish, I'll stop at urgent care on the way home."

Mary Elizabeth's wailing ratchets up another decibel. "Oh, Mommie, no," Mary Elizabeth sobs. She stomps her Jimmy Choo square-toed pink leather ballet-clad feet in the weeds. She shakes her blonde curls as big, fake tears dribble toward her trembling lips.

"I want to look now. We have all those other places to visit. Please, Cat. You must stay! It won't take long. We'll just whirl through here. Please?"

"Sure, I'll stay. Let me clean up a bit. I left my iPad and tape measure on the front porch railing. I've already taken measurements and made some notes. Y'all walk around the site. I'll join you in a few minutes."

My evil thoughts wonder if there's a possibility that the same person who tried to attack me would take on Mary Elizabeth. A chuckle starts to rise in my throat until I realize how serious this incident could have turned out. Maybe I should call the police.

But what would I say? Somebody tried to attack me? And where is that person? And who would believe me anyway? Most of the town knows I haven't been the same since I returned from Italy. Word got around quickly that I'd been whacked on my head and nearly killed during my time away. There are only three people in the Lowcountry who know the details: my friend Cassie, my therapist Dr. Ginny and the neurologist in Charleston. But small-town folks love to speculate.

I trudge around the house and up the steps. My iPad isn't where I left it. I tuck the measuring tape in my pocket and search the area. I poke through the tall weeds, but the iPad has vanished. Anger and fear arrive at the same time. Anger because it's a replacement expense I don't need, and fear because it contains all my notes, menus, events, photographs, and personal information. Who would take it and why?

Inside the car, I gulp water and wish it was something stronger. Grabbing an old towel from the back seat, I douse it with water and dab at the bloody spot on my forehead. Not too bad, I think, as I examine my face in the mirror—only a small scratch. I squint at my torn jeans and bloody knees, blot the blood, and pick a splinter out of my hand. Like so many of life's bumps, I'll survive this one. But it's hard not to go down that rabbit hole and recreate the Italian scene at the Zinzulusa Caves with Carlo skimming his knife across my forehead. The outward scars are barely visible, but the internal ones are never far from the surface. I sigh and frown at my image. Now is not the time to revisit this past nightmare. Mary Elizabeth is enough nightmare for one day.

With phone in hand, I tap in all the details I can recall. The earlier measurements that I collected and stored on my iPad will have to be redone.

A few speckles of rain plop on the windshield. Dried leaves scatter across the hood. They cackle like Macbeth's brood of witches. Taking a deep breath, I open the car door and step out. Stiffness has already settled in my joints. I hobble until I reach the back of the house. Before joining the Berkleys, I bend and stretch until I can walk without a noticeable limp.

As I round the house, Mary Elizabeth's face is mashed against the window. But Mrs. B isn't around.

"Where's your mom?"

"Oh, she wandered off somewhere. Cat, I want to see inside, but the windows are all black. Can't you get us in?"

"What?"

I move to Mary Elizabeth's side. She's right. The windows are blocked with some kind of black screens on the inside. There is no room filled with furniture. There's no fireplace or technical equipment. There's nothing except blackout screens. Did I see anything or was it only my overactive imagination? My neurologist and therapist suggested that the blackout spells might pop up from time to time. They also warned me I'd have nightmares until I could come to grips with the attempt on my life. But I'm sure I saw the inside of the house. I tug on the door handle. It doesn't budge. A heavy gust of wind swirls around the corner. My head begins a slow pounding as I'm sucked into the black abscess of Stella's death.

3

Six months have passed since my best friend Stella was murdered. Moving past the horror of her death and my own near-death experience in Castello del Mare has been slow. After all, the small village had been my childhood paradise. Now, it's my nightmare. And Stella, still dictating my life from her watery grave, left me her Italian villa. So far, returning has been too painful. My fear is that this beautiful place has become paradise lost rather than found. More healing has to occur before I can make that journey.

My neurologist in Charleston agreed with the records the Italian neurosurgeon sent home with me. Further tests revealed I had post-concussive syndrome with some structural changes to the brain. Initially, rehab's purpose was to teach me how to cope with memory and concentration problems, mood swings, headaches, fatigue, dizziness, and insomnia. The doctor said it was important for me to balance my need to rest and my need to work. Of course, after the first month, I forgot about the resting part and buried myself in work. It's the primary coping mechanism in my portfolio when life becomes unbearable.

My psychologist, Dr. Virginia Hollister, pointed out that while my visible wounds were healing just fine, the scars from grief, fear, and anxiety would take much longer. Every day is purgatory for me—no, not hell, because at least in hell, I would understand that I'd be shoveling shit for the rest of my life. But in purgatory, I live with the torment of never truly knowing what happened to Stella. I live with the constant fear that Riccardo will hunt me down. Every day, I wake up with anxiety crawling up my spine. But it is the grief of not knowing exactly what happened to Stella that tangles me in the darkness of ambiguity. Her body was never found. She simply floated away from me. I like to believe she was guided by the stars in the sky and a moonlit path on the sea—a forever star of the sea.

In the distance, I hear Dr. Virginia (Ginny) Hollister. I struggle to leave the void I'm wallowing in.

"Cat!"

Today, her insistent voice pulls me back into present time. The cool grays and blues of her office reassure me that I'm safely ensconced in the same plush navy chair. She leans forward, her shoulders tense, her eyes grave.

"Cat, where did you go? Are you okay? Do you want to stop the session?"

"No, I'm okay. Let's keep going."

"What I was saying before you drifted away is that you've submerged the worst parts of your experience. What happened to you in Italy was traumatic and debilitating. Your fear is alive and festering. It has to be exposed, but we'll do so with great caution."

She lets that sink in before continuing, "You have a lot to deal with. The residual weakness from the structural damage lingers, as do your lapses in memory, along with the scattered nightmares. It will take time, but remember how much progress you've already made. Now's the time to stabilize your life, so don't involve yourself in anything that increases anxiety and stress. It's important that you understand that, Cat. This plantation sounds like a place you need to avoid."

Her voice and words are kind. She could have easily said it's my impetuous behavior that has aggravated an already bad situation into something far worse. Maybe I shouldn't have told her about the potential attacker at Carrington Point. Of course, she's right. I need to stay away.

The horrific images of death still linger in my memory, popping up at unexpected times. The gun pressed against my skull, the knife slicing my forehead, and never knowing for sure what happened to Stella—no body to view, no last goodbye, only the Guardia di Finanza, a militaristic branch of the police, saying she was murdered and would I sign the papers. Lorenzo had stood next to me and guided my trembling hand as I signed all the required paperwork.

This isn't my first session with Dr. Ginny, and it's a far cry from my last. Shortly after I moved to the Lowcountry, my primary-care physician recognized I was struggling with anxiety and recommended I seek professional help.

For years prior to my move, I'd pushed all my unpleasant experiences into the depths of my soul. My bootstrap upbringing demanded I manage all of the pain on my own, but eventually, everything bubbled to the surface. Trying to extricate myself from the fear and sorrow on my own hadn't proven to be successful. My dreams had been filled with nightmares that left me drained and confused. A clammy cloak of suffocation hovered over me every waking hour.

The years I was married to Richard left me devoid of emotion—years of believing and hoping he would change. But every year, the abuse became more intense and lasted for longer periods until his sorrowful begging for forgiveness fell on ears that could no longer hear his voice.

Five days in a courtroom trial where he, a brilliant lawyer, tried to screw me out of my lucrative 401k and my share of what we'd built together. He also tried convincing the judge that my job at a prestigious accounting firm paid more than his. In his opinion, I was the primary breadwinner, and he should receive half of my investments as well as remain on my health care insurance. I was so mad I could have spit tacks.

Thankfully, the judge saw past his theatrics. I walked out of the courtroom with a divorce, all my assets intact, and half of the equity in the house. I was free, but what did freedom mean?

A week later, I packed up my personal belongings, stored anything I couldn't fit in the car, and headed to culinary school. My Italian *nonna* was the driving force from beyond the grave. Her beautiful, lyrical voice insisted I return to my roots and cook the way she'd taught me. Once I listened, culinary school was the only choice.

After the daily drudge of being a corporate accountant, culinary school was a place where I reveled in the sheer bliss of absorbing everything there was to learn about cooking. And I cooked for hours and hours, never thinking about Richard or regretting that I left a lucrative career in finance.

Then the next curve ball hit. Mom and Dad—gone just that—killed in a second by a drunk driver. No time for goodbyes, I love you or forgive me for all my transgressions and the grief I caused you during my growing up years.

I took a leave of absence from school and, with my dearest friend Stella's help, buried my parents and settled their estate. Richard popped up again. He tried to insinuate his way back into my life, appearing at the funeral all fluffed up like a peacock. He said my parents loved him, and they would want him to have a share of their assets.

If I had thought for one minute I could have gotten away with murder, he'd be dead. Instead, I called the sheriff and asked him to escort my worthless ex off the premises. The sheriff gladly obliged me. That was the end of Richard's presence in my life.

Back in culinary school, I put grief aside and continued my insane approach to learning with lightning speed. I rarely slept, ate only when I had to taste my assignments, and generally isolated myself from relationships of any kind. I was hell-bent on obtaining a Master's degree in as little time as possible.

I had minored in culinary arts when I was getting my Bachelor's degree in finance, so it hadn't been a stretch for me to be accepted into the Masters Program. While I had to pick up extra studies, I completed my degree in two years. During that time when I wasn't studying or cooking, I was searching for a place—not just any place, but a place where I could start over, a place to call home.

That sense of belonging happened the day I pulled into the Lowcountry of South Carolina. I had all but forgotten my uncle's fishing camp. It was the only part of my inheritance that I hadn't attended to. It was supposed to be a quick trip to sign some papers and put the place on the market.

But the giant oaks draped with dangling, silvery Spanish moss and the river flowing by the property changed my mind. This place, yes, this place where lascivious lushness rules the land and the water, captured my soul.

It's a setting that took my breath away then and still does today. Years after my arrival, I'm still in awe of storms marching triumphantly across the wide expanse of the saltwater river with lightening streaks strutting like drum majorettes leading a parade. It's the same when sea birds catapult through puffs of low-slung clouds or when star-kissed nights illuminate the universe.

Since that first day, I've learned that bedazzling beauty lies side-by-side with deceit and corruption. I call it divine decadence. The uniqueness of this place draws anyone who sees it into the syrupy sweetness known as the South. I wasn't born on this land, but when I moved here, I claimed it as my own. I chose this place, and the place returned the favor. Finally, a home of my own.

Dr. Ginny's voice breaks through again.

"Cat? You left me for the second time. Let's stop for today."

"No, I want to go on."

As I say these words, I can't help but think she rues the day I made the first appointment. Yet, she continues to be kind and supportive and never lets on she thinks I'm a total looney tune.

When we first started our sessions, she diagnosed me with situational depression brought on by trauma from childhood experiences with Stella and my family, my abusive marriage to Richard, and the sudden death of my parents. We were still working on these issues when I decided to pack up and spend a year in Italy. We both knew it would be problematic for me to take a year off from therapy, but Dr. Ginny was as enthusiastic about the trip as I was.. She encouraged me to go, and arranged bimonthly video calls to stay in touch. While it wasn't the best approach to therapy, my progress could still be determined through our conversations. I was reminded to keep up yoga, meditation, and jogging while I was away.

Since I returned from Italy earlier than anticipated and with far more trauma than I had left with, she's taking it slowly. Today, we are working on my intense need to count and organize.

She says it's a mild case of OCD, which was probably brought on by a stand-alone event that erupted during my childhood.

Before I left for Italy, we had worked our way through most of the abusive years of my marriage, as well as the death of my parents. She said those were the most important issues to tackle. The OCD could wait. Now that I'm back, in worse shape than before, she wants to start easy and clear up some of the less crippling behaviors before we tackle the Italian debacle.

"Cat, let's continue with the visualization."

"Okay, sure. I'm ready."

"Think about the first time you counted."

"Hmm, it seems like I have always counted, but—"

"Wait, Cat! Don't jump in immediately. You're so anxious to get it right that you rush in before I can finish. Give yourself time to think. Now settle back and close your eyes. Start the breathing exercises we've been practicing. Go back as far as you can into your childhood memories. Think about numbers and counting. Think about how it feels when you count. Does it give you satisfaction? Does it frustrate you? Start with recent memories of counting, then allow yourself to drift back to earlier years. Go ahead. Close your eyes."

At first, there's nothing but dark space. Then Dr. Ginny's soft voice—a sort of magical hum— reminding me to breathe. It's the first time I've noticed her words have a lyrical tone like my *nonna's*. Although Nonna only spoke Italian, it's the quality that's similar—like listening to a lullaby and allowing the little girl I once was to feel safe. Tears slide past my closed eyelids as I acknowledge the two strong women by my side—one from the past and one from the present. They see me. They hear me. They welcome me with open arms. They invite me to sing my song and dance my dance.

The years free fall. Big, bold numbers march into view. Without thinking, I count them. I counted during culinary school, through my marriage, and my job. I counted at university and in high school.

The years continue to tumble away to a playground. One minute, I'm swinging on the jungle gym. The next minute I'm eating dirt with Bobby Rigdon's knee pressed into my back. He's ten to my seven, already a boy-man. He clutched my right hand and ratcheted my arm up my back until tears dribbled from my eyes.

He leaned in close to my ear and hissed, "If you get in my space again, I'll kill you."

He said something else, but I no longer had the capacity to hear. He will kill me was all I knew. My entire body withdrew into a safe place—a place where I counted until he disappeared.

When I reach the magical number of thirty, I opened my eyes. He was no longer there. The numbers protected me. I picked myself up and brushed the dirt from my clothes while dabbing at my bloody knees. I never told anyone.

Counting never left me after that. It became my refuge. *Count,* I said to myself when the day I'd planned went off course. *Count,* I mumbled when I was disappointed with a grade or a class presentation. *Count,* I whimpered when Richard shouted or slapped me. I counted until one day, I realized I couldn't make it through the day without counting. It was too late to stop.

The afternoon sun poking through the window strokes my face. I open my eyes to Ginny's smile.

"Yes," she says. "Yes, you are making progress."

4

Most of my progress with Dr. Ginny vanishes after yesterday's incident at Carrington Point Plantation. The scary part is I don't know if the attempt to smash my head in by the unknown assailant was real or imagined.

All I know is that every single window was boarded over except the three running across the back of the house. The furnishings seemed real, but were they? When Mary Elizabeth and I looked in, those same three windows were covered with blackout screens that were on the inside of the house. Am I imagining things again? Was there really someone with a hammer aimed at my head? Or, am I trying to justify my behavior to convince myself the attempted attack was real?

After my headlong tumble, Mary Elizabeth and her mother traipsed all over the property but could not reach a decision before the storm plowed through, scattering us to our vehicles. Since I haven't heard from either of them, I'm hopeful they're looking for another venue.

My calendar is loaded with upcoming events. Keeping busy diverts my mind away from imaginary scary stories. The Fitzhugh dinner party for twelve is next on my list. It's coming up fast. There's no time for negative thoughts. I push them into the back of my brain's filing cabinet and focus on the menu and the shopping list. Today, I'm preparing the caramel flan.

Sarah Fitzhugh is bonkers about impressing the guest of honor. Her body jiggles with anticipation whenever we discuss the dinner party. When we met to select the menu, she breathlessly filled me in with a description of some descendant from a long line of Spanish royalty with a connection to a sailing vessel sinking off the South Carolina coast in the early days of exploration. Of course, she wanted me to create a Spanish-themed dinner.

Sarah is a favorite client. She's easygoing and lets me guide her in the menu selection. She loves that I take care of all the details. I love that she spares no expense.

The setting is their back veranda with impressive views of the marsh and deep water with picture-perfect sunsets. If the weather forecast holds true, it will be a gorgeous evening. The flan I'm preparing today is the dessert I have chosen to end the meal on a spectacular note.

After reading through the recipe, I assemble supplies. As I place the pan of cream on the stove, my phone jingles out Caruso. A crazy name from my past appears—Nick Cafaro, my first and only high school crush. With all the scams in today's world, I'm leery about answering. Why would Nick Cafaro be calling me after all these years? Does it have something to do with my iPad? But of course, it doesn't. That wouldn't make sense. As the call starts to roll over, I tentatively answer.

"Hello?"

"Cat, Cat, is that you? Kitty Cat? It's Nick, Nick Cafaro. You remember me, don't you?"

"Sure, Nick, but it's been ages. Twenty years or more, right? How are you? How did you get my number?"

"Hey, sorry it's been so long, but you know life and all. I'm as good-looking as ever, sweet Kitty Cat. How about you?"

"I'm good, Nick. Just surprised to hear from you. Where are you?"

"I'm here, in town on business which provided me with an excuse to call you. You won't believe this, but I'm on the search committee for our high school reunion. You and Stella are on the list of those I have to contact. You know it's our twentieth. You'll be there, right? And Stella, too?"

"Yes, Nick, I received my invitation. I've already responded."

Nick plows on as if he hasn't heard a word I've said.

"Since I already had business in this area, it seemed like a great opportunity to catch up in person. The reunion is going to be a blast, and the drive to Virginia isn't that far. You and Stella have to come. Stella Lombardi—the world-famous model and actress—the star attraction. She's the most prominent person in our class. It's my job to make sure she attends. The problem is we don't have current contact information for her. I told the committee not to worry because I knew you would have it. Right?"

"No, Nick, I don't have an address for Stella. I've already sent in my RSVP saying I won't be there, and neither will Stella."

"Humph! What's with the crappy attitude, Cat? After all this time, I thought you'd be delighted to hear from me. Twenty years ago, you'd have given anything to be my girl."

He laughs just the way I remember—boyish yet dismissive of my emotions. I shrink back into the shy self I used to be and cringe when he brings up Stella's name. If he doesn't know she's dead, I'm not about to tell him. I keep quiet, and slowly, it dawns on him to take another approach.

"Well, could you at least give me Stella's last address? I checked all my sources, but her last known address was in Italy. Without a phone number, I haven't been able to contact her. Do you remember Sally? Sally Boyd? She's on the committee. She said there was a writeup in *The Times* a while back about some gala in New York. Said you were in the photograph with Stella. You must be in touch with her. Why are you holding back information? Afraid Stella might come to the reunion and steal your thunder like she used to?"

Was I stupid enough to have a crush on this guy? I ask myself as I listen to his self-centered rhetoric. Nick Cafaro was my first kiss behind the bleachers at the park. Noses and foreheads bumped in confusion and uncertainty. He was "the man" on campus, a football star, and a basketball and baseball star, too. He'd asked to borrow my calculus notes, and I was hopelessly in love. I was so enthralled that he chose to spend time with me instead of Stella that I overlooked the reason. For a few weeks our heads were close together while I tried to explain the concept of change, the properties of derivatives and integrals of functions. But he was way too busy bedding the cheerleaders to pay attention. It's not accurate to say I lost him when I refused to let him copy my exam. He'd never been mine to lose. I had only been the smart girl who could keep him from failing. When I said no, he dumped me.

"Cat, is there a problem? Let me start over. Why don't we get together? I'm in town on business, but I have to eat. Can we meet?"

"So you're already here?"

"Sure am. Come on. Let's grab a cup of coffee. We can catch up. You'll never guess what I do for a living. You'll be shocked. What'd you say?"

"Sorry, Nick. Not today. I'm busy organizing for an upcoming event."

"Oh, I bet it's one of those charity functions. You always were a do-good type. Well, let's make it tomorrow. I'm going to be in town for a while and need to know where the action is, along with some good restaurants. Plus, my boss wants me to assess some property. Maybe you could shed some light on the real estate in the area as well as the community movers and shakers. Hey, it's gonna be great to catch up. I mean, twenty years and all is a long time."

Of course, I relent. What harm could there be in catching up with an old classmate? Maybe he's bald and has a beer belly, and I'll get the last laugh. We agree to meet for coffee the next morning.

5

Hesitating on the other side of the street, I peruse the café. The tables overlook the rushing river and the waterfront park. How will I recognize someone I haven't seen in twenty years? It's needless for me to fret as he's already seen me.

He pops up from the table, waves wildly, and gallops toward me. When he's within arm's length, he grabs me and hugs me so tight I push back. The last thing I need are cracked ribs. I nudge him away from me and take a look at my old friend. His eyes don't engage. Instead, they scrutinize the area as he stares over and around me. It's a strange way to greet anyone, much less an old friend.

"Well, Nick, it's good to see you. Are you expecting anyone else?"

"What? Ah no. No, I just got here. I'm taking in the scenery. Nice town. And look at you, Kitty Cat—aren't you just the picture of a small-town entrepreneur!"

I check out his bearded face, puffy eyes, shaggy hair pulled back in a ponytail, and tattoos on the parts of his arms I can see.

"Nice to see you too, Nick. I'm not so sure about the entrepreneur bit. What makes you say that?"

"Well, of course, I checked you out. Catering business, huh? Seems you're doing alright from the glowing reviews I read."

We cross the street and settle at the table. While the waiter takes our order, I give Nick another look. There's an air of mystery and unease about him—something I can't identify.

"I do okay. What about you? You indicated when you called that I'd be shocked at what you're doing now. So?"

I glance his way to discover his eyes are still roaming the area.

Capturing Nick's attention is going to take more energy than I have this morning. The old army field jacket he's wearing is frayed at the collar and cuffs, the drab green t-shirt and camouflaged pants certainly aren't freshly laundered, and the one boot poking from under the table is covered in mud.

"Nick? What is it you do, and why are you contacting me after all these years? You're dressed more for a hunting expedition than a conversation about a high school reunion."

He picks at the frayed cuff, sniffs the air like a terrier, and produces that award-winning smile I remember.

"Let's talk about the reunion first. I need Stella's contact information to pass on to the search committee. Do you remember Sandy Perkins? Or Martha Calhoun? Or maybe Doris Hendricks? They're the ones doing the actual search for missing classmates. We tried to reach Stella through her publicist, but no one returned our calls. That's when I thought of you."

His comment takes me right back to that place of being second best. I had such a crush on Nick, but he, like all the other guys, only had eyes for Stella.

"Sorry, Nick, I can't help you."

A piercing sound emits from Nick's phone. He pushes back from the table and walks away. His body hunches forward as if he's trying to protect the phone, the caller, the conversation, or himself. It's unusual behavior for someone in town on business, and his outfit is bizarre. *What is he up to?*

He gestures and shrugs before jamming the phone back in his pocket. He stares at the water for several seconds before coming back to the table.

"Hey, Cat, so sorry about that. I have to go. When *the boss* calls, there's no argument about where I need to be. Look, can we meet for lunch tomorrow? I'm supposed to have the day off, so there won't be any interruptions. I promise."

"Sure, Nick. I have an appointment at two, but if we make it an early lunch—say 11:30— that would work. There's a great restaurant in Port Royal. Maybe you could put your phone on mute when we're having lunch."

He laughs, throws money on the table, and grabs me for another excruciating hug.

"I'll text you tomorrow morning to confirm."

He half walks, half runs down the street and disappears between the buildings. The sun swings higher in the sky. Its heat penetrates my jacket. The cappuccino warms my stomach as I try to sort through what just happened.

The next morning I listen to a crack of thunder rolling across the marsh. From my bed, I watch the storm march forming on the other side of the river. The developmental stage of a good squall suits me this morning. I fluff up my pillows as lightning sizzles and crackles. When the first thick drops of rain hit the tin roof, I pull the covers up and settle into that blissfully drowsy state of mind, where my thoughts move from frantic to slow. My body slides into that rare spot between relaxed and blissful.

My phone vibrates. Nick's name flashes on the screen. What now? I don't answer. Instead, I let my eyes return to the marsh scene. The wind picks up. The grasses bend in supplication. The palms sway to some unknown melody. The Spanish moss falls in clumps from the giant oaks.

The chirping of the phone indicates a message has been left. As much as I want to linger in this perfect storm, I listen.

Hey Cat. Sorry, my boss came to town unexpectedly. Need to postpone our lunch. But I need a big favor. Could you drive out to Carrington Point Plantation? I know it's early and the weather's frightful, but I need some information about the place before I meet my boss. He's looking to buy in this area. You can probably give me some background or at least put me in touch with someone who can. Yeah, I know it's a pain in the butt to drive out here instead of talking on the phone. It's just that I have an international conference call at ten, and I need the information for that meeting. If you can't make it, give me a call. But I'm going to head out there now. I'll wait for you about a half mile past the driveway to the plantation. There's a rusted-out fence on the right. That's where the property line begins. Some surveyors are coming out later today, which is why it's important to meet with you now. I'm counting on you, Kitty Cat. Just like old times.

What a strange message. What if it's the person who stole my iPad, and they're pretending to be Nick? However, that makes zero sense because there certainly isn't anything on my iPad to connect me to Nick Cafaro. But why does he think I know anything about Carrington Point?

The storm slides off to the west, but the greenish-gray clouds indicate it's not over. My bare feet tingle from the cool tile in the bathroom. After throwing cold water on my face, I pull my red curls in a ponytail and grab weather-appropriate clothing. As my hand wraps around the doorknob, my internal voice yells: *Stop! What are you doing? You haven't seen Nick Cafaro in years.*

Dr. Ginny's voice chips away in my head. It's strong. It's telling me not to take unnecessary risks. There's also this niggling fear in the pit of my stomach. I text my friend Cassie:

Any chance you can ride out to the Carrington Point? I'm leaving now. Can I swing by and pick you up?

No sorry. At car repair shop. Broken taillight. Explain later.

Give me a call in 45. Meeting old school friend??? Having second thoughts.

Cassie responds to my last text by calling instead of texting. I can hear her angry voice in the insistent ringing. It's demanding me not to do anything foolish.

I text again:

Not answering. Call in 45.

This time, she texts back:

Caterina Maria Lucia Gabbiano, you are crazy—remind me to unfriend you. Please be careful!

I text back a kissy face just to antagonize her.

Cassie, aka Cassandra Burton, was one of the first people I met after moving to the Lowcountry. My first catered event had been booked. I was sure I could handle the entire gig alone. Suddenly, the initial number of guests increased. I was frantic. It would be difficult, if not impossible, to manage on my own. I was new in town and didn't know a soul.

Cassie and I bumped into each other at the grocery store. Actually, I ran over her with my cart. She had been very nice about the black marks on her new white sneakers and wouldn't accept money for a replacement pair. At the end of our conversation, just as she turned away, I blurted out that I ran over her because I was distracted. My desperation spilled out of every pore. I pleaded with her, asking if she knew anyone who could help me cater an event.

She threw back her head and howled with laughter. Her long black ponytail had swished back and forth as she hooted. I hadn't laughed in so long that I almost didn't know how, and I certainly didn't know why I should join in. But my body instinctively knew. Our combined hysterics had customers turning their carts away from us in a hurry.

When we surfaced to breathe, she handed me her card, which read *special event planner* and said, "I'll help you."

She's been helping me ever since, and so has her daughter Samantha. Cassie has been a lifesaver in other ways, too. She was waiting for me when I got off the plane in Savannah after my near-death experience in Italy and stayed by my side as I recovered. She listens to me instead of giving me "How to erase bad images from your mind" assignments like my therapist. While no one can take Stella's place in my heart, Cassie comes close.

6

This morning, my heart gallops ahead of itself as I drive out to Carrington Point Plantation. The missing iPad adds another layer of uneasiness. What if it was picked up by the crazy person who tried to attack me? Any halfway techie type could hack my password and find my personal information.

The possibility of a hacker/crazy person connecting me to Nick is an extreme thought. Yet, that's exactly the negative message pulsating in my mind. What's wrong with me? Why do I, after twenty years of not seeing Nick, think he's an okay guy? There's a dark side to me—one hidden under layers of my smiling I-am-okay fakery—one that keeps sending me down the rabbit hole.

The *For Sale* sign at the entrance of Carrington appears too soon. I slow the car to creep-along-speed. All is quiet as I pass. My convoluted thoughts tell me that if I drive slowly, I'll have time to make a snap decision about the person waiting. Maybe I'll have ten seconds to recognize Nick. If it's not him, I'll turn around and head back to town. Clever? Maybe. Maybe not.

The tires crunch on the gravel road. For the tenth time since I left home, I check to make sure the doors are locked. Massive overhead branches tremble against the storm-muddled sky. They twist and tangle into each other's canopies. Spanish moss whirls a flamenco staccato in the moist, breezy air. Big clumps of it whack the windshield. The road narrows, leaving no room for the quick turnaround I might need to make. I sigh into the thick, cloying humidity and, for the hundredth time, wonder what I'm doing.

Ahead, a rusted-out gate dangles from a partial fence leading to nowhere. A man dressed from head to toe in black darts from the tree line. He crouches in the dense bramble and signals me to stop. When I do, he approaches the car.

Is it Nick?

He lifts his hand in a careless greeting, but the baseball cap obscures his face. Fear percolates in my throat as bitter juices collect in my mouth. My brief encounter with Nick yesterday wasn't long enough to determine if this figure in black is the same person.

I slowly apply the brakes and roll to a stop. I'm not naive enough to release the lock. He grabs the handle and curses when it doesn't open.

"Shit, Cat," he says, banging on the window. I can't stand out here all day. Open the damm door."

"Show me your ID," I demand.

The man reaches into his back pocket. I'm sure he's pulling out a gun. Instead, he plasters a photo ID on the window. My eyes widen as Federal Bureau of Investigation flashes against the window. The face of a grownup Nick Cafaro stares back at me. I release the lock.

He lunges into the front seat but doesn't acknowledge me other than to say, "Drive another hundred yards. There's a small clearing ahead where you can pull off the road."

I press the gas pedal. We creep down the road until Nick says, "There."

It's so heavily wooded I don't see the turn until he says urgently, "Turn now."

I brake, turn sharply, and plow into the densely wooded area. Nick jumps out and removes a barrier of shrubbery. My mouth stays open as he signals for me to pull into the small space surrounded by giant oaks. My breathing accelerates, The trees close around the car, I'm trapped with this old classmate I haven't seen in years. When he replaces the barrier behind the car, I place my hand over my mouth to stifle a shriek.

Nick drops in the seat. He reaches across the console and pulls me to his chest. I push him away. He smiles with that same boyish grin I used to find so endearing.

"You're as feisty as ever. You have murder in your eyes. Talk to me."

"No," I snarl. "You talk to me. What in the hell is going on? You said you were on the search committee for our high school reunion, and now you're showing me an FBI badge."

He looks contrite but manages to sputter, "Ah, Cat, don't go jumping to conclusions. Hear me out."

But my anger is boiling over, mostly because I'm angry with myself for taking another unnecessary risk. Adrenaline pours through my body. It leaves me exhausted and scared.

"Why did you ask me to come out here? This place? And what's with the FBI? You seem to be familiar with these surroundings—far more than I am. Somehow, you failed to mention any of this in yesterday's conversation."

My pulse pounds. I pause for breath. Nick reaches over and takes my hand.

"Why are you so upset? Don't you want a little excitement in your life? Living in this small town must be boring. Settle down, and let me explain. That was my intention when I met you for coffee yesterday, but it didn't work out."

"Nick? You don't understand. Listen to me. I was at the plantation a few days ago, and someone tried to attack me. I'm guessing that same someone stole my iPad. Right after that, you call. Before we can have a proper conversation, you rush off. Then, today, you call and ask me to meet you out here. That's enough to make anyone nervous. I haven't seen you in twenty-some years, Nick. What's going on?"

"Ah, look, Cat. Let me explain."

I stare at him, "No, you let me finish. I can understand that the phone call you received yesterday was important, and you had to leave. But I changed my plans to have lunch with you today. You backed out of that and asked me to meet you in this dreadful place. Now you're flashing an FBI badge at me. Obviously, you know something about this place and my potential attacker. Did you see what happened? Or, perhaps you are the attacker? Did you lure me out here to finish me off?"

"Whoa—listen to you. Aren't you a wee bit paranoid? Accusing me of attacking you, finishing you off?"

We stare at each other—both with disbelief. Nick breaks the silence,

"Look, Cat, I'm sorry about what happened. No, I wasn't the attacker, but I was close by—even had you in my sight. I couldn't show myself. If it helps, I made sure you were okay. You managed to get yourself out of harm's way. But if you hadn't, I promise you I would have intervened—even if it meant the entire operation would go down."

"Operation? What are you talking about? This is insane. I want you out of my car. You're crazy!"

"Gosh, Cat. Don't get so worked up. Give me a chance to tell you what's going on."

"Well?"

"Okay, okay. Look, I can't tell you much, but I can tell you that Carrington Point Plantation is not a safe place for you to be. We've got it staked out. It's important that you tell me why you were out here and who you were with—those two women. Then I'm going to ask you to stay away from the place. It's dangerous and will continue to be for a couple of months."

"Ha," I huffily snort. "The people with me were clients—a mother and daughter—the Berkleys. They are looking at Carrington as a possible wedding reception. Do I tell them the FBI said it's off-limits?"

He laughs easily, but there are stress lines etched around his eyes. While he struggles to answer, I forge ahead.

"And what's this shit about you being an FBI agent? Since you lied about being on the high school reunion search committee, is this a lie, too?"

"Cat, if you stay quiet for a minute, I'll tell you what little I can about what's going on. You're right. I'm not exactly on the high school reunion search committee. I had to sweet talk my way with a couple of gals to get your information. I am an FBI agent and have been ever since I graduated from college or at least from the academy. Don't raise your eyebrow at me. That's the truth."

I feel one of those struck-dumb looks spreading across my face as I pretend this is a normal conversation. "But FBI? Why?"

"It's a long story, but I'm guessing you probably have a long story for the past twenty years, too. It's a bit complicated, and I don't have a lot of time."

"But you think I have time to drive all the way out here? You need to tell me as much as you can. Since you saw my attacker, do you know who it was? Do you know why I was the target? I'm not part of your operation. If you can give me a legitimate reason not to come back, I'll do my best to stay away.

"Cat, I can't say a lot. It's the nature of my work."

"Really, Nick? So, I'm supposed to believe you're an FBI agent? Am I supposed to tell my clients that this place is off-limits? Knowing Mary Elizabeth, that will make her want to book the plantation at all costs."

"You can't let that happen, Cat. If you keep quiet for a minute, I'll tell you what I can about the operation I'm involved in. We're reasonably sure this is the base for a human and drug trafficking operation."

I think I don't hear him correctly. "You're not talking about exploiting children, are you? How in the hell did you get involved in that?"

"Interstate activity means the FBI is involved. Trafficking and drug pushers go hand in hand these days. They use the children for sex and to move the drugs. When it crosses county and/or state lines, my phone rings. In many of these cases, we work with the local law enforcement. But not this case. It's a bit too complicated for the local sheriff. Maybe we'll bring them in later, but right now, only the FBI is involved."

He pauses, letting what he said sink in before he continues, "Here's what I can tell you. As fast as we break up a gang of traffickers, another one takes its place. The kids are always the losers. Sometimes, we manage to rescue them. But we can't guarantee what happens to them next. The courts often put them in foster homes— sometimes with abusive foster parents, or sometimes they land in jail, or if they're lucky, rehab. Some run off again, and another gang snags them. It's a dark, dirty, unspoken oozing wound in this country for a while, and it's making its way big time into South Carolina. We're trying to stop it."

I reach for his hand and say, "Nick, I'm sorry. I didn't know. I was only thinking of myself and how frightened I was. Your call came right after the incident at the plantation. That seemed suspicious. You're doing a good thing, but FBI agent? You hated school. The last time I heard, you had a football scholarship to Clemson. What happened?"

He shrugs but doesn't look at me. My side-view glimpse of his profile shows bits of gray woven through the dark, longer-than-usual hair that's pulled loose from a leather tie. There's a coarseness in his manner, his clothes, and his eyes that speak of the unspeakable.

After a long pause, he turns and says, "At mid-term, I got an offer to transfer to the University of South Carolina in Columbia. I changed my major to criminology and law and stopped playing football. There's no time to tell you all the details. Not now."

"When would be a good time?"

He turns away and stares out the window before saying, "I need you to fill in what happened on the day you encountered the attacker. According to the agents I'm working with, this place has been staked out for weeks without any sign of life. No movement, nothing but boarded windows and rotten wood. Before you went spiraling off the deck, I saw you look in the back windows. You stayed there a long time. I figured you saw something. It's important I know what you saw. The lives of these kids might depend on some inconsequential piece of evidence."

He studies my face, ready to pull the information out of my skin if I don't give him answers. I close my eyes and sink into the darkness that always keeps its hand tucked around my elbow. Nick touches my shoulder.

"Please, Cat."

"The first thing was the music. As I walked from the front of the house to the back, Viennese waltzes were playing."

"What? Well, that's strange. I guess I wasn't close enough to the house to hear music. But what could you see inside when you looked through those windows?"

"Why? If you're staking the place out, surely you've seen inside the house, right?"

There's a slight pause before Nick speaks. "Actually, I just joined the on-site operation a couple of days ago. Another agent and I take turns watching from the wood line while we wait on a search warrant. These things take time to secure, particularly in small towns. The local law enforcement doesn't like the FBI interfering unless they're involved in the operation. In the short time I've been here, those back windows have been blacked out, and there have been no signs of life. The structure is a rotten death trap, which makes it a good place for an operation like this. At the same time, it makes it difficult to stake out."

My mind wanders back to the room. I shake my head, "Well, you're going to be surprised when I tell you what I saw. It was totally unexpected."

"What do you mean?"

My mind roams through the file cabinet in my brain. It collects images and conjures up each item before I begin.

"I expected the outside of the house to be derelict and the inside to have a totally rotten infrastructure. When I looked inside and saw a completely furnished room, I was shocked. Everything was new. It's clear to me that someone lives there."

I pause. The memories flood.

"At first, I thought I was seeing things. That often happens to me, imagining things that aren't really there."

"What do you mean you imagine things that aren't there? Are you telling me you're not a reliable witness?"

"Like your story, mine is too long to tell you now. If we ever have that lunch, we can catch up, right? But yes, I'm telling you that I can't guarantee I'm a reliable witness. You'll have to decide if I am."

I pause. He pats my hand. When I don't continue, he says, "Take your time." But his body twitches. His urgency is obvious.

"The sofa faced the fireplace. There was a fire—gas logs, I think, from the flicker of the low flame."

He smiles and says, "That's a good start."

"The sofa was leather, a sort of mahogany color. There were two side chairs—maybe taupe. A coffee table was stacked with books and magazines, and there was a large rug underneath—a brown and white checkerboard."

I must have slipped away into the darkness of my memories without realizing it until Nick nudges my shoulder. "What else? Please go on."

Closing my eyes, I continue, "There was a fully stocked bar and a work area—computers, headphones, and all sorts of sophisticated-looking equipment—oh and a TV. That was shocking since the realtor I spoke with said there was no running water or electricity. Clearly, that's not true from all the electronics I saw."

"What else?"

"It was creepy looking through the window. I was invading some-one's privacy. It was so unexpected to see a fully furnished room. I stayed glued to the window because I thought I was imagining the entire thing ."

When Nick doesn't respond, I open my eyes. He's staring straight through the windshield. Maybe he's not listening.

"Someone is living in that dilapidated property. Is that what you think? Is this a hideout of some kind?"

He grabs my arm. He doesn't answer my question but asks one of his own, "Is that everything you saw?"

"Almost, but no, not quite. There was a screen at the far end of the room, some kind of room divider with a water theme. I don't exactly remember—maybe marshes, bamboo, lots of egrets—something like that. There was a bed. The end jutted out about two feet from the screen. That's a clear indicator that someone is living there."

"And?"

"It was around that time I heard the boards creak behind me."

I pause again, waiting for Nick to speak. He searches my face, tracing my hair, eyes, nose, and lips.

He blurts out, "Holy shit, Cat! You were always the smartest kid in our class. And now it seems you have a photographic memory. That's one thorough description. You only had a couple of minutes before that dude appeared and tried to smash you over the head. I'm impressed. Maybe you need to be an FBI agent."

Relief at someone believing what I saw has me close to tears. I'm also flattered that an FBI investigator thinks I know my stuff until he says, "Describe the guy."

"I can't."

"Why not?" His hand tightens around my wrist. "It's important, Cat."

"Gosh, Nick. You were there too! You said you saw him try to hit me with the hammer. Surely, you can describe him better than I can."

"No. I wasn't close enough. You must have seen something—his shoes, trousers, anything?"

I pull away and say, "Nick, a few months ago, I barely escaped with my life. I was in Italy searching for Stella. It's why I was so upset when you asked for Stella's address?"

He nods and says in a soft, sensuous voice, "Stella. She was the most beautiful girl I've ever known. You are still in touch with her, aren't you? What's she got to do with this?"

"Stella was murdered, Nick," my breath catches in my throat.

7

"What? What do you mean Stella was murdered? That's not possible. It would have made the headlines even here." He stops and stares at me and then says, "Is this one of the things you might have imagined?"

Blood rushes to my face when I hear his words.

"Stella's death is real. It's not something I imagined."

"Well, I'm sorry. Maybe when we meet again, you can tell me what happened. Right now, this operation is my only focus. I need a description of your assailant. It's critical to the investigation."

"You're sorry? You're sorry that Stella is dead? How considerate of you."

He grabs hold of my hands and leans in close, "Cat, nothing I say will change that. We'll talk about Stella later, okay? But now it's imperative that you give me a description of your attacker."

"I can't, Nick. It happened too quickly. He was only a blur."

He's still holding my hands. He tightens his grip until I'm winching with pain. I pry his fingers off and pull away from him.

"What's happened to you, Nick? You've become cynical? Is it your job?"

He doesn't look at me, just shakes his head.

"I'm still dealing with Stella's death and my own close call with death. Whatever FBI operation you're involved in, it doesn't include me. I didn't see the attacker."

"Shit, Cat. I didn't mean it to come out that way. I promise that once this operation is over, we'll spend lots of time together. Okay?

You can tell me everything, but right now, I need you to think. These kids deserve our help."

"That's a below-the-belt tactic, Nick. When I said I couldn't describe the person, I meant it. All I saw was a reflection. Male, taller than me by a head, with a dark hoodie covering most of the face. When I saw a hammer in his hand, I didn't stop to ask what color his eyes were. The adrenaline kicked in. I hit the deck. The next thing I remember was lying face down in the sand. That's it! Now, I would like to leave."

While I'm speaking, all his facial features tense. His jaw clenches and unclenches several times as if he's reminding himself to stay calm. His stare out the windshield is vacant.

He turns slowly and says, "Are you sure? It's crucial I get a detailed description of the person. Anything would be beneficial. It was probably one of the traffickers. We desperately need to ID them."

"I have nothing more to add, Nick."

We sit in silence.

Finally, he says, "If later on you remember anything about the attacker, text me. From now on, that's the only way to reach me. Whatever you do, don't call me. I can't have my phone vibrating in the middle of a sting. Understand? And not a word to anyone about seeing me. Okay? You have to promise; otherwise, these children will be in grave danger. I'll stay in touch, but you need to promise."

I nod in a non-committal way because I don't understand any part of this conversation. He grabs my hands in a vice grip and refuses to let go until I promise. Then he kisses each hand with a flourish and bounds out the car. He removes the shrubbery and vanishes. Red marks outline the imprint of his fingers on my skin.

The wind pushes the trees into a frenzied dance. Thunder bombards my ears. Lightning splits the sky. Trees sway into distorted monster shapes. Their branches clutch and choke each other before they release battle-weary limbs. One whacks the windshield like a gunshot. My arms wrap around my head. I cringe and coil into a cramped knot across the seat to stop the trembling. When it doesn't, I clasp the red starfish bracelet and count.

The magical starfish bracelet is only one of Stella's many gifts to me. It's like some strange talisman that I can't take off. With my body plastered on the car seat, the floodgates open. Fear penetrates deep into my core. My fingers rhythmically move across the finely cut ruby stone. The thunder rumbles. Lightning outlines the crashing tree limbs. My mind drifts off to Castello del Mare with Stella by my side. The years roll away.

Stella's seventeen year old eyes glowed like blue sapphires. She could hardly breathe or form sentences from the anticipation of showing me the bracelet.

"Look," she exclaimed with tears cascading down her cheeks. "Antonio asked me to wait for him—you know, marry him."

She thrust the box in my face and said, "It's a pre-engagement gift."

Inside the deep royal blue box nestled in the folds of white satin was a spectacular bracelet. She whispered that Antonio had it custom-designed by the famous jeweler Aldo Cipullo. At seventeen, we had no sense of what that meant. To us, it was the essence of romance, a shimmering declaration of love straight from our childhood fairy tales. We were so young, but we knew we were looking at a piece of jewelry out of our price range. The bracelet had spiraled gold bands on one side with clusters of leaf-shaped diamonds on the other. Suspended in the middle was a ruby shaped like a starfish. It, too, was surrounded by diamonds. We were spellbound and speechless.

Twenty-plus years later, in Stella's will, she left me both the bracelet and the starfish necklace that Antonio presented to her on their wedding day. Before I left Italy for home, I'd offered both pieces of jewelry to Stella's estranged husband. Although, it's probably time to call him Stella's widower since they never divorced. I wanted to keep the starfish bracelet, but I thought it was fair to offer him both. He refused, insisted the two pieces were a matching set and Stella wanted me to have both of them.

When I suggested he might remarry, have children and want to pass them on, he looked at me in horror. Then he begged me to take them, saying they meant nothing but pain to him. After an exhaustive conversation, I gave up and now I'm the owner of two priceless pieces of jewelry. The bracelet is part of my daily life, but the necklace stays locked in my safe. Will I ever wear it is the big question.

But in the end, bracelets, necklaces, fame, or fortune—none of them saved my beautiful friend Stella.

Once the storm abates and the trembling stops, I crank the engine and back out of the wooded area. The wiper blades slap into action as I twist the knob to high speed. My rapid breathing and the whack of the windshield wipers are in sync. A high-pitched whine tortures my ears as the blades strike debris and scrape it against the glass. A strange sort of rhythm plays in my head. It reminds me of yesterday's strains of Tales from the Vienna Woods. Those long-ago dancers swirling around the porch—lost forever in a single moment of grandeur that died too soon—like Stella.

Breathing deeply, I refocus my thoughts and speed up as I approach the driveway to the plantation. The brooding structure is barely discernible through the maze of massive oaks. As I pass the entrance, a big sigh of relief flows out of my body until a figure in a dark hooded pullover steps out of the bushes in front of the car. The wild waving of arms with what looks like a weapon pointed in my direction has me stomping on the gas.

I swerve to avoid hitting the person and fight the wheel to keep from pitching into the water-filled ditch. Accelerating without looking back, I don't slow down until I leave the heavy canopy of overlapping oaks. The asphalt surface of the road and the shrill ring of Cassie's call reassure me I will make it home alive.

He waited until Cat started the engine. Then Nick raced through the trees. He had to stop what he thought might happen. The under-brush grabbed his arms and legs, but he kept on plowing through the dense bramble. He could hear Cat's car catching up with him. He picked up speed and hoped he wasn't too late. He saw the hooded figure and the gun flailing in the air as he approached the edge of the plantation driveway. As Cat's car passed, he hurled himself forward, slamming into the body with enough force to block Cat from being shot. For a moment, the thought crossed his mind that there might be a wrestling match, and he might lose. He was too angry to care what the outcome might be.

Nick reared back and said, "Are you crazy? What do you think you're doing? Every time you show up, you cause trouble. You think the police wouldn't have been all over this place if you'd shot her?"

"Heck, Nick. What's your problem? I was having a little fun with the charming redhead you seem to like so much. Why were you snuggling with her in the car? What happens when I tell *the boss* about her?"

"You keep your stupid mouth shut. What made you attempt to attack her yesterday? What are you doing here?"

"Just checking on you like *the boss* asked. He likes to know you're doing your job and not getting squeamish."

"Get out of here. You're lucky I'm not going to tell him what happened here. What kind of idiot are you? I've told you to stay away. You have no right to use my place, drink my wine, or play my music. Do you understand? Why were you here yesterday? What made you raise the blackout shades on the back windows? Are you that stupid? What did you plan on doing with that hammer? Kill her? What do you think *the boss* would say to that?"

The man stalked away. Nick watched until he slipped out of sight. He stayed rooted to the spot until he heard the van rumble away. Now what? The entire operation was spinning out of control because of this stupid thug. God, what was he going to do? With this oaf and now Cat, he didn't see how things could get much worse. Cat had seen the inside of the house, and she was smart. She knows someone is living there. She'd even heard the music playing. He knew the promise she made not to tell anyone would probably not be kept. It would be a matter of time. Then what would he do?

8

"Is everything okay? I'm calling like you asked—forty-five minutes from the time you left your house. What's going on?"

"Nothing, really. It turned out this old classmate wanted some information on a piece of property his boss might purchase."

"Oh, is that all? I was worried some creep might abduct you?"

Cassie's warm laughter bursts into the car.

"Guess I wasn't enough of a trophy for him. Anyway, I'm on the way home. All is good. Thanks for checking on me, Cass."

"Oh gosh, you'd do the same for me. Want to grab something to eat tonight?"

"No, I'm going to stay in. This storm looks like it might hang around. But I'll see you tomorrow. You're still coming in the morning, right?"

"Sure, I'll see you then. We're prepping for the Fitzhugh's Spanish meal, right?

"Yes, that's the one. See ya."

After a long, very hot shower, I open a bottle of Grillo, pour a large glass, and take a big gulp before rummaging through the fridge. I balance a carton of eggs, porcini mushrooms, chives, Kalamata olives, and Fontina and nudge the door closed with my shoulder.

After another swallow of wine, I settle into the mechanics of cooking. The slow, rhythmic pace of counting while I slice mushrooms, chop potatoes, and mince garlic blocks all sinister thoughts. I love everything about food: buying it, storing it, preparing it, serving it, and especially eating it with friends. There is a lovely saying in Italian—*la cucina è il cuore della casa*—the kitchen is the heart of the home. I repeat these lyrical words over and over until a calmness gathers in my thoughts and movements.

After I whisk the eggs with Italian seasonings, I dump the mixture over the veggies that are already sizzling in the skillet. I lift and fold until the eggs reach the soft stage. Chopped Castelvetrano olives and grated Parmesan cheese are added. I run the skillet under the broiler. A few minutes later, a crusty, bubbling frittata emerges. I refill my glass and drizzle first cold press olive oil over a *caprese* salad. A couple of slices of olive-studded bread complete the meal.

Focusing on every single bite, I refuse to rehash any part of today's activities. It's the only way to hold onto whatever sanity I have left. There's no room in my life for more trauma. The only solution to recover is to ignore Nick and fill my calendar with work. Dr. Ginny assured me the nightmares will stop. She said one day I would remember only the good things about Stella and Italy. I want to believe her. I want to reclaim my love and my sweet memories of them both.

After I eat every morsel on my plate, I wash the dishes. I count and recount the utensils as I stack them side-by-side in the drawer. Little by little, the tension melts away. I check each door and window multiple times. The alarm system is set, but there is no peace in my body. I pace back and forth. Images of the bloodbath I experienced in Italy taunt me. After months of intense therapy with Dr. Ginny, the flashbacks have tapered off. But the recent scare at Carrington Point and today's meeting with Nick flood my mind with new fears that are piling up on top of old ones.

I turn the TV on and off several times. I open a tin of freshly made truffles and sniff the intense, dark chocolate with hints of raspberry. In the midst of trauma, or really any time, chocolate is my drug of choice. Oh, if only it were possible for me to have just one. Instead,

I stand in the middle of the room and mindlessly stuff two into my mouth. My fingers reach for a third.

Momentarily sated, I retrieve *The Tree of Life* by Hugh Nissenson from my nightstand and crawl under the covers. But this book unsettles me further. Why do I have a book called *The Tree of Life*?

When I unexpectedly returned from Italy after Stella had officially been ruled dead, I moved in with my friend Cassie. The person renting my house had signed a year's lease and wasn't willing to move out early. I even offered to reimburse him and find him another place, but he refused.

It turned out to be for the best, as I needed someone who cared about me when I woke up screaming during the night. Cassie was always there. Often, I'd find her sitting on the edge of my bed as I struggled out of another nightmare. She'd stroke my hair and mutter soft clucking sounds until a restless sleep returned.

When the day came to return home, Cassie and I cleaned the house from top to bottom. We thought we had boxed up and shipped everything the renter left behind. Some months later, when I was scanning my bookshelves for something to read, I came across several books about trees. As I flipped through them, I knew they weren't mine. Some were scientific textbooks, others were nonfiction, and several were fiction. There were books describing the ancient history of trees in great detail. One was about a species of tree called Moringa, known as the Tree of Life, for its healing power and nutritional value.

The renter must have left them. When I contacted him, he was adamant the books weren't his. Months later, I don't know why I have this small stack of books. Were they mine? Had I simply forgotten I had them? Were they part of my memory loss? When I couldn't explain them away, I accepted them as magical gifts. My plan is to read them all.

A few nights ago, I counted them. I reread the cover of each book before selecting this simple volume. It's been waiting on my nightstand. Tonight, I open it and read the introduction by Margo Jefferson:

Art and history (life as we have known it) do sprout from rot, and yet truth and beauty can be raised—resurrected—within us.

The vibration of my phone sends my heart racing. A text from Nick says, *See you made it safely home. Thanks for meeting me today. See you soon.*

I cut off the lamp and sleep without dreams or nightmares.

9

The Fitzhugh's dinner party glows with Lowcountry perfection. Guests stroll the lush green lawn as they nibble on tapas paired with a 2007 Gramona Reserva. A light breeze drifts off the water, enough to keep the mosquitos at bay. The moon hangs low over the marsh as guests glide toward the veranda.

Sarah pops into the kitchen. She leans against the counter as she surveys the feast we are preparing. She giggles and whispers like a child ready to blow out candles on a birthday cake.

"Cat, have you seen him? He's so distinguished."

I look up from plating the cold Spanish soup and smile.

"No, I haven't seen him. Does distinguished mean he's handsome, or does he dress well and look like a toad?"

"Oh, Cat, you have a warped sense of humor. Wait until you see him! Of course, he's handsome, and he's elegant, cultured, refined, dignified, not to mention sophisticated. I could ramble on forever. But if you're ready to start the dinner service, you'll see him, and you'll be drooling."

I smile, nod, and watch as Sarah, in her lovely green gown, sashays through the door and makes her way toward the dinner guests. As soon as she and the other guests settle into their places around the table, a La Fincas rosado is poured into chilled glasses.

The long table is draped with a pale yellow cloth. It shimmers like a field of sunflowers. Miniature red vases brimming with red and yellow roses are evenly spaced down the length of the table. Tapered red candles shoot flames into the already luminous night. Waiters attired in white shirts and black trousers serve the gazpacho along with baskets of crusty bread. Laughter, glasses, and silverware tinkle as Venus rises. The constellations display a magical light show.

I check the progress of the meal through the kitchen window. Cassie stands by my side and whispers, "I caught an eyeful of that good-looking count. Have you seen him yet?"

"Just a glimpse. I also saw his lovely dark-eyed companion. She's clearly keeping tabs on him, so don't get carried away by the royalty bit. I have a feeling she's got fangs."

Sarah and Henry Fitzhugh always invite eclectic guests, and tonight's list doesn't disappoint—a chief justice, the commander from the base, the mayor, a state senator, and the head of the Chamber with their wives or partners. The window only provides a partial view of the table, but the one glance I had of the count as he crossed the lawn made it clear why heads turned in his direction. The intrigue about his ancestor washing up on our shore is enough to keep tongues wagging. It's quite the coup for this small Southern town.

Once the empty soup bowls are returned to the kitchen, Cassie takes over and pushes me reluctantly into the spotlight. I hate this part of any event. But Sarah insists I serve the main course and the dessert table side. She likes to put on a big show. If it were anyone other than Sarah asking, I'd refuse. Cassie gives me a quick hug, whispers that all is okay, and holds the door open for me.

The paella is displayed on an oversized white platter shaped like a fish. The red hue of the saffron threads infuses the rice until it's a burnished gold. Piled on top and dispersed throughout the rice are lobster, shrimp, squid, clams, mussels, chunks of ham, and tiny peas. Extra clams and mussels in the shell are arranged around the outer edge. Barely steamed green beans and thin slices of crispy red bell peppers are intermixed. The presentation is spectacular.

Ohhhs and ahhhs and a splattering of applause erupt as the paella is placed on a serving table next to a stack of Flora Danica Orchid dinner plates—the kind I'm afraid to touch. After scooping out generous servings of the paella, I place a miniature ceramic cup of garlicky tomato aioli on each plate. The servers have instructions on how to add it to the paella once the plate is placed in front of the guest.

Wine and water glasses are refilled, and bread baskets are replenished. Before rushing back to the safety of the kitchen, I glance around the table until the count comes into range. He looks up. Our eyes lock. I can see why Sarah used all those adjectives to describe him—aristocratic is the word I choose before scurrying back to the kitchen.

Silence descends as the guests devour the meal. Gradually, conversation resumes, and empty plates are removed from the table.

Salads of mixed greens with cumin vinaigrette are served with platters of cheese and plump purple grapes. The servers clear plates and utensils, top off wine glasses and retrieve lost napkins. The idyllic scene disintegrates when a commotion erupts. A loud voice sputters obscenities. Cassie and I rush to the door, but Sarah stops us.

"It's okay. It's just Senator Madison in a tizzy," she whispers. "A bit of water splashed on his sleeve. He chastised the server—so unnecessary. He's such a rude man. I only invited him because the count wanted to meet some of the important people in the area. Oh gracious, I'll have to smooth things over. Instead of waiting another fifteen minutes to serve dessert, why don't you start now? That will divert attention away from him."

We watch Sarah work her magic as she shoos the server away, presents the senator with a clean cloth napkin, and says something to make him laugh.

"Wow," Cassie breathes into my ear. Her voice trembles with excitement. "When did we elect such a good-looking guy to be our state senator? I don't remember voting for him."

In my opinion, the man making all the fuss is a flushed-faced pompous ass. Why make such a stink over such a small incident? At least his partner has the decency to be embarrassed. I watch as she places her hand on his arm and gives him a very slight shake of her head—not enough to move the perfectly shimmering silvery blonde hair styled in the latest long bob. He jerks his arm away, but it seems her touch is enough to stop his tirade.

Cassie and I stand in the door a little longer and soak in the magical night. The moon rotates across the water, creating orbs of gold. I hum *It's a Wonderful World*. We return to the kitchen to prepare the dessert.

The dense, black coffee is ready. Cassie sets up a tray with sherry glasses and a bottle of El Maestro Sierra, a 15-year-old Oloroso, while I remove the flan from the fridge.

Flan, the Spanish name for cream caramel, is a showstopper if it comes out right. If it doesn't, then it's a collapsed mass of curdled custard. I run an inch of warm water in the sink and slide the rectangular container into the warm bath for thirty seconds. I pull it out and gently wipe the bottom and do a quick flip onto the waiting platter. The soft plop of the flan's release announces perfection.

All the work is worthwhile as I watch the caramel sauce ooze across the top, slide down the sides, and puddle on the platter. Blueberries, peach chunks, and strawberries are scattered around the outer edges, with a bouquet of mint on top. Cassie lets out a low whistle of appreciation. She pours the rich, slightly chilled sherry into the cut crystal glasses and follows me out the door.

Back in the kitchen, we gather platters and cooking utensils and begin the long, slow process of cleaning up. Cassie pours two glasses of wine and holds one out to me. As I reach across the counter, my hand hits the stem. A splash of deep red liquid dribbles down my chef's jacket. It joins a splotch of orange from the saffron, a smudge from the blueberries, and a red swirl from the gazpacho. I'm a work of art like Henri Matisse's *Red Interior*. Using a damp cloth, I smear the colors into a kaleidoscopic mess. Nothing I do makes it look better, and I forgot to bring a backup chef's jacket.

When I'm elbow-deep in soapy water, the kitchen door flings open. Sarah marches in with the guest of honor. I stare. Wow! Up close, the princely guy is far more than eye candy. He sweeps across the length of the kitchen, gently lifts my hand out of the sink, and pats it dry with a kitchen cloth before bringing it to his lips. The tickle of his mustache and his warm breath mingle on my damp hand.

He straightens but does not release my hand. His hair is squid-ink black, and his eyes are as blue as Royal Delft. His complexion is light olive. There's a mesmerizing, mysterious aura about him. He's tall with a slender frame. The exquisitely tailored Savile Row suit paints a picture of privilege: yachts, polo ponies, private planes, and villas on the Mediterranean Sea. He is elegant.

My hand remains firmly captured in his as he speaks, "I am Alfonso Fernando Felipe Francisco Perez, but you can call me Al."

To my dismay and his, I burst out laughing. "You can call me Al? Really?"

His eyes widen in confusion. His eyebrows raise in question. He shakes his head from side to side as I make floundering attempts to explain myself,

"Paul Simon? *Graceland? You can call me Al*—you don't know what I'm talking about, do you?"

No one speaks as I sputter and attempt to escape my own stupidity. Sarah frowns and taps the count on his shoulder. He turns toward her but does not release my hand. She explains through bits of Spanish and English about Paul Simon's *Graceland* album and the song "You Can Call Me Al."

I'm mortified. Flames of embarrassment lick red splotches up my neck and across my face. The count nods at Sarah, turns back to me, and says, "Yes, you can call me Al. I like that it makes you laugh."

His mouth curves into a captivating smile as he continues, "The meal was superb. Every morsel was delicious, as were the Spanish wine selections. Your attention to detail is exemplary. You are exactly the person I need."

"What do you mean?" I sputter.

"Oh, Señora, what I mean is the people of this beautiful Lowcountry have showered me with their magnificent Southern hospitality. A party to thank them is exactly what is required, and you must prepare the food."

Before I can think of anything remotely appropriate to say, the kitchen door flies open again, and the count's exquisite companion enters the room. Her black silk dress ripples in the whoosh from the swinging door. Her hair is as black and silky as her outfit. It's coiled in a knot high on her head. Her deep-set black eyes dismiss the wait staff, Sarah, and me with a steeliness until they light on my new friend Al.

"Oh, Alfonso," she gushes and lapses into Spanish.

Now, it's his turn for red splotches to creep up his neck and smear a flush to the roots of his hair. He nods at her rapid explosion of words, drops my hand, and turns his back.

He says to Sarah, "I am so sorry. Margarita is tired. We must leave. It has been a delightful evening. Thank you for your hospitality."

The entourage leaves the kitchen and moves onto the veranda. Their voices fade into the night air. When we can no longer hear the soft mutters, the entire staff, along with Cassie and I, dissolve into uncontrollable laughter.

Slipping out the side door, I watch the guests depart in their fancy cars or the more pretentious limos with drivers. One of the drivers stands out from the others. He's unusually tall with a shaved head. His muscles bulge in a clearly rented tux that doesn't fit. The senator and the count walk down the driveway, their heads bent as if their chat is serious. The senator stops at the limo with the ill-fitted tux driver. He nods at the driver and gestures. The count shakes the driver's hand. Rather strange, I think, which brings back images of Nick's clenched jaw and the assailant holding the hammer over my head. A current of fear runs through me.

10

Days drift by. I move in and out of the dark moments of my mind. There are no more ominous messages from Nick. I dismiss him from my thoughts. Numerous events fill my calendar as the year moves toward Mardi Gras, Valentine's, and St. Patrick's.

Additional meetings with Mary Elizabeth produce more whines about how Carrington Point Plantation is the perfect spot. I continue to coax her to choose Tidal Bay for the wedding reception. The view, the layout, the convenience to town, and plenty of parking—all fall on deaf ears—inconveniences and extra expenses do not deter Mary Elizabeth.

Dr. Ginny says I'm better, stronger. Her office is my safe space, as is listening to her lyrical what-I've-come-to-call "Nonna" voice. It lulls me to Castello del Mare and the good memories—memories that were made long before Stella disappeared and before the magic of those days had been tarnished by betrayal, destruction, and death.

As I sort through those memories, I remind myself to Zoom with Maria. It's something we do almost every week. Occasionally, Gino's head will pop onto the screen with a quick smile and wave. My lovely villa overlooking the sea, the one Stella left me, stays booked with vacation renters almost year-round. The rent more than covers the maintenance as well as Maria and Gino's caretaker salaries, little Gino's private tutor, and any special medical treatments he needs. We never mention Stella's murder or the close brush with death that Gino and I experienced at Carlo Rossini's hand. It hangs loosely and silently over our heads.

Often, during these floating-away times in Dr. Ginny's office, Stella joins me. I can't let her go—not yet. Ginny tells me to stop wearing the bracelet. She patiently explains it would be beneficial to me if I locked it away along with the necklace. She says hanging onto them are reminders of Stella, and it's detrimental to my progress.

Yes, I understand that, but it's the reason I keep them. It's not complicated why I clasp the bracelet around my wrist every single day. The mere act of wearing it keeps Stella with me. Her body was never found, leaving me with only a tiny flicker of hope and a huge plate of agony.

Dr. Ginny once asked me if I thought the red starfish would protect me. Maybe. All I know is that whenever I touch it, Stella magically appears. I'm no longer alone.

When Stella is not front and center in my thoughts, Lorenzo is. Some days, I see his face so clearly I turn, thinking his arms will embrace me. In his eyes, there is always a sweet tenderness. Occasionally, a text appears from him. When it does, my heart races.

Come va, Cat? How are you? Antonio is well. His sentence reduced for good behavior. Full-time practice will resume in a few months. With Carlo dead, we have destabilized part of the SCU (Sacra Corona Unita). When are you returning to Castello? Everyone misses you.

Dr. Ginny's voice breaks through, reminding me to continue my daily meditation and journaling and to practice erasing the dark tapes in my head, one frame at a time.

After my morning walk and shower, I take my laptop to the screened porch and consider the menus for my next two events: a business luncheon for twenty at the Lowcountry Golf Club and a wedding reception for two hundred fifty at Tidal Bay.

My cell phone jangles. Since I don't recognize the number, I let it go to message.

"Hello, hello, this is Alfonso Fernando." There's a long pause, then, "You can call me Al."

Another long pause, a chuckle, and finally, "Would you please return my call? I'm calling to see if you are available for lunch on Friday at the Waterfront Inn? Before I return to Spain, I want to plan a celebration. The one I spoke to you about at Señora Fitzhugh's dinner party. I think perhaps seventy-five guests. We could discuss the event over lunch on Friday. I'd be pleased if you would accept."

Not much detail, I think. He's not leaving me any choice other than to call him back if I want to know more. Clients used to be the driving force on whether or not I would cater an event. Not anymore. Not since Mrs. Harrington decided to destroy my reputation. These days, if the date is available, I take the event. The location, menu, number of guests, and host/hostess have almost become immaterial.

Seventy-five for the count's event is easily manageable if Cassie and her daughter Sam can help and if he budgets to hire extra wait staff. Even if I choose not to do the event, I have to return the call. There's some vague magnetism about the count that creeps under my skin. I can't decide if this is a good or bad thing. All I know is if the date is already booked, there won't be a need for a discussion over lunch.

I procrastinate calling Al back. The thought of seeing him makes me nervous. I remember how he held onto my hand—too long and too tight—and how his companion Margarita dismissed me. I'm sure she wouldn't be pleased with the idea of Al and me having lunch. If she joined us, that would be an added strain. The gleam in his eye when he kissed my hand said he liked women—a lot. He's a charmer and is used to getting his way.

Putting off the call won't make it go away. Reluctantly, I punch in the number. His assistant answers on the first ring. I state the reason for my call. He says the count isn't available. He clears his throat and asks if I'm available to meet the count for lunch. I respond only if the date for the count's event is one that's available. He gives me the date and waits while I check my calendar. I'm hoping it isn't available, but it is.

I want to tell him it's not available, but the money would be helpful. Insurance pays only so much for the therapy, and I have to cough up the rest. I'm far from destitute, but since my fall from grace, the events are not as frequent, and my income isn't as steady. I'd dipped big time into my inheritance for the failed sabbatical to Italy. I don't want to keep doing that.

The assistant asks if I'm still on the line and if the date is available.

"Yes," I respond.

"The count will expect you on Friday at one at the Waterfront Inn. Please do not keep him waiting."

I hang up and spend the next half hour berating myself for saying yes.

Friday, after my usual early morning walk and shower, I open my closet and plow through my wardrobe for something decent to wear. All of my time is spent in a chef's jacket, exercise clothes, or raggedy jeans or shorts, depending on the weather. I haven't had a formal business meeting or a date since John Ashley Williams demanded his engagement ring back. I chuckle sardonically as I recall a couple of lunch dates with Carlo, my would-be-murderer. It's the first time I've laughed about the deadly experience since it happened.

Yes, I think the therapy is working. As soon as I sigh with relief, the distorted black cloud of Riccardo's face appears. Shaking my head, I push the image away and let my hands sift through the few decent wardrobe items I own. They land on an emerald green dress with a flared skirt and scooped neck. I put emerald studs in my ears and snap Stella's bracelet around my wrist. I think about adding the starfish necklace, but it's too fancy and way too ostentatious. It would require a far more formal affair than lunch to wear it.

The image of Stella in the red Gucci gown she had worn to the gala in New York slides into my thoughts. She had just surprised me with a large packet of information and tickets for our 40th birthdays. Being born on the same day in the same year by mothers who were best friends made it inevitable that Stella and I would be best friends. When I had opened the packet, tickets to Andrea Bocelli's concert in Tuscany had spilled out. That had been the last time I saw her.

At that moment, it dawns on me to ask Maria to mail me Stella's dress. Yes, wearing it and the starfish necklace would be a way to honor Stella at the concert. I'll need to devise a plan, so Maria will mail the dress to me without becoming suspicious. She's already warned me not to go to the concert. But I must— it will be my final pilgrimage to honor Stella. I promised her I would go.

Lifting my hair off my shoulders, I twist my red curls into a shaggy knot and secure them with a hair clip. I add a dab of lipstick, shrug my shoulders at my cleaned-up appearance and grin. I feel pretty foolish spending so much time to appear glamorous for Al. What am I thinking?

Grabbing my purse and keys, I open the front door. My cell vibrates. I cringe when I see a text from Nick:

Need to talk. Meet me at the waterfront in ten minutes. Stand by the far end near the boat ramp.

Can't, I text back. *On way to meeting.*

The reply comes back quickly. *Sorry, but this isn't a request. This is the FBI. Be there.*

Five minutes have passed since I showed up at the waterfront. Now I'm five minutes late to meet Al.

I call his assistant, who says, "I'll give the message to Count

Perez, but do not expect him to wait for you. He has another engagement scheduled after lunch."

What a pain in the butt this count is, or maybe it's just his assistant. Now, I'm adding Nick to that same list. If black clouds were available for the asking, one would be dangling over my head as I pace back and forth on the promenade. Two more minutes, then I'm gone.

I lean against the concrete piling and watch the water full of debris from last night's storm. The choppy current ripples toward the ocean. Gazing across the river, I command my shoulders to relax and my stomach to untangle as my eyes follow the steel gray water pushing against the green burnished with gold marshes. Layers of palms and oaks shrouded with Spanish moss line the riverbank. Silent pools of water brim with sea creatures. They wait for the incoming tide. The wide river cradles sleepy sailboats. Cumulus clouds hover in hues of pearly silk and creamy marshmallow. The Norwegian Queen, with passengers waving from the deck, glides past on its way to Hilton Head.

The heat from his body alerts me. Before I can turn around, he pulls me into an embrace with my back planted against his chest. He whispers in my ear, "My, aren't you dolled up today. Meeting your lover?"

I dig my elbows into his stomach to get free. His arms tighten. His body presses into mine.

"Don't call attention to us, Cat. Stand still, don't struggle, and listen. Pretend I'm whispering passionate words in your ear. Can you do that?"

I nod. He continues, "Yesterday, those two women—the ones with you the other day—they came back to the plantation. You know who I'm talking about? Did you know they were coming? Did you agree to have a function there? If so, you have to cancel it. I thought you understood the danger. What else do I have to say to get you to understand that you have to stay away?"

Through clenched teeth, I say, "I don't have a clue what you are talking about. As far as I know, the venue for the wedding reception hasn't been decided. After speaking with you, I steered them away from Carrington Point. Trust me, I do not want to cater an event there."

"Well, they can't come out there again. Do you understand? The place is off-limits. It's too dangerous. It's your responsibility to make sure they understand that."

"Why do you think I can control who comes and goes out there? If the Berkleys choose to have the wedding reception at Carrington Point, I can't stop them. Yes, I can refuse to cater the event. That's the easy part. Don't you understand? They can easily hire someone else. That's out of my control. Nick, nothing about this makes sense. Why are you demanding I keep these people away from the plantation? It sounds like a threat? Is it?"

He's so close I can count his heartbeats. In my ears, it sounds like a drum roll. His hands slide down my arms and tightened around my wrists. "Cat, I can't afford to flub up this operation. I'm asking you to please stop these people from visiting the property again. They cannot have an event there. It's not your fault you stepped into the middle of a sting, but this isn't a request. It's mandatory. You and your clients must stay away from Carrington. You don't want to be responsible for anyone getting hurt, do you?"

He pulls my arms in opposite directions until I'm hugging myself, except it hurts. His arms are wrapped around my arms as he hisses, "This is the last time I'm telling you. Stay away. Tell those people anything, but keep them away from the property. Do you understand?"

When I nod, my head bumps his chin.

"I'm leaving now. Stay exactly where you are. Don't turn around until at least a full sixty seconds have passed. I'm sorry, Cat. I don't have a choice. Neither do you."

He disappears as quickly as he arrives. When I turn, there is no trace of him.

11

I sprint to the inn. Arriving in a breathless shamble, I locate the restrooms off the foyer, tuck a stray curl back in place, splash cold water on my face, and take five deep breaths. As I pause in the reception area to gain my composure before entering the dining room, a slight movement catches my eye.

A man hovers in the door to the restaurant It looks like the senator's limo driver—the one I saw at the Fitzhugh's dinner party. I wonder if the senator is having lunch, but my view is blocked by the guy. The ill-fitting tux has been replaced by black trousers and a white golf shirt. The muscles still bulge. His arms are covered with tattoos, as is his neck.

He strides toward the table where the count is sitting. A brief conversation occurs before the man moves toward a back entrance and disappears.

The count frowns at his phone while lifting a glass to his lips. I dab at perspiration beading on my forehead, smooth my dress, suck in my stomach, and amble in my best nonchalant manner toward the table.

A bottle of champagne nestled in a silver bucket is the center-piece. Droplets form and drip down the sides. The long-stemmed fluted glass belongs in the count's thin, elegant fingers. He shifts the glass back and forth, looks at his watch, and uncoils from the chair.

I bolt the short distance to the table and land in front of him just as he stands up. We collide, knocking heads. I've always wondered if those little tweety-birds appear when you bang heads: apparently, they do not. Instead, I feel irritable and silly.

"So far, this isn't going well," I say as I look into his dark blue eyes. He's close to fifty with a few threads of silver in his thick black hair. It adds to his aristocratic good looks.

"I'm sorry I'm late. Did your assistant let you know I called?"

He doesn't speak—just looks me over like I'm some kind of exhibit in a museum. Finally, he allows a slight smile to twitch in the corners of his mouth. "Well, when you didn't show up, I thought perhaps you had found something better to do. But here you are. Please sit."

There's something about his presence that reduces me to an awkward teen. I've catered events for dignitaries, celebrities, and heads of state. It was part of our training at the culinary institute, but this man confuses me. He gives off this essence of being interested and disinterested simultaneously. Perhaps it's the royalty bit. He probably doesn't associate with commoners like me very often.

"I hope I didn't interrupt your conversation with the man who was here before me."

"Oh no, not at all. That's George, my driver."

That was it. Nothing else followed. I'm curious, but don't probe. Our conversation is slow, halting—not to mention boring. *How are you? The dinner party was lovely. The food exquisite, blah, blah.*

Once I'm saturated with polite small talk, I say, "Please, I've kept you waiting long enough. You must be famished. Is there still time for lunch?"

He turns his head and tilts it at the waiter, who rushes to our table. My glass is filled with champagne, and the count's glass is replenished.

"A celebration?" I question.

"Yes, to new ventures," he says. We click glasses and sip the cold sparkling wine. Then he says, "Perhaps we need to start over."

"What do you mean?"

Creases cross his forehead as he ponders what to say next.

"There wasn't time to finish our conversation at the Fitzhughs. Perhaps I left you with the impression that I wanted you to cater an event to repay the hospitality I've received since I've been in the Lowcountry."

"Yes, that's exactly the impression you left. How was that misleading?"

"What I said is true. It's just that there's more. While the event is to show my appreciation for the many kindnesses I've received since my arrival, it's also about an investment opportunity."

"Investment opportunity? What does that mean?"

"Let me backtrack. I want you to cater an event, but it's more than a social occasion. It would also be to present a business venture. Initially, I thought the Waterfront Inn would be an appropriate venue, but I've changed my mine. Let me explain."

He pauses to watch my reaction. I nod for him to continue.

"It's been a few weeks since I suggested the event to you at the Fitzhughs. Much has changed during that interval—enough to include another location."

My fingers automatically fold and unfold the napkin nestled in my lap. A chill settles across my back. "I'd be happy to cater for your friends or business acquaintances as long as it's legal. It's your event and your call. But this inn is beautiful. I've worked with the chef and the staff on numerous occasions. They're always willing to create work space for me in their kitchen. It's convenient, and the water-front setting is lovely. Do you mind telling me why you want to change and what other location you are considering?"

He reaches for my hand, which I jerk away and let fall into my lap. He flushes and says, "Why do I make you so nervous?"

"Oh, it's not you. Please don't be offended. I'm a bit unsettled by the unexpected diversion I had earlier today, the one that made me late. I haven't had time to sort through it, and it's on my mind. I'm sorry. You have my full attention. Please continue."

"There's no need to apologize. You are here now. Is there anything I can help you with? Do you want to talk about it? I'm a good listener."

"That's very kind of you. I shouldn't have mentioned it, but I'm simply never late for appointments. It's one of those bothersome things, but I'll work through it."

He nods, straightens his cuff links, and continues, "I agree with you that the inn is lovely, and it would be a great setting. As I said earlier, a few things have changed since we spoke at the Fitzhughs. Let's have lunch first and become better acquainted. Then we'll talk business. Is that agreeable?"

"Yes. I'm ravenous."

He nods at the waiter, who refills our glasses.

"The menu is excellent. Today's special sounded delicious, so I placed our order when I arrived. But if you'd rather look at the menu and order something else, please do."

I tamp down my irritation at another man who assumes he knows best what I like. I growl at myself, determined not to make a big deal of it.

"I'm sure your choices will be excellent. There's so need for me to consider an alternative."

Our conversation comes to a halt when the waiter returns. He places a pale green porcelain soup bowl in front of me. It's filled with a creamy cauliflower soup, drizzled with golden olive oil. He stands at attention until the count nods. With a flourish, he produces a truffle shaver and a lumpy, rough-skinned nub of black truffle. The dense, earthy, and slightly funky aroma circles our table. I breathe it in, as the shavings settle on top of my soup. Drool collects inside my mouth as I wait for the truffle to be shaved over the count's soup. Then, I have to wait while he makes another toast to new endeavors. I'm not sure what he's implying, but my food genes take over. With the first bite, I'm lost in the magic of the velvety texture and the pungent richness of the truffles.

"You are so earnest," he says, shifting his chair closer to mine. "Your face is a picture of concentration and reverence as if every spoonful of the soup has to meet your approval. I like that. You understand food."

"Food is my salvation," I respond without filters. "My life

revolves around it. Without cooking, I'm not sure if I would have survived some dreadful years."

I close my mouth. Why can't I keep it shut? This is not a date or a personal chat. It's business. I try changing the subject, but it's too late.

"It's your passion for food that brought me into Mrs. Fitzhugh's kitchen to meet you," he says. "I've lived in Spain most of my life. I've never had a paella as good or as unique as the one you made. I couldn't leave without meeting the person who had created such a splendid dish. And to think I almost didn't eat it. You see, I was irritated that it was a non-traditional paella. No one in Spain would think to serve paella any way but hot. It would be sacrilegious."

I gasp and start to sputter out an apology.

"Please," he continues with a huge smile. "Let me finish by saying it was the best paella I've ever tasted. It was a unique experience— paella at room temperature with a garlicky mayonnaise? Unheard of."

He laughs. It's deep-throated and ripples out of his mouth.

"It was so good that once I got over the initial shock, I asked for a second serving. You see, I'm a bit rigid, and change can be difficult. My background is full of tradition and all the things I can and can't do. Your passion for food was in every dish you served and in the pairings of the wines. I had to meet you. Once I did, I knew you were the right person to help me with this event, but more importantly, I wanted us to be friends."

A flush rises from my toes. It slams a rosy hue across my face. I stutter, "I'm—I'm not sure what to say. Thank you. I am passionate about food. I learned how to cook from my Italian *nonna*."

"Ah, that explains a great deal. Tell me about her."

Tears fill my eyes as I tell the story of my naming. "I'm her namesake. For generations, the first girl in the Gabbiano family has been called Caterina. My *nonna* lived with us in her later years. She taught me not only to speak Italian but to be passionate about food. At the culinary institute, I learned the rules and the art of food, but it was Nonna who filled me with a love for food. She taught me about layering ingredients, understanding textures, smells and tastes, and, of course, the touch. You cannot make pasta and bread without the touch and without your heart involved from start to finish. It saddens me that I didn't become a chef until after she was gone. It was her dream for me."

He reaches for my hand again. This time, I don't jerk it away. I realize it's not a sexual gesture but one of understanding and friendship. For the first time in a long time, I relax. He releases my hand, picks up his glass and says, "To friendship and food and most of all to Nonna, yours and mine, who taught us to open our hearts."

The clicking of our glasses echoes through the restaurant. The waiter returns and removes our bowls. The breadbasket is refilled, and a perfectly baked salmon with dill sauce is placed in front of me. Grilled asparagus with toasted sesame seeds and roasted fingerling potatoes nestle on opposite sides of the salmon.

A chilled Château Minuty rosé splashes into tulip-shaped glasses. The count sniffs and sips, then swirls the wine in his mouth and says, "Ah, such an elegant taste of honeysuckle and wild strawberries with just a hint of peaches and orange peel. Taste, and tell me if it meets with your approval."

I sniff and sip. The exotic flavors burst in my mouth. Wow is what I think, but instead, I say, "Yes, it's a perfect match for the salmon."

As we linger over the meal, we share tidbits from our pasts. He asks that I call him Al, and I respond only if he'll call me Cat.

Al begins his story, "I'm a descendant of one of the Spanish explorers whose sailing vessel was wrecked off your coast in the late 1700s. That is my legitimate reason for the trip. I'm working with a research team who are trying to find the lost vessel. But my secondary reason is personal business. It's a rather covert project, and I want to keep it that way."

He stops mid-thought and asks if the salmon is seasoned correctly. When I reassure him it is, he continues, "The intention of this trip is to purchase property in the area and establish residency. I've found a place that's suitable. If I can procure it, then that's where

I want to hold the event. It will make a far greater impact if I can do that."

"Oh, that's wonderful," I exclaim. "Tell me about the new venue. The setting is one of the most important parts of an event—almost as important as the food and wine. But I have to warn you, I'm picky about locations. I've been known to turn down an event if the place isn't right."

He straightens the gold cufflink protruding from his jacket sleeve, repositions his napkin, and says, "I believe you'll like the property I'm considering. Once I get established, I'd like to open a world-class spa with a restaurant. The property is well-suited for al fresco dining and an outdoor kitchen. What do you think? Would you be interested in helping me design the kitchen?

I shake my head in amazement. "You've got big plans that cost big dollars. But if you're serious, I think guests would love having a chef in full view as they dine al fresco. It's easy to imagine an elegant dining area surrounded with lemon trees and hibiscus. But what a huge undertaking along with a resort. You do have big plans."

"Do you think it's too much?"

"Probably, but at the same time I'd enjoy working on a project like this. It's far more than planting trees. How did all this come about, and why did you choose the Lowcountry?" I stop and then add, "Of course, it's none of my business. Please don't feel obligated to tell me about your personal reasons. Let's start with the event so I can understand your motivation."

He gently pats my hand. I stop my rambling and wait.

"There is a story or two behind what is driving me to do this. As I was telling you earlier, my real reason for being here is to obtain property, something with a lot of acreage. Eventually, I'll open the resort, but my first goal is to establish a large nursery on the premises. My company will be experimenting with the Moringa tree. Have you heard of it?"

Is this a coincidence? I must have nodded *yes* because he continues. But my thoughts drift to my bookcase and the stack of books about trees—especially the Moringa tree. How strange, I think, as I tune back in to Al's commentary.

"There has to be enough property to build greenhouses to accommodate the Moringa plants. If you know anything about these trees, you know their normal habitat is in hot, arid conditions. But my goal is to produce hybrids that will survive in different climates. This plant is the answer to a universal food supply and prevention of hunger. It has the potential to both feed and heal the world."

The gnarly, lone tree in Castello del Mare, the one on the land jutting out into the sea, passes in front of my eyes. It's another connection. It has to be. That one lone tree gazing on the Adriatic still connects me to Stella. The books on trees I discovered in my bookcase are another connection. And now here's this man telling about his plans to grow trees. I don't think it's a coincidence or happenstance. I think it's magic. There are these small, precious moments when I'm open to magic, and the universe provides it. My reverie is broken when I hear Al's voice.

"Cat?"

I smile as if I have been following every word.

"Sorry, but it's so strange. I recently came across some books about the Moringa tree. And just a few weeks ago, I read an article in *The New Yorker* about the tree's possibilities."

He nods, "Yes, I read the same article. It stressed the importance of finding ways to combat world hunger."

I sort through a myriad of information stored in my brain before saying, "If I remember correctly, it emphasized all the amazing elements of the Moringa like the edible leaves which are rich in protein, iron, calcium, and essential amino acids, as well as vitamins A, B, and C."

Al's smile widens as he jumps back in the conversation. "Plus, the seedpods are high in protein and omega-3 fatty acids and can be pressed for vegetable oil and used to purify water. Even the residue is used as fertilizer. The leaves and the pods have strong anti-inflammatory and anti-diabetic properties. Every single part of the tree can be used."

"Gracious, we sound like a wikipedia synopsis about the Moringa."

Al's laugh is infectious. "Isn't it astonishing that one tree can do so much. It's been around for thousands of years, yet it's not well known. It is truly the Tree of Life."

I lean toward him and say, "What's really impressive is you're creating a hybrid and you have chosen this area. We need jobs during this economic downturn."

Energy and passion radiate across his face as he nods at everything I say. "Yes! Yes! You understand. You are the right person for this event. Please say you will help me."

He pulls his briefcase closer, his fingers hesitate on the lock, but he doesn't open it. Our eyes meet, and he says, "I know this is very early in our relationship, but I believe I can trust you. No one but you knows that I'm here to buy property and start a nursery. I'm putting myself at great risk to tell you. It's embarrassing to say that I'm basing my trust on the one meal you've prepared for me and our time together today. But I believe one great passion understands another, don't you?"

12

A l waits for my response, his eyes brim with expectations. Random thoughts dart around in my head—who is this person? What does he want from me? Why me? Would it be impolite to excuse myself and leave?

Instead, my need to please surfaces.

"Yes, you can trust me. You have my word that as long as your plans are legal, I won't betray anything confidential we discuss today. Why don't you tell me about the property and your plans? Then we'll discuss the event. Whether or not I'm the right caterer will come later. If the situation changes for me, I'll recommend someone else."

His smile dims as he says, "You must understand there is no other caterer I wish to hire. If somehow the location isn't suitable, you will tell me what is wrong. I will fix it. Is that acceptable?"

"Isn't that rather extreme?"

He leans closer and whispers, "You are the right person. That's enough."

"Why are you so sure I'm the right person?"

"Mrs. Fitzhugh said you were the best caterer in the area. She said you handle yourself well in difficult situations, you pay attention to the smallest detail, and you know how to balance the right amount of professionalism and friendliness. The most important thing she said is you can be trusted. These are all attributes I'm looking for, along with excellent food. I've tasted your divine creations. There is no one else I wish to consider."

I nod but still can't figure out how to respond, so I ask a question.

"Why is this event so important to you? Your enthusiasm is exciting, but it seems this is more than an event to celebrate a new business. Why don't you start at the beginning so I can better understand why you're here and what you hope to accomplish."

The power of his smile lights up the dining room. It also exposes a perfect row of white teeth. He sips more wine. The waiter rushes over to refill our glasses. Al waits until we're alone before continuing.

"I apologize for all the secrecy. It's important that my plans remain confidential until all the details are worked out. It's not my intention to pressure you, but can you agree?"

What the heck? This guy sounds like Nick. Just for a second, I wonder if there's a connection between them. Surely not.

"Of course," I murmur.

A frown creases his forehead, and his eyes narrow.

"You're hesitant."

"Yes, no, it's okay," I stammer, trying to regroup.

To redeem myself, I say, "I had no idea you wanted to establish residency here. I admire you for undertaking such an enormous project. Tell me how you became interested in the Moringa and why you want to create a hybrid."

"My story isn't that interesting, but I'll start with the reason I'm asking you to keep our conversations confidential. My family is not aware of my business dealings in the United States. I want it to stay that way. Little by little, I've been establishing myself as a business person here without their knowledge. If this last project is successful, then I will break all ties."

"Why don't you tell me your family story. We all have one of those."

Our eyes connect and hold. He sighs and begins.

"When I was a young man, my family required that each child participate in an activity that benefited humanity. It was only later that I learned these requirements were to benefit the family's coffers rather than humanity. Before I knew that, I spent my summers in Kerala, India. My job was to work with children. I taught a variety of things like basic English and reading skills and usually some sort of craft. While there, I learned about the Moringa tree. One incredibly hot afternoon, my group was taken to Maharashtra, where the farmers grow these trees as a crop."

The waiter approaches and asks if he can clear the table. We sit in silence until he finishes. The count picks up the conversation's thread.

"Most farmers in this area grew soybeans and tur. Do you know tur? It's a pigeon pea grown all over India. It's quite tasty—similar to edamame. However, the soil does not support these crops. They were not profitable, and families fell into poverty. Up until then, the Moringa was not generally cultivated. Although it's an ancient plant and has been used by healers for thousands of years, the scientific community largely ignored it. Do you understand?"

"Yes, but why did they ignore it?"

His eyes crinkle with pleasure, "At that age, I wasn't interested in the *why*, but I was fascinated by what I learned that afternoon. For several summers, I returned and worked with the farmers. Over time, I realized the Moringa was easy to grow and economical. Twenty years ago, I bought land in the Maharashtra region of India and hired some locals to cultivate the trees. They have been very successful. Their families no longer live in poverty. In fact, they purchased the land back from me. The entire village was involved in the process."

"How exciting for them and you. Why didn't you stay there and continue with expansion?"

"Ahh, that's when the family part of my life intervened, or I should say interfered. My brother, who is the oldest, discovered what I was doing and how successful my small project was. Since he is the rightful heir to the family estate, he persuaded my father to cut off all funds for the Moringa Project. He had those funds diverted to one of his frivolous projects. I believe the particular project was to create perfume using Asafetida, which is an incredibly stinky spice."

Our laughter ripples through the restaurant—not so much with joy but with a sadness that recognizes stupidity often prevails.

"So you decided that the next logical step was to cultivate these trees in another land? That's a huge leap. Why are you choosing the US instead of another impoverished country, one in a more suitable climate?"

He's almost jumping in his seat. "I discovered the Moringa is already being grown right here in your country, in Arizona. I've already met with the growers. They want someone to start the plants in a nursery environment. The young plants will be transported and planted on a Moringa farm near the desert. Since I have dual citizenship, thanks to my seafaring relative and my grandfather's marriage to an American, it's not difficult for me to start a company here. I can easily get the pods from the farm in Arizona without having to import them. Plus, it's far less complicated to make things happen in the United States than in other countries. At the same time, I'll start experimenting with hybrid plants under different climate conditions. I want this to be a worldwide project."

He pauses long enough to sip more wine. "This is why I want you to cater an event that is celebratory as well as an investment opportunity."

"What exactly does an investment opportunity mean?"

"It means I have the seed money to start the business but not enough to keep it running long-term. I need investors. This area is heavy with people who have large disposable incomes. It seemed like a good match, except I'm experiencing difficulties.

"Like what?"

I've been working with a realtor who promised to locate the holding company that owns the property I want to purchase. However, it's proving to be more difficult than expected. I've been assured it will happen, but so far, there's no time frame. I've hired an attorney to speed things up a bit, but I fear I'll have to return to Spain before all the details are worked out."

He lifts his wine glass to the light before taking a sip.

"Why did your assistant give me a date for the event when you haven't purchased the property? I don't understand."

"I was afraid you'd say no if I asked you to lunch without a reason. When I met you at the Fitzhughs and insinuated that I wanted you to cater an event for me, I thought finding and buying a property would be easy. Was it wrong to give you a date?"

"Well, it's unusual and a bit confusing."

"Yes, I can see that. I apologize that it's taking longer than I expected, but I will buy the property. The event will coincide with the closing. What I can't do is give you an exact date. In my excitement at finding both the property and you all in the same weekend, I got ahead of myself."

He lets that sink in. I nod, and he continues.

"This is a personal mission for me, but it's also a business one, as I intend to launch the Moringa Project at the event. My guest list will include friends and potential investors. Like I said a few minutes ago, I don't have the personal funds to finance an ongoing project as big as this. The event must create a dramatic impression, and that's where you come in. I need someone with your impressive credentials. You understand Spanish cuisine and our wine. Having an evening with these ingredients in a beautiful setting will have a positive impact."

He pauses briefly before saying, "You must think I'm crazy. I realize there are many loose ends, but in the next couple of months, I'll purchase the property, and finalize the plans. Are you willing to work with me?"

Since I'm not completely on board, I say, "I'm not sure, Al. It all seems to be up in the air without a date, a venue, guests, etc. You're chosen me because of my food, but I'm not sure that's enough."

He has the decency to tilt his head down. He fidgets with his napkin before saying, "I'm sorry there isn't a date yet. I won't have one until we can find the property owners and they agree to sell. But there's more, and you won't be happy about this. I also needed time to do a background check on you."

He holds up his hands as anger flits across my face. "Please listen, Cat. What I'm asking for is a bit more than what a normal catered event entails. This project requires a great deal of trust—preferably from someone who lives and works in the area and has a sense of the movers and shakers in the community. Plus, I require someone who can work magic and who is willing to work with me confidentially. You see, I haven't found many of the people I've met to be trustworthy. In fact, just the opposite."

"I don't understand what you mean. Who are these people?"

"I'd rather not say. But many of the guests I met at the Fitzhughs were invited as potential investors and confidants. I was less than pleased when the conversations focused on yachts, summer homes, and whose wine cellar was the best. When I mentioned creating jobs and solving world hunger, people changed the subject. In fact, you were the only person I met that night that gave me hope. You were natural and spontaneous, and you made me laugh."

"Is Margarita part of the Moringa Project?"

"Ahhh, yes, Margarita. Let me explain." His intense blue eyes lock onto mine before he continues. "We are divorced but remain on friendly terms. This is the last trip we will make together as she no longer has any interest in my endeavors. We've held on to each other for convenience. I realize that is foolish. She is already on a flight back to Spain. Today is a new start for me and the Moringa Project. She isn't aware of the project and has no role in it. I apologize for not providing much information, but I'm prepared to answer any questions you have."

He's so earnest, and his enthusiasm is contagious. I think of employment opportunities and the recognization it would bring to South Carolina. An infusion of new ideas, young people engaged in research, and perhaps a sustainable answer to some of the world's food problems. I'm prepared to forgive him for asking me to lunch on false pretenses—for a catering project that doesn't yet exist.

"You have piqued my interest," I acknowledge. "Even before you find a property, I can create a basic menu and an estimate. We can also discuss the movers and shakers in the community. While I know who they are, I have to warn you that I have made some enemies."

He nods with understanding. "Sarah told me a little about the current social scene and how your business has suffered because of a misunderstanding."

I glance at him, wondering where he's going with this conversation.

"She said you're a good person, the best caterer there is, and you know how to be discrete. She said I'd have to ask you to provide details about what transpired—something about a fiancé, a run-in with a client, and a trip to Italy."

To avoid sharing my story with a stranger, I say, "Sarah's my best client. I appreciate her recommendation. Why don't we start with your telling me about the property."

"Do you know Carrington Point Plantation? That's the property I want to buy."

Both of our cell phones shrill at the same time. Al murmurs an apology and slips out of his chair and moves toward the veranda. I check my messages and cringe when I see the text from Nick.

Who are you having lunch with? Text me when you leave.

My brain turns to mush. Carrington Point Plantation? Nick? Is it possible these two men are connected?

Al returns and signals the waiter.

"Cat, I'm sorry, but I have to leave. Please stay and have dessert or whatever else you want."

The waiter hovers.

"No, Al. Thanks, but I'm running late as well."

He reaches across the table and lifts my hand to his lips.

"Let's continue our conversation. Next week? Would you please check your schedule and leave me a message with dates and times? There's much about this property deal that isn't quite right. You've been here long enough to know people."

My stammering kicks in, "I, I, I might not be in a position to help you. Before our phones interrupted us, I was explaining that I'm not in the good graces of many of the grand families around here. They'd be the ones you'd want to invite to your celebration. They might even stay away if they found out you'd hired me to cater the event."

Maybe divulging that bit of my history will make Al look for someone else to confide in. And then there's Nick and his operation. Do I tell Nick that Al is trying to buy the property?

"I'm not worried about that, but I am concerned about the character of some of the people I've had to interact with regarding the property. As I said earlier, something is a bit off. I've done too many deals not to recognize that something or someone is purposely stalling my attempts to buy the land."

I push back from the table, as he continues, "Check your calendar and text me with some dates you have available so we can meet again. I'll call you in a few days to confirm."

Part of me is demanding I say no, but the other part of me is intrigued, in a doomsday kind of way—by this man and his plans. I nod in agreement.

13

Cassie hands me a glass of sweet tea and slumps down on the sofa next to me. She sighs and pushes her mop of black hair out of her equally dark eyes, and says, "Shit, Cat, how in the hell do you manage to get yourself into these weird predicaments? Don't roll your eyes at me. I'm sorry I wasn't able to go with you to Carrington the other day. First, some idiot backed into my car at Walmart and busted my taillight, which is where I was when you texted me. Then I had to fart around with the insurance and find someone to fix it before I got a ticket. Gosh, that seems like ages ago instead of just a couple of weeks. Have we not talked since then?"

"Actually, Cass, we haven't had any conversations except ones about food preparation. I've been distracted and you haven't been around. What's going on?"

"Well, I guess I've been a bit distracted too. I'm glad you called. It seems we both have been off having adventures. But finish telling me everything that happened when you met your classmate at Carrington Point. Then I want to know about lunch with the Spanish count. I thought I was hanging out with some elite personalities, but you always top me."

Cassie is a tell-all friend. We've spent hours together planning and prepping for events. As far as I know, we tell each other every-thing. Well, almost, except lately, we've both been a bit withdrawn.

So that's what I do—tell her the story. Well, most of it. I do omit the part about Nick being an undercover FBI agent and his warnings not to tell anyone. If I share this with Cassie, it might jeopardize his operation. She would suggest calling the police, and I would be stuck telling them a story without any evidence. I've done that before. It didn't work out well for me. If the police uncover Nick's covert operation, I would be in a cesspool of trouble.

The police would grill me about my potential attacker. What would I say? I could tell them what I saw inside the house—the furnishings suggesting inhabitants—but I won't because that's a good chance the whole thing was a figment of my imagination. The more I think about it, the more that seems to be the reality. I probably had a blackout and tripped and fell off the porch. My lack of mental acuity is not something I'm willing to share with the police. Everything that happened in Castello del Mare would come out.

My only goal since returning home has been to overcome that horrific scene in the Zinzulusa Caves—me bound and gagged with Gino bleeding out from a gunshot wound. And Carlo and Lorenzo in a shootout reminiscent of the OK Corral. At the time, I didn't know who was planning to kill me. I only recognized that death was on my doorstep.

Fortunately for me, Gino was only wounded. Thanks to him, I escaped with my life intact. That experience, alongside Stella's murder, has left my mental state a bit shaky. My thoughts are often confused. If I have to live through another police interrogation, I might fall apart. Somehow, Stella would be dragged into this, and all the grieving I have tried to work through would be resurrected.

Instead of telling Cassie the whole story, I vaguely tell her that there are telltale signs of squatters on the property or perhaps just kids out for a good time. The problem is I made the mistake of telling her I was frightened to be there alone.

"Oh, Cat, you have to have the police check the place. I don't want you going out there alone. You could get hurt, and nobody would know. If you have to go again, make sure I can go with you."

Cassie's voice fades away as the room crowds in, and darkness settles around me.

"Cat, Cat," Cassie's voice, thick with emotion, interrupts my trot down an excruciatingly painful road. She gently shakes my shoulder.

"What? I'm sorry, Cassie. I was just thinking about the events in Castello. Do you think it's me—that there's something about me that attracts catastrophe?"

"Haha," Cassie snorts with laughter. "The thing is, when evil visits me, the frogs come out and circle the wagons. With you, evil comes in the form of great-looking guys. Only you would meet a dashing commissario, a doctor, a property attorney—well, that one was deadly. But now you've met a charming count from Spain. I, on the other hand, meet all the creeps of the world. But forget about that. I want to hear about your lunch with the handsome count."

"The food was excellent, and he wants me to cater an event for him." Then I mumble, "He's looking at property in the area—specifically Carrington Point Plantation."

"Oh gosh! You can't cater an event there. You just told me it's not safe. Is that what's upsetting you?"

"Sort of—but not exactly. When Al first asked me if I would cater a party for him, he said it would be at the Waterfront Inn. Now it's changed to Carrington—that's if he can locate the owner. Our lunch was interrupted, so I'm not clear about what he wants me to do, and I'm not comfortable with him. I guess I'm not clear what his intentions are."

"Hmmm," Cassie says as she rummages through her purse until she finds a hair clip. She twists her hair in a quick braid before saying, "Are you talking business or personal?"

"After the lunch, I think both. He wants to hire me for the event, but he also seems to have taken a personal interest in me."

"And?" Cassie says as she inches forward on the sofa and leans toward me. "Well, what happened?"

"The lunch was amazing."

"Oh, good grief, Cat. Give me details—not the food, which you'll gush over for hours. I want the lowdown on the count. Who is he? What's he doing here? Why is he buying property? All the goodies, please!"

"Oh, Cass, he asked me not to discuss our conversation as it involves family issues, investment opportunities, and bringing business into South Carolina. His plans aren't confirmed yet. If any of the information is leaked, it would be to his detriment."

"So when has that stopped you from sharing with me? You know I won't tell anyone else. Come on, tell me something."

"Okay, but promise me."

Cassie is already crossing her heart and swearing never to reveal our conversation, even if threatened with death.

"You are such a drama queen, Cassie. But here's what I can tell you. He wants to buy Carrington and start a business that the property can support."

"What does that mean?"

"Well, a crop of sorts. Something sustainable. It would bring jobs and money into the Lowcountry."

"That sounds good. So what's the problem."

"The problem for him is no one seems to know who owns Carrington. For me, it's the location. It's scary—spooky. No, actually, the word is sinister. Why would I want to work in an environment that makes me uncomfortable?"

Cassie's brow creases. She shrugs and says, "You have two options: The first is to accept the job. If he buys the plantation and there are squatters, he will run them off before the event. You do have to tell him how you feel about the place. But at least for now, you know not to return without someone with you, preferably me, since I'll be helping you with the event. Right?"

"Yes, of course, you will. It wouldn't be a success without you by my side. And the second option?"

"You can say no—a big emphatic NO! Cat, you have to move on. You know that. Talk to your Dr. Ginny, although that might be the wrong thing to do since she championed your trip to Italy."

"That's not fair, Cassie. No one could have foreseen what happened to me in Italy. Dr. Ginny's been instrumental in helping me move past those horrifying memories. But you're right. I do have a choice—either do the event or not."

"It wouldn't hurt to get her opinion, would it?"

"I don't guess it would, Cassie. It's just not that simple."

What I don't tell Cassie is there's a third option—the one that features me dealing with Nick when he discovers Al plans to buy the property. That's an option I don't want to think about, but it could happen. I sigh and refocus. The best I can do is acknowledge that this situation does not require my suffering right now—it only requires my attention. I choose the option that works for me: Do nothing and let it play out.

Cassie turns her full gaze on me and says, "When was the last time you heard from Lorenzo?"

"A few weeks ago."

"Why don't you call him, Cat? Run all this by him—not because you need him to sort it out—but he'd be a good sounding board for you. You've often said you trust his opinion."

She hesitates a half second before adding, "You also need to remind yourself how you feel about him. It won't hurt to talk to him."

What Cassie says takes a moment to register. Cassie has never encouraged me to contact Lorenzo. She strings out clichés about him like good riddance, out of sight—out of mind, let sleeping dogs lie, he missed the boat and sweep him under the rug. Why is she recommending I call him now?

I look at her glowing face and say, "What's going on with you?"

She fidgets with her hair, a sure sign she's nervous about my question.

"What aren't you telling me? I've been so preoccupied with work and all the other crazy stuff going on in my life that I haven't been paying attention. It's been several months since our last big event at the Fitzhughs. We really haven't talked much since then. Yet here you are, bursting with something to tell me. What's going on, Cass? Whatever it is, it must be a good thing. You look amazing!"

Cassie's coy glance tells me there's going to be a big reveal. I'm not disappointed.

"I've met someone."

"Wow! When were you planning on telling me?"

"Oh, Cat, I always tell you everything. It's just, well, at first I wasn't sure. Plus, you've been so busy, and there's a bit of secrecy involved."

"What? That sounds pretty clandestine. You can't stop. Who is it? And why the secrecy?"

"You won't be mad at me, will you? I mean, the way I met him wasn't exactly professional."

"Okay, I'm interested."

"You're going to be so upset with me, but here goes. It actually started at the Fitzhugh's dinner party where we met the count, or *you can call me Al.*"

We both giggle until Cassie's face stiffens. She drops her head a little and says, "Well, I met someone there, too. One of the dinner guests flirted with me. I thought he was with his wife, so of course, I rebuffed him. Well, for that reason and because I know your policy on fraternizing with the guests. He read right through me and made a big deal out of introducing his dinner companion as his sister. I know —that doesn't let me off the hook, but I couldn't help but flirt back. He was so charming. Before he left, he gave me his business card with his personal number on the back. Oh, Cat, I know what you're going to say."

"Cass, it's okay. I mean, after all, I just had lunch with Al. It was supposed to be a business lunch, but I think the count likes me a bit more than most of my other business associates. He ordered truffles for our lunch. Somehow, that seemed a bit more than what one orders for a business luncheon, and then there was champagne. It all seemed a bit extravagant."

Cassie clasps her hands over her mouth. Her head falls back against the sofa. She breaks into a fit of giggles and finally manages to spit out, "You had truffles? Champagne? Well, that just erased all my guilty feelings."

"Okay, enough! It's time to tell me which guest got lucky."

She sighs mightily and says, "Please don't laugh until I finish the whole story. Okay? His name is James Middleton Madison, but he goes by Jim. He's a state senator, and he's running for reelection which is why we've had to keep our relationship under cover."

I lose control, and Cassie joins me. We laugh until we can't breathe. As we both gasp for breath, I ask, "You're in a relationship with someone named after a president? When I meet him, do I have to call him Mr. President?"

We burst into giggles again until I realize who she's talking about. "Wait a minute. Isn't he the guy that caused all the ruckus over some spilled water?"

"Oh, Cat, it really wasn't a *ruckus*. Sarah blew it out of proportion. It was the server's fault. Would you want someone spilling ice water on your clothes at an elegant dinner party?"

Hmmm—I heard the guy myself. Based on the decibel level, I'd say he was belligerent and rude. And later, Sarah told me that the senator had hit the waiter's hand which caused the incident. But I don't bring that up. In my opinion, a little water spilled on your clothes on a warm evening surely isn't bad enough to create all the disruption that occurred.

Instead, I say, "It's been a while since the Fitzhugh's dinner party. Why haven't you told me before?"

"I'm sorry, Cat. Because of his reelection campaign, he said he needed to be discreet. He really didn't want me to tell anyone, including you, but I told him that I'd kept it from you long enough. He was upset with me, but he didn't say I couldn't tell you. I promised him you wouldn't say anything."

"When do I get to meet the illustrious state senator?"

"Soon. I'm thinking about this weekend—maybe Sunday night unless you have plans. His sister Alice was with him at the Fitzhughs. I thought I'd ask her too. She seems sweet."

"Sounds good. I'm available as I don't think I'm on call for royalty that night. Is this why you suggested I call Lorenzo? You're happy, so you want me to be happy? Is that it, Cassie?"

"Partly, but I guess it's more that after meeting Jim, I better understand your emotional connection to Lorenzo. Over the years, I let myself forget how it feels to be so intoxicated."

"And you think I'm intoxicated by Lorenzo?"

"Cat, you're my best friend. I want you to be happy again. If Lorenzo makes you happy, call him."

I don't respond because she knows my story and understands my feelings for Lorenzo. Maybe I will call him—or maybe not.

14

Days go by without hearing from Nick. The silence makes me as nervous as when I hear from him. The Berkleys were more than a little miffed when I told them Carrington Point Plantation was permanently off the list of venues unless the owner could be found. Then I said even if the owner was found, they might not agree to rent the place out for the wedding reception. I created a story about the realtor's concern with liability issues surrounding the dilapidated condition of the house. My story said the police would impose steep fines if anyone was caught trespassing. It's the best I could come up with other than telling them that they might be killed if they went out there again. That seemed a bit too much.

Preparation for lunch is almost complete when I hear a car pull into the drive. I smooth my hair, tuck my shirt in my jeans, and slip my feet into my well-worn Cole Haan loafers, which I keep by the front door. I'm both surprised and pleased to see Al has driven himself. I open the door before he has time to ring the bell.

"Where's your bodyguard?"

He shrugs and looks puzzled as he hands me a bouquet of yellow roses and a bottle of champagne while balancing his briefcase under his arm, "What bodyguard? Oh, you mean George? I gave him the day off. Told him I wasn't going anywhere. I'm tired of him being at my beck and call every minute of the day and night."

"I would be too. Where did you find him?"

"Actually, one of the guests at the Fitzhugh's party recommended him. Your state senator. Do you know him? He gave me the information before he made a spectacle of himself when a waiter inadvertently spilled water on him. I considered not using his recommendation, but I needed a driver."

"Are you talking about Senator Madison?"

"Yes. During dinner, I mentioned I was looking for a car and driver. The senator immediately offered his assistance. I accepted before the altercation occurred. I'm not sure I would have accepted his offer afterward, but it was a little too late to turn down his offer."

"Are you comfortable with the driver? He doesn't exactly exude professionalism to me. He hovers like a bodyguard instead of a chauffeur."

"He's a bit obtuse, but I need someone familiar with the area while I'm looking for properties. George knows his way around, but he seems to have become a permanent fixture in my life," Al says with a frown. "The contract is only for a couple of months. He's supposed to be available anytime I need him, but I've told him numerous times not to hang around. He seems to think he's responsible for me every minute of the day."

"Hmmm, I guess it's nice he's so conscientious, but it's a little creepy, isn't it?"

Al laughs as he leans in for the traditional two-cheek kiss, "He's okay—maybe a bit too eager. The contract ends in a few weeks. I think I can manage. If not, I'll tell him I no longer need his services. Today, we don't have to worry about him, so let's not waste our time discussing him."

I step aside as he enters. His tailored navy trousers are perfectly creased, and the sleeves of the crisp white collared shirt are folded precisely to the correct length. He creates an aura only royals know how to project. I lead him through the house to the back porch.

"I hope you don't mind that I've planned lunch on the porch."

When he doesn't respond, I turn around to see he's lost in the magnificent view of the marsh and sailboats on the deep water. The sun tips the spartina grass with a burnished glow and leaves a path of sparkly diamonds across the river.

"This is spectacular. How long have you lived here?"

"The property has been in my family for a long time. I moved in a few years ago. It was originally a fish camp built by an obscure great-uncle."

A confused look settles on the count's face. I laugh and try to explain. "People first came to this area to fish in the ponds and rivers. Small pieces of property were purchased by the fishermen so they could pitch a tent, put up a shack or park a trailer. That's why they're called fish camps. It's only in the last thirty or so years that developers discovered how valuable these fish camps are."

I wait until Al nods for me to continue. "The property was left to my father. He built this lovely cottage and deeded it to me. I'd never visited, but I'd heard stories about the beauty of the Lowcountry. After a series of misfortunes, I needed a place—a new beginning. The minute I saw the house and the property, I knew this was my home."

"I'm sorry for the adversity that brought you here, but I'm also glad. We didn't have time to discuss any of your past at our last lunch. There's so much I don't know about you, Cat. Can we change that?"

My shoulders tense. My neck stiffens. No matter how nice this man is, I am not ready for anything other than friendship. I have to get that point across.

"Of course, and I'd love to hear more about your life in Spain. Let's have lunch, and you can tell me all about it."

He smiles, a quizzical eyebrow raised to let me know I hadn't answered his question.

I indicate the chair facing the marsh and say, "Sit here, please. I'll be right back."

He's right behind me when I enter the kitchen. Instead of protesting, I put him to work.

"There's a bottle of Marchese di Borgosole Fiano in the fridge. The corkscrew is in the drawer next to the dishwasher."

"Ah, Italian food for lunch?"

"Si signore. What other food is there?"

Our laughter generates a happy warmth in the kitchen. Al

maneuvers to my side as he opens the bottle of wine. He stands so close his cologne drifts into my space. Scents of wood and leather, along with a hint of citrus and a splash of sunshine, linger in the air. It's hard to resist burrowing my nose in his neck, but I manage.

"Of course, you're on my turf now. Italian is my specialty. Why don't you pour the wine? The glasses are on the table. I'll be right out."

As soon as I hear the door to the porch close, I breathe, gulping in huge hunks of air until my heartbeat settles into its normal rhythm. *Don't even think about it,* I tell myself as I pour the tomato-based fennel and potato soup into a heated tureen. I toss the *panzanella* salad with olive oil and lemon juice and sprinkle it with chopped green onions and crushed sweet red peppercorns. The rosemary focaccia I made earlier this morning is peeking out of the sweetgrass breadbasket. Everything is loaded on a small cart that rolls easily onto the porch. Al jumps up to help me.

"Please sit. You're my guest."

As he sits back down, I notice he's moved my chair and utensils much closer to his. I ladle soup into my nonna's Deruta bowls while I figure out the best way to correct this situation. When I serve the bowl of soup, I position myself between his chair and mine and nudge my chair ever so gently. I repeat the move when I place the basket of focaccia between our place settings and again when I plate his salad. My chair is almost back to its original spot by the time I slide into my seat.

"*Cin, cin,*" we both chorus before sipping the crisp, creamy Fiano.

Over espresso and a plate of cheese and fruit and pistachio biscotti, Al opens his briefcase and pulls out a file folder.

"I want you to see these aerial photographs of Carrington Point Plantation."

"Have you have any luck finding the owner?"

I don't mention that the realtor gave me the name of A. Andrews or maybe it was A. Aldridge as a possible connection, as I'm not sure the information is factual.

"Actually, I didn't until recently. Like you, I called the realtor and left messages for the holding company. I had my assistant dig up all the property information at the courthouse. It was quite a large file. He's still reviewing the contents."

He stopped to take a sip of wine. "George has driven me out there on several occasions. I've walked around the house and the property surrounding it. Since it's posted, I felt it better not to look any further. I've been told that people around here have shotguns, and trespassers are on their 'hunt-out-of-season' list. I don't want my head blown off."

He chuckles. I don't warn him that it's a real possibility.

"But a strange thing happened. It was either my good fortune or my misfortune to meet the owner."

I open my mouth, but nothing comes out. The words lock in my throat. Finally, I ask, "The owner? When? Who is it?"

"A man by the name of Mr. Richard Alistair Davenport. He says he's from Virginia. It was a few days ago. It was a coincidence I stumbled across him while I was looking around. He introduced himself. He said he was the descendant of Captain Richard Davenport, who arrived in the Chesapeake Bay Area in the 1660s. The property was part of the original land grants given by King Charles II. Mr. Davenport seemed knowledgeable, yet something wasn't quite right. He was nervous, agitated and in a rush for me to leave."

I knew without asking but asked anyway, "What does he look like?"

"Do you know him?"

"Why would you ask me that?"

"I thought the name might be familiar to you."

"No, I don't know the name, but it might be helpful if you describe him. Maybe I've seen him around town."

A lame excuse, but I know in the pit of my stomach exactly who he'll describe. My heartbeat picks up speed as I wait.

"He's about my height, six feet plus, dark, shaggy hair pulled back in one of those man buns. He needs a haircut, a shave, and probably a shower. I'd guess he's in his forties. He could be younger, but if so, he's lived a hard life. He was casually dressed in jeans and a hoodie and boots that needed polishing."

I smile, knowing the count's leather shoes tucked under the table are polished to a high gloss.

"Anything else about him you remember?"

"He didn't have a business card, but he took mine. He said he might be interested in selling the property, and he'd be in touch. The strange thing is there were no other vehicles in sight but my rental. The situation was uncomfortable. It was the one time I was glad George was close by."

Fortunately, there's no need to respond as Al continues.

"This is an example of why I need your opinion on the property as well as what the political climate is in this area. My assistant is looking into Mr. Davenport. Once I have more information, I will work on negotiating a price. I can only hope he is the owner. You're so quiet. What are you thinking?"

What am I thinking? If he only knew.

"Well, I think we need to look at these aerial shots, don't you?"

He nods and slides the photos toward me, and says, "The property is beautiful. It runs parallel to the river."

He opens the file and places it between us as he moves his chair closer to mine. He shuffles through the papers and spreads a plat and several photographs in front of me.

"Look at the house! It's magnificent! I need to get inside to determine if the interior structure is sound. If it is, I can restore it. I hope it is, as the workmanship on the outside is excellent. If it can't be restored, I will rebuild on the original foundation. What do you think?"

I pull the plat closer. The property is large and meanders along the tidal waterways and marshes. There are sections marked off for greenhouses and plots for raising other crops. The aerial shots reveal the waterways, the wooded areas, some buildings, and vast stretches of land.

His smile widens as he points, "These are old cotton sheds. They're close to the water. With very little expense, I can restore a few of them and turn them into greenhouses. They can be used for the seedlings while we are building the new greenhouses. It's ideal for my plans. I hope Mr. Davenport is legitimate."

Beads of sweat gather on my forehead. This venture could be dangerous for Al. While Nick isn't the property owner, he's not about to put up with anyone dropping by unannounced.

Al's voice is distant as he says, "What's wrong? You're so pale?"

I pour water into my glass and say, "Oh, sometimes I have lapses from a previous head injury. It's nothing. I'm fine. Really. Your news is exciting but disconcerting since there's no clear ownership."

How am I ever going to extricate myself from this mess? My mind races ahead as I try out different scenarios:

In a few days, I could call Al and say I checked with my doctor, and he prescribed indefinite bed rest. Of course, that won't work because I have numerous events lined up, and I can't afford to cancel them. In a town this size, he'd hear about it.

Maybe I can locate a caterer who specializes in Spanish food and convince Al that someone with a focus in this area would be a better choice. The problem is I don't know anyone who specializes in Spanish cuisine.

My third thought is the best—if Nick carries out his threat to harm me, I won't have to worry about what Al thinks.

15

A few days later, I think about Cassie's suggestion to call Lorenzo, but I don't. Instead, I Zoom with Maria and relax into the lull of her lyrical Italian. Tension melts away from my shoulders as she chatters about their daily life in Castello del Mare and the current renters staying in Villa Fiori. She lists all the maintenance work Gino has completed and asks if I have ever thought of installing a pool. When we exhaust our exchange of news, she asks the same question she always asks, "Caterina, when are you coming back? This is your home."

As always, I answer the same, "Maria, I'm not ready. The pain is still too great."

I dissolve into my work and spend time planning events, executing them, and moving on to the next. Nick and Al are silent images. They randomly float in and out of empty spaces in my mind. I practice mindfulness and always offer their names up on the altar of Houdini with the simple request that they completely disappear from my life.

Of course, that only happens in books and movies, so I'm not surprised when Al's assistant calls to say my presence is requested. This time, it's for dinner. It's urgent according to the assistant and must be tonight. I suggest we meet at a casual restaurant, but the assistant isn't impressed with my suggestions. He waits until I silence my prattle, then gives me the details. It's a formal dinner at the

Waterfront Inn on the private veranda overlooking the water. When I check my calendar, I discover a full moon is scheduled for tonight. I chuckle as I imagine Al has arranged that too.

I whine to Cassie. She raises an eyebrow and snorts about my inability to say no and how she'd love a free meal with a count. Ha, I think, my dearest friend has no compassion. But, of course, she does. She's making a point, and the point is well taken, except I have already said yes—and once said, I don't back out.

From the recesses of my closet, I pull out the black Versace dress and Manolo Blahnik shoes that Stella gave me on our last trip to New York. I shudder at the memories associated with the dress, but I can't bear to part with it. The conversation in New York still burns brightly in my memory. Stella and I had stood arm-in-arm admiring our dressed-up selves in the floor-length mirror. She said one day I'd wear her necklace. Was it simply a random conversation, or did Stella know? Of course, she didn't know. Yet, I can't help but think she sensed what was to come.

Tonight, with Stella on my mind, it seems appropriate to wear the dress and the necklace. I also want Al, who appears to be on the high side of wealthy, to know that I'm not a slouch. Of course, that's thanks to Stella.

The problem is I'm not a girl who wears sultry, revealing neck-lines. The night of the gala, which was in Stella's honor at the Metropolitan Museum of Art, she wouldn't allow me to pin shut the gap that plunged almost to my navel.

Tonight, the silky dress slides smoothly over my head and hugs my body. I look in the mirror, squirm and pull at the neckline. I search through my junk drawer until I find a rusty safety pin. As my hand hovers, I hear Stella's voice shriek, "Don't you dare stick that nasty pin in that Versace dress. What's wrong with you? Look in the mirror. You are gorgeous."

I turn back to the mirror. The dress swirls around me in a black cloud. The neckline magically lies in place. Reverently removing the starfish necklace from its box, I drape it around my neck. The clusters of diamonds blaze in the lamplight. The red starfish floats in its jeweled circle. Dare I wear it?

A shiver travels my spine as the mirror magically reflects images of Stella and me standing side-by-side in our hotel room in New York. She had fastened the starfish necklace around her neck. Then she quickly unclasped it and placed it around my neck. Her words return to me as if she's still by my side.

"Oh, Cat, look. It's perfect. Someday, it will belong to you. When that day comes, remember me, won't you?"

Sadness had seeped from the depths of her eyes and lingered on her face. She'd looked at me and smiled as if she had a secret. Neither of us could have known that now I would be the one wearing the necklace. Pushing away the morbid thoughts, I open the smaller blue velvet box and clasp the bracelet around my wrist.

My hair is coiled high on my head, with stray wisps rippling around my face. Make-up, which I seldom wear, makes my green eyes sparkle and mutes my freckles. If only it were Lorenzo, I was meeting, but that is a misplaced wish. And the count isn't a bad second choice.

The drive to the inn only takes minutes. When Al insisted George pick me up, I countered with a strong no. That man isn't someone I want to be alone with, but I don't tell Al, as he'd want to know why. What would I tell him? The guy's a thug?

Al backed off, so I'm driving myself. I turn onto the highway and wonder briefly if he would patch things up with Margarita. Cassie, as usual, learned from the bartender at the inn that a small scene between the two of them had played out in the lobby. Margarita had insisted he return with her to Spain. When he refused, she left in a huff with lots of Spanish words trailing behind.

The engine continues to idle after I pull into the parking area.

How I wish I could keep on driving and never stop. A feeling of doom edges its way into my thoughts as I watch the moon tip the branches of the grand oaks on the far side of the river. This is my home, I remind myself. This is where I belong. I turn the ignition off and open the door.

The cicadas blatantly serenade me as I glide across the fine, expansive lawn to the front steps. A young man dressed in a tux rushes out to greet me and places my hand in the tuck of his arm. The dramatic gesture has me giggling. He grins back at me. What a spectacle we make as he parades me through the inn like some grand duchess.

My jewelry more than compares with the snowbirds who shell out big bucks to stay in this elegant mansion. Another nervous laugh escapes from my lips, but this time, my escort doesn't join in. He focuses on the formidable figure of Count Alfonso rising from the shadows on the candle-lit veranda.

My hand is untucked and placed in Al's. He gallantly brushes his lips across my hand, then straightens and says, "Ah, you are beautiful tonight—more than beautiful—you take my breath away."

He is elegant in an outrageously expensive dinner jacket with diamond cuff links. His attire smacks of Brioni evening wear. It appears even a Spanish count chooses Italian attire.

Before I can remark on how extraordinary he looks, he nods toward the shadows and says, "I have a surprise for you. Remember I told you about meeting the owner of Carrington Point Plantation? I've invited him to join us this evening."

My heart thuds as I turn. I know who will be there. But why is Al doing this?

"Caterina, it's my pleasure to introduce to you Mr. Richard Alistair Davenport of Virginia."

"What...what...?" I stutter as a man steps out of the shadows and stands before me.

"The count has told me so much about you, Ms. Gabbiano. I'm enchanted to meet you."

The intense eyes of my old high school friend lock with mine. I freeze in place as Nick Cafaro's treacherous smile encompasses me. He takes my hand, crushes it in his grip and says, "Why, you're even more beautiful than the count said."

I swallow hard and barely nod at him before jerking my hand away. I glance toward Al. He avoids my eyes as he pulls out my chair and guides me into the seat. He whispers in my ear, *play along* and then says aloud, "You're surprised I asked Richard to join us, yes?"

"Yes, of course, I'm surprised."

"Let me explain. I mentioned to you that I'd met Mr. Davenport a few days ago. When I told him I was interested in buying his property, he suggested we meet again after he spoke with the estate attorneys. He left a message at the inn, and I invited him to join us tonight. The disappointing news is it will take some time to settle the estate. But he's agreed to stay in touch and consider my offer."

I am gobsmacked into silence as Al rambles on, unaware of my state of shock. I stare across the table at Nick's sardonic smile. I slide into repetitious counting. I keep time with the flurry of my heartbeats. My fingers twist the elegant linen napkin into a wad as I try to decipher what game Al and Nick are playing and why I'm in the middle of it.

The bottle of champagne waits patiently in the crystal bucket. I'm too annoyed to ask for some. My body, as well as my hands, is shaky. The last thing I want is to drop a glass and draw attention to my distress.

Nick Cafaro, I think. *You little rat. What are you up to?*

Al and Nick (aka Richard) strive to outdo each other with charming platitudes that ooze like butter. The words slip and slide from their mouths, landing with greasy plops on the spotless white tablecloth.

What's going on? It's as if I've been invited to a theme party, and everyone is in costume, including me. The conversation is slick. Anger begins to boil in my stomach. Al exhorts Nick to join in his venture to save the world. Nick nods and appears interested, but his hooded eyes read loud and clear that the plan he has in mind doesn't combat world hunger.

Focusing on the surroundings, I look for anything to provide relief from this insane situation. Strains of *Moonlight Serenade* drift through the French doors. The music clutches me in a cocoon that feels like a stranglehold as the moon skims the horizon on its ascent into the heavens. Perhaps, I think without much hope, an earthquake, a hurricane, or some other disaster will descend to save me from participating in this evening of deceit.

Finally, the champagne is poured. I unclench my napkin and move my hand slowly, checking for stability before I lift the glass to my lips. Al gently shakes his head. I stop short of downing it in one swallow.

"Let's toast the occasion, Cat. Richard tells me he's given instructions to his attorneys to put all their efforts into settling the estate quickly. And he's also interested in investing in my new venture."

I nod my head and wait. I cannot speak for fear my voice will give me away. My fake smile hurts my face. I glare at Nick. When did he add con artist to his list of deceitful endeavors? He ignores my stare and gives all of his attention to Al.

"To lucrative times ahead," Nick proposes.

Al looks only slightly flustered as he rejoins with, "To combating world hunger."

They both turn to me. I stupidly say *hear, hear* like I'm a member of the British parliament. Fortunately, I stop short of saying, *hear ye, hear ye.*

With my glass of champagne emptied in a few seconds, I nod to the waiter for a refill. Al frowns, but my ability to reason has vanished. My eyes latch onto his. I wait for a signal that he's in control of the situation, but the strange half smile on his face says differently. So I chug a second glass of champagne. I become quite talkative with a second glass of anything alcoholic.

A rambling monologue pours from my mouth about my villa in Castello del Mare, my vacation plans, and, ultimately, my intention to move to Italy. I paint a picture of Villa Fiori against the black velvet of the night. Both men smirk—Nick in annoyance and Al in disbelief —but the volcano inside of me has erupted. There's no putting the stopper back in.

Al leans in close to me. His pupils dilate, and his nostrils flare as he grabs my hand.

"You are in such good spirits tonight, Caterina. I had no idea you were moving to Italy. Do you have a date in mind?"

"What?"

"A date when you're moving to Italy?"

"Oh, did I say I was moving? No, not exactly—well, not right away."

He pats my hand again in that patronizing way that men have. My anger ratchets up a notch.

He turns to Nick. "Well, let's enjoy our meal. Cat, you and I can finish this conversation later."

"When would that be? Hmmm? What makes you think there's a need for us to have a conversation? I'm not so sure Mr. Davenport's property will ever be for sale. If your heart is set on that property, I think you're going to have a long wait."

Alcohol and my mouth are not a good combo, as my mouth automatically spews out words better left unsaid.

I look Nick in the eyes and continue my sarcasm, "It appears to me that Mr. Davenport isn't really interested in selling Carrington Point Plantation. Isn't that true, Mr. Davenport?"

Nick glares but doesn't respond.

Al puts his hand over mine and says, "Cat, why would you say such a thing? Of course, he's willing. Mr. Davenport and I will work out the details later. Let's enjoy the evening."

He signals the waiter. The meal begins.

16

For the remainder of the evening there is nothing pretty about my behavior. My anger toward Al and Nick numbs my ability to reason. I refuse another glass of champagne and stick to sipping one glass of red wine throughout dinner.

The conversation is awkward. I do nothing to improve it. When I can no longer tolerate either one of the men, I tell Al that I have an event tomorrow and need to leave. He insists George drive me home. When I refuse, he pushes back and says, "Cat, I think you've had too much to drink. I will drive you home."

Then Nick chimes in, "No, I'll drive her home. It's on my way."

I stand and say, "I am driving myself home. I am not intoxicated, I know the way, and I am perfectly capable."

Al doesn't wish to make a scene in the restaurant. He nods in my direction, "Would you please text me when you arrive? If you don't, I'll stop by."

Common courtesy has left me. I nod curtly at Nick and turn to go. Al rises and pulls me into an embrace and whispers, "I'm sorry, Cat. I'll call you tomorrow."

Jerking away, I storm off the veranda. Once inside the restaurant, I turn to see Al deep in conversation with con man Nick. I don't know what to think.

Driving the distance home is a bit hazy. Thankfully, it's a short drive, it's late, and no other vehicles are on the road. Once inside the house, I send a terse text to Al, douse my face with ice water, and brew a pot of coffee.

Cassie's voice to call Lorenzo sounds like a drum roll in my head. Nick Cafaro's behavior makes the decision easier. Whoever Nick is—the person I used to know, a crazy undercover FBI agent, or a hustler—he's acting suspicious. Now I have to wonder if Al is part of this scheme, too? Why am I being included? Those questions provide enough reasons to call Lorenzo. The slight buzz I'm feeling supplies the false courage required to place the call.

It's well past midnight when I flop down on the sofa and open my laptop. My finger hovers over Lorenzo's number. He'll be up by now drinking espresso before he leaves for the station.

If I think too long, my courage will fail me. I hit the button. The screen opens. It's been a while since I've seen him, as we usually text. My heart clinches. I suck in my breath and inhale his rugged good looks. My heart feels soft and mushy as he runs his fingers across his chin—it creates a longing so strong that I reach out to touch him.

Before my hand touches the screen, I pull it back and pretend to brush hair out my eyes. I focus on controlling all my impulses. I smile.

"*Ciao*, Lorenzo."

"*Ciao*, Cat. *Come va?*"

"*Bene e tu?*"

"*Sì*, yes, *bene*."

We stare at each other. As I wrestle with my desire, the conversation comes to a standstill.

Finally, he says, "Are you on your way to a party, or are you just coming home?"

The spell is broken. I must look like a bedraggled Cinderella who waited too long to leave the ball. It didn't dawn on me to brush my hair, wipe smudged mascara from under my eyes or change clothes before hitting the call button—maybe my head isn't as clear as I thought it was.

I laugh, blush, and dump my words out all at one time.

"Yeah, sorry about that, but I wanted to catch you before you left for the station. I didn't think about how I must look."

He smiles, "You look stunning, Cat. Maybe a little overdressed for morning coffee and conversation, but the necklace suits you."

I blush again and wish I'd taken the damm thing off. I reach up but stop when he says, "Don't, Cat. Leave it on. *Allora*, tell me, what's so important?"

"I'm in kind of jam, Lorenzo. I need to talk to someone with connections to the FBI. Do you know anyone?"

"Whoa, hold on. Why are you asking me about FBI connections? Cat, have you forgotten you were almost killed in Castello?"

"No, Lorenzo. I haven't forgotten."

"You promised me you'd stay out of trouble. You swore your only plan was to return home and reopen your business. I'm sure the FBI isn't involved in your business unless you are doing something illegal. What's going on?"

Blood floods my cheeks. He's going to be so angry when I tell him, but my choices are limited. I don't personally know anyone in law enforcement in this town. Sheriff Blackwell is a friend of Cassie's. She talks about what a grand person he is, but I believe this situation with Nick has gone way past local law enforcement. Plus, I trust Lorenzo. Trust is what I need right now.

So I begin, "A while back, I received a phone call from an old high school friend—Nick Cafaro. He asked me to meet him for coffee to talk about our twentieth high school reunion."

"This is someone you've know for a long time? Does he live in the same town?"

"No, he's here on a business trip, but let me finish, then you can grill me. *Va bene?*"

Lorenzo huffs, but doesn't say anything else.

"We had just ordered coffee when our meeting was interrupted by a call from his boss, or at least that's what he said. He had to leave, so we arranged to meet for lunch the next day. The next morning, he contacted me and said lunch would have to wait as he needed to participate in an international call."

"So you didn't meet him, right?"

"Actually, I did but not for lunch. He asked me if I could meet him right then to look at some property his boss was interested in purchasing. When I asked why he didn't contact a realtor, he said he didn't know anyone in the area. He thought since I lived here, it would be helpful to have my opinion."

"Where was the property? Did you know anything about it?"

"A little. It's an old plantation, maybe fifteen miles outside of town. I'd met clients out there a few days earlier. They were interested in the location as a possible wedding reception venue."

"So you decided to meet him?"

Yes. But when I arrived, this guy dressed all in black popped out of the woods and demanded I let him in my car."

"You're still alive, so I guess you got out of there, right?"

"Well, no, but I did ask to see identification. That's when he showed me his FBI badge.It looked legitimate."

Lorenzo was groaning, but I kept on.

"Once inside the car, he said he was an undercover agent, and he was involved it a covert operation. The plantation that I had shown to my clients is being staked out as a place for illegal activities."

"Okay, so far, this is interesting but not life-threatening."

"Well, the threats come later."

"Cat?"

"I'm getting to that part, but first, Nick kept pumping me for information about the plantation. He said he'd seen me at the property, and he accused me of snooping in a place I didn't belong."

"Why would he accuse you of snooping? Were you?"

"Gracious, no. I just told you I was checking out the place for a wedding reception."

"So you weren't doing anything illegal?"

I start to sputter until I realize he's joking.

"No, I wasn't doing anything illegal. I had permission to be there

—well, sort of. But before my clients arrived, someone tried to attack me."

"Oh, Cat. Don't tell me you're messing in stuff that's none of your business."

"Just listen to me. My only purpose for being on the property was to access it and meet my clients. I didn't have being attacked on my list of things to do that day. Okay?"

"Sorry, continue with your story."

"The strange thing is Nick said he saw the guy with a hammer posed to knock me in the head. He made no attempt to stop it. I could have been badly hurt or killed. All the time, he was spying on me—and my clients. Does that sound right to you?"

"It does sound unusual. However, if he was staking the place out, he couldn't reveal himself unless it was a life and death situation."

"Don't you imagine it felt like life and death to me?"

"Were you attacked?"

"No, I managed to get away. Then my clients showed up, and whoever it was ran off. But don't you think it's weird that an FBI agent was watching me—us all that time?"

"I'm not sure. Keep talking."

"When I drove out to meet him at the property, he wanted to know what I saw the day I was nearly attacked. He wanted me to describe my assailant. Oh, I forgot he said I had to promise not to tell anyone I was meeting him."

Lorenzo interrupts, "Cat, are you crazy?"

He rubs the stubble on his face and glares at me.

"Oh, Lorenzo, please let me finish the story, then you can say whatever you want. Okay?"

"Sorry, Cat. But your story sounds risky. The last thing you need is more trouble. Go ahead. I promise to keep quiet."

"Hmmm, where did I leave off? Oh, yes—Nick grilled me with a million questions."

"Oh, *merda*, Cat. *Fermare*! Stop right there."

"What? You don't want to hear the rest?"

"No, stay away from this guy. Do not meet him or respond to him. I can be there by the end of the week. It sounds like you need someone to ensure you are not a target. I have a contact with the FBI in D.C. I'll place a call before I leave. They can protect you until I arrive."

"Lorenzo, I called you for advice, not because I need a knight in shining armor. Either you listen, or we sign off—your call."

The silence is staggering. For a moment, I believe he might sign off. His hair is standing on end from the numerous times his fingers have plowed back and forth.

Finally, he says, "Okay. I promise, but you are in over your head. I'm not sure I can help you."

"Just listen. When I finish, you can ask me anything, but let me get through this. Okay?"

"*Va bene.*"

This time, he listens without interrupting. I zip through everything that happened, even adding the story of human trafficking.

"Okay, that's all except for the Spanish count."

17

"Cat, you're joking? There is no Spanish count. You are making it up, so I will forget to tell you how crazy you are."

"No, Lorenzo. I'm not joking. There is a Spanish count. He wants to buy the property—the same property Nick told me to stay away from. Until tonight, I had no idea Nick and the count were connected."

"What do you mean—connected?"

"I mean, I met the count for dinner tonight—well, actually, last night. It was supposed to be a business dinner to discuss the event he's hired me to cater. When I arrived, Nick was with him. He not only gave a fake name to the count, but he told him he owned the property."

"That's how you dress for a business dinner?"

Lorenzo is toying with me. I know, but I still sputter all over myself.

"I'll dress however I please for dinner—business or personal."

"Okay, I deserve that. I was joking, but you're touchy this evening. From what you've told me, you don't like this Nick guy, do you?"

"I used to. We were great friends in high school, but that was a long time ago. He was crazy in love with Stella. Yet, when I tried to tell him she was dead, he refused to listen. He said the FBI operation was his only focus. He brushed off her death so fast that I became suspicious."

"Sounds like he has other things on his mind. In his position that's not unusual."

"Oh, Lorenzo, listen to the rest of the story before you take Nick's side."

He nods, and I continue.

"Nick kept persisting me to describe the person who threatened me with the hammer. The only thing I saw was a distorted reflection in the window. It happened so fast that I couldn't describe anything about the person, but Nick kept probing. He was relentless. Then he told me to stay away from the location and to keep my clients away."

"Did he tell you anything about the FBI undercover operation?"

"Nothing much, but I didn't ask questions. It's a topic that makes me squeamish—young children being trafficked—sex and drugs. I didn't ask for details."

Neither of us speak for a few minutes. Since Lorenzo already thinks I'm nuts, I make a quick decision to tell him the rest.

I take a deep breath and say, "A few days later, Nick contacted me again and insisted I meet him."

"And you did? Yes, of course, you would."

I ignore his comment and continue, "The rendezvous was on the waterfront. He came up behind me so fast that I never saw him. He used his body to block me against the concrete piling, and he threatened me."

Lorenzo groans a low growl kind of sound, "What did he say?"

"He said my clients had returned to the property, and it was my responsibility to keep them away. When I said I had no control over my clients, he said that was my problem, not his. He's supposed to be an old friend, but his behavior was frightening."

"How? What did he do or say?"

"The park was devoid of people that day. But that's not all. He physically made me uncomfortable, and he threatened me."

"Oh, Cat. You are a walking advertisement for trauma. You need someone to take care of you."

"I do not need or want anyone taking care of me," I say, jutting out my chin and compressing my lips in a tight line.

"*Va bene, so che.* Go ahead and tell me the rest of your story."

How is it that he always manages to make me angry? I'm not helpless. He knows I'm not. It is so disconcerting until I remember he's an Italian man. I smile. Our eyes connect. He smiles back. His entire face radiates warmth. I'm wrapped in his arms as we stand on the terrace in Castello. He tucks the white flowers in my hair and—"

"Cat, I'm waiting."

I crash land in front of my computer.

"The Spanish count," I begin. "He wants to buy the property that Nick told me to stay away from. Not only does he want to buy the property, but he also intends to start a nursery business on it. He asked me to cater this grand reception where he plans to announce his business intentions and ask his guests to invest in the project. That's why I agreed to have dinner with him last night. When I arrived, the count said we had a guest joining us. Then he introduced me to Nick as Richard Alistair Davenport and told me this Richard person owned the property."

"Did you reveal Nick's real name?"

"No, of course not. If Nick is telling the truth, then I would be interfering with the federal government."

"What if he's not telling the truth?"

"That's why I am calling you, Lorenzo. I believe Nick is lying. He doesn't own that property any more than I do. Why would he lie about that? What else is he lying about? What if he's not an undercover FBI agent? Nothing about this makes sense."

"Okay, send me Nick's full name as well as the alias he is using, along with the count's name. You didn't mention his name."

Laugher spills out before I can stop. I sputter, "Count Alfonso Fernando Philippe Francisco Perez."

Lorenzo joins in my laughter before asking, "What do you call him?"

Tears slide down my cheeks as my entire body shakes. I snort out, "Al."

Much to my dismay, I have to find a tissue and blow my nose. That's when I decide the knock on the head in Castello del Mare had rendered me senseless. Here I am once again involved in another dangerous mess, and I'm practically rolling on the floor every time I say the count's name.

After I answer all of Lorenzo's questions, he says, "Let me make some contacts. A few years ago, I was invited to attend some international training sessions at the FBI National Academy. I've kept in touch with several of the agents and helped on a few international cases. I'm sure they'll do the same for me. I'll be back in touch soon. Cat?"

"Hmmm?"

"Cat, promise me you'll stay away from Nick and the count until I check them out. *Va bene?*"

"*Va bene*, Lorenzo."

18

Cassie's giddy with the prospect of entertaining her friend State Senator James Middleton Madison and his sister Alice. We've discussed the perfect meal endlessly and finally decided on a Southern menu with a twist or two. The kitchen is full of her laughter as she provides me with tales of her escapades with the senator.

The shrimp have been slathered with herb and garlic-infused butter and are waiting to be popped on the grill before our guests arrive. The pork loin has been smoking all day and will be sliced and plated on a bed of arugula surrounded by slow-roasted tomatoes. The cheese and garlic grits are ready to pop into the oven, along with the barbecued butter beans.

I'm putting together an old-fashioned soak salad. It's a favorite, as it's made 3 to 4 hours in advance and stored in the fridge. I've already washed and picked over a bunch of watercress, spinach, and turnip greens. Next, I cut the freshly picked juicy tomatoes into chunks and add them to the greens. Then, I mix olive oil, white wine vinegar, fresh lemon juice, minced garlic with a dash of salt, pepper and sugar and drizzle over the salad until every morsel is infused.

My last job is the lemon curd for the pound cake. It's almost ready. I glance up from my work and watch Cassie frosting the triple chocolate layer cake, as she hums *The Shape of You*.

We work well together—sometimes with long periods of silence and other times with so much chatter and laughter that we barely get the job done. I sigh with contentment. Having a friend like Cassie has made my life so much better.

She looks up and says, "Big sigh, what's up?"

"I talked to Lorenzo last night."

"You didn't! How could you not tell me? You are so mean."

"Me, mean? You who have kept the senator a secret for weeks and weeks?"

We laugh easily but not for long as Cassie continues, "Okay, how did it go?"

"Not bad. He's thinking about coming for a visit. He said he didn't understand what a Lowcountry was and wanted to see what it looked like."

"How could you keep that from me all day? Do you think he'll come?"

"Hmmm, I don't know. He's busy, but at least he's thinking about it. Now, you need to get out of here. Wear something sexy for your senator. I'll clean up and run through the checklist to make sure everything is perfect. See you back here around six."

"Thanks, Cat. I really appreciate you pulling out all the stops for Jim and his sister. I'm a wreck about you meeting him. You promise you'll like him?"

"Get out of here! If you like him, how could I not like him?"

Of course, I don't like him. I try, but his character is deeply flawed. I can't quite figure out what it is. I puzzle over it as I listen to the table conversation. It's there, lying just below the arrogance. It bothers me why I can't figure out what Cassie sees in him. He says all the right things—dotes on Cassie—but there is a deep, down, rotten smell of deception about him. His sister Alice has this vacant, otherworldly look in her eyes. She floats on the conversation with smiles and nods but with very little participation. Whenever her eyes light on Cassie, a shadow crosses her face. When her eyes turn to the senator, she glows. There's a moment when a look passes between them, but I dismiss those negative thoughts. Yet, I can't stop thinking that it isn't a normal brother/sister look.

Cassie is radiant in cobalt blue. She's one of those people who looks great in anything, but tonight, she smolders with excitement.

"Cat?"

"What?" I say, knowing I'd left the conversation. "Sorry, did I drift away? You know how I am, Cassie. I'm already thinking about our next event. What did I miss?"

Jim chuckles, which, for no obvious reason, irritates me. Then he says, "Well, I've heard about your reputation as the best dang caterer in the Lowcountry. All I can say is the movers and shakers in this community got it right. *Woo doggie*, girl, you know how to cook. This meal was scrumptious—Southern food like I've never had before. You know I'm going to recommend you for all of our functions, little lady. Your dance card will be full."

Oh yuck! Did he really say girl and little lady?

I keep my increasingly stressful thoughts to myself and respond, "Maybe not, senator. Once you dig into my resume, you might reconsider."

"Oh, please, call me Jim. Why don't you save me the trouble and tell me what I'd find? As far as I can tell, you're charming, a fabulous cook, and mighty fine-looking too."

He reaches for Cassie's hand and continues, "Cass, baby, y'all didn't tell me what a looker Cat is. She's enough to make a man jump ship."

His hearty laughter echoes around the table. My body lifts out of the chair automatically. I stop short of reaching across the table and smacking the crap out of him. My eyes turn pleadingly to Cassie, but she's enthralled—even fawning a bit.

Shit! I keep my head down as I collect the plates. When I try to remove his, he grabs me around the waist and says, "Let me kiss the chef."

I stare across his head at Cassie and push back with all my might. The plates clatter to the floor. The crash reverberates around the room. Cassie jumps up. Our eyes meet over broken shards. She gives her head a little shake—sign language for let it go.

I'm stunned, livid. Bile backs in my throat as I contemplate smashing the guy's face. But Cassie is signaling for me to back off. Why?

We pick up the large pieces of broken china and head to the kitchen. My first thought is to kick this creep out of my house.

Cassie places her hand on my arm and whispers, "Please let it go, Cat. I'm sure he didn't mean to make you uncomfortable. He's had a bad day, and perhaps he's had a bit too much to drink."

I grit my teeth and forcibly swallow angry words instead of spilling them out in every direction.

"Cassie, this isn't good. You know that. It's not the first time. Have you forgotten the scene he created at the Fitzhugh's dinner party? From what I've heard, he's mighty quick to lose his temper. That's a dangerous characteristic."

"It's okay, Cat. Really. Please let it go."

We're interrupted when he barges into the kitchen. He leans against the doorjamb and says, "Hey girls, we need a dustpan and broom to clean up the mess Cat made. How 'bout one of you rustle them up? Alice will do the sweeping. Won't you sis?"

I glare at him and turn away. Cassie finds the broom and dustpan and says demurely, "I'll take care of it. Alice is a guest. I can't have her cleaning up our mess."

The rest of the evening is pure hell. I am civil, but just barely. As soon as the last forkful of cake is devoured and the last sip of coffee drunk, I stand and say, "You'll have to excuse me. I have a full day tomorrow and an early start."

Cassie casts a sad side-long glance my way, but I ignore it. I want these people gone before I say or do something that will ruin my friendship with Cassie. I force my breathing to slow down. I unclench my hands. My anger isn't going to resolve this situation tonight.

Thankfully, Alice jumps up from her chair. She gives me a small hug and a half smile and says, "It was lovely, Cat. Thank you. Come along, James. Cat and Cassie have plenty to keep them busy. We'll only be in the way. We don't want to overstay our welcome."

"Well, now, I was counting on staying with Cassie tonight. Isn't that so, sugar? Alice, you take my car. How's that?"

Before I heave up my dinner, Cassie has Jim by the arm and maneuvers him out the front door. She whispers so low I can't hear what she tells him. His shoulders hunch up. He shakes his finger in her face before grabbing Alice and pushing her toward the car.

19

A faint strand of dawn tipped across the horizon as Nick scanned the road through binoculars. He was positioned in the thickest part of the wooded area. He checked his watch for the fifth time and texted the driver again. He'd heard nothing since they turned onto Highway 21. There was only silence.

His hand strayed to the waistband of his jeans. He muttered when he realized the Glock 19 wasn't in its usual place. Cold sweat ran down his back. Stupid to be out here without it. He'd wait a few more minutes for the cargo vans to show up. If they didn't, he'd go back to the house and retrieve the gun.

Carrington Point Plantation had been a great location at the beginning of the operation, but it was time to move on. It wouldn't be long before someone—maybe the count—figured out he was not the owner. Cat already knew and was suspicious. He wasn't sure he could trust her. She was too inquisitive, nothing like the sweet, submissive girl he'd known in high school. She was also angry. It wouldn't take much for her to talk to someone.

To pass the time, he thought about what he'd found on her iPad. When she left it on the front railing, George had nabbed it. But he was such a dumbass he couldn't crack the password. Nick's background had made it an easy task. He'd spent time scanning the emails and looking at the files. He'd scrolled through numerous menus and proposals for upcoming events. When he opened the photo file, he was inundated with images of food. He browsed through them rapidly. The good news was there were no photos of the interior of the house. That would have been a game changer.

There were a few photos of Stella and Cat, arm-in-arm at some big function. Stella peered out at him, startlingly beautiful in a dramatic red gown—she was every bit the movie star. But it was Cat who radiated in a simple black v-neck gown. She had an ethereal glow about her—a joy radiating from the inside out.

He pulled back into the thicket and wondered how he was going to tell *the boss* that Cat had seen the inside of the house and could describe the furnishings. Maybe he should withhold that information for a while. But probably not, since the possibility was strong that George would tell *the boss* some half-assed concocted story full of lies. He wasn't sure why George kept snooping around. It had taken all his willpower not to throttle him. The guy was stupid. If he had harmed Cat in any way, the entire operation would have crashed. He needed to talk to *the boss* soon.

The one thing he didn't want was for Cat to get hurt. How she wound up in the midst of all this was beyond him. Nick's phone buzzed with a text.

What's going on with the latest haul? I'm ready for some entertainment.

Nick felt pure evil radiating from the text. He had no option but to respond.

No word. Contact you as soon as shipment arrives. Nothing for you tonight.

Nick shook his head wearily. He had to delay as long as he could or at least until he could figure out what to do next. It'd made him sick when George had demanded he cipher off the cream of the crop for sexual encounters with *the boss* and his cronies. When the operation had first started up, he'd been stupid enough to believe they were helping the girls. Now, he desperately wished he could remove himself. So far, there were no roads out of this stinking hole.

When his little brother Ted had been killed, Nick had lost control. It was supposed to have been a peaceful demonstration. No violence. He'd been there and watched as the bullet struck his brother in the forehead. He'd stood stone still as his brother had crumpled to the ground, never moved again. Just eighteen.

Nick's life was over. His most important job had been to protect Ted. With his little brother dead, he'd turned to alcohol and drugs. The FBI put him on administrative leave with the understanding that if he sought psychiatric care, went to their drug and alcohol rehabilitation program, and joined one of their bereavement groups, there was a chance for reinstatement. But Nick was lost. He knew it and didn't care.

That was when *the boss* had told him the Bureau would never take him back. After all, the FBI had killed his brother, hadn't they? He'd posed that as a question to Nick. Led him in that direction and left him hanging. He'd been so overcome with grief, drugs, and alcohol he'd believed *the boss* and had followed him down this dark path. A path without a way out.

He pushed the morbid thoughts back into the deep recesses of his mind and focused on Cat. It had been a colossal blow to her when he showed up for dinner with the count. What she didn't know was it had been a shock for him to see her sashaying to the table dressed like a starlet in the same black gown that she had worn in the photo on her iPad. The count had neglected to mention the name of his dinner companion.

Running into the count had been his own stupidity. He knew better than to leave the confines of the plantation house during daylight. Every time he'd done it, trouble had ensued. It was almost as if his unscheduled strolls outside were on some dark web calendar. Otherwise, how could it be that every time he decided he couldn't stay inside a minute longer, it seemed to be the very day strangers came to check out the plantation?

The surprise visit by the count had pushed him to create the story about owning the property. It was the best he could come up with on short notice. He'd hoped it was enough to blow smoke up the count's royal ass.

But Cat? The look on her face when he joined them for dinner would have been funny in another situation. She'd been furious, and an angry woman was something he didn't have time to tangle with. Cat had been his friend—had helped him during those difficult high school years. And now he was threatening her. What kind of person had he become? The entire operation was a disaster. It was on a collision course. When it collapsed, he was sure he'd be the collateral damage.

He scanned the road again and exhaled when the first of the vehicles turned into the driveway. He waited until both vans pulled up behind the house before he left his hiding place.

"What in the hell happened? Why are you late?" he snarled at the driver of the first van.

"Hey man, don't blame us. We had to detour. Roadblocks on Highway 21. Lucky for us, the scanner was on, or we would have rolled right into a sting. They're out in force tonight. No time to contact you."

"Okay, but don't pull this stunt again. If anything is going down, I need to know about it, ya hear? Now move on. I'll be along shortly to check the cargo."

The driver nodded and pulled down the dirt path without headlights. The second van followed.

Nick walked into the house, turned off the gas fireplace, grabbed a jacket from the rack by the door, and picked up a flashlight. His hand was on the knob when he reversed direction and moved toward the desk. From the bottom drawer, he removed his Glock 19. He placed it in the waist of his jeans. He took a deep breath and tried to steel himself for what was waiting for him. It was something he'd never get used to.

20

"Shit," James Middleton Madison said to no one in particular. "Did you see that? The bitch just made a fool out of me."

He turned to watch the back of Cassie's cobalt blue dress disappear into the house as the door closed behind her.

"Well, James, what did you expect?"

"Shut your mouth, Alice. You're simpleminded, just like that Cat woman. Don't be talking to me unless you have something civil to say. You understand?"

Alice flinched and backed away from his outstretched hand.

"James, let me drive. You're tired."

He turned around, jerked her close, and whispered, "You're a stupid woman. Don't you dare think you know better than me. You're always forgetting your place, opening your mouth when nobody wants to hear from you. Shut the fuck up and get in the car. I'm driving."

He released her so suddenly that she lost her balance and crashed into the door.

"Don't you go making any noise. Ya hear? You sure didn't come to my rescue tonight when that woman tried to castrate me. Nah, you sit there all smug with that ridiculous smile on your ugly face. You think I'm going to put up with that? No, not me. In fact, I'm not putting up with her or you. I've got plans for tonight. You'll have to find somewhere else to stay. You're not going to ruin the rest of my evening. I'll drop you at the inn, or you can drop me off and drive to the condo."

Alice slid into the passenger seat and fastened her seatbelt. Silent tears dripped down her face in slow-moving streams. She whispered so low, he didn't hear her, " You promised you wouldn't bring anyone to the house."

"Yes indeed. You're jealous, aren't you, Alice? Always have been, my little sister wishing for her big brother to give it to her. You know you're sick, Alice?"

Alice pressed her forehead against the cool glass window and sobbed as James wrenched the car away from the curb without turning on the headlights.

Cassie leaned against the front door and took a deep breath. I stop clearing the table and wait. She's so lovely and such a splendid friend that I don't dare yell out, *how can you let that despicable man touch you?*

Finally, she pushes away from the door. I move to the sideboard, pick up two glasses and a bottle of red, and nod toward the living room.

"What happened, Cass?"

The damn breaks as she drops on the sofa and curls into a fetal position. She presses her face into the cushion and sobs.

"Shush. Don't Cassie. He's not worth it."

"But, Cat, he didn't mean it. He's never acted like that before. Never! And we've been together ever since the Fitzhugh's party. He's been wonderful—kind and considerate. He just had too much to drink. He was only flirting with you. It was harmless. He didn't mean to upset you. Can't you understand that?"

I shove a box of tissues next to her and don't respond. What can I possibly say that won't offend her? This guy is a first-class slime ball, but Cassie isn't going to appreciate my point of view. At least not tonight.

"I'll call Sam to tell her you're staying over."

Cassie whispers, "You don't have to call her. Spring break is over. She's back in school."

"Okay, then go take a shower. You know where everything is. Clean pjs are in the bottom drawer in the guest room. Your glass of wine will be waiting when you finish."

With a big sniff, Cassie stands up. With shoes in hand and shoulders hunched, she pads across the hardwood floors. Her cobalt blue dress billows out, swirling in what should have been a happy dance instead of a funeral dirge.

I finish clearing the table, load the dishwasher, and stack the pots and pans in the sink. They can wait. There's no hurry since I lied about having a busy day tomorrow.

How can I help Cassie? Her pain is razor-sharp. A failed relationship is the last thing she needs. Yet, after seeing the senator up close, a failure from my point of view would be a welcomed relief. He's is a creep and a manipulator. Plus, my gut tells me there's something else going on with him. What it is, I don't know, but this guy is going to hurt her. Cass can't see it. No amount of me spouting wisdom will change that. She's always been the levelheaded one to my craziness. How much honesty does anyone want when it comes to romance?

If I say anything, she'll be defensive, just like I was when Dr. Ginny told me I had enabled my ex-husband's behavior. She didn't say it with malice but with kindness so I could better understand my own behavior in order to change it.

Cassie doesn't want to hear anything negative about Jim. Even if she were to listen, what I have to say won't change her mind.

I pace the entire length of the kitchen and back again. Damn, this is a mess. This jackass isn't about to play nice now that his false veneer has been exposed. What if he takes in out on Cassie? I stop in my tracks when the shower is silent.

James' cell chimed out *Highway to Hell*. The car lurched as he struggled to remove the phone from his coat jacket.

"James. Please. Stop the car!"

"Shut your mouth, Alice."

The front wheels careened into the curbing as James rolled to a stop and tapped his phone. Before he can read the text, *a* blue light flashed in the rearview mirror.

"Ah, shit! I should have asked George to drive us tonight. Alice, slide over here in the driver's seat. I'll pop out of the car and pretend to be sick. You tell 'em you've been driving the whole time. Ya hear me?"

21

The vans pulled under the trees just off the road that led down to the river and the old cotton sheds. Once Nick inspected the cargo, the product would be delivered there. He hated the name "product" that he'd been forced to use for the young girls. The sheds were the holding pens until further instructions arrived. Then, the girls who weren't picked to service *the boss* and his buddies were delivered to the next distribution point. Before checking the vans, he texted *the boss* to let him know that they had arrived.

Nick slipped silently through the wood line. He watched the drivers smoking and chatting as if they had a load of construction materials waiting behind the cargo doors. Nick pulled back into the shadow when he saw George was one of the drivers. The deadly feeling in the pit of his stomach returned. He hadn't seen or heard from George since their last encounter when he thought George was going to kill Cat. Nick stepped out of the shadow.

"What are you doing here? Where's the regular driver?"

George drew himself up to his full height and crossed his arms over his barreled chest.

"He didn't show. *The boss* asked me to take his place."

Nick felt the hair on the back of his neck stand up. *Why would the boss interfere? He'd made it clear that his name wasn't to be associated in any way with the operation. George driving a van meant trouble.*

Nick was worried. After he'd stumbled across the count and had lied about owning the plantation, he'd discreetly followed Al back to his car. And there was George, waiting with the door open. Something was going on that *the boss* hadn't bothered to discuss with him. It was an ominous sign when George showed up. He wasn't just a driver. Nope, he was a whole lot more.

Pushing the dark thoughts away, Nick walked up to the first van and nodded. The doors swung open. The putrid smell of urine, defecation, sweat, and filthy bodies filled the air. He snapped on his flashlight. Rows of big empty eyes stared back at him—mostly brunettes but a few blondes and a scrawny redhead. They all had that drug-induced emaciated look. They clutched at each other, some of them whimpering.

He backed away and said, "How many?'

"Twelve in this van."

"Get them cleaned up. Go on. Get out of here."

The doors slammed shut, and the vehicle, without headlights, pulled back on the path and headed toward the river. Nick inclined his head toward George. The doors to the second van swung open. The same nastiness pervaded the night air. He flashed his light into the black recesses.

"What the hell? You know the girls are supposed to be at least sixteen. That one barely looks twelve. You're crazy to pick up a kid this age. She's not a runaway. Is she? George, is this your doing? Get rid of her. Now!"

George wiped his hand across his mouth. To Nick, it looked like he was wiping away a grin, but how could that be possible?

"*The boss* ordered this one."

"What do you mean?"

"He wants them young and untouched. Says you're not doing your job."

One of the older girls scooted toward the opening. Her hand was clasped firmly around the wrist of the small fair-haired girl—the one that looked so young. She inched forward and pleaded, "Please let us go. I won't say anything. We just wanna go home, please."

He couldn't afford to act weak in front of George. The Glock made its way out of his waistband. He pointed it in her face and watched as big tears slid down her cheeks and snot dripped from her nose.

Nick didn't look her in the eye when he said, "It's too late for that."

The entire time he was talking, she was inching her way closer to the door.

Nick nodded to George, "Close it up and get out of here."

The girl bolted, screaming at the younger girl to run. She kicked Nick, scratched his face and tried to bite him. The struggle was fierce as Nick attempted to bring her under control. She wailed like a screeching bobcat until he whacked her into silence with the butt of his gun. While Nick was grappling with her, George grabbed the younger girl and held her in a stranglehold.

"My sister," sobbed the young girl as she beat on George's arms. "You've killed her."

Her long, loud, high-pitched scream pierced the night air.

"Shut her up. Throw them back in the van and get out of here. These two are trouble. Tell Marissa to separate them. I don't care what *the boss* asked you to do. This isn't acceptable. You won't do this again. Is that clear? These girls need to be released."

George sneered and said, "I only take orders from *the boss*."

He turned to walk away. Nick grabbed his jacket and jerked him around.

"Listen, you stupid fuck. We're talking statutory rape with a kid that young. I'll make sure *the boss* understands. Get the hell out of here."

George towered over Nick. His lips rippled in a smirk. The thin white scar that ran up the side of his face zig-zagged when he forced a smile.

"Man, you don't wanna mess with me. If I say the word, *the boss* will dump you, quick like."

He jerked free of Nick's hands and climbed into the van. Nick watched it disappear into the dark shadows of the enormous oaks.

He shook his head, stuck the Glock back in his waistband, and limped toward the house. He couldn't let his guard down in front of George. Didn't let on that the girl had kicked the shit out of him. Sooner or later, this was bound to happen. He knew *the boss* preferred young girls, ones that didn't come from the streets. George's involvement let him know *the boss* was displeased. If *the boss* was unhappy, it meant he might be eliminated. After years in the FBI, Nick had acquired a sixth sense about operations. He was pretty sure this one was going to end badly for him.

22

When Cassie doesn't return after her shower, I tap on the door.

"You okay? Can I come in?"

Silence. The door opens a slit. Cassie's eyes are swollen and red. She stifles a sob and says, "Cat, I don't want to talk tonight. I need time to think about what happened. Okay?"

"Sure, Cass. That's fine. I'm here if you want to talk or just need a hug. It doesn't matter what time."

"Can I have the hug now?"

I push the door open and give her my biggest and best hug. I whisper against her head, "It's OK. You can count on me for anything."

Her shoulders relax a tiny bit. She nods her head against mine.

I give her another squeeze before letting her go.

"We'll talk in the morning."

I close the door and walk away so she doesn't see my tears. She's had a hard life. Unmarried and pregnant at seventeen. A good-for-nothing scoundrel leaving her the minute she told him about the baby. A family that deserted her. For eighteen years, her total focus had been raising her daughter Samantha, and she's done a damm good job. Sam's in her first year of culinary school, and Cassie, after all these years, believes she's found someone who loves her. *Shit— same ole crap with different characters.*

The gas logs blaze, throwing off a warmth that doesn't take the chill out of my heart. I plop down on the sofa and take a swallow of wine.

Earlier this morning, I told Cassie I had called Lorenzo. I let her believe it was a social call. It was anything but that. At the Fitzhugh's party, when Senator Madison had his temper tantrum, I'd pegged him. Maybe that's not fair, but Dr. Ginny is teaching me discernment.

My antenna shot right up when Cassie said they'd been dating for a while, yet she hadn't confided in me. It's so uncharacteristic of our friendship. Somehow, her excuse about his running for reelection didn't hold up. It wasn't like he was married. Or maybe he was, and that was the problem. But she invited him to dinner, so that can't be it. There must be other reasons for all this secrecy. Yet, Cassie hasn't told me anything that makes sense. Whatever is going on isn't good for Cassie.

I'm thankful I didn't tell her about Nick or the real reason I called Lorenzo. With a guy like the senator, she might have accidentally shared that with him. While she would never do or say anything intentionally to hurt me, pillow talk makes idiots out of all of us. Senator Madison is the last person I would want to know about Nick or Lorenzo or anything about my personal life.

As I sort through what happened tonight, Lorenzo floats right into my thoughts. It was clear during my conversation with him that he wasn't happy with me, but I've come to expect that. The stars never line up for us. I've been in love with him since I was a kid. He'd always been in love with Stella, but she was in love with Antonio until she wasn't. Lorenzo waited for her all those years. Then she was murdered. All of our childhood dreams were packed with hormones and everlasting crap, and now we're picking our way through the rubble.

After years—maybe twelve—Lorenzo and I met again in Castello del Mare. We stupidly fell into bed when our grief for Stella caused us to momentarily lose our sanity. It was not the best way to renew the one relationship I had longed for all my life. There was a small window of opportunity that would have changed the course of my life when Lorenzo asked me to stay in Italy. But I said no. For once, I realized I hadn't had time to sort through all the reasons for my previous unhealthy relationships.

Now Lorenzo and I are at this impasse—he's cool and aloof. I'm still crazy in love with him. But I don't need love in my life. I certainly don't need Stella constantly cropping up between us. If, and only if, Lorenzo can one day let Stella go, would we have a chance. The thing is, when I'm in a tight spot and need someone to talk to, Lorenzo is that person. He's always had my back. He will always be my friend, if not my lover.

Before we hung up from our last conversation, he strongly suggested I sign up for self-defense classes. He recommended something called Krav Maga. He said if I didn't sign up, he wouldn't help me with my current dilemma. According to him, this Krav Maga is a practice developed by the Israeli Army in the 1940s. It's used as the official hand-to-hand combat for the Israeli Defense Forces.

Lorenzo said he was trying it out with the Guardia di Finanza. Since he's the commissario, I'm sure he knows what he's talking about. He also said I seem to attract trouble. Maybe martial arts would give me the basics to fight back. When I didn't respond, his lecture continued.

"Cat, the best way to win a fight is to not get into a fight in the first place. Given that you're prone to seeking out conflict, it's imperative that you learn how to neutralize a threat. I don't want to receive one of those calls—the one that says you didn't survive one of your sleuthing activities."

He went on to say other stuff like I'm crazy—of course in the sweetest way—*pazzo, pazzo*. But he was serious about my need to defend myself. After the close call in Italy and at Carrington Point Plantation, he's right.

Once again, I've managed to put myself in an ominous situation, and the cast of characters breathing down my neck is growing.

There's Nick, possibly Al, and the weird limo driver, George. Add to that this James Middleton Madison person. And what about his sister Alice? She certainly seems a bit out of touch with reality. These people may or may not want to hurt me, but being prepared makes sense.

I sigh loudly. I hate it when Lorenzo is right, but I'm following his advice. Tomorrow night I have an appointment at Club Karate.

23

The two vans emptied their cargo and left after a heated argument between George and one of the guards. The girls, afraid to move, huddled in the middle of a large barracks-style facility. They were surrounded by burly men in black turtlenecks with AR-15s slung over their shoulders.

Diana squinted. The room was poorly lit and drafty. She held Stephanie close to her body as if they were one person. Any other time, Stef would have wiggled out of her grasp. Tonight, she clung like plastic wrap.

The room was large, with cots lined up against the walls in military style. On each cot, a small pillow rested on top of a folded olive drab blanket. Her eyes adjusted to the dim light and covertly swept the room. Their only salvation was escape. She had to find a way out of this place.

The door they'd been pushed through was guarded on the outside. The only other door was at the other end of the room. Diana scrutinized the walls without windows. She was sure she'd seen windows on the outside of the building. She slowed down the frantic movement of her eyes until they landed on a sliver of light. They followed the thin outline where plywood sheets were nailed over the windows. Her head swiveled. She could just make out the uneven lines. She counted the ones she could see—possibly six windows.

A large woman in black jeans, a gray sweatshirt, and knee-high black boots entered from the closed door at the end of the room. Her hair was pulled tightly into a bun—neither her mouth nor eyes smiled. She stood silently in the middle of the floor. Her eyes roamed over the girls. Her head nodded up and down or left to right as she surveyed them like cattle and determined each one's fate.

When the woman entered the room, Diana pushed Stephanie behind her back and whispered, "Don't let go of me."

Stephanie's heaves vibrated through her body. Her tears soaked through Diana's thin tank top. Diana turned slightly and whispered, "Please, Stef, don't cry. I'll get you out of here. I promise."

The sudden grip on her arm caught her by surprise. The woman grabbed her face and squeezed until tears leaked from her eyes. She nodded at one of the guards. With one jerk, the two girls were separated.

"Please, no, no. Let her stay with me," Diana begged.

The violent slap across her face knocked her to her knees.

"Listen, you little bitch! You'll only hear this once. You have no say in your life from this moment on. You are worthless. What you want does not matter. You'll do exactly what I say. That applies to all of you low-life. Well, except for this pretty little one. She shook her finger in Diana's face. If you get out of line, she will suffer. You will watch."

The woman gripped Stephanie by her hair and pulled her across the room. She opened the closed door and pushed her through. Stephanie's screams echoed throughout the structure. Then, there was silence. The agony of that moment was one Diana knew would stay with her every day for the rest of her life.

A few minutes passed. The woman returned with a large baton in her hand and spoke, "Line up."

The girls hesitated until the one closest to the woman was hit behind the knees. Before she fell to the floor, one of the guards jerked her up. The rest of the girls shuffled into a disjointed line.

"Each of you will be allowed a few minutes to use the bathroom. The door remains open. Go now," she said as she poked the first girl in the back.

Humiliation cowered the girls even further into their separation from each other. The first step in divide and conquer had begun.

When the first girl finished, she was dragged to a cot. One hand was cuffed to the bed.

The line staggered forward as each girl entered and exited the bathroom. Each was led to a cot and cuffed. Three girls remained ahead of Diana. She watched and counted as the cots were filled. The odds were good that she would be assigned one of the cots under a boarded-over window. It was her only hope. Three cots were left— one by a window and the other two against a wall. She looked at the girl standing before her and realized it was the one from the club, the one she'd loaned her red hair clip. She leaned in close and whispered, "Please let me have the cot next to the boarded-over window."

She thought she noticed a slight nod, maybe a tiny tilt of her head. She wasn't sure as the girl's thick, honey-colored hair hung in wild tangles over her face. The red hair clip hung on a matted clump of hair.

When Diana came out of the bathroom, she saw the cot she wanted was vacant. When she passed the cot before hers, she glanced down and saw what she thought was a tiny smile on cracked, swollen lips.

Desperation clung to Diana like a form-fitting wetsuit. At seventeen, she'd just been handed the death penalty and not only for herself. Her little sister, if she lived, would bear the scars forever.

The baton struck her in the back as she was pushed onto the cot.

24

The next morning, Cassie didn't come out of the guest room until after the coffee had been made. I was dressed and on my way out the door. We stood in the kitchen. The morning light filtered across her face. Lines of pain and fatigue were etched there.

"Did you sleep?" I ask, knowing she didn't.

"A little."

She pushes her mop of dark hair out of her eyes and glances at the coffee pot. I swoop up the pot and fill a mug. She gives me a weak smile as the coffee transfers from my hand to hers.

"Cass, maybe we can talk later—if you're up to it. If you're not, I could check with Dr. Ginny. I'm sure she could find a slot for you this week. Want me to call?"

"No, Cat. I know you want what's best for me, but I'm not ready to talk to you or Dr. Ginny. I need more time. You understand?"

"Sure."

I managed to hug her around the coffee mug without splashing the contents on either of us. We are both grateful, as I'm notorious for my klutzy ways.

It's close to eight in the evening when I pull into the strip mall. The shops are typical: a grocery store, a Subway, a Chinese take-out, a dry cleaners, and a UPS store. Club Karate anchors a long, sprawling section on the far right end.

After parking, I sit in the car and wonder what the heck I'm doing here. Me, martial arts? Ha! I remind myself it's just a meeting with the owner to discuss Krav Maga—what it is and whether or not I should sign up. If I'm lucky, there's a chance I'm not fit enough to join. Except, I know I'm fit. Since the incident at the Zinzulusa Caves, I've been advised not to run anymore. That's been difficult for me as running and cooking were the two things that saved me until I began sessions with Dr. Ginny. Now, I work out with a personal trainer, and I walk at least 4-6 miles most days so I'm fit.

A big sigh escapes as I pull myself out of the past and check the time. Being punctual is another habit of mine, along with my endless counting. I glance at the clock again and leave the car. The lights in the parking lot illuminate a gravel pathway as I weave among the towering oaks.

The glass windows on each side of the building are loaded with trophies. I push through the door and come face-to-face with a class of mostly little people who exhibit lots of bravado and high levels of energy. There's no one at the reception desk. I find a seat and watch.

The man in charge is easy to recognize from his posture, the command of his body and the way the children's eyes are riveted on his every movement. His black trousers and jacket show off a slim, fit body. He nods in my direction without interrupting the flow of the class. He calls for attention. The small bodies line up and pair off as he issues commands.

Of course, I'd Googled the owner before arriving. He's a ninth-degree black belt in karate and also a three-degree black belt in Krav Maga. My research revealed that Krav Maga is a sort of street fighting. It's not a sport, and there are no contests to declare a winner. Its purpose is to teach you techniques that will save your life if you're forced into a brawl without rules.

Glancing around the room, I take in the mirrors that stretch across the entire back wall. The floor is matted so children, as well as adults, are cushioned when they take a fall. One wall contains shelves with fake guns, knives, sticks, and an assortment of lethal-looking weapons.

I open my notebook and reread my notes.

Training is simulated to produce the actual pressure of being in a fight, including tricks to increase your adrenaline and your fear level. Expect to be insulted, yelled at, hit from behind, a gun rammed in your back, or a knife at your throat.

Well, that sounds like training I could live without. What in the heck am I doing here? The far wall is lined with placards reminding students to consider their *Posture, Lines of Power, Methods of Generating Power, Footwork, Timing, Sequencing, Focus,* and *Mental and Emotional Activation.*

I review the signs several times to determine if reading them will somehow inspire me. I think not. Turning back to my notebook, I squint at the last line I wrote down, which says that the purpose of Krav Maga is to teach you how to strike back and how to fight against weapons and multiple attackers.

None of this research produces warm fuzzies. My adrenaline and fear were already ratcheted to a higher-than-normal level before I entered the building. Now, after watching the little kids slamming each other into the floor, I'm pretty sure I'm in the wrong place.

A hand hovers in front of my face. I look up to a generous smile and kind eyes. Our hands touch. His is strong, steady, and warm—mine cold and clammy. The kids continue to perform as Charles Williams introduces himself.

"Hi, call me Chuck. You have to be Caterina, right?"

Before I respond, he slips effortlessly into the curved plastic seat next to me.

"Yes, I am, but please call me Cat."

His face creases all over in a brilliant smile.

"Nine lives, huh? That's a good start. How many have you used up so far?"

His eyes dance with laughter as he waits for my response.

"Well, let's see. While I'm not exactly sure what constitutes usage of one of my lives, I'd say I have at least seven left."

He chuckles as he bounces back up from the chair and resumes his stance on the mat. He bows to the children and says *Kida*. It's clearly a show of respect. I'm enthralled at the stillness in the class and watch as they bow and respond, *Kida*. Then all hell breaks loose as twenty kids scramble to change clothes, pick up book bags, and hunt for their rides.

Chuck returns and picks up the conversation as if he'd never left my side. "Krav Maga teaches you that your body is a weapon. That's the first step. If you understand that small premise, your next step is to make that weapon as strong as possible. The most important lesson is to learn that your body is your only defense."

I nod without really understanding the physical part, but the mental part makes sense. If you believe your body is a powerful weapon, then it is.

Tuning back to the conversation so I don't miss anything, I ask, "Is that what you teach? How to believe your body is a weapon?"

"In a way, yes. It's all about the building blocks. My purpose is to work with my clients until they arrive at the moment when they believe in the power of their bodies. Do you have doubts? Tell me why you're here."

"I don't know anything about self-defense or martial arts, but a friend seems to think I would benefit. He specifically suggested Krav Maga."

"So someone else is behind you coming? Someone who cares about you, right?"

I blush. What else is there to do when I find myself closed in? A red hue spreads across my face. My embarrassment touches him.

"Sorry, that's none of my business. As I was saying, our classes start with a warm-up. Next, there are power drills and exercises. These are a combination of cardio and strength training. What you learn here will save your life. You'll learn to condition your body to carry out each technique effectively and without thinking. Your reaction over time will become instinctive and immediate at the first sign of a threat. It doesn't matter whether it's in your face or behind you."

"Wow!"

"There's a class starting in fifteen minutes. Why don't you participate? It might help you make a decision?"

"I didn't dress to participate. These clothes aren't exactly right for a tumble on the floor," I say as adults garbed in white tunics and trousers filter into the building.

"Guess what? When you're on the street, your clothes aren't going to be suitable for an attack. Come on. I promise we won't hurt you on the first night."

25

A few weeks later, I realize that Krav Maga sessions with Chuck are liberating and exhilarating. He was careful not to overexpose me early on to the perils of street fighting. I watched a lot and participated at his direction and only when he partnered with me. The experience was a little frightening, but it was also reassuring to discover my inner strength.

After the end of the first session he looked at me intently and said, "You'll be back, right? We meet every Tuesday and Thursday at seven. You can sign up when you return for the next session."

His eyes smile along with his mouth. Right away, I like him. His persona is steady and non-threatening. I nod and hope this is the beginning of a healthy relationship.

This morning, I swipe at the steamed mirror with the same towel I'm using to blot my hair. Through the foggy mist, my red curls sprout in every direction. The mirror smiles back at me. I'm less tense these days. Krav Maga has certainly helped. I drag the towel across the mirror, scrunch my hair and pull on an oversized sweater and lounging pants before heading to the kitchen.

The shrill of my cell reminds me I have a lot of work to do before my next event. The incoming call is Mrs. Berkley. I moan with dread. She's already left me several messages about Carrington Point. It seems Mary Elizabeth refuses to have her wedding reception anywhere except the old plantation. Somehow, they think it's my job to find out who owns it and get permission to use the grounds.

Every time I hear the name Carrington Point Plantation, bile rises in my throat. It's the last place on earth I want to cater an event.

What a pickle to suddenly have so many people enamored with the place. My hand is poised to click on the call when I notice movement outside the window. A sleek, black limo pulls into the driveway and parks in the back of the house. Aww crapola, here comes Al. I've been avoiding his calls ever since the disastrous night at the Waterfront Inn.

Al's driver, George, slams the car door. He skirts the piles of Spanish moss in the driveway. Lately, there hasn't been any time to sweep up. He looks around, tugs at his jacket, and runs his hand over his bald head before ringing the bell.

Should I answer or ignore him? There's an aura of danger that clings to this man. He hovers. I'm sure he listens to every conversation Al and I have, but for what purpose? I watch through the glass panel as he shifts restlessly and looks over his shoulder in a casing-the-joint kind of way. Time slows to a snail's pace while I chew on my bottom lip and wonder why in the hell I can't be a simple caterer with some good clients and a stable income in a sweet Lowcountry town.

I twist the deadbolt and crack the door to the arrogant sneer on the man's face. He clears his throat and says, "The count asks if you will see him."

What is the perfect comeback to this kind of request, I wonder.

"Sure, why not," is all I come up with—the last of the great orators clearly isn't me.

The man nods and stomps back to the car. Muscles bulge and ripple under his suit jacket, but it's the bulge outlined in his waistband that gives me pause. The guy is packing. It's a new day when a chauffeur looks and acts more like a bodyguard than someone hired to shuttle you around to look at property.

He opens the car door. There's a brief consultation. Seconds pass before Al, in full regalia, steps out of the car. My still-damp hair, braless pullover and oversized trousers are a far cry from royal attire. It's too late to change so I swing open the door and await his royal highness.

He marches toward the house. I can almost hear him counting off the cadence. He arrives in full military bearing and clicks his heels. I move aside. He quick-steps into the foyer.

He looks around and says, "Hello, Cat. I apologize for dropping by unannounced, but you're not answering my calls or texts. The air between us must be cleared. I'm sorry I didn't warn you ahead of time that Richard would be having dinner with us. Let me explain. May I come in?"

I don't welcome him any further than the foyer. "I'm not sure I want to hear your explanation, but go ahead."

Al hesitates. I could invite him into the house, but I want this conversation to be short. When I don't comment, he begins. "Before our dinner, George drove me to the plantation to have a look at the cotton sheds. Richard popped up again. During our conversation, I mentioned that I was having dinner with a local caterer. He said he'd like to meet you as he'd heard good things about your catering business and might need your services."

My mouth drops open. I quickly shut it before I say too much. When I reopen it, I say, "Do you want a cup of tea?"

Before he can answer, I walk toward the kitchen. He follows. We stand shoulder to shoulder and gaze out the long expanse of window showcasing the marsh and the fast-flowing river.

"Al, this is my home. When you were here for lunch, I told you my story about moving to the Lowcountry after I finished culinary school. The property has been in my family for a while. I was a broken person when I arrived. When I stood in this spot and took my first look out this window, I decided to stay. Peace reigns in this place. That's why I'm here. I don't need or want chaos in my life. Do you understand?"

His warm breath blows against the back of my neck. He clears his throat and barely whispers, "I do understand. You are connected to this place. Your heart and soul belong here. Because of this, I believe you understand my dilemma. After all these years, I've come to this small town—just like you. Your place is here. Mine is at Carrington Point Plantation. I won't be satisfied with any other."

"What if it isn't for sale? Are you saying that you won't look for another property? You won't move here?"

He shrugs and says, "You are full of questions this morning. Well, I have a few for you. But first, will you accept my apology?"

It's strange, but I honestly don't want to accept it, so I say, "Culturally, we are from different backgrounds, but you're on my turf, and your actions toward me were unprofessional. I will accept your apology this time. If it happens again, it will be the end of our business relationship and our friendship."

Al's face is a photo image of dismay. He traces an imaginary line on the windowsill with his index finger while he stares at the sailboats on the river.

"You're right, Cat. I put my business interests over our friendship. It won't happen again."

"Good," I say. Then I pat his arm and say, "Okay, what other questions do you have?"

He turns away from the window and says, "Most of them are about this Mr. Davenport. Are you sure it's okay?"

"I suppose you want to find out as much as you can about him. I'm probably not the right person to help you. But go ahead and ask."

The whistle of the tea kettle interrupts our conversation. I pull cups out of the cabinet, along with a jar of local honey and a selection of tea bags. We don't speak as I prepare the tea. With a nod of my head, we move to the table.

"Okay, let's have the questions."

26

Al beams his smile on me. It's his eyes that first attracted me. They are a steely blue and are constantly observing others. When he recognized he had disappointed me, sadness had spilled out of them. Now that we are no longer adversaries, his smile is deep and genuine and his eyes sparkle.

He begins, "How can we locate Señor Richard Alistair Davenport? He refused to leave me a contact number. Every time I've asked, he says he'll be in touch. I've been out to Carrington several times since the night of our dinner. He seems to have disappeared and the place seems vacant. Why do you think he wanted to be at that dinner? And finally, do you know anyone in this area who might know him or where he's staying?"

"Sorry, he's not a person I want to know anything about. I have no desire to help you find him."

"Cat, he's not telling the truth about the property or himself. That's why I invited him to join us. I thought we could call his bluff, but that backfired. Yet, I sense some history between you two. Is that right?"

"Perhaps if you'd warned me, I would have been in a better position to help you unmask him. What possessed you to include him and not tell me?"

"Cat, you haven't really forgiven me, have you?"

"It's not you, Al. It's this entire situation. You hired me to cater an ordinary event for you. If you had mentioned all the intrigue surrounding the event, I would have declined."

"Oh, Cat, I honestly thought it was a simple request. How could I have predicted that the property owner would be some mysterious unknown entity who may or may not sell the place? Yes, I'm suspicious of Señor Davenport, but there was no reason for me to question his ownership, was there?

"No, you're right."

"It was my mistake to invite him to dinner. I thought maybe you'd recognize him or at least question him to determine if he was the real owner. I didn't realize the encounter would upset you or that the entire evening would be a disaster."

I smile before saying, "You're right. It was a disaster. I was under the impression you and I were having a nice, quiet dinner to discuss your event. You were the one who suggested your project was confidential. Gracious, Al, you wanted me to swear in blood that I wouldn't discuss your plans with anyone else. Do you think that inviting a stranger to dinner and not telling me and then discussing your project with this man instills trust? Or perhaps you planned to use me right from the beginning. Maybe all this friendship and trust conversation is just baloney."

He leans away from me. His eyes widen, and his mouth drops open. I really don't care, so I dig deeper.

"You could have texted me that Mr. Davenport would be joining us. Any little hint would have been helpful instead of a whispered *play-along with me*. I had no clue what you were talking about or what you wanted me to do."

"Cat, you are far more upset than what you're telling me. I believe you know this man. If that's true, we need to figure out how to work together. Tell me what's going on. Tell me what you know."

The view outside the window has turned into a Monet painting—all blurry, leaving an impression of soft green-gray water against bright lime-colored marsh grasses, all burnished with golden kisses of sunlight filtering through pink cotton clouds.

I weigh my words before saying, "Al, I'm not sure what's going on. My track record with trust and men hasn't been favorable—in business or my personal life."

He nods. "I appreciate your honesty. You're right. I put you in an extremely awkward situation. From this day on, it will not happen again."

"That's acceptable, but it's also possible I'm not the right person for your event. Your expectations are more than I bargained for. I'm good at straightforward. All this confidential mumbo jumbo isn't what I agreed to when I said I'd cater your function. Perhaps it's better if we agree to end our tentative contract."

"Cat, listen to me. This is no longer about catering an event at Carrington. I suspect Señor Davenport is some sort of a hustler. When he forced himself into our dinner plans, I saw it as an opportunity to expose him. I thought we'd have dinner, conversation and discover something useful from him.

"Al, he's a con artist. You said so yourself. He wasn't about to tell us anything."

Al's sigh is weary, but he continues. "Yes, you're right. He didn't reveal a thing. However, your vehement reaction changed the direction of the evening. It didn't take me long to realize you recognized him, but it was too late. Why didn't you tell me you knew him when I gave you a description? In retrospect, I remember the strange look on your face when I described him. You have to understand I had no idea you might know him."

His eyes brim with regret but stay firmly anchored on my face. It's hard to remain in that fixed stare position. I blink and turn back to the window.

"If we're to work together, there can be no more surprises. Agreed?"

Instead of answering, Al shifts his chair closer and clasps my arms. "No more surprises. Your friendship makes this endeavor worthwhile. I want you to be part of it."

He settles back in his chair. His smile brightens the already luminous yellow kitchen. He turns to me and says, "Let's forget about Richard for a little while. Is that possible? Can we talk about something pleasant? Like the menu?"

Reluctantly, I say, "I roughed one out. Your file is in the next room. Let me get it."

Al is right on my heels. My office is stacked with files, cookbooks, party decorations, and a variety of odds and ends. Framed certificates, awards, and photos of events I've catered adorn the walls. He leans in to examine them. He lingers on the selfie of Lorenzo and me on the boat in the marina at Castello del Mare. Our arms are entwined. My head is nestled against his shoulder.

"Let's go back to the kitchen; otherwise, we'll be buried alive in here. Would you like more tea?"

He nods. The gas flame pops into life. I refill the kettle and place it on the burner. This time, I check the pantry for a tin of freshly baked cookies. I pile a variety on a platter splashed with red poppies. A pitcher of cream, sugar, and lemon slices fill up another tray alongside my mother's teapot. I slide the tray next to Al and open the file while he bites into a chocolate walnut toffee cookie.

Pulling out a sketch pad, I point out the rectangles in a horseshoe shape in front of the plantation house. I'm still a tiny bit miffed, so I say, "I'm not sure it makes sense to continue with this project since the property doesn't appear to be available. But if you insist, here's a rough sketch of what I recommend. If you decide to find another property, the same plan could be utilized with some minor adjustments. For now, it's based on the space at Carrington. These are all food and beverage tables arranged in stations, sort of like Stations of the Cross."

He smiles and slides his chair closer to mine.

"Each station would consist of small plates—tapas and beverages. You would stand here—at the entrance and welcome the guests. We could put a small table next to you with a guest book and brochures about your project."

"Yes, I like that idea. Would you consider standing with me at the entrance?"

"Oh gosh, no. Not that I wouldn't be honored, but it's a work night for me. I'll be overseeing all the stations along with my friend

Cassie and her daughter Sam. I'll hire wait staff for each station and ask some of the local young people to cover valet parking so your guests don't have to walk through the fields."

"What about the outside kitchen? We haven't discussed the design yet."

"Most kitchens in these old homes are usually at the back of the house. My suggestion is the outside kitchen be located in proximity to the inside kitchen. I have another set of sketches for that. Do you want to see those or continue with the food and beverage layout?"

"Oh, please continue with the food and beverage setup."

"Okay. Here's the first station. It's positioned to the left of the grand staircase and helps to block those attending from exploring the premises. The rest of the stations would circle like a horseshoe with the last one next to the dance floor. How does that look so far?"

He leans in close to me as his fingers trace the design. "Yes, I like it."

"The first table will have a simple pickup nibble. It's the first stop for food, so we don't want long lines to form. When the guests arrive, they will see all the other food and beverage possibilities in front of them. Since they'll want to taste everything, they'll keep moving. We'll use miniature cups—some with salted almonds and some with cracked marinated olives and pair these with a sparking Spanish wine. He smiles and nods,

"Yes, that all sounds good. What's at this station?" He points a finger at a rectangle on the right of the staircase.

"Mini cheese omelets and little shot glasses full of gazpacho and a Spanish rosado wine to complement. Over here is the veggie station. We'll serve garlicky sautéed mushrooms, stuffed cherry tomatoes, deviled quail eggs, and mini Española tortillas along with a nice Spanish white. Is this still okay?"

Over a series of minutes, he has managed to move his chair so close to mine that his very light, exotic aftershave hovers in the space — citrus and crushed peppercorns. He nods his head in approval.

Nice, I think and continue, "Then a station for seafood, poultry, and meat. There will be spicy sizzling shrimp, crispy chicken and ham croquettes, and chorizo empanadillas. The last station will display desserts: dulce de leche brownies and churros with chocolate, caramel and guava dipping sauces. This is the showstopper as a line-cook will make the churros to order. This station will also feature platters of fresh fruit and Spanish cheeses along with a few Spanish cordials, coffee and hot chocolate."

When I look up, the intensity of his stare plays scales up and down my spine. Without a bra, I feel more naked than usual. He's very attractive—more elegant than handsome. His stare devours me. I'm on the verge of freaking out when he reaches for my hand and lifts it to his lips.

"It's perfect and exactly why I asked you to cater the meal. Would you also handle the flowers? What do you suggest?"

He continues to hold my hand in a grip as tight as a tick on a yard dog while he guides me closer.

As I struggle to remove my hand from his grasp, I say, "Red and yellow roses and white calla lilies in towering vases for the stations and smaller arrangements of the same on the tables around the dance floor. And, of course, plenty of candles."

A discrete cough has us both jumping apart. Al abruptly releases my hand and stands.

"You told me to interrupt you at three for your next appoint-ment," George says and silently vanishes.

Al sighs. He stands and pulls me up with him. Our bodies almost touch. If I lifted my head, his lips would be on mine. But I don't.

"You will hear from me very soon."

The click of his heels down the hall, and the soft thud of the front door brings me back to reality just as my phone buzzes. Dread gathers in the pit of my stomach as I know before I look that it's Nick.

Backroom Fox Tavern in 15.

27

The Foxy, as locals call it, is a favorite watering hole for locals. It's a fun place, except the decibel levels are off my hearing chart. At the end of a long day, the last thing I want to do is stand in a crowded bar and scream at my companions. It's too bad because the food created on the premises is delicious.

Muttering, I search my purse for coins. Downtown parking is such an annoyance—not only do I have to find coins to feed the meters, but I have to parallel park. My car is squeezed, after many attempts, between a red Miata convertible and one of those monster black Ford pickups. Of course, I'm already annoyed as Nick seems to think I'm at his beck and call. This whole situation stinks, yet I'm of two minds—the old classmate versus the sinister undercover FBI agent—split personalities that puzzle me in ways that are both intriguing and frightening.

As I feed the meter, branches swat at my back and a light breeze tosses potential rain clouds overhead. When I straighten, I'm looking directly inside the cab of the black truck. My heart gallops when I see masses of blonde curls spilling across the dashboard. My hand reaches out. Stella's name slips from my lips. Of course, it can't be Stella, but for one single second, I believe it is. My heart thunders in my ears.

Telling myself to breathe, I stand glued to the spot until my heart rate returns to normal. I step forward until I'm next to the window. The blonde head lifts. The tear-stained face rips at my heart. I take a few steps away from the vehicle, then turn around and walk back. I rap on the window.

"Are you okay? Do you need help?"

The mass of blond curls shakes. She raises an arm and uses the sweatshirt sleeve to swipe her cheeks and nose.

I hesitate, searching for the right words while I assess the situation. She's in her late teens, which means she's in the throes of emotional upheaval. Probably a fight with parents or a boyfriend.

"Are you sure I can't help you? Do you need anything?"

Again, she shakes her head. Then she whispers, "I'm fine, thanks."

She's not okay, but short of dragging her out of the truck, what can I do? I fish around in my purse, find a business card, and slide it through the small opening in the window.

"If you ever need anything, that's my direct line. You can call me anytime."

She nods and drops her head down. Before the blonde curls curtain her face, I see a raised lump and bruise on her forehead. As I walk away, I pull out my phone. I fluff my hair and smile on the pretense of taking a selfie. I position the camera to include the truck and license plate.

Big sobs hung in Diana's throat. From the side mirror, she watched the lady taking a selfie. Her whole body ached from suppressing her screams. Her brain clamored that it wasn't too late. All she had to do was roll down the window and yell. The lady would come back.

She bit her bottom lip until blood broke the surface. She couldn't cause a raucous. If she did, the man would kill her little sister just as he promised before he left the truck.

"You try anything stupid, and your kid sister is dead." Then he added maliciously, "You'll be responsible for her death."

Diana didn't know if Stephanie was still in the warehouse, but it didn't matter. It was her fault they were in this mess. If anything happened to Stef, she was to blame. She couldn't shriek at the woman for help. She had to protect her little sister. She no longer cared what they did to her as long as she could save her sister. Stephanie was only a child. She deserved a life.

It had been such a stupid mistake. Stephanie had begged and begged Diana to let her tag along on that Friday night. It wasn't the first time she'd begged. Diana had always said no. But that night, Diana had a big blowup with her mom. The conversation rewound in her mind a thousand times as sobs shook her body.

"You can't go out, Diana! Stephanie can't be left alone! I have to work! My schedule has been on the calendar for a month. It doesn't matter that you didn't look. You have no choice but to stay home tonight."

"Mom, she's fourteen. She's old enough to stay alone. It's not fair that I have to stay home because of her. I hate you both!"

Diana had slammed her purse on the table in the foyer. She'd almost been out of the door. Now, she was stuck with her bratty sister. She'd promised Alex she'd meet him at seven.

It was almost 7:30 when her mom finally left the apartment for her second job cleaning office buildings. The door wasn't firmly shut before Stephanie began to nag Diana to keep her date with Alex and take her along.

"Mom will never know," she whispered as if Mom might be listening at the door. "We'll be home and in bed before she returns."

And stupid fool that she was, in her anger, she'd said okay.

By the time Diana had slathered Stephanie with makeup, created a sophisticated upsweep and dressed her in a sexy outfit—far too old for someone fourteen, they had to run to catch the 8:35 pm bus. Of course, Alex hadn't waited for her. But once there, Stephanie had reveled in the whistles and catcalls and begged for just a half hour in the sleazy bar where uptown funk was pumping out of the door.

The only thing Diana remembered was that she and Stef had danced, the strobe lights had pulsated, and the smell of sweat had permeated the bar. She'd only gone to the place because Alex had said it was cool and a lot of kids hung out there. She didn't see Alex, but she recognized several kids from her high school.

Men had brought them drinks and made fumbling attempts to persuade the young girls to go off with them. When her head started spinning, Diana left Stephanie for a few minutes to go to the bathroom. It was only in retrospect she realized someone had spiked their drinks. In the bathroom, she discovered a girl sprawled over the toilet bowl, heaving her guts out. Her whimpering sent Diana into mother mode. She'd grabbed paper towels and mopped the girl's face and clothes. Vomit was tangled in her hair. Diana washed it out as best she could. She removed the red hair clip from her own hair, pulled the girl's wet hair back, and fastened it out of her face.

"Hannah," the girl had whispered. "My name's Hannah. Thank you."

Diana had helped her stand up and maneuvered her out of the bathroom, only to discover Stephanie had disappeared.

She had a vague memory of stumbling out of the bar and seeing Stephanie being pushed into a van. She'd screamed, abandoned Hannah, and ran toward Stephanie only to find someone forcing her into the same vehicle. It had been crammed with other girls, all screaming and crying. Just before the doors had slammed and locked, Hannah had been thrown in.

After driving for what seemed like hours and having her head bashed in when she tried to escape, she, along with all of the girls, had been locked in a building in the middle of nowhere. Then they took Stephanie. But where had they taken her? What would they do with her? She tried not to think about it as she had a vague idea of what was going on. She kept hoping and praying that the stories she'd heard weren't true. Her only thought was to figure out a way to escape and to find Stephanie.

Now sitting in this truck, she knew she could walk away, except she couldn't—not without Stephanie. The man they called Nick had made her come with him. He said she was a troublemaker, and the matron would eliminate her if she kept acting up. She didn't care about herself, but when he threatened Stephanie, her only choice was to stay in the truck. She held up the card the lady had pushed through the window. Her tears splattered on the green logo:

*Cat's Catering For
Every Event In Your Life*

Caterina Gabbiano,
Lowcountry Caterer

catering@CatGabbiano.com
843-555-1212

On the card was a beautifully photographed plate of food and a glass of wine. Below it was an email address and phone number. Diana repeated the number over and over and then folded the card until it was no bigger than a postage stamp and buried it in the pocket of her jeans—the tiny one for coins that no one ever searched.

28

Since the early 1800s, The Fox Tavern has stood on this same corner. The original oak door is faded but solid as the day it was first installed. I turn the brass knob and push. The door swings open into a vacant room. Maybe three in the afternoon is an in-between time. Although I've walked by here often enough to know that by early afternoon, it's usually packed.

I squint into the dimly lit interior before relinquishing the door. It closes with a solid thump that echoes through the empty space. I linger inside the doorway until my eyes adjust to the gloomy atmosphere. The long ebony bar comes into focus. Then, the bartender. He glances up but continues to swish sudsy water in glasses. He nods toward the back. I furtively glance in that direction, but no one is visible in the shadowy space.

Is Nick there? Waiting for me? My lack of courage keeps me rooted in the same spot. Chuck's voice whispers to breathe deeply. I slowly shift my weight away from my escape route, take another deep breath, and shuffle away from the door. As I creep down the length of the bar, I can feel eyes on my back. My invisibility cloak doesn't seem to be working.

Tentatively poking my head into the poorly lit room, I see only one person at a table in the rear. From my viewpoint, the man looks like a cross between Sam Spade and a pervert. He's wrapped in a trench coat. Instead of a tattered fedora with a brim, a Phillies baseball cap is pulled down so low it touches the top of oversized Ray-Bans. There's a *deja vous* moment from a scene in *The Maltese Falcon* or *Return of the Thin Man*.

I pick up speed, chuckling as I approach the table.

"Well, hello, Sam Spade!"

Nick reaches across the void, grabs my wrist, and jerks until I tumble into the chair.

"What the?"

"Cat, this is not a joke or some sordid novel you're reading. No one knows who I am or why I'm here. There's nothing funny about what's going on here."

I sputter with indignation, push back against the chair, and try to stand.

"Nick, you've lost your mind. What happened to the funny guy who was always playing practical jokes? Isn't that what this is? Am I supposed to say you got me? You've been scaring me on purpose, right?"

He tightens his clamp on my wrist. His hold is strong enough to force me to fall with a whack in the chair. Pain radiates in my wrist as he snarls, "Listen, Cat. You've gotten yourself messed up in something serious. I'm sorry for that, but it's too late to undo. You know too much about the operation. Until we get it cleaned up, you have to keep your mouth shut. Do you understand? If you don't do what I say, this could end badly for you."

Chuck's soothing voice in my ear encourages me to relax and breathe. And just like that, Nick loosens his grip. Fear sticks in my throat as Nick's words lodge in my brain. Trying to get a grip on my emotions, I scan the surroundings. Since this is the favorite watering hole in town, there has to be a reason it's deserted on a late weekday afternoon. As I glance toward the bar, the scowl on the bartender's face tells me I can't count on him to come to my rescue.

"What's so important, Nick?"

"How did the count find out about the plantation?"

"What? You think I told him?"

"The man's from another country, Cat. How in the hell would he just happen to wander onto that deserted road if he hadn't been pointed in that direction? Can you enlighten me?"

"No, I can't. I never mentioned it to him. Why would I after you threatened me?"

His finger slides his sunglasses down his nose. Anger makes his eyes large and dark. His mouth is curved in a slight grimace. This character is a far cry from my old friend Nick. The person sitting across from me has a cruel streak—like it would give him great pleasure to hurt me.

"Cat, you don't know what it means to be threatened. I was lenient with you because you're a friend from my past. But not anymore. You tell that count of yours to stay away. The place is not for sale. It never will be. You make up a story that will keep him off the property. I've warned you. This is the final time. Anyone setting foot on the property is subject to a bullet between the eyes."

"Nick, you can't be serious? Kids wander out there all the time. I can't force the Berkleys to stay away or, for that matter, Al. Are you telling me that you're going to murder these people? You've lost your flipping mind! You're an FBI agent, aren't you? Please tell me you're joking! You are joking, right?"

He renews the grip on my wrist, jerks my body halfway across the table, and leans in close.

"Cat, there's a huge difference between FBI and undercover FBI. You're smart enough to understand that. My intention is not to hurt you or anyone else, but I'm warning you and your friends to stay away. This operation cannot be compromised. Do you understand?"

I open my mouth, but the pressure from his fingers is excruciating. Words crawl up my throat but remain stuck. How can this be possible? I'm sitting across from a former classmate, and I'm petrified.

"It will be over by the end of the month. Then you and your friends can dance naked on the lawn for all I care. But don't go near the place until I text you that it's clear. I won't see you again unless you ignore my warnings. If you do, I'm not responsible for what happens to you or anyone else who wanders onto the property or interferes in a government operation."

My mouth hangs open, a buzzing noise sounds in my ears, and a gray film shimmers in front of my eyes. Chuck's steady cadence travels into my awareness. Breathe deeply, center your body, and focus on your personal power. My eyes remain closed until the back of Nick's trench coat brushes against the chair. The front door shuts with a loud thud that ricochets throughout the building. Quiet descends with only the sound of the bartender stacking glass on glass.

I count to thirty as I wait for my breathing to settle. Then I push back from the table and stroll out as if I owned the place.

Standing in the shelter of the awning, I search for a glimpse of a trench coat, but Nick's already vanished. Two blocks down the street, the black Ford pickup parked behind my car inches out of its spot. I'm too far away to see who's in the driver's seat, but it seems unlikely that it would be Nick. He couldn't possibly be driving the truck with the young girl in it. Or could he?

29

Diana waited until she heard the soft moans and snorts of sleep. She'd overheard one of the guards say they were moving out in a few days, and this place would no longer be a drop-off point. Time was running out.

That first night, when that woman had pushed her sister Stephanie through the door at the end of the barracks, had only been the beginning. That same night, Hannah also disappeared. Every day, a few more girls vanished. The first to go were the youngest and those who were not habitual users. Tonight, it would be the same— picking and sorting until no one was left. She couldn't let her mind dwell on Stephanie or Hannah.

Diana gave a little pull on the plywood, but nothing happened. She picked at the wood nailed to the window until her fingers were bleeding. What she needed was something to slip between the two. But what? She slumped back on the cot. Tears trickled into her hair-line, but she stopped them immediately. There was no room or time for tears. She had to break out. She had to find Stephanie. She repeated the phone number she had memorized from the card the lady named Cat had given her. If she could get out of here, that's who she'd contact.

She thought about it every waking moment. At some point, there would be a chance. She had to be ready. Their days were regimented so she ran through her mind and came up with one possibility. Twice a day, she was allowed to go outside for fifteen minutes. There were usually two guards, but they never paid close attention as long as she stayed within the perimeters. Surely, there would be a piece of glass or a sharp stone, some small item she could pick up to help her pry the plywood off. There was the tiniest possibility the guards wouldn't notice if she slipped into the wood line, but she knew that would be a really stupid move. She'd be dead in seconds if she tried.

The night finally ended. Over a breakfast of lukewarm oatmeal, Diana looked for anything she could use to pry the plywood away from the window. The guards were restless and appeared on high alert. All the plates and utensils were plastic. Plus, if she created a scene inside, all the girls would be punished. If everything else failed, she wouldn't hesitate to jeopardize the other girls. She'd take any chance to rescue Stephanie.

Her reverie was broken when the matron shouted her name. It was time for her daily exercise. As she walked through the door into the humid dampness, she saw that instead of the usual two guards, there was only one. It was unusual but to her benefit. Perhaps this was another sign of the operation moving on to another location.

The perimeter was outlined with strings tied on small stakes protruding from the ground. Diana checked out the stakes, but she'd never get away with pulling one out of the ground without being seen. Then what would she do with it? It was too big to hide easily.

She walked to the furthest point and stopped. There was no wind —only the sound of restless creatures in the brush and birdsong. Yet, there was the distinctive feel of water close by—saltwater. It collected on her skin. The dampness curled her hair. But it was the rotten-egg smell of sulfur and methane that penetrated the lining of her skin. She'd learned about the Lowcountry marshes and pluff mud in her upstate high school literature class when they had been assigned Pat Conroy's books to read. She'd fallen in love with the places he described, and she had longed to visit. Maybe she was still in South Carolina. Maybe there was a chance to escape. She had to believe.

Just for a moment, a sob racked her body. School—so long ago when she hadn't understood the good life her mom had given her. She stopped the sob midstream. She had to plow through this—there was only one goal.

She turned toward the guard and smiled as her eyes swept the ground. Any sharp object would do. He watched her suspiciously through narrowed eyes. He was short and squat. His bulky muscles indicated it would be easy for him to smash her with one punch. A permanent sneer crossed his mouth. As she approached, he placed his finger on the trigger and shifted the AR15.

"Whoa!" she said, adding a bit of sultry to her voice.

He took a long puff on the cigarette.

"Can I have a puff?"

She kept the smile on her face and moved closer.

He handed her the butt. She took it from his nicotine-stained fingers and turned her back so he wouldn't see her cringe. The wet butt stuck to her lips. Repulsion shook her body, but she forced herself not to gag or cough.

"Sounds like water is close by—a river, the ocean?"

"What's it to you? Looking for an escape route? Just a few steps away from this staked-out area is the marsh and a fast-moving salt-water river. It's not something you want to put your pretty butt in. It's full of snakes and gators and lots of spiny poisonous creatures. Those bare feet of yours don't look like they've had much experience in the wild." He chuckled with delight when Diana shrunk away from him.

"Time's up," he said as he opened the door and shoved her through.

As she stumbled into the dark barracks, she lost her balance. She hit the doorjamb and ricocheted into the lamp table. Under her weight, the table tipped, and the lamp crashed to the floor. Before anyone could react or see what happened and before the matron arrived, Diana pocketed a small shard of pottery and a pair of pocket-sized needle nose pliers that had fallen out of the drawer.

As she raised herself from the floor, the slap came swiftly across her face.

"You stupid idiot!" The matron screamed, spittle spraying her face. Diana automatically reacted, raising her hand to wipe away the spit. Her arm was grabbed from behind and jerked up her back. Pain shot through her body. Darkness hovered as she fought against losing consciousness. The baton cracked across her knees. She dropped into the broken shards of pottery.

The matron twisted her chin with such force that Diana involuntarily screamed. As the guard and the matron dragged her through the barracks, the front door slammed open. Diana shuddered as she recognized the man—the one who'd hit her with his gun when she first arrived and who had made her ride with him into town. More importantly, he was the one who had threatened Stephanie's life.

"What the fuck is going on?" His voice stormed through the room. It landed at the feet of the guard and matron.

"She's nothing but trouble. We're getting rid of her."

"Take your hands off her!"

The matron looked up, eyes wary.

"Why? I've always eliminated the ones who cause trouble."

"I'm in charge now. This one stays. She's clean. No drugs, no prostitution, no criminal record. Although she's too old for some of our clientele, she'll still bring a good price on the open market. Somebody will want her."

Diana's body was released to the floor. She lay in a trembling heap.

"You," he nodded to the guard, "get an ice pack for her face. You," he shouted at the matron, "get her some decent clothes, get her cleaned up. Now! I'll be back with a buyer. She better not be banged up. You understand?"

As soon as the man left, the matron pushed her onto the cot and cuffed her hand. She leered into Diana's face and said, "You little bitch. You're lucky he showed up. You were close to being dead. Don't be getting any ideas about that man. He's not your savior. In fact, he'll screw your pretty little head off before he sells you."

Her cackle permeated the barracks. The few remaining girls stared and then turned away—fearful they might be next in line for the matron's wrath.

30

A fine drizzle follows me back to the car. I lean against the door and text Lorenzo the photo of the license plate because I can't think of anything else to do with it. I ask if we can Zoom in an hour. Then I dial the number at the karate studio. Chuck answers on the first ring.

"Hey, Cat. I was just thinking about you. Are you coming to tonight's class? I sure hope you are."

I cut him off mid-sentence, "Chuck, do you give private lessons?"

"What? Uh, I guess I do. Well, sure, if they're for you. What's going on?"

"Nothing, really. It's just that I often work at night. Would it be possible for me to take private lessons during the day?"

"Is there a particular day that works best for you?"

"Mondays are good as I try not to schedule any events. It's my catchup day. Is that a possibility?"

"Sure, it's the day I usually do the books, check the equipment, and have the cleaning people come in. But they're out of here by ten. Would that work? Around 10? Or 10:30?

"Let's make it 10:30. Can we start this Monday?"

"Sure, that works for me. Cat?"

"Hmmm?"

"Cat, is something wrong? Your voice seems I don't know—maybe a little stressed?"

I pause. Chuck is one of those genuinely nice people. If I tell him what's going on, he'll want to help. He doesn't need to be involved in whatever mess I'm in. And what would I tell him? I don't have a clue what's going on. If I do need help, I'm pretty sure I'll call the police and not Chuck. So I say, "No, I'm tired. That's all. My busy season is gearing up, and I'm working a ton of hours."

"Okay. Well, I'll see you Monday at 10:30." There's silence, then, "Cat, if you ever need a friend, I'd like to be that person. Maybe after our lesson, we could have coffee?"

"Thanks, Chuck. I'd love to. See you Monday."

During my conversation with Chuck, the rain had drifted off. Sweltering humidity takes its place. Knots gather in my neck and shoulders. I shrug my shoulders in an attempt to ease the tension. Instead of getting in the car, I walk toward the waterfront park. It's one of my favorite places to sit and ponder the stuff in my head that's creating anxiety. The park includes seven beautifully landscaped acres on the river. The swing bridge crossing to the next island is one of only eight in the state. It's either a blessing or a curse, depending on whether or not you're stuck in traffic and you're late. For me, it's an opportunity to hit the pause button, roll down the windows, and let the ocean breeze ease the day's stresses.

Crossing Bay Street, I stop to peek in the window of the River Glass Shop. I spot a red starfish necklace in the window that would be perfect for Sam. She's a real beauty like her mom. I turn to go inside when I spot Alice, the senator's odd sister, coming out of Bay Street Beauty Shop. I duck my head. Meeting up with her isn't something I want to do. And neither does she as I watch her pretend she doesn't see me. She stops, looks away, and turns in another direction. I teeter back and forth but finally call her name.

"Hey, hi Alice," I breathlessly pant out in my cheery voice as I pursue her down the street.

I pat my tousled hair and hope I don't look like a raging wild woman. Slowing down, I match my pace to hers.

She smiles timidly and puts a fake look of surprise on her face.

"Oh Cat! How lovely to see you. James and I were talking this morning about the delicious meal you and Cassandra made. It was divine. Y'all sure know how to put on a spread. I guess that's been a while now. Did I write a thank you note? I'm so forgetful these days."

"Yes, Alice. You sent a lovely card. I'm sorry the meal didn't end on a better note than it did."

"What do you mean?"

"Cassie and Jim? Didn't you know? She hasn't seen him since that night."

As soon as the words slip out of my mouth, I know Cassie will be furious with me for interfering.

"Oh, tell Cassandra not to worry. The legislative session is starting, and there's the reelection campaign. James is simply too busy to indulge in any frivolous activities. Oh, not that Cassandra fits that description."

Clearly, the frivolous was meant to fit Cassie, but I don't say so.

"It's too complicated for him to have a social life with the long hours and the travel. It's a temporary situation for James since every year isn't an election year. But Cassandra needs to move on and find someone more attentive than James. From what little I know about her, she seems to require a lot of attention. James doesn't have time for that sort of thing."

Short of slapping her or walking away in a huff, I grit my teeth and say ever so sweetly, " I'll suggest that to her. She does deserve the best."

Alice doesn't respond. She keeps her eyes on the pavement as if she's walking a tightrope. Neither of us is in the mood to continue the conversation. I say *it's nice to see you again,* and we part ways.

Checking the time, I take off in a run to the car. If the swing bridge isn't open for boating traffic, I'll be home in time for Lorenzo's call.

Alice paused at a shop window. She watched the reflection of Cat crossing Bay and turning down West Street. Of all days to bump into her. Not that it mattered. Any day was a bad day to cross paths with that woman.

James was right. She's a bitch, but then so was Cassandra. Alice could take the fly-by-night sex he had with street girls as long as he didn't parade them in front of her. But the moment he introduced her to Cassie, she knew there'd be trouble. He'd tried to lead a normal life once before, and look what had happened—the wife and kids sequestered in Switzerland with money pouring out of their businesses to keep them there. As long as that ex-wife continued to live the good life, they were safe. But what if one day?

Well, she wouldn't think about that now. She had enough to deal with as she was aware of something Cat wasn't. James and Cassandra had gotten back together. Interesting Cat didn't seem to know. In fact, it might suggest that Cat and Cassandra weren't on good terms—a small bonus if true. And James, he wasn't nearly as smart as he wanted people and, particularly her, to believe. He'd left his phone lying around. It had been easy to listen to the disgusting messages Cassandra left. All the years, she'd kept him out of trouble. Here he was thinking of replacing her again and with a stray. That's what Cassie was—without a pedigree.

No, she didn't think that would happen. She wouldn't let it.

She walked the distance to the marina parking lot, where George waited for her. He was leaning against the limo. She waved, and he immediately opened the door. She wondered just how loyal he might be to James. Maybe he had a price. She planned to find out if he did.

Lorenzo Zoomed in. "I got the photo with the license plate number. The truck was rented by JMM Properties. It's located in South Carolina. Does that name sound familiar?"

"No, it doesn't. Did you find any information on the owners or employees or a specific location of the company? It sounds like a real estate firm."

"You're right, it is. It appears to be legitimate. The surface check on employees indicates all have appropriate real estate licenses. The owner's name is A. Aldridge. Is that a name you know?"

"It's not. Where is the company located?"

"It's out of Greenville, South Carolina. I dug a little deeper and discovered there's also a JMM company with a listing address of Spartanburg. It appears that the JMM and A. Aldridge might be connected. Ever heard of either of these companies or the two towns?"

"They're both in upstate South Carolina and are neighboring cities. Also, the city of Anderson is part of that triangle. It's one of the hot spots where drugs come through. Recently, there was a big bust, and the court determined that a cartel out of Eastern Europe is operating in the area—both drugs and human trafficking."

"Crap, Cat, that's a good lead and something that will make the FBI pay attention if they think there's a connection. I'll put in a call to my friend after we finish this conversation."

"Lorenzo, can you check further on the two property companies? While I'm not familiar with A. Aldridge Properties or JMM, there might be a connection that would lead us to Nick or Senator Madison. Is there a board of directors for either? Maybe some of the same names will show up, and we can track them."

I lean in toward the computer screen and say, "Also, Al dropped by. He wanted to tell me that he thinks Nick is some kind of hustler. I agree. Are you having any luck with obtaining information from the FBI on him?"

"There's a lot of secrecy around his file. It's taking time to find someone who has the level of security clearance required. My contact's working on it. So far, the information on Senator Madison is sketchy and hasn't yielded anything of interest. He's not exactly a nice man, but there are no ties to organized crime or kickbacks so far. But we've just started. Do you know him?"

"Not exactly, and I really don't want to know him. But a few months ago, Cassie and I were working on an event, and he was a guest. In my opinion, he made a complete ass of himself. But Cassie was smitten. For a while, they were an item. So, of course, we invited him and his sister to dinner. Up close, he's even worse. His behavior at dinner was despicable and cruel. He dropped Cassie because he was mad at me. Now, she's barely speaking to me. The problem is I'm reasonably sure she's seeing him again. He's a narcissist and a control freak, and he's messing with my friend."

"Cat, we can't arrest him for being a miserable person."

"Well, then keep digging, as I sure as hell think he's involved in something illegal."

"Cat, my relationship with the FBI is fragile. It's based on the time I've spent with a particular agent in Quantico. I'm not in a position to make demands. We work together across international lines. It's only because of our mutual respect and friendship that I'm able to make these inquiries. Do you understand?"

"Sort of. You're telling me it's a balancing act."

"That's right. I'm asking my friend for a huge favor. I need you to back off. People are working on it. Let them do their jobs. *Va bene?*"

31

"Cassie, what do you think about this arrangement? Do these Purple Moonlight carnations look washed out next to the dark purple irises? Maybe more baby's breath? More greenery? I don't know. Maybe in lowlights, they'll be okay. Cass?"

There's no answer. Turning toward the stove, I watch Cassie's lost-in-an-earthquake expression as she mindlessly stirs the sauce. It's the first time we've worked together since the disastrous Sunday dinner with the repugnant senator. She's concocted all sorts of reasons not to work with me. Fortunately, the events have been small, and I've managed. But the wedding reception at Tidal Bay is huge. Thankfully, she showed up today, as I wasn't sure what I'd do without her help.

"Cass, put the sauce on the warmer. We need a break. I'll make some tea if you'll set up the chairs on the deck. Okay?"

Cassie nods, moves the pan, then walks to the French doors. She looks back over her shoulder and says, "Cat, I'm good. Really, I am. You don't have to keep tiptoeing around me."

I nod, but somehow, I believe tiptoeing is the right thing to do until Cassie gets her head around this situation. She's smart enough to figure it out without me providing a sermon on the senator. I want good things for her, and that dang creep isn't one of them. He's just flat-out despicable, and his behavior frightens me. The way he treated his sister suggests something nasty just below the surface.

My reverie is broken when the kettle whistles. I pile freshly made almond and chocolate chip biscotti on my favorite piece of Deruta pottery. Alongside, I place mugs, wedges of lemon, and a small pot of local honey and pour the boiling water into my mother's Arthur Wood vintage teapot.

Cassie is already settled on a cushioned lounge and has made room on the table for the tray. I slide it on the table, as I think about the many cups of tea we shared on this deck. It's become our place to sit quietly, puzzle through catering logistics, or simply have a chat. We've had enough chats and cups of tea out here for me to know Cass likes a squeeze of lemon and a big drizzle of honey. But not enough chats to understand why she won't talk to me.

"Thanks, Cat. Let's get this over. We have lots of chopping and dicing to do before Saturday's event."

That's Cassie. She's either all in or not. She gives me the opening I've been waiting for, but I'm not sure what to say. Her black eyes drift to the water view behind me. Her mop of raven hair is twisted in a knot on the top of her head, and wispy pieces float in the light breeze.

"Cassie, the odds are John Ashley, and Jim will be at the wedding Saturday evening. I'm sure they've been invited. Tell me where you stand with Jim, and tell me how to behave if he shows up and messes with you."

"Why don't you tell me how you'll react to John Ashley and what support you'll need from me?"

I sip my tea and realize I've blundered again. Going first means letting Cass off the hook. The conversation will be about John Ashley and me. The silence drags on a little too long, so I plunge in.

"Ha, that's easy. After what happened to me in Italy, the John Ashleys of this world don't amount to much. It was my own stupidity when I overlooked his controlling behavior. I'm over him. I have no lingering feelings for him, not even a smidgen. It won't upset me in the slightest to see him or his bride. My biggest problem will be to keep my mouth shut so I don't say something snarky where others might hear me. But if he looks at me cross-eyed, I'll throttle him. Why do you think I'm taking Krav Maga classes?"

Cassie's dimples show for the first time in days.

"Actually, Cat, I was worried when you took up self-defense. I thought maybe Al was messing with you."

"Oh gracious, Cass. Not, Al. He's stopped by the house a few times, but he's always a gentleman. Our time together has always been about the event he wants me to do. We're working on the menu now. He's lovely, and we're becoming friends."

"If he were interested in something other than friendship, would you be?"

"Okay, now you're stalling, Cass. This isn't about me or Al. It's about you and Jim. Tell me where you stand and what you need my role to be if he's at the reception. Or perhaps you don't need support if you're still seeing him."

She doesn't react to my comment. Instead, she drifts off into some foggy landscape that doesn't include me. Finally, she looks at me with tears glittering in her eyes.

"What do you want me to say? That I'm upset? Well, okay, I'm furious. You get anything you want. And now you've decided that the one man I want in my life isn't right for me. Why?"

Blood drains from my face. It slugs through my body and dumps in the pit of my stomach. Something's off—something she's not telling me. Whining and blaming me is so out of character for her.

"Cass, you don't mean that? I'd never do anything to hurt you. The guy is a first-class asshole. You are so smitten with him that you haven't noticed the sadistic way he looks at Alice. He likes to humiliate people. I was married to a violent man, and Jim has all the markings."

I shut my mouth in horror. Once again, I have said all the wrong things, all the things I promised myself I wouldn't.

Sputtering all over myself, I shrill, "Oh, Cass. I've hurt you. I do understand how you're feeling. I've been there. That's the reason I want to protect you from having the same awful experience I had with Richard and John Ashley. I, I didn't mean to upset you."

There's no need for me to continue. The damage is done. It's in

Cassie's eyes, in her pained facial expression, in the slouch of her shoulders.

She gives me a limp smile before saying, "Don't be. You've had your say. But why bother? I already knew how you felt about Jim. You're not good at keeping your feelings a secret. As far as I'm concerned, this is the one and only conversation we'll have about him. It's off-limits from now on. You don't have a right to tell me what I should or shouldn't do with my life or who I should or shouldn't see. If it's okay with you, I'll finish the sauce. But I'm taking the rest of the day off. I'll come in early tomorrow morning."

Cassie picks up the tray. She didn't look in my direction. Her footsteps are heavy and angry. She bangs around in the kitchen, utensils fall to the floor, and dishes slam in the sink. I stay on the deck until the house is eerily quiet. It's only after I hear the crunch of tires on gravel when she drives away that I unfold myself from the lounge and walk down to the dock.

Why do I think it's my job to fix people? I chew on that question for a while, searching for an honest answer. Maybe it's because it's so much easier to fix someone other than myself. When I think about the advice I freely hand out to others, I realize it's exactly the same advice I need be following. What a mess. Will Cassie ever forgive me?

The water is so calm I can hear its heartbeat. After only a few years, this place has taught me so much about the ebb and flow of life —about healing and restoration. The warm breeze wraps its arms around me. I lean into it as a child to its mother.

32

T idal Bay is my secret desire. If I had a zillion dollars, I'd knock on the door and demand the house, no matter the cost. It was built in 1853, has over 7,000 square feet, and is surrounded on three sides by water. The owners recently restored the house to its former glory. The fresh oyster-white paint gleams in the afternoon sunlight. The golden rays strike against the towering columns and sweep up the front staircase. Windows sparkle. The lawn and landscaping have been meticulously groomed. Round tables are ladened with pale Purple Moonlight lilacs, deep purple irises, and variegated purple and white carnations tucked with baby's breath and ivy—all spilling out of crystal vases.

I only have seconds to admire our earlier work before an army of staff greets us at the back door and begins the process of unloading the van. Cassie and Sam take charge of the kitchen, where they arrange the meals on massive platters and chafing dishes. My job is to check the flower arrangements throughout the house and to make sure the correct table setting is at each place.

My final assignment before the festivities start is the wedding cake. With pre-filled pastry bags, I pipe purple carnations and add tiny crystallized white flowers. I sink giant blackberries in between the flowers. On each side of the cake are vases of the same hue of purple carnations and white calla lilies. I smooth the pale purple tablecloth, straighten the candelabras, and realign the plates, forks, and napkins, which are embroidered with miniature purple carnations. My last job is to construct pyramids of sugared blackberries on silver platters on each side of the cake.

My breath is slow and even as I tuck the last blackberry on top of the stack. When I step back to admire my work, an arm is flung around my waist. I gasp and recoil. Without turning, I tuck into my body, jab as hard as I can with an elbow, catch the person's calf with my left foot and jerk just like Chuck taught me.

I turn in time to see my attacker, John Ashley, thud against the wall. His face is infused with a brilliant red much like a neon sign as he clasps his stomach and groans. Hooting with laughter would draw attention to the situation, so I stifle the chuckle in my throat and put on my *I'm so concerned* look.

"Well, John Ashley, you might have said something before touching me. It would have been less painful for you. Should I call your bride or an ambulance?"

His only acknowledgment is to glare before he stalks off.

Laughter flows from Cassie and Sam, whose heads poke out of the kitchen door. I join in until the hostess, Mrs. Joshua Marshall Armstrong, arrives with a less-than-happy face.

"What seems to be the problem, Cat? It would be more seemly if whatever joke you and your people are sharing is relegated to a time away from this event. If you need something, please let the house-keeper know. I do not wish to be interrupted again with this type of disturbance."

She huffs and abruptly marches off. Our faces brim with suppressed laughter as we collapse against each other in the kitchen. How do I find these people? Yes, of course, this is the aftermath of Mrs. Harrington's war on my business. Once again, I've taken on a client that I wouldn't have before my trip to Italy. But the joy of Cassie's laughter is worth getting fired over. I sigh, pick up the next platter of food, and move to the buffet table.

The band swings into a lively rendition of *Carolina Girl,* and guests take to the dance floor. All the traditions of a Southern wedding reception are executed along with the appropriate toasts and a dance card lineup of who's who.

The food platters are replenished in the kitchen. Sam and I circulate. We whisk away used plates, glasses, and napkins. Half-empty platters of food are transitioned into full platters by Cassie.

I keep an eye out for John Ashley, but he's going to great lengths to stay far away from me. The senator hasn't made an appearance, but I expect he will. He wouldn't want to miss an opportunity to pontificate about his upcoming bid for reelection.

I watch Cassie begin the process of toting empty containers to the van. She loves the work as much as I do, but at the end of the day, it's a relief to wrap up an event. I can tell her back and feet hurt because mine do. She's probably thinking about sinking into a bubble bath with a big glass of wine, but there's still lots to do. It will be another couple of hours before the party winds down enough for them to do the final clean-up.

I wonder if she and Jim have plans to meet after the wedding reception. He still hasn't shown up yet, but I'm sure he will.

Cassie glanced at the time. She should be happy, but her inner voice kept telling her she was making a mistake. The last time she and Jim were together, they had discussed going public with their relationship. With the election date so close, Jim had pushed back. He wanted to hold off, but Cassie wasn't buying it. Their clandestine meetings in dingy motels were taking a toll. The relationship was floundering. She had invested everything. She needed it back on track. The wedding reception at Tidal Bay would be a good place to start. Nothing blatant, just a conversation that others might hear— something as simply as saying he'll see her later. Even a nod or a smile would be okay, but there had to be some indication they were a couple.

Her biggest concern was Cat. She hadn't told her she'd started dating Jim again, but she suspected Cat had guessed. Their friendship hadn't been on solid ground since the fiasco dinner party, and lately, it had started to unravel more. Cassie had been defensive every time the topic came up. Cat was her best friend. Was she right about Jim?

His behavior was often strange. When he didn't contact her after the disastrous meal at Cat's, she'd thought the relationship was over. She had been devastated. She had called and texted and begged, but he hadn't responded. Finally, she'd decided it was for the best. It was almost as if he knew when he'd broken her as he had called.

The relationship had resumed with far more intensity, but a couple of things had really bothered her. She had called him James a few times, just as Alice did. He'd snapped at her and said only Alice was allowed to use his given name. Then, he'd insisted she couldn't tell Cat they were back together. That felt wrong too. He'd blamed it on the election being so close. When she suggested it would be a positive if the citizens knew he was in a solid relationship, he'd said no—that it was not the time to announce anything new with the election only a few weeks away.

She was tired of meeting him in out-of-the-way places where they wouldn't be seen. She had finally worked up enough courage to say it was time. In her mind, tonight was the night. Cassie's cheeks flushed, and her heart accelerated at the thought that soon everyone would know. She pushed her misgivings away.

She closed the van doors, then remembered Cat had asked her to get the invoice from the glove compartment and leave it on the kitchen counter for Mrs. Armstrong's housekeeper. She absently punched the release button on the compartment. It was locked. While unusual, Cassie didn't think about it. She dug a set of keys out of her pocket and popped open the compartment. Her hand rummaged under the vehicle manual and through a stack of papers. She felt the cold metal against her skin and poked her head lower until she could see inside. Nestled in all the junk was a small pistol. *What the heck? Cat must have forgotten to put it in the safe after her practice.*

She picked it up and immediately dropped it. Damn, what if the dang thing went off? She leaned in closer and tentatively pulled at the stack of papers underneath the menacing weapon. After ruffling through them, she found the invoice. She threw the other papers back in, slammed the lid, and locked it. She had to let Cat know she'd found the gun. It wasn't like Cat to forget to secure it in the home safe. Well, perhaps it wasn't unusual since both of them were out of sorts these days.

Cassie was still thinking about the gun, as she stepped out of the van. A black limo sped down the road and pulled into the circular drive. It was Jim. She hadn't told Cat she knew for sure he'd be here or that they planned to acknowledge each other publicly. Cat would not be amused.

After tucking the invoice in her pocket, she crept around the side of the house. She hesitated only a second before tiptoeing across the screened veranda. She slipped into the hallway and positioned herself in a strategic location to view the entrance hall. She tucked into a corner behind a giant potted plant and waited for the right moment.

Jim glowed in his custom-made tux. He never missed an opportunity to be at the gym, and it showed. Alice clung to his arm. She looked ethereal in a dove-gray gown with a gauzy silver overlay.

Cassie watched from behind the column. Jim hadn't been enthusiastic about going public tonight, but he hadn't forbidden her. She whispered to herself, *go back to the kitchen*. Instead, she paused for another look at Jim's handsome face. At that same moment, Alice leaned into him and whispered in his ear. He kissed her lightly on the cheek and touched her hand in such an intimate manner that Cassie felt sick. They glided across the floor in her direction.

33

After I cut and packaged the wedding cake in white take-home boxes with elegant purple and gold ribbons, we began the long process of cleaning up. Cassie had asked to stay in the kitchen, which left Sam and me out front with the wait staff. I had't seen Cass in a while, so I poke my head through the door. The kitchen is empty.

An unknown dread churns in my stomach. I check the staff bathroom and the dining area. She's not in either. That leaves the solarium. Surely, she wouldn't attempt to talk to Jim. I'd seen the limo pull up. That George person had opened the door and assisted Alice from the car while Jim preened like a peacock. He and his driver give me the creeps.

Before crossing the threshold to the solarium, I notice most of the crowd has moved to the dance floor or outside. There are only a few malingerers still hovering around the bar. A strident male voice breaks through the muffled hum of conversation.

"What do you want? Get out of my way."

As soon as I recognize the senator's voice, I rush toward the racket without thinking. The harsh words can only mean disaster. As I enter the solarium, Cassie's hands are raised in the air as if a gun is pointed at her chest. Her face is chalky white against the dark mop of her black hair. Jim's index finger wags back and forth in her face. His words are loud enough to stop the dancing in the next room.

"It seems you've mistaken me for someone else. You're hired help. I will be speaking to Mrs. Armstrong about your inappropriate behavior."

Five feet from the catastrophe, I pass a table with platters of food. I grab the first dish and stroll into the middle of the group surrounding Cassie and Jim. Sliding in between them gives Cassie space and time to disappear. Once I sense she's gone, I look into the creep's eyes, smile and begin to babble.

"Well, Senator Madison, did you just arrive? Goodness, you've missed a lot of the festivities. Why you must be starved. Can I fix you a plate? Would you prefer something to drink? Or maybe you'd like to show us your moves on the dance floor. If you want to say hello to the bride and groom, they're outside along with most of the guests. The photographer is taking photos. I'm sure he'd loved to have a picture or two of a celebrity like you."

He snorts like the belligerent oaf he is and storms off with Alice trotting after him.

I drop the platter on the bar, and race to the kitchen. Cassie's not there. Sam pushes through the back door with tears drizzling down her face.

"Where's Cass?"

"I gave her the keys to my car. She's going home," Sam said, snatching a paper towel to wipe her eyes.

"Sam, go with her. She doesn't need to be alone."

"I can't leave you to clean up this mess."

"Yes, you can! Hurry! Catch her before she leaves!"

Sam blows me a kiss, grabs her purse, and runs out the door. Her yells for Cass to stop the car bounce back through the kitchen door before it slams shut.

34

Hours later, I pull into my driveway. After putting away all the catering equipment, I change into my favorite baggy jeans and an oversized t-shirt, the one that says *Love is Temporary Chocolate is Forever*. With a glass of water and my favorite Nero D'Oro, I collapse against a pile of plump pillows on the swing bed.

The sun has long faded, and a dusty pinkish-gray haze hovers over the marsh. Nocturnal birds take flight in a swirling arc before resettling in the expansive oaks along the marshy banks of the river. The tide slugs against the eroding embankments. My imagination gives me free rein to believe the swing bed glides under the influence of the rising moon's pull. This little patch of heaven is my sanctuary, my magic carpet. Some days, like today, it's the only place I find joy.

Although I'm sure Cassie won't answer my calls, I leave messages and check my phone constantly. She's hurt, humiliated, and angry. She needs time. I understand that feeling of total humiliation. I've lived the devastating degradation that Cassie faced today. I was fortunate not to have an audience other than strangers in a restaurant when John Ashley broke off our engagement. But the divorce trial with Richard was the topic of tabloids. My personal life was ripped away while the entire community looked and listened. I was left wounded and exposed.

Now I'm on the other side, looking in as Cassie flounders in the throes of being dumped in public. Yet, something keeps bugging me. Why would she approach Jim at a private function? She said he'd made it clear he never wanted to see her again.

I demand my thoughts to cease and desist, but they ramble on out of control. I realize that Cassie had started to see him again, but she decided not to tell me. I don't want to believe it, but in affairs of the heart, stupidity always wins. Our unreliable emotions take us by surprise and lead us down the path to perdition. My head slowly shakes out a sad, yes. Cassie had some expectations about tonight that didn't quite work out the way she believed they would.

The desire to lie down and let the night music lull me to sleep is strong. But the desire to help Cassie is stronger. What can I do? How can I help?

Google makes it easy to answer that question. I start by keying in the senator's name. If I'm lucky, there will be some dark secret in his past that I can unearth. I skim through the usual stats not fully understanding why I'm doing this.

Age: 48; Married, divorced-no-fault, currently single.

Children: Benjamin and Mia reside in Switzerland with their mother, Anna Karlsson. The children attend TASIS American Boarding School in Switzerland

High School: Bluffton High

College: University of Georgia, 1987; Columbia Law School, 1991

Practice: Brindle, Hastings & Madison

Career: Private practice 15 years, State representative 2007-2013, State Senator 2013 to present

The no-fault divorce is the only flag on the profile. There are only five reasons for divorce in South Carolina: adultery, habitual drunkenness, physical abuse, abandonment, and no-fault. Jim's public persona would require a no-fault divorce, but I wonder? I flip back to the information on the ex-wife's location—Switzerland? What if this was one of those hushed-up divorces?

Alice's name pops into my thoughts. While I'm sure she wouldn't intentionally reveal anything about Jim's marriage and family, she might let some tidbit slip with the right questions. I make a note to call her for lunch, or even better, I'll ask her to meet me for a drink. In the meantime, this is something I can pass on to Lorenzo.

I scan through pages and pages of bills the senator voted for or against, political rallies and slogans, and photos until my eyes tear and the motion of the bed spins my head. My finger is ready to click the off button when a newspaper clipping with of a bunch of guys catches my eye. A group of young men with a caption that reads: *Columbia Law School Poker Club Wins Tournament for Sixth Year with a Little Help from the Alumni And All for a Good Cause.*

Nick Cafaro clasps a trophy to his chest. Dollar bills overflow from the mouth of the brass cup. Cigars, rolled-up sleeves, and suspenders appear to be the dress code for the event, even in the black and white photo, smoke circles in the air. Bottles of whiskey and decks of cards are carelessly displayed on a nearby table.

A sudden gust of wind penetrates the air and moves the swing bed enough for me to pause. The sweetness of gardenias rises as the breeze sweeps across the porch. The bushes that surround the house are covered in blossoms. The powerful aroma temporarily distracts me. In the soft twilight, my view of the universe is kind, a safe place away from the evil that roars through the earth—evil that slaughters whatever lies in its path.

The photo pulls me back to the reality in which I'm suspended. Nick Cafaro, a poor boy from the wrong side of the tracks who hated school and almost flunked out in his senior year, is a graduate of Columbia Law School? Impressive.

I scrutinize the others. Then I follow the hand clasped on Nick's shoulder until I meet the eyes of the man standing behind him, holding a sign that proclaims *the boss*. Recognition dawns. What an unlikely pair!

35

The light cotton throw is plastered to my skin. Wiping the sweat from my face, I reach for the glass of water that's usually on my nightstand. I fumble around until I realize there is no nightstand. It has disappeared.

At five in the morning, the air is already dense with humidity. Moaning and sighing, I struggle to sit up and shake off the night-mares, but everything is moving. My muddled dreams hover in the shadows, not ready to let go of the darkness and face the light. The dreams are still alive—the sneering face of the senator and Cassie's blood-curdling scream. It's as if I'm watching a live-stream movie, and the remote won't let me shut it off.

The swinging motion creeps up on me again. My stomach heaves. Did I drink too much last night? No, I only had one glass of wine, so that's not it. My mind fumbles around as I crack open a crusted-over eye.

The sigh of the river and the tilt of marsh grasses gliding with the tide propel me upward. I mutter obscenities as I realize that, once again, I've fallen asleep on the swing bed. My allergies are in full gallop. I rub the eye gunk away and squint at the sun, itching to burst out of the night's restraints. Little by little, the nightmares subside.

My laptop sits open on the coffee table. I stretch to reach it and click. Last night's research pops open to the old newspaper clipping of Nick—the one with the boss's hand still clasped firmly on his shoulder. No wonder I had nightmares. I follow the hand up the arm and look into the sinister face.

"Well, well, well," I murmur under my breath. "If you lie down with dogs, you get up with fleas." Ol' Ben Franklin just might be on to something. So this is Nick's boss. How the heck did that happen?

Rising unsteadily from the swing bed, I close the computer and tuck it under my arm. The porch is damp on my bare feet. There's time for coffee and a quick shower before my Krav Maga lesson. I plan to stop by Cassie's unannounced and force her to go with me. There will be no conversation about the nasty incident at Tidal Bay. As usual, I probably won't keep that promise.

Before showering, I leave a message with a realtor friend. Maybe supplying Al with a list of properties for sale with large tracts of land would be beneficial. I don't want this area to miss out simply because Carrington Point isn't available. The other real reason I call my friend is to ask her if she knows anything about A. Aldridge or JMM Properties. I believe there's a connection.

My mind returns to the old newspaper clipping and the hand clasped on Nick's shoulder. Nick would have been about twenty-two. Wheels whirl in my head. Logic suggests I find out how Nick got into Columbia Law School and how he was tagged for the FBI Academy. Whose imprint will show up as a reference? I'm guessing *the boss*.

With that thought, I message Lorenzo, asking him if his connections in Washington can find a common thread between the two men. I forward a copy of the clipping.

Mondays are habitual. At my private Krav Maga sessions, Chuck and I duke it out for an hour and then have a cup of coffee before going our separate ways. We've developed a comfortable friendship. Coffee, a review of the lesson, and then moving on to food, wine, and travel, which we discovered are topics we both enjoy. Occasionally we have lunch.

Chuck is such a nice guy. There's something about him that reminds me of Lorenzo. My match-making mind is busy formulating plans. Which is why today, I have Cassie by the arm. I pull. She lurches reluctantly toward the studio. Ever since the wedding reception and Jim spewing vile words in her face, she's been lethargic and depressed. She won't make an appointment to see Ginny, and she won't talk to me.

I've been searching for ways, even if they're wrong, to steer her away from the black hole. She's my friend, and I don't want her in that hole. Part of me is frightened I'll follow behind her. I'm always just a step or two away from nestling down in the warm muck and letting go of all the trauma and terror that life has a habit of dumping. But when I picked Cassie up this morning, I promised her there will be no conversation about Jim. I try so hard to keep my word, but of course, I don't.

"Come on, Cass. Chuck's a nice guy. He'll teach you how to kick Jim in the cojones."

Cassie grabs a tree branch and hangs on.

"I don't want to do this. Let me sit in the car. I'm not ready to face anyone. This guy's probably going to ask why I want to learn this Krav, whatever. Neither of you is going to be happy when I say because I want to kill someone."

A giggle slips out before I can stop it.

"That's exactly why I'm dragging you here, Cass. The guy deserves whatever happens to him. But I would prefer that someone else does the deed as I don't have enough money to hire one of those super lawyers for you."

A slight smile strokes her lips upward before she drags them back down into her current frowny-face look.

"Look, just go in with me. It won't hurt to watch. You don't have to participate. We'll go to lunch after—my treat. Okay?"

I let go of her arm and walk across the parking lot. I don't look back, but the shuffle of her feet signals she's behind me. I tap on the glass. Chuck cracks the door. His grand smile beams through the opening.

He gives me a quick hug and whispers, "Wow, who's the dark beauty?"

I kick his foot before he can say anything else and announce, "Chuck, this is my friend Cassie. If it's alright with you, she's joining us today—maybe to watch, or perhaps you can persuade her to participate."

Chuck's eyes, which I had never noticed before today, are silvery green. They flicker ever so slightly as he gives Cassie the once over.

He extends his hand and says, "Hello, Cassie. I'm Chuck. Are you interested in Krav Maga?"

"Hell no," she snarls, a bit of saliva dangling on her lip. "This is Cat's idea of how I should spend my time. It's only the promise of lunch that brings me here."

"Well, that's honest. Come on in. You can join us, or you can sit on the sidelines and be grumpy. It doesn't matter to me."

Cassie takes a step back and looks Chuck over, maybe seeing him for the first time.

"Hmph," is all she says.

Chuck opens the door wider. Once we're inside, he locks it, turns on the lights, and grabs me from behind. I give a flick of my leg behind his calf. We struggle our way to the mat.

"Y'all are crazy," Cass says as she slams her hand into Chuck's back. He takes her down to the mat and pulls her up so quickly she can only gasp.

An hour later, slathered in sweat, we sit outside at Herban Market, devouring hefty sandwiches while the breeze from the river cools us down. Cassie isn't exactly smiling, but from time to time, she contributes to the conversation.

Chuck is smitten. He has that goofy schoolboy look on his face as his head nods to whatever Cassie says when she does speak. If he likes her when she's on her worst behavior, like today, maybe down the road, there's a chance for a healthy relationship to flourish. Cassie needs to laugh again, and Chuck just might be able to break through her misery. *Yes*, I think, *this is good.*

But I was wrong. Not that it wasn't good, but Cassie had already gone down the rabbit hole.

36

It's another lunch with Al today, but I dress casually—jeans, a blue and white striped shirt, and blue sneakers. According to his message, we're driving out to Carrington before lunch. He wants to see if we can ferret out the notorious Richard Alistair Davenport, aka Nick Cafaro. My fingers hover over the phone as I consider texting Nick. I'm actually afraid of what he will do if we arrive unannounced. That's if he's still there.

Would he really hurt us? Possibly shoot us? The answer is frightening. Nick is so involved in this covert operation that I truly believe he would hurt me or anyone else who interfered.

Who is Nick Cafaro? What has happened to him since our paths last crossed? Is he really an FBI agent? What if someone else is behind what he's doing, and it's not the FBI?

My thoughts are all over the board. Here I am again, dabbling in something every bit as dangerous as searching for Stella's murderer. The one thing I know is that neither Al nor I are going back to Carrington Point anytime soon. My head clears as I finish dressing. If I don't accomplish anything else today, I will keep him away—at least until I hear back from Lorenzo. Once I make that decision, relief floods my body. I no longer have to consider texting Nick.

Al, prompt as usual, is still being driven by George. But Al, instead of George, is out of the car and at the door before I can open it. He bows over my hand, brushing it lightly with his lips. He lifts his head. His usual bright smile is missing. His eyes are puffy from lack of sleep. We chat for a few minutes before I say, "Al, what's wrong?"

"The time is approaching for me to go back to Spain. I came here with such high hopes. I'm disappointed that my plan to grow Moringa trees in the Lowcountry no longer seems possible."

"Oh, Al, please don't give up yet. Your dream is so worthwhile. It would benefit so many people. Surely, you can find another place. I'll help you."

"If you're ready, we can discuss it in the car."

I close the door and key the deadbolt. The morning breeze ruffles through my still-damp hair. Al takes my hand and tucks it in his elbow. George, driver and all-around do-everything for Al, is ready with the limo door open. I smile and start to say good morning, but he ignores me. His eyes turn away and focus on Al. It's as if I don't exist. There's a harshness in his face and brute force in his body movements. He spooks me every time I see him. A tiny ping in my brain signals I'm looking at someone who was not hired just to drive Al around. Does this mean he's somehow involved and not the innocent bystander he claims to be? Or is it Jim who is somehow involved with Nick and the operation? Perhaps for some reason unknown to me, George has been hired to watch Al. If that's true, then George is listening to everything we say and reporting back to Jim or Nick or maybe someone else? My heart thuds as my feet sink deeper and deeper into the muddy mire of this mess.

As I slide into the limo, it's impossible not to feel the luxury of the cushy seats. For a second, I forget all the deceit. It doesn't last long as the lavishness cannot ease the fear settling in my stomach. A small sigh escapes. Al reacts by reaching across the seat and taking my hand. His voice is tense, hushed, and a bit draconian when he suggests there's a problem.

"Cat, there's something I need to tell you. The man who had dinner with us the other night is not who he says he is."

Perhaps he expects a startled look, a gasp, or at least a question from me, but I look him in the eye and nod.

"You already knew? Ahhh, that explains what happened the night we had dinner. I didn't realize you knew the man. Why didn't you tell me?"

A tiny *yes, I know him* slips out as I clap my hand over my mouth, but it's too late.

"Well, it appears you don't trust me. When we last spoke, I told you I was suspicious of bumping into him at the plantation. It seemed more than coincidence to come across him strolling on the property, particularly when no one in town had a clue who owned Carrington."

When I don't respond, he shifts in the seat and leans in close, "I tracked down the real Richard Alistair Davenport."

"What?"

"Don't worry, I didn't reveal anything. I simply asked if he was the owner of a property in South Carolina. Of course, he said no. But at some point, he'll have to be informed that someone is impersonating him."

Out of the corner of my eye, I watch George follow every word of our conversation. I turn to Al and pull him into an embrace that he enjoys way too much.

I whisper in his ear, "George is listening."

I hold the embrace for a few more seconds before releasing him. He pats my hand. His face sags. He looks decidedly older than the last time I saw him. His fingers restlessly straighten his already perfectly creased trousers.

"It's okay. George can be trusted. He's ex-military and comes highly recommended."

Maybe, but my gut tells me otherwise. I meet George's steely eyes in the rearview mirror. Since the senator recommended him, my level of distrust is deep.

"George and I drove out to Carrington yesterday to look for Davenport. Before I tell you what we found, can you recommend a restaurant—something out of the way where we won't be recognized? I'm getting spooked by all this intrigue, but I'd also like to get out of town if you have someplace you'd recommend. The change would do us both good."

"Do you mind a forty-five minute drive?"

"No, not at all. What are you thinking?"

At my suggestion and Al's okay, George taps the address of the Crystal Beer Parlor in Savannah into the GPS. There's a high probability we won't bump into any friends or acquaintances. It's a down-home place, a bit off the beaten path. It's not a place someone like Al would try unless encouraged. He's right we need a change, and what's better than a food adventure?

"Alright, that's taken care of. So tell me what you found at Carrington."

"My purpose in going back yesterday was to find this Señor Davenport—to call him out. No one was around, so George and I drove down the road as far as we could. It ended a short distance from the old cotton sheds. We had to leave the car and walk the rest of the way."

Al sits forward and leans toward me, "After what George discovered, I'm pretty sure something illegal is occurring on the property. You and I don't need to be poking around. I believe it's too dangerous. I suspect we need to contact the authorities. You'll know better than I who to contact."

All of a sudden, I'm exhausted. How is it that I keep meeting people involved in something illegal or bordering on corruption, or at the very least, they exhibit weird behavior? I want to scream at George to turn the car around and take me home. Yet, I've already stepped over the line by involving Lorenzo. He, in turn, has involved the FBI. I have to see this through. When I nod, Al continues. It's important I hear what he has to say so I can pass the information on to Lorenzo. He'll make sure it's passed on to his FBI buddies.

Al says, "Before I continue, I need you to tell me what you know about this man."

I squirm around in the plush seat as I search for an eject button. Finding nothing to help me out of the jam I'm in, I stall.

"Why don't we wait and finish this conversation over lunch."

Al considers my suggestion and nods in agreement. I'm so thankful, as having George listen to every single word is unsettling. Of course, Al might invite him to have lunch with us, but I can't worry about that now.

We spent the rest of the drive chattering about characters around town and the possibilities of who to put on the guest list for Al's event if it ever occurs.

37

Forty-five minutes fly by, and soon, we're pulling up outside the Crystal Beer Parlor.

Al nods at George."Come back in a couple of hours. Cat tells me this is a major food experience. I want plenty of time to savor the meal."

George frowns and says he can grab a quick lunch here and wait in the car for us, but Al is adamant.

"No, go somewhere nice and have lunch. I'll text you when we're ready to leave."

George braces his lean, athletic body against the shiny black limo. He looks like a Stephen King character with a hint of vampire about him. More and more, I think George is involved with Nick and Jim. But how? And why? It's as if a million threads are floating in front of my face. If only I could capture a few, I'm sure a pattern would form. For now, they dangle—just out of my grasp.

Al straightens his jacket, tucks my hand in his arm, and waits until George is in the car and has turned the corner. He turns his smile on me and says, "Let's go in. I can't wait to taste whatever is on the menu. I'm guessing it must be some unusual Southern cuisine you want me to experience. Am I right?"

I shrug and lead the way into the Crystal Beer Parlor.

Al looks a tiny bit impressed as we stroll past the polished to a high-shine mahogany bar. I request a booth in the back and ask the waiter if the owner, John Nichols, is on the premises. Of course, since he's the chef, he's in the house.

Al opens the dog-eared menu and looks at it with disdain. Have I made a mistake bringing a Spanish count to one of my favorite spots? But I know I haven't when John shows up all smiles. He slaps Al on his back and scoots in the booth right next to him. He grabs Al's hand and proceeds to pump it vigorously. Al's mouth drops open. His eyes dart around, looking for an exit. But John's all-encompassing personality and generous spirit make everything okay.

Without asking, John plunges into the story of the historic structure and its occupants and how it became the Crystal Beer Parlor. He starts in the early 1900s when it opened as the Greken Family Grocery Store. He doesn't take a breath until he reaches the part of the story when he buys the place in 2009.

Al, who at first looks put out, relaxes under John's magic storytelling. He asks remarkably good questions for someone who has probably never eaten in an establishment like The Crystal. Once John leaves to make his rounds of the other patrons, I order for both us.

Appetizers arrive. I hold my breath until Al takes his first bite of fried dill pickles with ranch dressing. A goofy smile spreads across his face. I push the plate of fried green tomatoes with a horseradish cream sauce closer to him. He doesn't hesitate.

Finally, he asks, "What kind of food is this?"

"Pickles and green tomatoes."

His laughter bounces around our booth. For a moment, I forget why we're here. Al's face spreads into a wide-open grin like a child discovering for the first time that strange food can be delicious.

"It's amazing! Such unique tastes. Pickles! Who would dream of frying pickles?" He says while scooping another serving onto his plate.

Next comes Shrimp 'n Grits for Al and Bowl O'Soul for me. Al pokes at the jumbo shrimp nestled on top of creamy grits surrounded by slices of roasted red bell pepper and chunks of andouille sausage.

"What is this?" he asks, waving a forkful of grits.

"It's grits. It's the same as polenta," I say.

"*Polenta?*"

"Harina de maíz."

"Whatever it is, it's delicious. What did you order? It looks a bit messy."

"Oh, it's delightfully messy. Bowl O' Soul also has grits, but it's topped with pulled pork, collard greens, and pimento cheese."

But he's already lost in the shrimp and grits. *Hmmmm* is all I heard as he digs into the bowl with gusto. Eventually, he gets around to tasting my Bowl O'Soul and says that's what he'll order next time.

Without asking, John sends a sample platter of desserts to our table: mud pie, peach cobbler, fried pound cake, and a slice of six-layer carrot cake. We are both moaning with joy and distress.

The table is cleared. We're sipping coffee when Al says, "Why don't you tell me everything you know about this Richard or Nick person."

There's a long stretch of silence while I practice Chuck's Krav Maga breathing routine and try to figure out what I can tell Al without giving him information that Lorenzo wouldn't want me to. Finally, I blurt out, "Nick said if I told anyone what was going on at Carrington I'd be interfering with an undercover FBI operation."

"What? Of all the things you could have told me about him, that one doesn't seem likely. Do you believe him?"

"Initially, yes. He's an old classmate of mine. Many years ago, we were close friends. When he contacted me, I was surprised but not fearful. This whole thing started a while back when I took some clients to look at Carrington Point as a possible wedding reception venue."

Al nods as he sips his espresso.

I pause and then say, "Nick, the man you know as Richard, later told me that when I showed up with clients at Carrington, I compromised his undercover operation. He demanded I stay away from the property, and he said I had to keep my clients away. If I didn't, he wouldn't be responsible for anyone getting hurt or possibly killed. He also said it would be on my conscience if that happened."

Al leans away from the table. He pushes his head back until it presses into the padded cushion and closes his eyes. His forehead and around his mouth are etched with lines of fatigue. He sighs before he responds.

"Cat, this has been a dream of mine for a long time. For years, I've been searching for something that would give me a chance to redeem my life of indulgence and idleness. Moringa is a project I believe in. Carrington Point is the perfect property. Now, my dream is collapsing. We've stumbled across something that appears to be illegal and possibly deadly. I think your friend is involved."

"Al, tell me what happened on the last trip? When you and George decided to go out there."

"I didn't actually see anything. We were almost to the cotton sheds when George insisted I return to the car and wait for him. He was concerned that there might be druggies, prostitutes, or homeless people on the property. When I protested, he reminded me that he's trained in all aspects of military warfare and could protect himself. He said I needed to stay out of the way as he couldn't guarantee someone wouldn't take a crack at me. When George returned, he said some unsavory characters were holding up in the sheds. He also said he'd contacted the police, but we needed to get out of there because he'd called in anonymously."

"Why would he call in anonymously?"

"He said that someone in my position didn't need to be involved in negative publicity. He's right. My name in the newspaper as part of some kind of drug bust or prostitution ring wouldn't exactly put the Moringa Project in a good light with new investors."

In my mind, George is not doing this to save the count's reputation, but I'm sure he's doing it to save someone else's. But who besides himself? Possibly Nick, maybe, or both?

38

George pulled out of the parking lot of the Crystal Beer Parlor, drove around the block, and parked. He pulled up the boss's name on his cell and texted, *Can you talk?*

The call came through right away.

"Yeah, I know you're busy, but I thought you'd want to know we're in Savannah. They're having lunch at the Crystal. The count dismissed me. No, it'd be obvious if I tried to eat lunch there. The place is wide open. He was adamant I disappear."

George listened for a bit and said, "Sure, I understand it's my job to stay close, but there are limits. That's not why I called. They know Nick is lying about the stupid-ass story he told about being the owner of the property. Yeah, yeah, the count did some research and discovered this Davenport guy that Nick was impersonating lives in Virginia and didn't know anything about a property in South Carolina."

George shrugged and continued, "Cat went to school with Nick. I thought you'd be interested to know he's been seeing her. Yes, I'm sure. Didn't tell, did he? I told you the guy's a huge liability. Let me get rid of him and her, too. She's smart, which makes her dangerous."

George squinted in the afternoon sun. He pulled down the visor and nodded at his image.

"Yesterday was a close call. Yeah, I understand I'm supposed to keep the count away from the plantation, but he was determined. In his mind, I'm just a hired driver. He'd be suspicious if I started telling him what he can and can't do. If he weren't such a wuss, we'd have been fucked. But he went scurrying back to the car when I told him it would be a disadvantage for him to be involved. I told him he didn't need any scandal attached to his name. Yeah, yeah, I know. I'll hold off. But every day we wait, there's a chance this operation is going to blow apart."

George ended the call and slumped against the seat. He thought *the boss* was a wuss, too. The entire operation was a pile of shit. It had been poorly planned. Now that Nick's day-to-day control was floundering, the whole thing was a disaster. It wouldn't take much longer to push Nick out. Once he was in charge, things would change. *The boss* wouldn't recognize what was happening until it was too late. No one was aware of his ties to the Russian bosses.

He was ready to push the plan forward. He'd been indentured to *the boss* for a couple of years now, and it didn't seem as if there was any cut-off point. It was time to put an end to this indefinite contract and secure his position as head of the operation. If not, then he needed to get the hell out of this place and head on down to Mexico.

He'd been a convicted murderer and rapist in Mangaung Maximum Security Prison in Bloemfontein, South Africa until outside contacts in Bratva had secured the money for his escape. Some other miserable creature had been pushed into his cell and burned to death right in front of his eyes. There was no autopsy, and the prison authorities filed a report informing the authorities that Thabo Bandile, now known as George, was dead. He'd slipped out the back door and never looked back. He'd covered his tracks, but sooner or later, his South African connections to Bratva, the Russian mafia, would catch up with him. They wanted a piece of the action.

It had taken him a while to get forged papers and to sneak his way into Canada and finally cross the border into the US.

In the US, he'd hooked up with the Albania mafia, Rudaj, and found the kind of shady work he expected—illegal gun deals, drug runs, pimping, and forgery until his luck ran out. He messed with the wrong people a few times and got picked up for possession with intent to distribute. Stupid mistake. His court-appointed lawyer advised him to plead guilty, but George had been around far longer than the snotty-nosed kid pretending to be his counsel. He'd plead not guilty and asked for a criminal defense lawyer, which made Judge Daniel Wingate's ears perk up.

The hearing was postponed while a new lawyer was brought up to speed. George was put in a holding tank until bail could be raised. He wasn't there long before he'd been collected and put in an interrogation room. His new lawyer approached him with a proposition. Charges would be dropped if he agreed to participate in an experimental rehab program. The details were sketchy. George smelled a rat, but then he knew how to outsmart any rodent. He accepted the terms and went to work as a driver/security guard for *the boss*.

They'd reached an agreement early on about what sort of job this would be. It seemed *the boss* had a weakness for young girls. George knew he'd hit the jackpot. A couple of years was nothing to win *the boss's* trust. As he procured goods that met the man's expectations, he found a foothold and made inroads into gaining power. Nick was the only person that stood in his way, and that wouldn't be for much longer. And if his plans for taking over the operation didn't work out, Alice had offered him a sweet deal. He'd been stunned and told her he needed some time to think about it. But a cool million in unmarked bills was looking pretty good. He'd leave the country for good.

39

Cassie sat on the painted bench, one of many scattered throughout town. Each was crafted with great love and was scripted with an exuberant message of optimism. The air was smooth, warm as melted butter. Cassie didn't notice. She sobbed into her hands. The tears smudged her mascara. She was sick with fear. She stank of it. Fear had its own smell—sour, foul. She hadn't smelled it in a long time, not since she'd discovered she was pregnant with Sam.

She'd just turned seventeen and had been voted Homecoming Queen. Her world had bottomed out. The boy who had filled her head with dreams and her heart with love had also filled her with a child. She'd been ecstatic, radiant, and full of hope when she stood before him and told him he would be a father in the New Year. He had laughed. With tears drizzling down her face, she begged him to marry her. He'd slapped her, called her a slut, and screamed the baby wasn't his. He left. She never saw him again but heard he'd joined the Marines.

Her good Christian family, once over their disbelief, said she'd gotten into the mess on her own. It was her responsibility to figure a way out. Eventually, her dad found a job out of state. Before moving, he'd met her one last time, gave her a check for five hundred dollars, and walked away without saying a word. She never heard from them again. She was alone. She'd never tried to find them and was thankful Sam had never wanted to know them.

She dropped out of school, minus her homecoming queen crown.

She thought about killing herself. Her fear was so strong she knew death would be better.

A friend's parents took her in. She was given a room in the basement, dank and dark. To pay for her stay, she cooked and cleaned for the family. While cleaning, she'd snooped in the master bathroom vanity and found enough pills to end her life. She was scared. It was one thing to kill herself, but what about her baby? Her upbringing had been strong regarding the sin of taking a life. Yet, she had no reason to live. Every Saturday, she'd slipped one or two of the pills in her pocket. Collecting the pills had taken too long. By the time she had enough, she was over four months along. The baby had moved. That one tiny kick saved their lives.

Once Samatha was born, Cassie was told she needed to move out as a baby was too disruptive to their lives. It seemed that no one wanted a teenager with a baby. Again, she contemplated suicide. She still had the pills. But Sam was so beautiful and such a good baby. Cassie hung on and grew into the role of motherhood.

A family law firm gave her a job and a small apartment above the office while she completed her GED. One of the employees let it slip that Sheriff Blackwell was the reason she got the job. He and his wife were good people. She'd always been welcomed in their home and had played with their girls, but she wanted to make her own way. She almost didn't accept the job, but the people in the office were kind. They even let her bring Sam to work. She figured this was her only chance.

Later, she realized the sheriff had been behind that as well. She kept the job until she received an associate degree in hospitality management at the technical college and got hired by an event planner. Later, she got her B.A. and added restaurant and hotel management to her resumé. Then, she'd opened her own event planning business.

One day, in the grocery store, she bumped into Cat and knew instantly she had a friend for life. Things had been good right up until she introduced Cat to Jim. There wasn't any point in rehashing that miserable dinner party. It was destroying their friendship.

She had to stop the tears and focus on her next steps. Whatever decision she made would impact Sam for the rest of her life. The years since she'd first held Sam in her arms had flown by. Sam was now grown up and in culinary school.

Cassie had created a will and trust fund for her. Financially, Sam would be okay, but what about emotionally and mentally? She hated herself for contemplating suicide and leaving Sam behind to deal with the aftermath. But she hated herself more for letting that monster slither back into her life.

She'd been lonely and vulnerable. Jim had taken her by surprise. She'd never been the center of someone's universe. He hooked her right from the first moment she met him. She believed that with Sam in college, there was time to think of herself—to give herself a chance at love and sharing her life with someone.

When Jim abruptly dumped her after the dinner at Cat's, she had been frantic, out of her mind with grief. All of her old insecurities came flooding back. She wasn't worthy. How could she have imagined that an important man like Jim would love her?

She wrestled with the suddenness of his departure from her life. It didn't make sense. Yes, the dinner party had been a total flop, but that wasn't her fault. It had been Cat's. *No, wait,* she told herself. It wasn't Cat who created the problem. It was Jim. Yet, he had immediately blamed Cat, and she had agreed. She'd been so angry with Cat that she never noticed how Jim had mistreated all of them that evening. Her desire for him and the need to belong overcame her rational thoughts. She had chosen what she thought was love over the strong friendship she and Cat had shared for years.

She thought back to meeting him for the first time at the Fitzhugh's dinner party. It had been magical. He had given her his card and asked her to call him, but she hadn't. Cat was a stickler about not fraternizing with their clients, but he was persistent. He went out of his way to find her. When he pursued her, she illogically categorized his behavior as romantic instead of controlling. They met for coffee to discuss a cocktail reception he was planning for his reelection campaign. In retrospect, she remembered he had requested she not tell anyone they were meeting. It had made the time together mysterious and exciting.

That one meeting was all it took. A cocktail reception had never materialized. Cassie couldn't remember now if they had even discussed such an event. The passion between them was palatable to the point that they were in bed before the afternoon was over. The whirlwind affair began.

He had been attentive and a passionate lover. He showered her with gifts and compliments. Everything about the affair was perfect. Of course, now Cassie could see the telltale signs of control. She had chosen to ignore them. It had been easy to blame it on Cat's behavior at the dinner party. When Jim had dropped her over such a small incident, she'd been shocked. In her mind, it was only a slight misunderstanding. In those few weeks with him before the dinner, she had fallen in love with all her being. When he didn't call, she'd been crazy with grief. The days went by. Her messages went unanswered. Darkness and panic had gathered in the pit of her stomach.

Cat hadn't understood her pain. Had said good riddance. That's when the gap in their friendship opened. Cassie felt lousy about that, as deep down, she knew Jim's reaction to the misunderstanding was out of proportion to what had happened.

When he finally called, he asked her to not tell Cat. He sent a limo to pick her up. She was impressed, except the driver, who said his name was George, kept her in his sights in the rearview mirror the entire drive to Charleston. It wasn't the first or last time his scrutiny made her feel uncomfortable. Whenever George picked her up, his constant staring implied she was under some kind of surveillance. When she'd asked Jim about George, he'd brushed her off.

They had made up over a spectacular Chef's Tasting Menu at Circa 1886. She had been so happy to see him, to be with him again, that she didn't ask why the breakup had happened. She knew he'd explain, but he didn't mention it.

When nothing was said, she blurted out, "Jim, tell me what I did wrong. I don't understand why you dropped me over such a small faux pas. Can you explain?"

"Oh, shush, Cassie. I've had a lot to contend with. Alice hasn't been well. I'm preparing for the next legislative session, and you know I'm running for reelection. I have to focus. I can't have my life disrupted. And frankly, your friend Cat irritated me so much I was willing to let you go. She's not good for you. But after I thought about it, I realized I can't blame you for Cat's mediocrity and ignorance. You and I, hell, we're meant to be together."

40

S he should have defended Cat. She should have demanded he take her home. Instead, she let him back in her life.

The royalty treatment went on for a while—long enough for him to hook her again. A couple of weeks later, George had picked her up for a mystery weekend. A "kiss and makeup tryst," Jim had called it. She'd been dazzled when she was dropped off at the Wentworth Mansion in Charleston and escorted to the opulent Grand Mansion Suite. The manager took her luggage and said Jim was waiting for her on the roof as he pointed the way. She had never been in a place as elegant.

Champagne, chilled in a crystal bucket, caviar and a 360-degree view had left her breathless. Love songs played in the background as the last burst of sun sighed its way into the ocean.

Later, Jim had carried her over the threshold. He'd kissed her hand and then told her the history of the floor-to-ceiling marble gas fireplaces, the original Italian chandeliers, and the Tiffany-stained glass.

They'd made love, but for the first time, the magic was missing. He had been distracted. Instead of the tender romantic intimacy she longed for, it had been rough, brutal. But after, he'd cuddled her and said how great it was and how lost he'd been without her.

Of course, she didn't tell Cat. She couldn't bear it if he left her again. Plus, Jim had said it was their secret, and telling Cat would spoil it for them. Another red flag she chose to ignore. They continued to meet secretly, although never again in the grand style of Wentworth Mansion. She kept telling herself she was happy to be with him. Gradually, things changed—the secret rendezvous became the opening of doors in motels on lonely country roads. Ones with window units, beds that sagged, water that dripped, and floors that stuck to her feet.

When she questioned him, he said he needed to travel the state in his bid for reelection. He told her he couldn't have her staying with him at hotels paid for by citizens. It wouldn't look right.

She packed picnic dinners since there were rarely decent eating establishments anywhere near the rundown motels. Sometimes, she'd wait the entire night sitting on a corner of the filthy bedspread. He often didn't return. If he did, their time together was filled with him grabbing at her clothes and forcing himself on her, then leaving. He treated her as if she were some two-bit slut he'd picked up on the street.

Every time she pulled away or came close to ending the relationship, it was as if he knew her breaking point. His attitude would change. The hotel room would improve, and the sweetness would return to his voice and lovemaking. He wound and rewound her. Then he'd leave her dangling like a rock-the-baby yo-yo.

At first, the changes were subtle, from grand hotels to chain hotels and then the back country road hovels. When they were together, Jim would grill her about the events she was planning. He seemed interested in the clients, locations, the food, and wine. Then he'd ask if she was still working with Cat.

"Of course, I'm still working with Cat. We're a great team. She's my friend. She's asked me to be her partner."

"Why would you do that?" he'd asked. "Don't you want to be in charge? Didn't you have your own business before? You used to make all the decisions. The money was all yours. Even in a partnership, Cat will run the show. Surely you know that. She's top dog. She makes sure everyone knows that. But, sugar, make sure you don't tell her we're back together. She'd do anything to split us up."

When Cassie hadn't responded, he'd continued. "You're smarter than Cat. I could bring you all the clients you'd ever want. Why don't you dump her? She's holding you back."

In lucid moments, she'd said to Jim, "Cat's not holding me back. Together, we have more than enough clients. Our business is steady, our profits are good, and we love working together."

She thought a great deal about what a partnership with Cat would mean. In the shabby motels on the back roads, she'd questioned her motives to continue the affair with Jim. She told herself she was in love, and that was enough.

But her rational side knew she owed Cat a lot. When Cat had asked her if she wanted to be a partner, she'd said she'd like to think about it. Of course, she couldn't confide in Cat. She wouldn't approve or understand why Cassie was seeing Jim again. She didn't have the courage to tell Cat that her real intention was to become his wife.

Gradually, Jim's voice in her head became louder and stronger. Maybe he was right. Perhaps she should go out on her own again. With Jim's backing, she'd never have to worry about clients. But if he asked her to marry him, she wouldn't have to worry about leaving Cat or starting up another business. She wouldn't have to work. She couldn't even imagine what that would be like, as she'd had a job since she was ten years old.

Jim continued to feed her ego and encourage her to leave Cat. He'd look at her, smile in that lovely way he had, shrug his shoulders and say, "Look, Cassie. Don't be stupid. This is your chance. It would be easy to get rid of Cat."

The panic in Cassie's voice spilled over, "Get rid of her. What do you mean?"

"What do you think I mean? Kill her? Oh, silly girl, what are you talking about? I mean, undermine her. She's talking about you behind your back—ruining your reputation. Never gives you credit for anything. Calls you hired help. That's all you are to her. She misled you, and you gave her all your clients. She'll keep treating you badly until she destroys you. Don't let that happen, sugar."

A long, slow chuckle escaped from his lips, "Oh, by the way, I do know people. For a price, they can make anything happen. What? Oh, come on, Baby, don't tell me you haven't thought about it. We all have those moments."

Cassie's eyes filled with tears. The long-ago memory of Jason slapping her and calling her a slut appeared alongside her father, handing her a check like she was a cheap pickup before turning his back and walking away. She wasn't worthy. She'd never been. Perhaps even Cat was using her. Everyone else had. She really didn't want to believe that, but the seed was planted.

She grimaced as she pushed up from the bench. Now Jim had dumped her again—in a public place for the entire town to witness— the wedding reception at Tidal Bay. People had looked at her as if she were a pile of vomit. They'd snickered and formed little circles around Jim. She'd betrayed Cat for this creep.

She pulled a tissue from her pocket, dabbed at her mascara-smeared eyes and walked to the top of the Bluff. The wind had picked up and whitecaps danced, rippling the waves into gray foam. She moved slowly up Bay Street with the wind beating against her back.

She stopped at the Old Federal Courthouse and sat on the concrete bench that faced the river. She watched the flags flap like the large wingspan of a brown pelican. This was her home. She'd lived here all her life. She knew the history and the families of this town, including the grand building in front of her. It had been one of the oldest homes in town—built around the time of the Revolutionary War. The history of this place spanned three hundred years, trans- forming from a home to a hospital, a federal court, and then a museum. Recently, after a three-million-dollar renovation, it had become the sheriff's office—and not just any sheriff, but her friend, Sheriff Blackwell. He was the one man in her life who had treated her right.

Cassie briefly wondered why she was on a bench outside the sheriff's office with a gun nestled in her purse. Sheriff Blackwell would be disappointed. Even when she was a kid, he'd always talked to her like an adult. But she couldn't, wouldn't tell him that the gun belonged to Cat and that she'd stolen it from Cat's van. She couldn't tell him that, once again, she had given herself to a miserable man who had sucked the will to live right out of her. If he knew what she was planning to do, he'd take the gun away, but not before asking her what was wrong and how he could help her fix it. She wondered why she just didn't stop this foolishness and go inside and ask him for help. But she couldn't.

She thought about the gun. When Cat returned from her life-threatening ordeal in Italy, she'd been a wreck. Cassie had been surprised that she'd been able to purchase a gun after what had happened to her. But she had obtained her concealed weapons license and spent hours at the practice range. She'd told Cassie she didn't feel safe anymore, particularly when she was leaving an event in the wee hours of the morning.

After seeing the gun in the glovebox at Tidal Bay, Cassie took a chance that it was still there. Earlier, when she knew Cat was on her morning walk, she stopped by the house and stole the gun. She wondered if Cat had discovered the gun was missing. Probably not. It didn't matter anyway. It was too late for anybody to stop her.

She was on her way to Jim's house. Still, she sat on the bench in front of the sheriff's office. In her heart was a wistful hope that maybe Sheriff Blackwell was there and would look out the window and stop her. But the door didn't open.

It was time to make a decision. She had sorted and resorted the evil thoughts hanging like an albatross around her neck. She had three choices: suicide, murder, or both.

Once the plan was in motion, there'd be no turning back.

41

My mother's tea set comes out when there's a need for comfort or when my brain is freeze-dried and needs to be steamed open. The spicy aromas of cardamon, cinnamon, ginger, star anise, and black pepper bob on the breeze as I place the tray on the teak table by the swing bed. The big screened porch facing deep water is my sanctuary—my place to think things through with a strong cup of Chai.

Today, I turn to the first page of a new notebook. While I would love to hang up a giant evidence board as all the best detective novels and TV shows use, this will have to suffice. The quote on the front cover is appropriate: *Sure, Let Me Drop Everything and Work on YOUR Problem.* My hand rests on the page as I consider my assignment from Lorenzo. He said the FBI requested it. It seems I'm one of the few people who has met most of the potential suspects or people of interest. My assignment is to describe everyone I've interacted with since my first visit to the plantation.

I open the notebook to the first blank page. I lift the pen and write in bold, capitalized letters NICK CAFARO, aka Richard Alistair Davenport. The pen of its own volition traces the letters while I pull images of what I know about him from thin air. How long have I known Nick?

Sinking back against the cushions, I recall the snaggle-toothed boy who entered our third-grade classroom. When was that? Twenty years ago? Oh gosh, no! This fall, it will be twenty years since we graduated from high school. It's closer to thirty years. How can that be?

A couple of months ago, I received the high school reunion invitation. It took me back to those glorious, carefree days when Stella was still alive, and the world looked bright with possibilities. Knowing Stella would never be able to attend a high school reunion made my answer to the invitation a big NO!

Even if I momentarily thought I might want to go, I can't. It's on the same weekend as the Andrea Bocelli concert—the one Stella and I had planned to attend for our birthday celebration. Now I will go to the concert alone. It will be my last pilgrimage to honor her life. Nothing will stop me from going. It's the only reunion I plan on attending.

Thirty years ago, Nick transferred from out of state to Patrick Henry Elementary School in Richmond, Virginia, and we became good buddies.

My pen hovers. No words come as I realize how very little I know about him and zero about his family. If Stella were here, she'd fill in the blanks. She had a knack for ferreting out the current gossip about people. Closing my eyes, I visualize Nick as a boy. Little by little, I add words to the list.

NICK CAFARO, aka Richard Alister Davenport
high school quarterback, played basketball and baseball
dated Stella - three months before she dumped him
not the best student
good-looking in a macho kind of way
popular with girls
family background?
former close friends?
current friends?
football scholarship to Clemson but transferred and graduated from the University of South Carolina - Why?
attended Columbia Law School — how?
attended FBI academy—how?
FBI undercover agent? Is this true? How did that happen?
Connection to State Senator James Middleton Madison?

Connection to George?

Connection to Al?

Connection to the girl in the truck?

Married: no—according to records.

After adding a physical description, I search the internet but find nothing new.

The next name I write in bold letters is

COUNT ALFONSO FERNANDO FELIPE FRAN-CISCO PEREZ from Madrid, Spain aka Al

his royal credentials check out from my earlier sleuthing

Divorced from Margarita

No children

Is he sincere about his save-the-world Moringa Project?

Is he a scammer? A liar?

Is he connected to the senator or, even worse, to Nick? Or George?

Does he have Lowcountry connections?

After that, the names tumble out. Next is James Middleton Madison. I already have his information from my previous research. I highlight the no-fault divorce and put a question mark by his ex-wife and children living in Switzerland.

Alice is next on the list. When I write her name on the page I remember A. Aldridge Properties. I make a notation for the FBI to research Alice's full name. It's a long shot, but Lorenzo asked me to put down anything I considered unusual. A. Aldridge makes me think about JMM Properties. I gasp at the possibility that JMM could be James Middleton Madison. If that's the case, there's a possibility that either Alice or Jim own Carrington Point, or maybe it's in both their names. I backtrack to the page with the senator's name and add JMM Properties.

George is identified as Al's driver and the senator's henchman. I note he was recommended to Al by the senator and highlight my thoughts about his eavesdropping on conversations and the possibility he is reporting all his findings to the senator. I clarify this is all conjecture. I add that I don't have a last name for him and indicate he appears to be armed. As I scribble down my thoughts, I wonder if any of them will be of interest to the FBI.

The Berkleys are added to the list: Margaret and Mary Elizabeth, but they are certainly not involved. I make that clear in my notes.

Next is the girl with the blonde curls—the one in the truck. I hadn't planned on adding her, but something was off about her being in that truck. If the vehicle is registered to JMM and if JMM is the senator, then that means he's connected in some way. In retrospect, I believe the girl's tears were from fear of something or someone. Could that possibly be Nick or maybe even Jim? Was it a coincidence that she was in a truck parked close to the Foxy? I pause in my scribbling and wish I had done more for that young woman.

The dreaded moment arrives when I consider Cassie's name for the list. If she's still involved with the senator, then her name has to go on the list. My hand doesn't move to add it. She's my dearest friend. How can I betray her? Yet, I know her relationship with the senator puts her in a tough spot—one I can't ignore. My fear is he's brainwashed her, or at least he's controlling her and using her for his own purposes. If there's any chance of saving her, I need to add her name. For me, this is betrayal of the worst kind. She might never forgive me. But I'd do anything for her, even if it means losing her friendship. Her name goes on the list.

Turning to a blank page, I write Lorenzo's name at the top—not because he's a suspect but because—I stop and chastise myself for acting like a teenager. My pen curves around the "L" in his name. Steve Terrell's soft musical notes drift from my playlist: *I'll be seeing you in all the old familiar places—that this heart of mine embraces—all day through.*

Lorenzo's sad smile, his eyes full of light, and his magical touch all crowd into my thoughts. A longing so strong leaves me breathless, the cup of tea abandoned, and the list of names forgotten.

42

Nick slammed his mobile on the desk. The insistent texts continued—one after the other.

Where's the girl? You promised her yesterday.

I want her now.

Don't mess with me, boy!

Nick had run out of excuses. The last text was clear.

Don't force me to call the FEDS! You'll lose this time. Prison won't be to your liking.

Nick was heavily embroiled in this trafficking ring. *The boss,* which the senator had insisted on being called when they'd first met, was the driving force behind the illegal operation. At first, Nick believed in the program. It had been described as a way to help street girls come clean, find jobs, return to school, or be placed in foster homes. He'd been a little confused about some of the processes, particularly when the senator said the girls would be warehoused at Carrington Point. He'd called it a halfway house where the girls would have a chance to rest and be treated for any illnesses. They'd be given some decent clothes and a process would be put in place to determine their needs before they were placed. Nick had wondered, but he hadn't questioned the senator. Why would he?

Nick's job was to be responsible for the security of the entire plantation which included making sure no one trespassed on the property. It provided a place for him live, and he'd been happy to fix up a room in the old house. He'd done all of the work himself, including the electrical and plumbing jobs. The senator said this was a secret mission that only the FBI was aware of. It had to be kept that way as they couldn't afford to have trafficking gangs learn their location. Initially, that had made sense.

Nick's other responsibilities included counting heads when the vans arrived, keeping Marissa, the matron at the warehouses, informed about deliveries, and finally sending the senator statistics on headcount, approximate ages, and a summary of the overall condition of each girl. He was told all this information was needed for funding reasons. He now knew that was a lie. The senator had requested the stats so he could pick and choose the best for his sordid, illicit activities.

Nick knew he was lucky to be working at all, much less receiving a paycheck, and it was a generous one. Slowly, over time, he realized the girls were not part of a rescue operation. Instead, the ones that were controllable, decent looking, very young, and not deep into addiction were being groomed for sex and drug trafficking. The others were being churned into street prostitutes and dealers.

Nick had approached the senator with his findings. He was sure the senator couldn't possibly know what was happening. Jim had laughed in his face and said, "What'd you think? You're not stupid enough to believe that I'm some kind of saint? And look, any merchandise I don't like or turn back in, you're welcome to try out."

Nick had been revolted. But after being blacklisted by the FBI, he knew he'd never find another job. He ignored his better nature—the one he used to have. He told himself the girls were losers anyway and sooner or later would wind up dead. Maybe what he was doing gave them a chance. Of course, he was lying to himself. Then he did the unpardonable. He quit viewing them as humans. That had worked until the last batch when the girl had kicked him. She'd been fierce and courageous. She'd fought to protect her sister. He wished he'd fought to save his brother, but he hadn't.

When George told him the young girl was for the senator, Nick knew he could no longer tolerate the senator or the situation. He also knew he was signing his own death sentence if he went against the senator and reported their activities. He had to do something. But what?

It had been a spur-of-the-moment plan to take the girl into town—the one who had kicked him. He thought for sure she'd flag someone down, and it would all be over. It turned out he had frightened her into submission with threats on her sister's life. He had a dark, ugly side. It had emerged after his brother's death. No one meant anything to him. He had no future.

Yet, he couldn't get away from the image of the big flop of blonde curls spilling over her face, her entire being trembling but docile. Begging him not to hurt her little sister. When he'd told her that her sister would soon be sold into sexual slavery, she'd lashed out. Her small fists had pounded him. Her wails rattled through the truck like a dying animal. To silence her, he'd backhanded her. That had made him feel worse—small and mean.

Then she did the cruelest thing. She told him her name—Diana. She begged him to let her and her sister Stephanie go. When he hadn't responded, she'd said she'd do whatever he desired if he would release her little sister. She had sobbed over and over, "She's only fourteen—please don't hurt her."

Never had he known a single one of their names. That had made the difference. Diana had awakened something deep inside of him. He hadn't been able to put the girl out of his mind. Both were so young, so innocent—just like his brother had been. Carrying the guilt of his brother's death was already too much. He couldn't add anyone else to the burden he was already saddled with.

George would soon be picking up the youngest girl for the senator. Something old and primitive struggled in his gut when he thought about George. They had been adversaries from their first meeting.

It was George who told him that the senator was demanding younger and younger girls. They had argued. Nick said the purpose of the senator's mission was to save young girls from sex trafficking, not enslave them. George mumbled it was the senator's call, not theirs. The senator had overruled Nick and sent George in search of the kind of girls the senator wanted.

Nick knew when George opened the back of the van that those two girls were not the norm. Although their disheveled appearances and smells were the same, their hair, make-up and clothes were not. They didn't fit the mold of druggie, prostitute, or runaway.

He should have sent them packing immediately. But after the girl kicked him, he reacted out of spite. He'd wanted her to be sorry. He'd wanted her to pay. But that was his own stupid ego. That was why he was on the wrong side of the law. His ego, his idealism, his narrow view of what had happened all those years ago to his brother. And now, Cat was involved. Was her life to be sacrificed too?

Or, was this his moment to do something right—to save lives and to honor his brother?

43

Diana listened to the night sounds inside the warehouse—light snores and shifting bodies. A nightlight had replaced the small lamp on the table by the door. Shadows drifted and flickered—long, dark shapes weaving among the cots. The tears held back for so long flowed. As quickly as they appeared, they stopped—replaced by the image of Stephanie's small, trusting face.

Diana gritted her teeth and then inched her way across the cot until her hand touched the wall. She arched her back as far as the cuff would allow. Her fingers traced the edge of the plywood. She felt for the shard of pottery and tiny pliers she had tucked between the thin piece of plywood on the frame and the battered mattress.

During the last three evenings, she'd loosened four nails. Last night, when she'd pulled on the board, it had given. There was a slim chance that one or two strong jerks might rip it far enough away from the window for her to jump through. But then what? She was cuffed to the bed. Even if she weren't, the noise would wake up the other girls. Would they scream and make enough noise to alert the guards? Or would they stay silent? It was a risk she had to take. The only thing stopping her was the cuff.

She was sure Stephanie had been removed from the warehouse. There had been no movement behind those closed doors for several days. Only a few girls were left in the holding room. Most were suffering from withdrawals. The odds weren't in their favor. They would probably be discarded in the river or on a dark country road. She hoped the girl, Hannah, had escaped her captors, but she knew hope was not realistic. Soon, the man would be returning for her. If she were still here, her life would be over.

Last night, she'd tried to loosen the cuff with the pliers but realized it was impossible. Tonight, she tackled the links chaining the cuff to the bed. One weak link was all she needed.

Her hand shook from the effort. Every missed thrust of the pliers sent rivulets of blood cascading down her wrist. She wasn't deterred. When the pliers did grab the right place, and she was able to apply the right amount of pressure, the tiny opening in the link widened a millimeter. Finally, the link pulled away enough for her to separate the chain from the cuff. She trembled with her new found freedom until she remembered that although she was no longer shackled, she was not truly free. Her journey was just beginning.

The task had taken hours. The first glimmer of dawn peeked through the cracks around the plywood. Darkness was her only protection. She needed to go. She checked to see if the other girls were asleep, then she slid across the cot and raised up on her knees. Then, with all her strength, she lunged at the plywood. The screech of wood ripping from the window frame sounded like a barrage of bullets from early morning training on Parris Island. She kept jerking and tugging until part of the board ripped away.

She hurled her body through the window with arms wrapped around her head. The shattered glass tore at her skin. She landed with a thud and a loud crack. Even before she touched the large knot swelling just below her elbow, she knew her arm was broken. With her undamaged arm, she pushed up from the ground and, in a low crouching position, stumbled through the bramble and low-lying shrubs.

Angry shouts and pounding boots slammed through the door. She ran. Bullets whizzed by her head and thudded into trees. She tore through the heavy underbrush. She didn't stop running until the slimy pluff mud squished between her toes. She hesitated, taking stock of the blood oozing from multiple glass cuts. Her limp arm dangled uselessly by her side.

Every part of her body screamed surrender as she turned and faced the marsh and the river beyond. She quieted her mind with images of Stephanie. She wouldn't surrender. She was a survivor.

She heard the fast-flowing current as her eyes strained to see the river in the blackness of early morning. She shuddered, wondering what kind of creatures were lurking, ready to attack her tattered body. But it really didn't matter. She was willing to take her chances with any of the wild creatures. She was sure they weren't as dangerous as the humans she was fleeing.

The waning moon tipped-toed across the river before slinking behind low-lying clouds. Streaks of light played along the flat gray horizon. The surrounding woods were alive with yells and thundering footsteps headed in her direction. She waded out further and plunged into the river. She wasn't much for praying, but she offered some words into the blackness that somehow the current would carry her to freedom. She surfaced and floundered until she could get her one good arm moving toward the lights of what she hoped was a marina and someone to help. Her body shook from the cold water, the shock of what she'd done, and the impossibility of her situation. She repeated the phone number of the caterer over and over as she looked at the stars and wished with all her might that she'd be in time to rescue Stephanie.

44

Sheriff Blackwell scratched his head, leaned back in his chair and glanced out the window again. Cassandra Burton had been glued to the bench, the one by the war memorial, for a good half hour. He vacillated between getting some work done and checking on her. Why was she out there? Was she upset or maybe frightened? He couldn't see her face. She was sloughed over, and every once in a while, her shoulders shook like she might be crying.

He'd known Cassie since she was a shy little girl of seven. Her father had been stationed at Parris Island and had gotten into a brawl or two. He'd been a fool for not reporting him, but he'd felt sorry for the young Marine. Instead of reporting him, he had hauled his ass back to the base a few times. The family had stayed on after his discharge, but the father had never been able to keep a job—lots of anger issues. Sheriff Blackwell and his wife Annabelle had befriended Cassie early on. Since his girls were infants, it had been easy for them to invite Cassie around to play with their girls. As she became older and more responsible, she was their regular babysitter. They'd included her in their circle of love for years.

He remembered when that nasty Hamilton boy got her pregnant and ran off. That was bad enough, but to have her family abandon her was just pure meanness. He'd made it his business to keep an eye on her. She didn't have anyone else. He hadn't let on that he was helping her out. She was fiercely independent and would have rejected any of his offers.

But without her knowing, he'd made sure she got the job at the law firm along with the apartment. He convinced them to let her bring the baby to work. He'd created an anonymous scholarship for her education. He'd backed her because he knew how tough life could be. He also suspected and had been proven right that she had a lot of fortitude and would make her way. She had. He'd been as proud of her as if she were his own.

When Cassie was pregnant, he and his wife Annabelle kept her in their sights without trespassing on her privacy. She had stopped by less often as she felt she was a bad example for their little girls. He was glad about having girls. They drove him crazy, but his love for them and his fierce need to protect them was what he lived for. The miracle was they loved him back. They'd always be his girls. One married, one in college, and the youngest Lindsay, a real handful, in her last year of high school.

He looked out the window again. Cassie had moved into the circle. The one with all the flags and little plaques about the early settlements. For a minute, he thought about the parade of Europeans who'd come to this area—the French and Spanish in the 1500s, the Scottish in the 1600s, and, of course, the British. They took the credit for settling the area in the 1700s and stayed the longest—until the Revolutionary War was over. But his favorite flag in the circle was the American Colonial from 1776. This flag spoke of freedom and equality, although in today's angry society, it wasn't working out quite the way the Founding Fathers had imagined.

He turned back to the stack of papers on his desk. The one on top was another Amber Alert. Two sisters in the upstate. He perused the information: 17 and 14—that was another heartbreak of this job. These young girls, so bright and innocent, plunged into darkness and despair. He glanced at their photos and saw a barrette in the older girl's hair. For a brief moment, he wondered if this was the first girl they'd pulled out of the water just a couple of weeks ago. The hair clip looked the same. But since these two young'uns were upstate, they had probably already been spirited over the state line into North Carolina.

He also needed to wrap up his report on the young girl whose body had washed up at the marina a few nights ago—the second one this month. He needed to seriously consider if there was a connection between the two. The first girl hadn't been identified, which broke his heart. It meant no one was looking for her. Now, his head was spinning from the second girl washing up at the marina less than forty-eight hours ago.

That night his sleep had been restless. He'd been thinking about the surge of crime in his small town when the call came in the wee hours —another dead girl had washed up at the marina.

"Yeah, I'm sure," Sergeant Barrett had said when he'd questioned him about the body. But he'd learned never to leave these things to chance. The sheriff didn't care that the sergeant had grumbled when he'd instructed him to call the coroner and the ambulance. One thing he'd never do is declare a person dead without medical personnel.

Annabelle had rolled her eyes and given him a sleepy smile when he whispered he didn't know when he'd be back. She was used to his late hours and erratic schedule. She'd snuggled under the duvet as he pulled on a pair of socks and put his boots on.

He didn't activate the siren or go over the speed limit to the marina. There wasn't any point since the girl was dead. Man, he was tired. He hoped they'd at least pulled her out of the water.

The young girl's body was bruised and broken. Cuts everywhere and one wrist with deep gashes. One arm was limp with a large knot that appeared to be a broken bone. At first, he wondered if she'd tried to kill herself by slitting her wrists and, failing that, attempted suicide by drowning. Then he saw the handcuff and broken chain.

"What the hell?" Spewed from his lips. It looked like she'd attempted to cut off the cuff but hadn't been successful. It was still attached, but he saw she'd been smart enough to pry open one of the links. He examined her wrist and saw where her flesh was picked and torn from some crude instrument.

Poor child. She must have gone through hell to get free. He knelt beside her to do one last official check before she was pronounced dead. Tears backed up in his eyes. He thought of his own daughters and squeezed her small, limp hand.

A tiny twitch in her body had him yelling to start CPR. A few seconds later, there was a faint pulse. He bellowed at his team to alert the ambulance to put some speed on. He didn't stop bellowing until she was wrapped in a blanket and sputtering.

As the oxygen mask was placed over her nose and mouth, the girl opened her eyes and thrashed about wildly. The EMTs quickly strapped her in, but Sheriff Blackwell saw she was trying to say something. When he got close, it sounded like a bunch of garbled numbers. He didn't waste time trying to find out what she was saying. Instead, he slammed the door and hit the side of the van so hard it vibrated. He had to save her. With sirens at full tilt, the ambulance jumped the curbing and disappeared. He was right behind, with sirens blaring and lights flashing.

45

After they'd patched her up and declared her alive with hypothermia, they let him in the room. She also had an arm broken in two places and some cuts that required a few stitches. Heck, he'd been as shocked as anybody when she wheezed out that she had an aunt in town, some caterer with the unlikely name of Cat. It was her aunt's phone number she'd been trying to tell him. He knew who she was talking about but only because he knew Cassie worked for a caterer named Cat. He figured Cat was the name the kid called her aunt. It made sense the girl wanted to contact a relative. But why not her mother? It was a bit strange when she kept repeating the number over and over but couldn't say anything else. The doctor said she was in shock and that she must have memorized that particular number. He said it would have been the last thing on her mind when she hit the icy water.

He'd waited to make the call until after 6 am. He hadn't wanted to leave the girl until he was sure she was going to survive. She told him her name was Diana and asked him to call her aunt. Then she'd closed her eyes. He'd walked into the hallway to place the call. The voice answering had been awake and alert. He guessed a caterer was up all hours cooking for those fancy events.

He asked the woman, who identified herself as Cat, to come to the hospital. He mentioned her niece had been admitted. She'd hesitated as if she didn't understand. Then, after a deep breath, she said she was on her way.

Twenty minutes later, a lovely but wild-eyed redhead had

arrived. She said her name was Cat Gabbiano. She insisted on seeing the girl. She'd leaned over the bed and cradled the girl in her arms. Tears poured down her cheeks as she muttered, "Oh God, I knew something was wrong, and I didn't help her."

The head nurse had barged in and demanded she leave, but Sheriff Blackwell said she was a relative and had his permission to stay. Although he wasn't sure about the relative part—something didn't add up. However, her concern for the girl was real and that's what mattered.

Eventually, they'd been shooed from the girl's room so more heated blankets could be brought in, meds given, and the oxygen adjusted. He and Cat had moved to those impossibly uncomfortable plastic chairs in the cold, sterile waiting room. That's when he'd challenged Cat about being the girl's aunt. She was right up front and said no, she wasn't, but it was her fault the girl was in the hospital. Her story unfolded as unlikely as his winning the lottery. But he believed her. She didn't hold back.

He was shocked that this dynamic woman was involved in the middle of a mess that he knew nothing about. It made no sense that she had answers to questions he didn't know he should be asking. From their conversation, he discovered there was a drug and human trafficking operation right in his own backyard. It seemed Cat had a lot more information than he did.

Now Diana, this fragile banged-up girl, bound them together. Their mission was twofold—find out all they could about this young girl and discover who was behind this miserable, evil operation. And then to put the culprits behind bars for a very long time.

He'd been more than surprised to hear the words FBI operative come out of Cat's mouth, but that was nothing compared to her connection to the Guardia di Finanza in Italy. Who was this Cat person? How come she knew more than he did about drugs and young girls sold into sexual slavery?

He looked at the bulletin again before dropping it in the to-be-posted box. He picked up the next notification and begin to peruse it. Then, he stopped mid-sentence as it dawned on him he recognized the girl with the hair clip.

"Damn!" He needed to get back to the hospital.

He glanced out the window again. Cassie was still there. He pushed back from his desk. He needed to get to the hospital but he needed to talk to Cassie before he left—make sure she was okay.

The ping of his private email turned his attention back to work. He saw the red flag alert and watched as an FBI logo printed out. Some bad things were happening in his town. He wasn't happy. He was sick of the gangs, the pushers, the hustlers—evil, greedy sons of bitches. But to have the FBI invade his territory was something that had never happened before. He was angry, frustrated, and concerned. But he needed to get back to the hospital and he needed to talk to Cassie. He had to make sure she was okay before he plunged into this next craziness.

He pulled out his handkerchief and mopped his forehead. Because of Cat, he was involved in something far bigger than he and his staff had ever handled before. He had no choice but to plow ahead. He couldn't let these despicable people harm more of these young girls. He leaned forward and glanced at the photograph of his own daughters. He felt the intense pain of losing one of them to this kind of scrum.

He reached for his reading glasses and skimmed through the attachment the FBI had sent. It contained a list of people and their possible involvement in the operation. He skimmed the list until his eyes landed on Cassie's name. He bolted out of the chair, coffee and paper flying across the desk.

The glass in the door shuddered as he slammed it open, but Cassie was gone. His stomach clinched. That girl was in a heap of trouble. Why hadn't he checked on her earlier? A few minutes of his time, that's all she needed. Someone to sit by her side so she'd know she wasn't alone. He needed to find her before the wrong people did. His anger motivated him to place the call to Sergeant Barrett.

He yelled into the phone, "Put out an all-points bulletin for Cassandra Burton. I'm sending you a photo now."

46

So much has happened in the past few days. I get dizzy thinking about it. The list of special interest people I compiled and passed on to Lorenzo was given to the FBI.

I'd no sooner completed and handed off my list to Lorenzo when Sheriff Blackwell called. He said my niece Diana was in the hospital. Of course, I dropped everything and raced to the hospital to discover my so-called niece was the young blonde woman who had been in the black truck—that day I met Nick at the Foxy.

I had to explain all of this to Lorenzo, who wasn't happy with me because he had to enlighten the FBI that, once again, I had stuck my nose where it didn't belong. Since Sheriff Blackwell discovered Diana and I disclosed the possible ties to the trafficking ring, the FBI has reluctantly agreed for local law enforcement to be involved.

By now, Sheriff Blackwell has received a copy of my list. I can only imagine how upset he's going to be when he sees Cassie's name. She'd had mentioned her friendship with him more than a few times and often talked about how much he'd helped her out. But she'd never shared exactly why or how.

When I was at the hospital with Sheriff Blackwell, I learned a lot more about how strong their friendship is. Now that I've seen how protective he is of Diana, I can imagine he's the same way with Cassie.

Within twenty-four hours, Diana regained some of her strength. Once she was aware of her circumstances, the sheriff and I suggested she call her mother. At first, the teenager refused. Her guilt and shame were so great she feared her mother couldn't forgive her. We showed her the bulletin with the information her mother had provided the police. But, it took a lot of talking to convince her that no matter what had happened, her mother would still love her. While it was heartbreaking Stephanie was missing, her mom deserved to know that at least one of her daughters was safe.

She finally relented. It had been hard to watch the reunion of Diana and her mother. Their sobs were heart-wrenching. While the odds of finding Stephanie are slim, Sheriff Blackwell and I created as much hope as we could. While we didn't spare them the seriousness of the situation, we told them the FBI was in charge. If anyone could locate Stephanie, it would be them.

A few days ago, Diana was released from the hospital. The FBI moved her and her mother to a safe house. They are now under round-the-clock protection. Our greatest fear is that the traffickers will discover Diana is alive and willing to testify against them. If they do, they'll come after her.

The sheriff somehow got the local newspaper to run a story about a young girl washed up at the marina without admitting the girl is alive. The FBI hopes the coverage will cause the traffickers to believe she's dead.

Diana provided the FBI with valuable information about the place she was held prisoner and the people who were involved. Although she didn't know where she was, she told them about hearing the military artillery. They also were able to estimate of how long she was in the river.

It's darn good to know Sheriff Blackwell is involved. When we met at the hospital, I told him about my connection to the FBI and the Guardia di Finanza. He still shakes his head in disbelief whenever he sees me.

Later today, the sheriff, Al, and I are Zooming with Lorenzo. He said it isn't normal to have civilians engaged in law enforcement investigations, so this would be an exception. He admonished me to keep my nose on my face and out of other people's business. He's even more irritated that Al is involved.

Lorenzo said an FBI agent would be on the Zoom call, but his video would be off, as we are not allowed to see him. He said the call was only to pick our brains, and he emphasized we are not allowed to ask questions.

So far, there are no clues involving Carrington Point Plantation. Al and I want to rectify that. We've agreed that during our interview with the FBI, we will disclose the suspicious activities out there. Not only is the plantation close to the water and Parris Island, but it's also fairly close to the marina. That property is worth examining from one end to the other. Of course, no one is particularly interested in what Al and I think.

I push back from my desk and stand for a stretch. The saddest and scariest part of the entire operation is that Cassie is mixed up in this mess because of Jim. We've been together often in the past few weeks in the throes of marathon planning and cooking for upcoming events, but not a word has left Cass's lips. The worst part is she didn't trust me enough to tell me that she and Jim had reconnected after their initial breakup. Of course, now I understand her reaction at Tidal Bay. She was devastated when he trashed her in front of the guests. I learned from Sam that the reception was supposed to have been the time and the place where Jim publicly acknowledged her. Instead, he abandoned her. He did the one thing that could send her over the edge.

The last thing she'd said to me was she wouldn't be my partner because she was leaving town and she didn't know if she'd ever come back. She refused to say why. But she had that haunted look—a look I know well—a look that means she's desperate and not in a healthy state of mind. I haven't seen her in a few days. She doesn't answer my calls or texts. When I've stopped by, she's never home. My gut is telling me she's in big trouble.

Through the large expanse of windows in the kitchen, the burnished marsh grass and the swift current of the river steal through the window and creep into my heart. It creates this intensity of movement. It calls me to join the flow—become part of the joyful surge of life. But knowing Cassie is in trouble dims my eyes to its beauty.

As I watch waves rippling toward the ocean, a sudden thought comes to mind. I shriek as my heart clutches with fear. I race to the kitchen. Dumping everything out of my purse, I scatter the contents on the counter until I find the keys to the van. Holding my breath all the way, I sprint. My knuckles hit the door handle with a whack, but I ignore the pain. I jerk open the glove compartment and shuffle through the papers. There's no gun. It's gone, and Cassie is the only person who knew it was there.

47

Nick tried to reach the senator all day. At their previous meeting, they talked about pulling out of Carrington Point Plantation—maybe moving further south. That was before George told the senator that Nick had been meeting with Cat, had allowed outsiders on the premises, and had told a Spanish count that he owned the plantation. George had been eager to let the senator know.

Yesterday, the senator had texted Nick and said they were not moving, and George would be more involved in the daily operations. The problem was local. Those obstructing the operation would be eliminated.

Nick was shocked until he thought about George's movements over the past few weeks. The thug had been charting this course from the beginning. He'd filled the senator's head with false promises while stroking his ego, feeding his greed, and squeezing Nick out of the picture. Eliminating the obstructions meant killing Cat and Al.

That's when the question popped into his mind as to why the senator would hire a thug like George. Everything about him—his muscle-bound body, the smirk on his face, the shaved head, and the tattoos creeping out of his shirt collar and along his arms—all screamed thug or, even worse, a mafia type. From previous experience, Nick knew George was a hired killer. He feared the senator wasn't aware that he had gotten involved in something far bigger and more dangerous than he understood.

Nick had no recourse other than to extricate himself from this nightmare. The pleading eyes and terrified screams of those two girls haunted him. Maybe he couldn't save himself, but he sure as hell could save those two girls and any others that were still in the warehouses. And he could save Cat and Al. They were simply bystanders in this debacle.

Nick adjusted the flame in the fireplace. The weather had turned cool during the night. Leaves swirled across the porch. Even if the work was dirty, he'd enjoyed living in the old house.

He rested his head in his hands and, not for the first time, wondered how he had strayed so far from justice and morality. The oath of office he had sworn to as a federal employee had been forgotten when his brother was murdered. His world had collapsed.

The flames flickered in the fireplace as he realized the senator had been grooming him for years. How else could he have gotten into Columbia Law School or the FBI Academy? Now he understood that the senator had sponsored him at law school and championed his admission to the FBI academy. If the senator hadn't intervened, Nick would have never graduated from college. He would have been fired from the FBI instead of being allowed to resign.

It was the good senator who had enough pull to get his records sealed and enough money to send him to a private rehab clinic until he dried out. When no one would hire him, the senator came to his rescue once again. He had created a job for Nick and paid him well in cash to perform miscellaneous tasks—errands just shy of being shady. Nick had been too lost in his own grief to question what he was asked to do. Then, the mercy project came along and changed everything.

Rescuing girls from drugs and prostitution and placing them in caring homes seemed like a worthy penance. He had been excited and enthusiastic—something he hadn't felt in years. He was eager to be part of the program. As far as he knew, all the kids had been placed in safe environments.

Nick believed he had been given another chance to redeem himself and to pay back his indebtedness to the senator and society. His brain had been too muddled to understand that the operation was just a front for the human trafficking and drug smuggling business.

Fortunately or unfortunately, it was his dislike of George that had forced him to examine what was really going on. He'd watched in horror through his binoculars when George had almost bashed Cat's head in with a hammer. Even after all these years, he'd recognized those red curls. By contacting her, he thought he could keep her safe from danger. That had backfired, and he had gotten her in deeper and now Al was in the mix. The entire operation was in shambles. He needed to get out.

He saw himself through Cat's shocked eyes when he'd threatened her. She had the same look his brother had given him moments before the bullet had entered his head. It was as if he'd killed his brother with his own hands. Was that going to be the end result for Cat? He was running out of time. He simply couldn't let her, Al or one more of these young girls be tossed away. It was time to confront the senator. He pushed up from the sofa, opened the desk drawer, and picked up his gun.

48

C assie drove around and around without a single thought in her head. Her brain was numb—nonfunctioning. Her thoughts were groggy. They darted in and out without offering anything cohesive she could focus on. She pulled off the road to get her bearings and realized she was close to Jim's house, or she supposed she should say his mansion. She didn't know as he'd never invited her to his place. That was another obvious clue anyone else would have seen. Everything about his life was a secret.

Of course, she'd asked him where he lived and suggested he invite her over. He always put her off with some excuse. After they'd reconnected the second time, curiosity got the better of her and she'd followed him. She only wanted a glimpse of his lifestyle, the one she hoped would be hers one day. She suspected that his driver, a creepy guy named George, was some kind of bodyguard, so she kept a good distance behind the limo.

The area was posh, from its elegant stone entrance to the lush landscape trailing to the water's edge. The acreage for each home offered complete privacy. The limo had turned in a driveway with large brass eagles on each side of the stucco archway. On that sunny day, she'd been full of excitement at the prospect of where she'd live in the future—her new life as a senator's wife. She dismissed Cat's concerns about the senator's behavior and had felt disappointed when her best friend didn't support her.

Today, as her car idled across the road from what was clearly a mansion, the clouds hung low and heavy like massive cotton fields. She put the car in gear and drove by the house. Instead of stopping, she continued to the high ridge behind the property. She pulled onto what looked like an old hunting trail in a wooded area. Taking the gun out of her purse, she slipped it into the waistband of her jeans. She left the car and walked back to the road to ensure her car couldn't be seen. Then she slipped into the woods. Slowly and with great caution, she tread through the underbrush. She stopped at the steep incline leading to the senator's house.

The senator's black limo was parked near the pool. At least he's here, she thought although she wasn't sure what she was going to say or do. Maybe she'd know after she confronted him. She grimaced as she considered how easy it would be to point the gun and pull the trigger. Could she really do that? Was she angry enough to murder him? Was she willing to pay the price? Would she end her own life as well? If only she'd listened to Cat.

Nick rounded the bend to the senator's house but kept driving after he saw a black limo in the driveway. He was sure it was George, and he wasn't about to tangle with him. Nick continued driving until he found a spot above the senator's compound. He pulled off the road, pulled his binoculars out of the glovebox and walked to the edge of the slope.

He swept the binoculars over the wooded area and spotted a car pulled off the road. When he didn't see any movement in the car or the woods, he refocused on the majestic house standing below the wood line. His gaze continued to the limo. It was empty.

Nick leaned against his car and waited. Birds squawking in the trees caught his attention. Nick swung his binoculars in place and noticed a slight movement in the trees. A dark-haired woman was creeping through the woods. He figured she belonged to the car he'd seen parked in the woods. He didn't recognize her, and wondered what she was up to. While he was relieved it wasn't Cat, he still had to figure out what she was up to. She could easily botch whatever chance he had of catching the senator alone.

George stood in the doorway to the senator's office. He'd knocked just once and stupidly barged in without asking permission. His eyes swept the room and its occupants. At first, he thought he'd walked into a family squabble. The senator's face was red and bloated. Alice was crying.

He was standing behind his desk. His hairy, barreled chest was exposed as his robe slid halfway down his arms. Alice, kneeling in front of him, told George this was way more than a squabble. Even he was revolted.

It only took a second before the characters in the bizarre scene sprung into action. Alice shrieked and jumped up. She tried but didn't succeed in covering her naked body under the gauzy gown that had slipped off her shoulders and hovered around her waist. The senator bared his teeth and screamed, "Get the hell out of here. Get off this property, and don't show your nasty face around here ever again."

George backed out of the door and closed it with a slam. He didn't leave. He waited. He knew the senator would regain his composure and regret his words. George knew too much. He had no qualms about using what he knew to blackmail the senator.

Only a few minutes went by before the door opened, and a fully dressed senator stepped into the sunroom where George was waiting. They stood facing each other, neither willing to break the silence.

"Sorry for the intrusion. I only came to tell you the girl is ready whenever you want her."

"You scumbag! Don't you ever come into my house again without an invitation from me. Ya hear?"

George looked squarely at the senator and said, "Either you want the girl or you don't. I have no interest in anything else you do. I have her stashed close by. I can get her now, or I can take her back to the warehouse. We're moving the rest of them out tonight. There's been a breach. One of the girls broke out. It appears she didn't survive, but it's time we get rid of them. We need to vacate the premises for a while—at least a couple of months, thanks to your pal Nick. If you don't want the girl, that's fine with me. I can easily move her out with the others. I'm dropping them off in Anderson or anywhere you say. It doesn't matter to me."

The air stirred for only a second as the door to the senator's study opened a whisper. George was sure Alice was listening to the conversation, but he didn't change his expression or acknowledge the slight sound and movement.

"It's going to matter if you cross me. Don't think I haven't been watching you honing in on my operation. You've tried to turn me against Nick. It's easy to see you want him out of the way so you can take control of the operation. But I see right through you. You're nothing but a thug. I've got everything I need to send you to prison, or even better, have you transported back to South Africa where they'll pluck out your eyes before chopping off your balls."

George didn't move, didn't acknowledge anything the senator said to him. He didn't have to. His plan was already in motion. It was just a matter of time.

"You want the girl or not?"

"Of course, I want the girl. Now."

James pushed past George and retreated to the master suite. He didn't want George to see his fear or his excitement. He already knew too much. It was time he got rid of him, but not before he delivered the fourteen-year-old virgin. His blood rushed hot through his veins and pulsated in his groin.

Cassie was halfway down the hill when the back door opened. George walked briskly to the car and opened the door. Alice appeared on the terrace and called his name. He left the door open and walked back to the terrace. When he reached Alice, he put his arms around her. She leaned against him. He pulled away and gripped her shoulders.

Cassie squinted but wasn't sure from this distance if Alice was crying. Her body was shaking, but her face was turned away. They spoke for a few minutes. Then he rushed down the steps and jumped in the car. He backed up and swung onto the circular driveway. He gunned the engine and pulled away with wheels screeching.

Cassie hesitated for a minute, then pulled back into the wood line. She couldn't imagine why George and Alice appeared to be much closer than a chauffeur and client, much less why Alice was nearly naked. She wondered where George was going in such a hurry, although it really didn't matter. Her goal was to confront James. She hoped she could do that without Alice interfering.

She pushed up from the rotten stump she'd been leaning against and dusted off the seat of her jeans. When she reached the edge of the wood line, she stopped and listened. She froze into a low crouch as nearby twigs snapped and broke as if someone was rushing through the bramble.

She waited—not breathing, not moving. During those minutes, frozen in place, Cassie questioned what she was about to do. God, she was almost forty years old, and here she was, squatting in the woods with thoughts of killing another human being. What had possessed her? Cat was right. No one, and particularly no man, was worth ruining her and Sam's lives. She jumped up and raced back to her car. She dropped the gun in her purse and backed out of the woods.

Nick watched as the woman ran back up the hill and drove off. He made his way down the slope without much interest in her purpose. He guessed she'd changed her mind. But as he leaned into a giant oak to assess the back of the house, he saw her car slow down and pull into the circular driveway. Nick pivoted from tree to tree. He stayed in the shadow as waited to see what she'd do next.

He was intrigued by the woman. It was only after George and Alice appeared on the terrace that she had changed her mind and left. Did she see or hear something that sent her around to the front door? Maybe she decided to approach Alice or the senator directly versus sneaking through the back.

Well, he'd have to wait until she left as he didn't want any witnesses to his conversation with the senator.

49

Al and I sit shoulder to shoulder at the kitchen table. It's noon in the Lowcountry. Outside the river lies placid. The humidity hangs heavy without a breeze to lift the veil of overbearing heat. The weather, just like this transatlantic call, makes me sweat. Even Al's pristine elegance languishes from the few minutes he endured walking from the car to the air-conditioned house.

Al clears his throat and reaches for the tall glass of iced tea in front of him.

"Cat?"

"Hmmm?"

"Is it really necessary for us to participate? Can't the local sheriff deal with this? It's my fault all of this is happening. I involved you after I already had suspicions about the place and Nick. Don't you think it's time for us to bow out?"

"Oh Al, I was involved before you approached me to cater your event. We've already gone over this. Let's see what Lorenzo says. I'm pretty sure after he debriefs us, he'll tell us we are no longer needed in the investigation. He wouldn't put either of us in danger, and the FBI is not about to let civilians mess things up."

Al shakes his head and shrugs. Because of the proximity of our bodies, his small movements feel like my own.

The computer comes to life. Lorenzo's dark scowl fills the screen. His eyes meet mine before they flit over to Al. He scrutinizes him as I make the introductions.

"Before Sheriff Blackwell and the FBI join us, here's what I need from you today. You are to provide us with any information you have regarding Carrington Point Plantation. Cat, you've already given us a list of those you've met that might have a connection. Al, sorry to say, but your name is on that list—not because we suspect you of anything, but because your interest in buying the property connects you. We have to check you out. If you or Cat think of other names we might have missed, let us know. Once we've debriefed both of you, I'll ask you to sign off the call. Is that understood? Cat?"

When I don't respond, Al nudges me. I nod.

"Also, the agent's face will not appear on the screen."

I open my mouth before thinking, "But Lorenzo, I need to know who the agent is. What if we need help? How would I recognize whether or not the person at my door is an FBI agent or a mass murderer?"

"Cat, listen to me. You are not going to need help. After this phone conversation, you and Al are sidelined. Stop your sleuthing! Now! That's an order. Al, make sure she stays out of the investigation. Can you do that?"

For the first time since the conversation began, Al laughs and says, "I think you know this woman better than I do. If you have pointers on keeping her out of trouble, I could use them."

Both men laugh. It's not funny, but then they're men. I dismiss them both and say, "What about Diana? As soon as these people discover she's alive, they'll come after her. Can the FBI guarantee her safety? And what about her little sister? Has she been found? No one has given us any information. I imagine Diana and her mother are in agony. Can you tell us anything?"

"Cat, I can tell you exactly what the FBI told Stephanie's mom. They think she's alive. The way these trafficking operations work is first to groom the girls. Usually, the girls they pick up from the streets are already groomed at some level by a boyfriend or relative, which is why they're on the streets in the first place. Diana and Stephanie are the exceptions. We're pretty sure they were picked up by mistake or were targeted. But either way, they are not streetwise and would initially fight any attempts to be groomed.

I nod my head in agreement. "That makes sense."

"Fortunately, this gives us a little extra time to find Stephanie. Diana has given us valuable information about the people she came in contact with—one of her descriptions fits yours of Nick. There's another that vaguely lines up with your description of the chauffeur although she said he was driving a van. The woman she described hasn't surfaced on the data base yet, but I think she will."

"What about the location?"

"She's given us an excellent description. It could be any one of several places up and down the river. We'll check them all out. I know you and Al think it's Carrington Point, but we've been watching the warehouses the last few days, and there's been no movement. It looks like they've been used recently, but they appear to be vacant now. We haven't moved in yet, but expect we'll find some interesting items for forensics. We're waiting on a search warrant, and then we'll go in. Now Cat, all I need from you is a promise that once this Zoom is over, you'll cease your involvement."

I nod with a non-committal toss of my head. It could mean yes or no. Lorenzo sighs and rubs the stubble that's heavy on his face.

"Cat, there's something else I need to tell you so you'll realize how dangerous this really is."

"What do you mean?"

Lorenzo stares at the screen. He shakes his head and then says, "This human trafficking ring is connected to both the Russian and Albanian mafia with ties to the SCU—the one that killed Stella. The Sacra Corona Unita that Carlo Rossini was running."

"How can that be true? This is the United States. Yes, alright. I know the mafia is here too, but surely not the SCU."

I wait for Lorenzo to tell me that it's a mistake. But he doesn't.

Instead, he says, "I didn't tell you because I don't want to alarm you. If we catch these people, it will come out. There's no point in you being blindsided. Based on your recent experience with the mafia, you are fully aware of the implications. You don't have to participate in this Zoom. You've given us a lot of information, and I don't want to put you in further danger."

"No, no. I want to be part of anything that involves Stella's death. I won't be satisfied until all of them are dead or behind bars for life—and not just sentenced to a minimum of ten years like Riccardo."

"*Va bene*, let's get started."

The sheriff and the agent are invited into the Zoom call. Al and I share all the information we have. The only thing new is my information on what I saw inside the plantation house. The agents were still waiting on the search warrant. As the conversation continues, I think about Cassie. Do I tell Lorenzo about the missing gun? And what about the romantic ties between Jim and Cassie? When I added Cassie's name to the list, I only mentioned that she knew the senator. I'm not sure why I think the senator is involved. It's just a gut thing, but if I don't tell Lorenzo, Cassie could be in danger.

I'm still deciding what to do when Lorenzo announces it's time for Al and me to leave the meeting.

"Well, there is one more thing. I'm not sure it's connected. But it might be."

Lorenzo stares at the screen, anticipating that I'm going to drop something he doesn't want to hear. Of course, he's right. I plunge in.

"My handgun is missing. I think Cassie took it. She's the only person besides me with a key to the glove compartment of the van. I'm concerned, given her state of mind, that she might shoot herself or the senator."

Curses explode from Lorenzo. Sheriff Blackwell rises from his seat.

"Damm it, Cat? Why didn't you tell me this earlier?"

"I'm sorry. I didn't want to get Cassie into trouble."

Sheriff Blackwell sputters, "Shucks, Cat. Cassie was just sitting outside my office. Commissario, I'm going to leave and go after that girl. I've already put out an alert to pick her up. When I saw her sitting on that bench, I figured she was in some kind of trouble."

I interrupt, "What alert? When? Why do you think Cassie's in trouble?"

Lorenzo raises his voice over my shrill questions and the sheriff's attempt to leave.

"Stop, both of you. Cat, be quiet. Sheriff, sit down. Creating panic isn't going to help us. Cat, you start. Once you finish, Blackwell, you go next. After that, Cat and Al, you're out of this meeting. Understand?"

Tears hover. Al reaches for my hand. I hold tightly onto his.

50

Cassie slowed down as she passed the entrance to the house. What the heck? She had nothing to lose. She backed up and swung into the long, circular drive. Some madness was directing her to get out of the car and knock on the front door. Some final act of defiance, she supposed.

She parked right next to the dramatic front steps. It was one of those wow-factor entrances, exactly what she expected from Jim. The steps were full and round and flared at the bottom. On each side were massive black planters. Giant hibiscus with white blooms the size of grapefruits nodded in the afternoon breeze.

Cassie swept her hand through her hair and twisted it into a knot. She found a clip in the coin tray and snapped it in her hair. She pulled down the mirror and applied lipstick. Then, she straightened her shirt collar, brushed imaginary dirt from her jeans, and checked her purse to make sure the gun was still there before she stepped out of the car. Not that she planned on using the weapon, but it gave her the extra confidence she needed to take this step.

She'd heard other people's stories about the long walk but had never thought much about it until now. Her knees stiffened as she approached the massive staircase. Her sandals stuck to the pavers. Her body was yelling at her to turn around and get the hell out of this place. These people were evil. She didn't need to waste any more time on them. Her deep anger, pain, and sadness had lessened as the morning had worn on. Cat was right. No man, and certainly not Jim, was worth suicide or the murderous thoughts she'd been harboring.

She turned away from the steps. Her only thought was to find Cat and apologize.

She had almost reached the car when the front door opened, and a voice called out, "Why Cassandra, whatever are you doing here?"

Cassie spun around. Alice stood in the open doorway. She no longer had on the see-through negligee, but vestiges of swollen eyes and puffiness remained on her semi-composed face.

Cassie paused at the bottom of the staircase, not sure what to do next. Alice gestured with her hand. The movement broke whatever spell had its hold on Cassie's body. Her right foot and then her left moved up the staircase. By the time she arrived at the top, Alice had regained her composure.

"Now, Cassie, James isn't home, and I'm on my way to Doris's for bridge, it being Thursday and all. So I don't have time to offer any hospitality, but perhaps you'll step inside and tell me the purpose of your visit."

Cassie tiptoed into the grand foyer. She was immediately struck by the interior staircase. It duplicated the exterior one except it was finely burnished wood. Its high luster and golden tones gleamed under the crystal chandelier. The white marble floor, sparkled like a skating rink in the afternoon sun. A round mahogany table was centered under the chandelier. A crystal vase filled with white calla lilies added to the cold stillness of the house.

Cassie was so in awe that she didn't comprehend anything Alice said and stuttered out a silly "What, what?"

"Oh, it's okay, honey. I'm just prattling. I don't think you're part of the bridge club group, are you? That's where I'm headed. Is there a reason you're here? Like I said, James is out. I'm not exactly sure where, but I don't advise you to wait as sometimes he brings *friends* home with him."

Cassie immediately understood what Alice was implying when she stressed *friends*.

"Of course, I have no intention of waiting. Was that George who just left? He almost drove me off the road. Is Jim okay?"

"Why, of course, he is my dear. George had a quick errand to run for him. He'll be back shortly to take me to my bridge game. What is it you wanted, Cassandra? Anything in particular I can help you with?"

Heat rose up Cassie's neck. Her face flushed, but her voice was strong as she said, "I simply stopped by to apologize for the incident at Cat's. Yes, I know that was a few months ago, but we never spoke about it. At the time, I didn't consider how rude James was to you. If I had paid attention that evening, I would have recognized how controlling he is. Is that how he usually treats you?"

She held her breath and wondered how in the heck she'd come up with such a foolish question. It was the furthest thing from her mind.

"Oh no, dear. James is never rude, unlike your friend Cat. He's a sweet, gentle soul, but he was confused by Cat's lack of manners. I was, too. We simply don't surround ourselves with adults who throw temper tantrums."

The urge to reply with as much venom as possible reared up. Cassie slammed it down.

"Alice, you were kind to invite me in, but I must be on my way. If you do see James, please tell him goodbye. Tell him I'll always remember the weekend we spent at the Mansion in Charleston. But it's time for me to move on with my life. I have better things to do, and I want to do them with people who are more refined than the likes of you two."

Alice seethed when Cassie mentioned the Mansion weekend. It was the first she'd heard about it. Her face went white. Her lips clenched in a tight line. She fidgeted with the buttons on the jacket of her perfect little bridge outfit. Cassie smiled at her discomfort.

"I'll see myself out. Now, you have a nice day."

Cassie sauntered down the steps like Scarlett. At the bottom, she turned around and extended her right arm down to her side and bent her elbow to 90°. She made sure her fingers and elbow formed one vertical line. She slightly cupped her hand and rotated it without moving her forearm. She waved. It was the perfect Miss America wave, the one she'd practiced for years as a child but never had the opportunity to use in real life. She turned her head slowly as if admirers were lined up for miles. She smiled her biggest and best smile. *Cat will be so proud of me* was her last coherent thought.

Fifteen minutes later, She pulled into the driveway at Cat's. The only thing she remembered was putting the car in park. The engine was still vibrating as she ran to the door and banged with all her might.

A relentless banging on the door echoes through the house. Al and I simultaneously jump up from the table and collide. When I open the door, a wailing Cassie falls into my arms. It takes a while to calm her down enough to hear her story about her encounter with Alice, how I was right about Jim, how she was wrong, and whether I would forgive her. A cup of tea with a shot of rum restores some color to her pale cheeks.

Al understands and slips out the door.

Cassie hands me the gun, accompanied by another teary apology. Then I have to tell her the sheriff put out an APB on her.

"I need to call him, Cassie. He needs to know you're safe. Is that okay?"

Cassie looks at me in the way that close friends do and collapses into fits of laughter and snorts.

"Oh my goodness, Cat," she says in-between hiccups. "Now I'm an outlaw and on the lam," as she bursts into loud hoots mixed with sobs.

I weep with joy, relief, and gratitude that the day is ending far better than it began.

51

Nick crept through the wooded area. The woman had finally left, and George hadn't returned. There was no reason to suspect anyone else was near the property, but based on the traffic between the front and back doors, he wouldn't be surprised if someone else popped in or out. He continued to text the senator, but there were no replies.

He wondered what George was up to but figured he'd left to get the girl. If he had, Jim would be preoccupied. Nick needed to see him before George came back.

He scampered down the slope and crouched under the portico next to the wall. He'd hoped Jim would be poolside or fishing off the dock. Before he had driven here, he'd checked to make sure the Senate wasn't in session or that Jim wasn't on the campaign trail.

The pool was deserted, but someone had recently been in as puddles of water trailed toward the French doors. Nick skirted the puddles, climbed the stairs, and raised his hand to knock on the already slightly open door. He wondered where Alice was and why she and George appeared to know each other well enough to embrace. He had no idea those two were connected or that Jim would let George anywhere near Alice except to drive her around. Maybe that's how it started. He wondered how long it had been going on and if Jim knew.

He was hesitant to go in as he'd never been invited to the senator's house. He guessed he wasn't considered fit company. He knew Alice was inside, but he wasn't sure if she lived here too. He thought briefly about what would happen if she saw him. Would she invite him in or ask him to leave?

He stuck his head through the door and called out, "Anybody home?"

No one answered. He waited a couple of minutes, then used his elbow to push the door open. He stepped inside, careful not to touch anything. The first lesson at the FBI academy was never to leave fingerprints. He looked around and called out.

"Senator? Jim? Hello? Anyone here?"

His voice echoed throughout the house. There was no response. The quiet was strong.

Following the trail of water spots, Nick walked across the long, enclosed sunroom and entered the hallway. He paused, thought about leaving. The voice in his head was loud—warning him to get out of the house, but his feet kept moving toward the closed door—the one he thought might be the senator's office.

He knocked on the burled walnut door. He noticed a turquoise silk scarf draped on a chair outside the door. He used it to turn the handle. The door cracked open.

"What do you think you're doing?"

Nick jumped and dropped the scarf. He turned slowly and raised his hands in the air. A SIG Sauer P365 was pointed at his face.

"I'm here to see Jim."

Alice didn't waver. She held the gun just tight enough so her hands wouldn't shake.

"Who are you? Why are you sneaking in the house through the back door?"

Nick didn't back down, "I'm a colleague of the senator's. I have an appointment."

"You're lying. I keep track of his appointments. His entire afternoon is free. Now, tell me who you are or I'll call the police?"

"Nick Cafaro. I need to go over some strategic planning with him. We're relocating some of his assets. He asked me to stop by. Maybe it didn't get on his calendar."

Alice lowered the gun a fraction and snarled, "I've never heard of you, but I know you're lying. You can make your way out the same way you came in. I have no qualms about shooting you in the back. Do you understand? Now get out."

Nick slowly retraced his steps, walked out the French doors, and ran. He prayed that he'd reach the car alive.

He didn't look back until he reached the safety of the wood line. Alice had disappeared. He made his way to the car and settled in to wait. He was pretty sure George would return with the girl. It would probably be his only chance to rescue her. She was his priority, and then he had to make sure Cat was safe. He'd have to tell her everything.

The girl was terrified. George had cuffed her and dragged her to the car. She'd fought like a wild animal. She'd scraped the cuffs across his face before he'd punched her—not hard, but enough to shut her up. He made sure she was breathing before he cuffed her legs, shoved her down on the back seat, and threw a blanket over her small, trembling body.

He looked in the mirror. A big red whelp meandered down the right side of his face. It was puffy, but the skin wasn't broken. He was a long way from South Africa. He sure as hell wasn't going to go back. This gig was just about over. He had to be patient for a little longer. Then he'd move on.

Before he'd picked her up, he'd returned to the plantation. He'd planned on destroying the cotton sheds along with any evidence that might have been left behind. He'd parked behind the old house and waited a few minutes to see if there was any movement. Then he got out of the car and used his key to open the back door. It didn't take but a second to see that Nick wasn't around. They needed to talk as Nick was part of the scheme. Now, he'd have to drive back to town and pick up the girl. Once he dropped her off at the senator's place, he'd return. Nick would probably be back by then.

The fallout with the senator meant he needed Nick on his side until the senator could be eliminated. He knew from the earlier encounter that his days were numbered. He'd made a huge blunder when he opened the office door. Until he dealt with the bastard, he'd need to keep looking over his shoulder. There was no way the senator would let him live now that he'd discovered what was going on between him and Alice. Although she'd told him her brother was abusive, she hadn't divulged the level. Knowing this made it easier for him to do what needed to be done.

He'd eliminate the senator, Cat and the count. Then he'd destroy the old cotton sheds. That would be his last act before blowing this backwater town. Everything was in place. He only needed to strike the match and disappear before anyone noticed.

52

A lice fidgeted with her cards. She used her cocktail napkin to wipe the beads of sweat off her forehead. Her bridge partner scowled and tried to get her attention. But Alice bent over her cards like she was playing The Big Game, and her life's savings were on the line.

At the last break, she'd left the table, headed to the bathroom, and dialed James's number. This was the third time she'd called. She knew he wouldn't answer. She'd left two previous messages to tell him the games were being played slower than usual as there were a couple of new people. It was all part of the plan she and George had worked out, except it really was taking too long.

It was just her luck that these new players showed up tonight and were slowing the game down. Her stomach heaved. She turned on the cold water tap and splashed her face. She patted it with the hand-stitched guest towel. She loved the old genteel Southern ways and traditions still so prevalent in the Lowcountry. She felt sad that so much of the tradition of the South was a thing of the past. The younger generation laughed and poked fun at the charming way she viewed the world. She looked at her watch again. It was time to place another call. This time, she needed to show a little more concern in her voice.

She'd told Jim she'd be back by five. It was already five-thirty. It would be a few hours before she could leave. These duplicate games could go on well into the night. In fact, Doris had already instructed the cook there'd be eight more for dinner. The plan required that she be back at the house around nine. She needed to play her hands carefully in order to make that happen.

She frowned in the mirror, patted her hair, and carefully outlined her lips before filling them in with the new Jimmy Choo lipstick 'Oh My Pink.' Putting the cap on with a firm twist, she stared at the fancy tube. Never had she spent so much on a lipstick, but she deserved it. She dropped it into the purse. A clank rang out as it hit the nose of the gun. After the plan was carried out, she would need to get rid of the weapon. She snapped the purse shut. She wouldn't think about it now, if she did, she'd fall apart. But that man showing up—the one who called himself Nick—was a problem. He'd seen her with a gun. She wasn't sure who he was, but George would know what to do. And Cassandra—what had possessed that girl to show up after James had humiliated her in public? This game she was forced to play was unnerving. The stakes were high, and she was in too deep. She couldn't afford to lose. She tossed her head, squared her shoulders, and opened the door.

All her life, Alice had been the child in the background—the forgotten child. James had already established himself as master of the house when she arrived some five years later. He was adored and could do no wrong in their parents' eyes. She had believed the myth of James as the golden child until the day she turned six.

He'd come to her room after her miserable birthday party, which had consisted of a single cupcake with six candles and a spoonful of melting ice cream set on a plate and later a hastily sung stanza of "Happy Birthday." Her parents said that they'd spent so much money on James' party there wasn't enough to do anything special for hers—and besides, there was nothing special about being six or being a girl.

Once she was allowed to leave the table, she locked herself in her room and cried until there were no more tears. She'd changed into her pajamas and crawled into bed.

The knock had been soft, almost indiscernible. Her heart beat rapidly in anticipation of a forgotten gift or even a belated hug. When she unlocked the door, James stood there with his finger to his lips. She felt giddy with excitement when he said he had something special to show her. He pushed her back on the bed as he unzipped his jeans and pointed a big swollen thing at her. She's been scared but strangely attracted and curious. She hadn't hesitated when he asked her to pet his friend Jimmy.

Later, after wet stuff had spilled on her pajamas, he'd whispered that it was their secret. No one was to know. If she ever told, he and Jimmy would never speak to her again. Over the years, the frequency of his visits and his demands increased. She had no choice as he was bigger and stronger. She succumbed. Deep down inside, the secret became a heavy weight. He violated every orifice of her body and threatened to kill her and their parents if she ever spoke about it. She was shamed into silence.

And so it began. Years of guilt, humiliation, self-incrimination, and servitude—the worst kind of self-perpetuating enslavement. Oh yes, she'd allowed it to continue. What else could she do?

As James found his way in the world, she was left to fend for herself. College, affairs, a career, nothing filled the void as James could. Once, she considered marriage and the possibility of a normal life. When he learned about her engagement, he returned home. He told her he'd never let her go. He reminded her that he was in charge of her life and no one could ever replace him. He told her to break off the engagement, or he would tell her fiancé her dark secrets. She was so mentally broken by then that it never dawned on her that he'd never tell. If he did, he would be destroying his own life, too. He was already in the political arena, but she had been too frightened to understand this. The abuse had continued.

Before his engagement was announced, he came to her and said he had to marry and produce children to be successful in politics. He assured her he would always need her. He set her up in the real estate business and bought her a condo in Hilton Head. He chose to marry a foreign girl, someone who needed a green card and someone he thought he could control. It worked for a while until Anna became a self-assured young woman.

Alice hated Anna and had done everything to make her life miserable. The only time James came back to Alice was when Anna was pregnant, and only because the doctor told him his wife might miscarry. Jim wanted children because of the family-man status it gave him, so he left Anna alone. Twice for nine months, he had once more belonged to Alice.

Alice had understood she would never have a normal life, but she had been shocked when she'd opened the door one day to a small knock. She had never thought that her sister-in-law's life might be pure hell.

Anna had stood in the foyer, her face bloodied, with a broken tooth and bruises on her arms. She'd asked Alice if being beaten during sex was normal. She'd pleaded with Alice to help her escape. She said she was willing to do anything to get out of the marriage. She never bothered to question why Alice was so willing to help her.

Alice hired a private investigator, and soon, they'd accumulated a long list of the girls James had violated. He had gotten away with his clandestine affairs for so long that he had become sloppy. It had been easy for the private investigator to obtain compromising photos. Threats of the photographs being sent to newspapers, TV stations, and plastered on social media had paved the way for the marriage to be dissolved. Anna and the children fled the country with a promise never to return. Of course, the restitution had been steep.

For the next couple of years, Alice had James all to herself. She had tolerated the fly-by-night affairs because he had promised her she wouldn't lose him to another woman. She had been content until Cassandra appeared. Initially, she believed it would be a short-term affair. She had been right as James had ended the relationship after the disastrous dinner at Cat's. She had watched Cat's eyes so alert and cautious. James hadn't been able to reel her in like he had Cassandra. That had meant trouble. She had tried to avoid looking at James all night. The one time she'd slipped up, Cat's knowing look frightened her.

James's ego was so large that when Cat humiliated him, he dropped Cassandra. But not before Alice had reminded him of the slanderous photographs. It had taken a while to calm him down enough to let him know she would never think of using them. He told her he'd break up with Cassandra immediately, and he had. He'd pleaded with her to give the photos to him, and she did. He beamed and hugged her. What a stupid man he was to think she'd actually give him the originals.

Of course, Alice had been shocked when she discovered James had reconnected with Cassie. He'd kept it a secret—something he'd never done before. That's when she realized the affair was serious.When she discovered they were back together, she had placed more photos on his desk along with a copy of the witness statements from the private investor as well as Anna's statement of abuse.

When she learned Cat and Cassandra would be the caterers for the wedding reception at Tidal Bay, she'd told James that he had to create a scene in public. He needed to humiliate Cassandra in a way that would guarantee the relationship was dead. Alice pointed out that there was no room for a mistake on his part. If he chose to see her again, Alice would go public with the photos.

The threat scared him. Alice had never challenged him before. If she went public, he'd be ruined, and more than likely wind up in prison as some of the girls were underage. He had no choice but to promise her what she wanted. Of course, he hadn't bothered to tell her he was already finished with Cassie. George had given her that bit of information. According to George, James had informed him that Cassie was a bore and way too old for him. He'd said he only wanted the young girls.

Alice thumbed through her cards, but her mind was not on the game. All these years, she had only wanted one thing, and that was for them to be together. The irony was that so much had changed she no longer cared. She had another offer—a chance to get out and start over. It was happening tonight. After all these years of abuse, she'd made a different decision—one that would change the trajectory of her life.

She clutched her cards and tried to focus. But the scenes from this morning circled like sharks. When she had joined James at the pool, she could tell he was in one of his nasty moods. She'd placed a tray with a French press and two coffee cups on the table. She had smiled at him with such love and stretched her body in the sunlight so he could see she was naked under the sheer robe.

"Go away." He'd snarled from the edge of the pool.

"My darling, what a nasty mood you're in this morning."

"You heard me, go away! I'm not listening to you whine or preach to me. I've got more important things on my mind."

But Alice stayed. "George told me he's bringing one of the girls here. He said you asked him to. You know that's not allowed. I don't care what you do when I'm away. But this is our home—mine and yours. I won't allow you to bring filth into it.

"You won't allow! Ha! Your word doesn't mean anything around here, Alice. The girl will be here this evening. I want you out of the house! Grab a few things and go to our place in Hilton Head. In a week or so, we'll talk about whether or not you can come back."

"James, you don't mean that... you can't mean that."

He'd smiled that nasty smile.

She'd had enough. "James, if you bring one of those girls here, you will regret it. I promise you that."

Alice repositioned the purse in her lap. She patted her hair, smiled, and bid Three No Trump.

53

Between wet sobs and hugs, Cassie told her story. Eventually, after repeatedly asking me to forgive her, I tucked her in bed. My last promise before she closed her eyes was that I'd totally forgiven her. But Cassie and I are enough alike that we'll continue to hash it out until we're both sure we can move on.

Sometime during the night, the sound of tires on gravel wakes me. I slip into the kitchen and look out the door. Cassie's car is gone. There's a big note taped to the door.

Sam called crying. Of course, affairs of the heart. She's driving home and needs her mom. Don't worry, I promise I'm not with Jim. It's really over.

There's a heart-shaped smiley face, just like the pre-Jim Cassie would have added to her messages.

I slide back under the sheets, but my mind is on overload. Until I speak to Cassie and know she and Sam are both okay, I can't help but worry. How I wish none of this had happened. How I wish Cassie and I were getting ready to announce our partnership. She might change her mind, but it's too soon to ask her to stay and reconsider. She needs time. And I need sleep.

Hours go by as I thrash around in bed with my muddled thoughts. Should I call Cassie? And what about Al? After he left, he sent several messages. He wanted to know how Cassie was, how he could help, and when we could finish discussing yesterday's Zoom meeting. Would I go with him to look at other properties, and would I consider dinner without a business agenda?

Closing my eyes and breathing deeply doesn't help—nothing helps. I'm wide awake in the pre-dawn hours when my phone shrills.

"Cat, sorry to call you at this ridiculous hour."

"It's okay, Al. I wasn't asleep. What's up?"

"George just called with some disturbing news. He said something is happening at the plantation, and he'd like us to meet him out there."

"That doesn't sound right. What does he want? You're not going, are you? Whatever the news, it needs to be handled by the authorities."

"Cat, he told me that your friend Nick Cafaro is holding Stephanie hostage in one of the old cotton sheds."

"What? Why would Nick do that, and why would George know about it? How does he know Nick? Why didn't he call the police?"

"Listen, Cat. George knows we've been looking for Stephanie. He called me, but it's really you he wants. He thinks you can talk some sense into Nick. Would you be willing to go with me? I'm on my way to your place now, but I can go alone if you think this is a bad idea."

"Yes, of course, I think it's a bad idea. Lorenzo will kill me if he gets wind of us doing this. Al, nothing about George's story makes sense. What else did he say?"

"Just that Nick was waving a gun and yelling about somebody called *the boss*. He said Nick was threatening to kill the girl. Cat, I think you have to talk to Nick. We can't let him kill Stephanie."

"Ok, I'll go with you, but I'm calling Sheriff Blackwell to back us up. And I'm asking him to get the FBI out there."

A couple of hours had passed as Nick waited. Where was *the boss*? A few lights had automatically come on in the house, but there was no sign of movement. Where was George? He should have returned with the girl by now. He returned an hour ago, but left again to drive Alice somewhere. From the looks of her attire, it was some kind of social event.

As the shadows of night edged across the deep water, the senator walked out of the back door. Nick eased the car door open and slipped into the woods just as the sun sunk into the world of twilight —much like his life as he approached the end.

He moved quietly until he had Jim in his sight. He watched as he stepped to the edge of the pool, discarded his robe, and plunged buck-naked into the water and began a slow breaststroke.

After he finished his swim, he slipped back into his robe and disappeared into the house.

It was close to nine when the limo pulled into the circular drive-way. Alice left the car and entered the house. George drove away.

Nick stayed crouched in the same spot. It wasn't long before George returned and parked under the portico. Nick watched George as he removed the shackles from the girl's ankles and jerked her up off the back seat. This would be his first rescue, next it would be Cat.

George's voice was a low growl. "Don't be giving me any trouble. Your job is to give the man what he wants. If you fight or scream, you'll die."

Her trembles pulsated through the hand that he laid on her shoulder. The matron had dressed her in a long, white dress. It flowed to her ankles. Her feet were bare. Her hair was loosely tied back with a gold satin ribbon.

The back door stood ajar. He pushed the girl through and stopped. The house was deadly quiet. He wondered where the senator was. He'd called ahead to say he was on the way with the girl. He had just dropped Alice off and expected her to be here too.

The boss usually greeted him at the door as eager as a new bride-groom. George always got a kick out of watching him smack his lips like some sex-crazed teenager. This girl was exactly what he'd ordered, but where was he?

George pushed Stephanie further into the house.

"Hey, is anybody home? Jim, you here? Alice?"

He drew his gun and swirled around as Alice slipped into the room. "What's wrong with you? I could have shot you. Where is he?"

"Don't worry about James. Everything's under control. Leave the girl with me. Come back in about thirty minutes as we planned. I don't expect problems, but you never know. Earlier, a man I'd never seen before showed up."

"Who?"

"Said his name was Nick. I didn't catch the last name. He said he was a colleague of James."

George handed over the girl and said, "He's lying. Don't let him in the house again."

"Oh, I sent him packing. He won't be back."

"Does Jim know Nick stopped by?"

"No, I didn't see any point in telling him."

"Well, I imagine after I barged into his office morning, he doesn't ever want to see me again. Didn't mean to stumble in, Alice. Just remember you won't have to worry about him much longer."

Alice nodded and said, "You better get out of here. You have a few things to do before you return. Make sure all of the plans are in place to eliminate any witnesses and all evidence—including that Cat woman. She's too smart. I wouldn't be surprised if she's already gone to the police."

54

Nick waited until George pulled out of the driveway. He stayed in his crouched-down position for a few minutes before creeping through the woods toward the house. While he waited, he'd surveyed the doors for surveillance cameras and alarm systems. He figured with all the comings and goings, they weren't activated. He doubted the senator would want his naked body exposed to scrutiny if there was a break-in and the cops were called and wanted to see the security videos.

The door to the sunroom was open. Nick slipped in and waited, listening. He crept into the house and headed toward Jim's office. The silk scarf was still on the floor where he'd dropped it on his earlier visit. He drew his gun and pushed the door open. The room was empty. A chair was turned over, and papers were strewn across the floor. Nick slipped out of the office and moved further into the house. Voices, soft at first and then increasing in volume, came from a partially opened door at the far end of the hallway. Following the sounds, he inched along the wall.

The gap in the door was wide enough to see a king-sized bed. In the center was a body in a white garment curled tightly in a ball. He couldn't tell if the body was dead or alive. There was no movement, but there was also no blood spread on the pale blue coverlet. Maybe he wasn't too late.

The senator was standing next to the bed with his hands partially raised. A voice too low to hear was speaking. The plush runner in the hallway silenced his steps as he moved closer. He slid into an alcove just outside the door. He crouched low and waited.

"Now, Alice, put down that gun. What are you doing with a gun anyway? Where did you get it? Alice, listen to me. I'll call George to come back and take the girl with him. Just put the damn gun down."

During the senator's little speech, Nick changed positions. He moved to the left of the door jam out of the senator's vision. He could see the bed and the lifeless body. From the conversation, he surmised Alice was also in the room. But she was out of his sight.

"James, I've done everything you've ever asked of me since I was six years old. This is how you treat me. You've hurt me for the last time."

"Ah, Alice, I'm sorry. Don't know what I was thinking. Come on, let me call George."

"Shut up, James! I'm talking now. You've run out of second chances."

"But, Alice, if you shoot me, who'll take care of you? You'll go to jail."

"You think I'm stupid? You've always thought I was stupid, and you were right. I was stupid to let you abuse me. But how could I have prevented it? I was a child! You killed me when I was six years old, James. Killing you now won't bother me one bit. I'm no longer an innocent child. I have an alibi. I'm still at Doris's house. I've called you three times and left messages giving you updates about the bridge game and how I'm going to be very late getting home."

James sneered, his lip curled into a cruel thin line. "Well, if you're so smart, how can you account for being here and at Doris's playing bridge? Huh? Don't you think your bridge partners will notice your absence?"

"Why, my darling James, we're taking a short break before dinner. Right now, I'm taking a walk on the dock. Everyone can see me. That's if anyone's looking, they'll see someone who looks like me —in the fading light, with the same outfit, hair color and body shape. It wasn't difficult to hire someone to duplicate me. Our break before dinner is about thirty minutes. Doris asked me to ring the old school house bell on the light post when it was time for everyone to come in for dinner. I have another twenty minutes before I have to do that. Perhaps I'm not as dumb as you think."

"Come on, Alice. Let's talk about this. "

A shot rang out, glass shattered. The senator dropped to his knees. His hands waved frantically above his head. They flopped like broken wings. He whimpered, his face alternated between ghostly white and brilliant red—beaded with sweat. Nick was ready to barge in until he realized the senator wasn't hit. He should intervene, but he waited to see what would happen next.

Alice laughed a low throaty chuckle, "No, James. I don't have time to talk. Remember all the times I wanted to talk, and you ignored me? You've held me hostage for years, but no more. Your power over me no longer exists. Stand up and face me. When I pull the trigger, I want to see your sorry face."

Nick crashed through the door at the same moment Alice pulled the trigger. The door slammed into her back. The gun spiraled out of her hand as she fell against the bed. The bullet ricocheted and shattered the mirror over the credenza. James lunged for the weapon.

55

It's another couple of hours until the sun comes up. I throw on an old pair of jeans and a couple of layers to combat the early morning chill. My heart is galloping like a fine-tuned racehorse. After all that's happened, I know George is not someone to trust.

When I try Sheriff Blackwell's number, the call rolls to messages. I briefly describe my conversation with Al and tell him we're driving out to Carrington Point Plantation. I pause, take a deep breath, and say I'd feel better if I knew he was on the way—and I'd love to know the FBI was with him.

The sound of Al's car pulling into the drive has me racing out the door. I'm already sliding across the passenger seat before he put the gear in park.

"Tell me again why George called you and what he said."

Black shadows created by the motion light filter across his face as he turns toward me.

"After yesterday's Zoom meeting and Cassie's sudden appearance at your place, I was at loose ends. I contacted George as I thought it would be a good time for him to drive me around to look at more properties. Although I've booked my flight back to Spain, there's some time left to consider other properties. I haven't totally given up on Carrington Point, but for now, it's out of the picture unless I can find the real owner. The strange thing is George didn't return my calls or texts. You know how he hovers and won't leave me alone for a minute. It was out of character for him not to respond right away."

Al turns his headlights on bright and pulls onto the highway. The majestic oaks that are so welcoming in daylight now sway in grotesque shapes. They look like giant raptors from millions of years ago. We are suspended between the blackness of night and the dusty gray of morning. The time of *chiaroscuro*. I shift uneasily in my seat.

Total chaos ensued as the senator grabbed the gun. He shot wildly. Nick ducked beside the door. He heard Alice hit the floor with a thud. Dropping to his knees, Nick swung the door open all the way just as the senator fired. His aim was high and hit the wall. Nick shot low. The gun flew out of the senator's hand and slid under the bed. The senator dove to the floor and grabbed the gun at the same time as Nick's hand grasped his collar. He twisted it tighter and tighter until the senator gasped for breath and released the weapon. It fell with a clatter to the floor. Nick swooped it up by the barrel and whacked the side of the senator's head. He placed the gun on a small table by the door and pulled out his own.

Alice whimpered. The body on the bed uncoiled and began a high-pitched wail. The senator lay face down on the floor, a deep moan escaping from his lips. Nick cuffed him and checked his breathing before turning to Alice. She was sprawled on the floor, blood gushing from her shoulder.

What a mess was all Nick could think. The girl sobbed and wailed. Alice's feeble cries for help could barely be heard over the racket the girl was making. Nick crossed the room to quiet her. He was shocked to see she was chained to the bedpost. What kind of perverted person was the senator? Since she wasn't wounded and couldn't go anywhere, he tried to reassure her. But she was way past the point of reason. He begged her not to scream, said help was on the way, and returned to Alice. He knelt next to her with his gun aimed at her head. He figured none of these people were trustworthy. When he saw that neither the senator nor Alice was in any condition to jump him, he lowered his gun to the floor. He grabbed a throw off the bed and pressed it against Alice's shoulder.

A voice rang out, "Don't move. Raise your hands."

Nick was inches from his gun but knew if he made a lunge for it, both he and Alice would be shot. At first, he thought the voice belonged to the senator until he heard a soft moan coming from that direction. Slowly, with his hands raised, he glanced around. George was standing in the doorway with a smirk on his face.

"Get up," he snarled.

Nick stood and faced George.

"Well, well," George said, "It looks like I arrived too late to be of much help. Were you going to kill them all? Then what?"

"It wasn't my intention to kill any of them. I walked in on Alice. She was pointing a gun at the senator. When I pushed through the door to stop her from shooting him, it hit her in the back. She lost her balance and dropped the gun. The senator grabbed it and shot her. We need to call an ambulance. She's lost a lot of blood."

"Hand me your phone. No one's calling an ambulance or the police. I suggest you leave immediately. Get yourself back to the plantation, pack up, and move out before morning."

"Alice is badly wounded, and the girl needs medical attention. If you're not going to call for help, what do you plan to do with all these people?"

Nick glanced at the girl whose screams had died to whimpers. She had curled back in a knot.

George glanced at her briefly and said, "I'll drop her off on a back road somewhere. In the morning, I'll make an anonymous call to the sheriff's office. That way, they won't make the connection between the girl and the senator. He won't be found until someone reports him missing. That will give you and me more than enough time to disappear."

"What about Alice?"

"I'll check out her wound and patch her up as best I can. No one will be the wiser. Alice and the senator will have to explain the situation. I could be wrong, but I don't imagine they'll want to call anyone. Perhaps they can concoct a believable story to cover whatever nastiness was going on here. But I doubt they'll want to have an investigation. They have too much to lose. Give me the keys to the cuffs, your phone and gun, and get out of here. Be gone before morning. That's all the time you'll have before the plantation is turned upside down."

"My gun and phone?"

"You heard me. Get out of here now. I'll dispose of your gun once I'm through here."

"If I'm on the run, I'll need a gun and my phone."

"Okay, give it a rest. I'll drop them off at the plantation once I tidy up here. It's just a precaution. I need you on my side. I can't take a chance you won't use the gun. That would draw attention to what's going on here. I'm giving you a chance, Nick. I suggest you take it."

"Why are you letting me go?"

"Why not? The senator used both of us. It only makes sense. Sooner or later, this little operation would have collapsed. He's set it up so that you and I would take the blame for everything while he walks away. I'll be out of the country in twenty-four hours. I advise you to do the same. Go on, get out of here before I change my mind."

Nick glanced at the girl on the bed. He knew it was Diana's little sister. He felt like crap leaving her. He hoped George was telling the truth and would drop her off in a safe place, but he doubted George's sincerity. He figured once he was close to the border, he could place a call about the girl.

As he walked by Alice, she grabbed his foot, "If you tell anyone about this, I'll personally track you down and kill you."

Nick shook loose, nodded at George and walked out of the room. As he strode down the hallway, he figured the last sound he'd hear would be a shot entering his back. But nothing happened. He was in a full sprint by the time he reached the car. He pulled the burner phone from the pouch hidden in the top of the glove compartment and texted Cat to warn her. When she didn't answer, he called, but it went directly to messages. His time was running out. He would try again when he reached the plantation.

56

George waited until he heard the engine turn over and Nick's car pulling back onto the road before he walked over to Alice.

"Please help me," came faintly from her lips.

"Sorry, Alice. Don't get me wrong. I want to help you, but you're wounded. I know we planned to go away together, but you'd slow me down. Don't worry. I'm going to patch you up."

"What about Jim and the girl?"

"Don't worry," George said as he slipped on a pair of gloves and retrieved Nick's gun.

"I'm going to patch you up first. From the looks of the wound, it's clean. Once I stop the blood flow, you're going to be fine."

"George, you promised you'd take me. Please don't leave me."

"Yeah, I promised, but that was before you got shot. In a way, this will work out better for you. You won't be on the run like me. It's a horrible life—always looking over your shoulder and knowing there's a price on your head. It'll be easier for me to leave the country without you. Once you're cleared of any wrongdoing and some time has passed, no one will question your leaving the country. We'll hook up then. For now, all you have to do is tell the police you found Jim with this underage girl and tried to stop him from raping her. He turned on you and tried to kill you."

"But what about my gun? It's got my prints and James' prints on it."

"Soon enough, it won't. I'll wipe it clean. Then I'll put it in the senator's hand. Forensics will show only one bullet was fired. That's the bullet they'll take out of your shoulder. They'll believe the gun was Jim's."

"Then what?"

"You can say one of Jim's colleagues stopped by and heard screams."

"Who do I say the colleague was?"

"God, Alice, don't be so dense—Nick, of course. Listen to me. You'll tell them that Nick tried to separate the senator and the girl. When the senator knocked him across the room, he pulled out a gun and shot the senator in the back. Then he grabbed the girl. She fought and knocked the gun out of his hand. He didn't stop to pick it."

"What? What are you talking about? That's not what happened! What about the girl? She's a witness."

He looked over at the girl who was still in a fetal position.

"Alice, the girl's in shock, practically comatose. She doesn't have a clue what happened or what's going to happen. They won't subpoena her. If they do her, her parents or an attorney will say she's not competent to be a witness. It will take a lot of therapy before that kid says anything to anyone. Listen to me carefully. I'm going to put her in the car, then I'll come back and clean up this mess. Okay?"

George half-drug, half-carried the girl from the room. Alice struggled to sit up. She looked at Jim and whispered his name, "James, James, wake up. Hurry before George comes back."

The senator moaned and cracked open an eye.

"Alice, get these dammed cuffs off me. What in the hell happened? Get over here now."

Alice tried to push away from the floor but was too weak. "I can't, Jim. Whatever happens is out of my hands. If you'd trusted me or even loved me just a little, none of this would have happened."

"Oh, shut your mouth, woman. I don't care if he kills you. Get over here now."

George slipped back into the room.

"Not thinking of helping this idiot, are you Alice?"

She said no, but giant tears leaked from her eyes.

"Okay, do you have your story straight about what happened? It's critical that you do. Your testimony will seal the senator's fate. The tricky part is convincing them that Nick was the one who shot him. But you can do it. Remember, Nick is guilty. He shot the senator. Repeat to me what you're going to say and how."

Alice's voice trembled, "I, I came home from a bridge game at Doris's house—about nine. I heard voices and found Jim with a young girl. She, she—oh my God! I can't do this."

The senator reared his head in the air, "Of course, you can't do it, Alice. You love me too much. You've loved me all your life. You've proven it over and over. George, you'll have to let me go or kill us both because there's no way Alice will testify against me. Isn't that right, little sister? You don't want your name dragged through court and associated with incest. I know you, Alice. Appearances mean every-thing to you. Come on, George. Let me go. There's plenty of time for you to get out of the country if you leave now."

The senator let out a piercing scream as George's foot slammed into his lower back.

"Shut your mouth, you idiot. Now Alice, if you don't get your story straight, you're going to end up in jail. You don't want that to happen. Go on. Tell me what comes next. I want the fine senator to hear how his life is going to end."

Alice swiped at her tears, "She, she—the girl was chained to the bed. He was raping her. I screamed and tried to pull him off of her. He slapped me. When I persisted, he pulled out a gun and shot me."

"That's not too bad, but where did he get the gun? They'll expect you to be in shock, but you have to have some details."

"Alice, don't you listen to him. He's going to kill you too. Alice, do you hear me?"

George's foot, which had relaxed, stomped into the senator's back. Another ear-shattering scream filled the room. George ignored it and moved his foot to the base of the senator's neck.

"Shut your mouth."

A low groan was the only sound.

"Okay, Alice, if you get this right, you won't be charged with anything. You'll be free. You hear me, Alice. You won't have to go to jail. You'll testify that as you were screaming for your life, Nick barged in and shot the senator and took the girl."

"But what about this Nick person? He told me he was a colleague of the senator. Why would he shoot Jim? Why wouldn't he help him? If he did shoot him, wouldn't he call the police and tell them a story that's different from mine?"

"Nick Cafaro will get his gun back, but not exactly as he planned. Only his prints are on his gun—a suicide seems logical after the operation he's been involved in, don't you think?"

"Oh, George, I don't think I can do it. You never said this would happen. You promised to kill the senator and take me out of the country with you. I paid you to get rid of James. He's still here. What are you going to do about that?"

"Don't you worry, Alice. Once I'm settled in South America, I'll contact you. It'll take longer, but soon you'll be able to join me. Now, let me patch you up. We'll work on your story some more while I'm doing that."

Before Alice could protest, George picked up her gun. He wiped off her prints. He picked up Nick's gun and tucked it into his jeans. He strode over to the senator, knelt next to him, and unlocked the cuffs.

The senator smirked and said, "Good man, George. Now help me up. Go ahead and finish off Alice. Then you need to find Nick and bring him back here. Why in the heck did you let him go? We can pin Alice's murder on him. Man, my head is hurting. Help me up."

George placed his knee on the senator's back and flattened him onto the floor.

"What the fuck do you think you're doing? Get off of me, you scumbag. You're gonna pay for this."

"Listen up—I'm giving you a gun so you can protect yourself. Come on now, open your hand."

"What? What's going on?"

George's knee pressed deeper. The senator bellowed and opened his hand. George slipped the gun into place and forced his fingers to wrap around the barrel and his index finger on the trigger. Without releasing his knee from the senator's back, he pulled out Nick's gun, stood up, and fired.

Alice flinched. Unexpected relief flooded through her body. James lay sprawled face down in his own blood. He was dead. He couldn't hurt her anymore. Maybe George was right. Perhaps she could start over.

"Okay, " she said, "Tell me what happened after Nick shot Jim. Why would he leave his gun behind? Tell me again what I'm supposed to say."

57

Al took the next curve a little too fast. I'm close to telling him to pull over so I can drive. Instead, I say, "What did George say when he called you?"

"Cat, he was in such a state that I barely understood him. You were right. All this time, he has been listening to our conversations. But he did it to help us."

"Oh, Al, how can you think that? George doesn't strike me as a helpful person. He's more of a mercenary type—a gun-for-hire kind of person. What is going on? Since George didn't call the police, why didn't you? I'm confused. This whole thing doesn't make sense."

"Cat, it's a good thing George called us first. The police would only have made the situation worse. They might react too quickly and shoot Nick or worse, Stephanie."

"Al, George works for the senator, a guy who I'm reasonably sure is corrupt. Why else would he recommend someone like George to drive you around and listen to all your conversations? That is not the usual role of a chauffeur. Did you even check his credentials?"

"No, why would I? Your state senator recommended him. I thought he was a reliable source."

"Ha, some state senator. As I just mentioned, I'm sure he's corrupt and involved in illegal activities. I just haven't had time to prove it."

Al grabs my hand. "Cat, now's not the time. We need to help Stephanie."

"Sorry, what else did George say?"

"Do you remember the day George and I went to the warehouses? George sent me back to the car because there were a couple of squatters. He didn't want me to get involved, so he ran them off and called the police."

"Did you actually see the squatters? Did he really call the police? If he called anyone, it should have been the sheriff. But I don't believe he called anyone."

"No, I didn't see the squatters. He said he called the police. Why would he lie?"

When I don't answer, Al continues, "When he called just now, he said he was at the plantation. Every few days he'd been making early morning reconnaissance out there to make sure the riffraff was gone."

"At this hour?"

"He said it was the best time to catch them. That's how he found Stephanie. The problem is Nick has her. He said she's tied up, gagged, and hysterical."

"If she's tied and gagged, how can he tell if she's hysterical?"

"Oh, Cat. Listen! If Stephanie's in trouble, we just need to get out there. The details can be sorted out later. But for right now, George says she's hysterical—in shock and freaking out. Nick told George to leave the property or he'd kill him and Stephanie. Nick held a gun on him and walked him back to his car."

"Where is George now?"

"He's back at the plantation. He drove a short distance away, pulled off the road, and walked back. He said it could take a while for the police to arrive. He somehow knew that you and Nick were friends, which is why he suggested I bring you. He thinks you could talk Nick into releasing her."

"Al, none of this makes sense. How in the world would George know that Nick and I are friends, and why would he think I could talk him into releasing her? This is not a good idea. How do we know he isn't setting some kind of trap for us?"

Al shakes his head. "Where does all your creative imagination come from? Why would you even think that? George is trying to help her and us. Once we're there, we can assess what's going on. Then, you can decide whether or not to talk to Nick."

I shrug and shake my head. "Al, I left a message for Sheriff Blackwell before you picked me up. I don't believe George. He's been driving you all over the place, listening to every conversation and probably reporting back to the senator. He certainly knows the plantation is in the county and would require a call to the sheriff and not the police. Nothing about this sounds logical to me."

Al has never seen the dark side of George, and no amount of talking on my part is going to change his mind. We ride the rest of the way in silence. As we approach the drive, Al turns off the headlights.

"Why did you turn off the headlights?"

"George told me to. He doesn't want Nick spooked. Let's just see what's going on. All we have to do is get her out of Nick's hands and safely in the car. It will be okay. You'll see."

While I don't believe anything George told Al, I don't want to take a chance that Nick does have Stephanie or maybe knows where she is. We coast down the gravel road until it turns into a muddy path. The tires make a sucking noise as the car moves through the night's rain puddles. Al slows down to a crawl and stops when the road abruptly ends in a washed-out gully.

58

N ick threw a few things in a satchel. He retrieved the extra gun he kept hidden and added it to the bag. He needed a plan, but he wasn't sure where to start. George wasn't going to return his gun. He'd pretty much figured out that whatever scheme George had in mind would include Nick's gun and fingerprints.

He was reasonably sure George would kill the senator. Nick didn't like Jim, but even the worst person deserved their day in court. What he worried about was what George would do with Alice and the girl. But what could he do about it? Nothing.

Someone would find them—the senator, Alice, and the girl. With his fingerprints on the gun, the best he could do was keep a low profile for a few more hours and then disappear. But where would he go? He'd have to steal a car. He couldn't be caught driving one of the senator's vehicles.

He turned on the coffee maker and opened the door to the back deck. The cool early morning air felt good before the heat and humidity ratcheted into misery. It was a stupid thought, but he didn't want to leave. This house had become his home. The deck was the only thing he hadn't completed. He walked to the place in the railing where Cat had busted through to escape from George's almost brutal attack. He rubbed his hand over two day's growth of prickly beard and wondered if there was a way to let her know he was sorry.

He heard the low rumble of an engine and dropped to his knees. He flattened his body and hoped the headlights wouldn't pick him up. The crunch of tires approached. The headlights were off. The car slowly made its way down the dirt road. He didn't recognize the vehicle but figured it could only mean trouble.

He jumped up and ran into the house. He slid into a pair of jeans and stopped briefly to cram his feet into loafers. He grabbed the gun and snatched his jacket from the peg by the door.

Al pulled the car a little off the path and cut the engine.

"This is as far as the car can go without getting stuck."

With the aid of a Nitecore flashlight, the old cotton sheds emerged from the cluster of giant oaks. The dark wooden structures were in various stages of disrepair. As we move closer, I see they're lined up one after the other—ghostly shapes outlined against the gray of dawn. As we approach the end of dilapidated shapes, the last two appear to have been recently repaired, or at least an attempt had been made to cover decaying wood. My feet crunch on broken glass. Looking up, I see the ripped plywood dangling and a shattered window. Although Diana had no idea where she had been held prisoner, this has to be it.

Whispering, I call Al's name. "Shine the light over here—on the broken glass."

The bright stream of light moved back and forth over the shards.

"Wait! Go back! Here!"

The light passes over what looks like blood. We kneel in the dirt but don't touch the evidence. We're in enough trouble already. Lorenzo will be furious when he discovers we came out here without waiting for the sheriff or without asking him to contact the FBI. Here we are, standing in the middle of evidence and messing with the scene of a crime—although I'm not sure Diana jumping out the window is a crime.

As the first gray light of dawn tips the tall pines and grand oaks, the land where cotton was once king stretches before me. White fluffy balls flowing endlessly to the river must have been a grand sight. There are times, like now, when I'm so frightened my mind derails. We are crazy to be here. As I crouch in the dirt and broken glass, I gear my thoughts into some sort of self-preservation mode in order to protect myself from thinking about what is actually happening. It's another exasperating habit I have of switching my mind into some obscure overdrive. This time, I plow through my school file and pull out everything I've ever known about Sea Island cotton. I rock back on my heels and groan. This is something else I'll have to discuss with Dr. Ginny when this craziness is over. I shut down the cotton dissertation and resume skulking behind Al.

A chill dances along my spine as I pick my way out of the broken glass and move from one patch of weeds to another. Turning back is a strong force in my thoughts, but I push on. The need to find Diana's little sister overcomes any rational fear I should have. Shivers continue to navigate up and down my spine as the past and present enslavement of people on this property merge into a bleak outline of dawn. How can it be that this is still happening?

Al turns off the flashlight and glances back to make sure I'm following him. As he rounds the last structure, I pick up my pace only to smack into his back when I turn the corner.

"Sorry," I say as I extricate myself from his body. "What's wrong?"

His voice lowers to a whisper, "I heard a thumping sound."

We hold our breaths and listen. The wind rustles and sighs through the pines. The staccato peck, peck, pecking of an early morning downy woodpecker permeates the silence. A blue jay jeers as my heartbeat settles into a holding pattern. The morning sky multiplies its shades of gray and pink.

It's in this still, quiet moment that my stupidity hits me. This is a dangerous place. Al and I are not equipped to solve whatever is happening here. What if George kidnapped Stephanie and is holding her for ransom? We could be putting her life in danger, and we sure are putting ourselves there. I pull out my phone and scroll to Sheriff

Blackwell's number to place another call to him. We need to go back to the car and wait until he arrives.

"Put your phone on the ground."

Panic rushes through my body. My first instinct is to run, but I am paralyzed in place as I look into the eyes of death. George has an AK-15 with a suppressor trained on us.

Al lifts his hands in the air in a friendly manner, still believing the guy is okay. He whispers, "Goodness, George, quit pointing that thing at us. Tell us where Nick is holding Stephanie. Is it in one of these sheds?"

The hopelessness of the situation sinks in. We are doomed because we are idiots—at least I am. My gut warned me, and once again, I ignored the warning.

When the gun remains trained on us, Al's voice quivers, "George, what is the meaning of this? Why do you have a gun? Where is Stephanie?"

The muffled thud of a shot vibrates through my body. I'm not sure who's been hit until Al slumps to the ground. I automatically drop and cover his body with my own.

"Stand up! Move away from the body!"

Blood is pooling beneath Al as I force myself into an upright position.

"Are you mad? Why did you shoot him? Where's Stephanie?"

George looks right through me before saying, "It's going to give me great pleasure to put a bullet through your head. Didn't you know it's dangerous to be so inquisitive? I'll tell you where Stephanie is— she's with the senator. Once he's used her, she'll be sold to the highest bidder and will be transported out of state before anyone notices."

The morning breeze whispers through the old cotton fields. Birds chirp as they search for food. The marsh grasses rustle in anticipation of the first caresses from the sun. The cotton fields in front of me blur into images of that day in Italy—the caves, the rocks, and the sea. Another day when death hovered as Carlo had pressed the gun against my head. I try to follow what George is saying, but I'm losing ground.

"You two have been nothing but trouble. Your interference in the operation has created problems for a whole lot of people. It's the end of the road for both of you."

He repositions the gun and aims at my chest.

A voice yells through the trees, "Cat, get down! George, stop! Put the gun down now!"

We both turn in the direction of the tree line. Nick's jacket billows as he races toward us. A volley of bullets sprays into the trees as Nick dodges and ducks. Bits of earth erupt into the early light of dawn. The sound ricochets. Birds scream and flutter into the air. Nick is still yelling at me to get down as he breaks through the woods. I hit the ground seconds before George takes aim. As I tumble backward, the earth explodes. The last sound I hear is the dull thud of bullets.

59

G eorge stared at the bloody heap of bodies and grunted. He hadn't counted on Nick interfering. That was a stupid misstep on his part. He pulled Nick's body off the girl to make sure she was dead. She was covered in blood. He didn't have time to determine exactly where she'd been hit. But it didn't matter. He had to figure out what to do with the bodies.

The van was packed with all the necessities: water, food, a satellite dish for high-tech surveillance, and a drop-down bed in the side panel. He'd made sure the VIN was removed. The van had been modified to the point of being unrecognizable as any particular model. The custom magnetic sign on the door panel proclaimed Canon Enterprises ∼ Plumbing & Remodeling ∼ 1 800 326-5148. As he drove from state to state, the sign would change.

There was one other thing inside the van—a cool million in cash along with a newly minted passport and identification papers to cover every possible encounter on his way south. It didn't really matter what story Alice told the police. He'd be long gone.

Right from the beginning, he counted on her as his alibi. He had agreed to take her with him when he left town. It had been easy to string her along. He ran his hand over the stubble on his head and his face. By the time he reached the border, there would be hair and a neatly trimmed beard, and the tats would be covered. The new look would match the latest passport.

He planned to set fire to the cotton sheds as a diversion tactic. Once the flames were seen, the fire department, sheriff's department, police, and EMTs would flood the area. That would give him a good head start. But he hadn't counted on the bodies. If they were discovered, the FBI would be on his tail immediately. There would be roadblocks and alerts going out all across the southeast. If no one knew about the bodies, they would assume vagrants started the fire.

Muttering under his breath, he focused on a plan to dispose of the bodies. His original plan hadn't included all these bodies or how long it would take to dump them. He remembered the swampy waters around an old fish camp on the marsh side of Tybee. He was familiar with the place, and it wasn't too far out of his way. He unrolled a plastic tarp, spread it on the floor of the van, and began the arduous task of moving the corpses.

Then he moved from shed to shed, leaving a trail of gasoline. He worked steadily, as rushing led to mistakes.

A sudden movement jolts me into a conscious state. I open my eyes to blackness. The coppery smell of blood floods my nostrils, accompanied by soft groans. Confusion reigns while I work through the jumbled maze of my thoughts. My worst nightmare is always waking up in the Zinzulusa Caves with the smell of gunpowder and the stench of death in the air. Chuck's voice pulls me back to the present. *Breath! Focus! Strategize!* His words are strong. I concentrate.

Where am I? Why is everything moving? I pat my body. My hands come away, covered in blood. Tears leak as I gently open my jacket. Blood oozes from scraps on my body and face, but there are no gapping holes. When I try to move, intense pain is all encompassing. After a few unsuccessful attempts, I manage to flex my legs and arms without screaming. As long as I'm alive, there's a chance I can get out of here—wherever here is.

A sudden sharp turn sends my body crashing into metal. My hands flail into space before landing on a body. I stifle a scream and let my eyes adjust as low moans empty into the desolate space.

Twisting my head in all directions, I see the outlines of bodies—one next to me and one further away.

We're in some kind of vehicle, and it's moving fast. Another sharp turn has the body closest to me shifting. I scoot over and tentatively touch the person. Looking for wounds, I pat the body until my hand jerks away from a patch of sticky blood seeping from the chest. My eyes adjust as faint light leaks around the panel doors. Slowly, the outline of Nick's face comes into view. My eyes and hands return to his wound. Although I know next to nothing about gunshot wounds, this one looks nasty and close to the heart. My fingers check his pulse. It's so fast I can't count the beats.

"Nick, Nick?" Can you hear me?"

His body shifts a fraction. I remove my jacket and fold it as small as I can. Somewhere along life's way, probably the Girl Scouts, I learned when there's blood, you need to compress the wound to stop the flow. Elevating a person with a wound near the heart is something else I vaguely remember. But is this the correct thing to do? I don't know, but I have to do something.

"Nick? I'm going to try to move you—just a tiny bit. Can you help me?"

His head wobbles. I'm hopeful it means okay. Grasping him around his torso, I ease him into a semi-sitting position with his head and shoulders against the back wall of the van. I press my jacket against the wound. A small yelp and whimper from him signal he's alive.

"Nick, can you hold the jacket in place? There's someone else in the van. I think it's Al. Don't move. I need to check on him, okay?"

In the darkness, I can't tell if he nods or even understands. I place his right hand against the jacket, press, and then release. His hand stays in place, so I crawl to the next body.

Al is crumpled against the van door with his right leg in a peculiar twist. I shake him gently, but he doesn't respond. His pulse is weak and erratic. As I run my hands over his body, the shooting flashes in front of my eyes. Al was shot first—in the leg, I think. I gently uncoil his mangled leg. First compression. I pull my sweater over my head, wad it up, and apply it right on the wound. Al jerks but remains unconscious. With one hand, I yank his belt from his trousers. It feels too narrow and might do more harm than good. I unbutton my shirt, thankful I put on layers this morning.

The wound is in the calf. I use the arms of my shirt to make a tourniquet and place it below the knee. The tiny Nitecore flashlight protrudes from Al's pocket. I click the light on briefly to examine their wounds. After I'm sure I've done all I can, I sweep the light over the interior. I'm astounded to see it's outfitted like living quarters.

On high, the battery life of the flashlight is only a couple of hours. Since I don't know where we are or where we're going, I cut it off to conserve the battery. I tie a half-knot in the shirt sleeves, insert the flashlight, twist, and then tie a full knot.

Sitting back on my heels, I realize there's not much chance of us getting out alive. My body trembles with fear. My thoughts are as confused as a swarm of bees without a queen to lead them. I revert to doing what always centers me, the one thing that brings me back to calmness—I count. The trembling stops as I mutter numbers. My thoughts turn from terror to stillness as the hum of numbers leads me into quietness and deep breathing. In the vast darkness of the van, the sweetness of life returns. Both of these men are important to me. They are in danger of dying. By default, I've been elected queen bee. It's up to me to do whatever I can to save them.

Putting aside my fear, I assess our limited possibilities. I'm sure George is driving the van. I'm sure his only intent is to kill us. The reality of our helplessness sinks in. I feel myself sinking into a black hole until the numbers march back into my head. I allow myself to believe that we will survive.

Nick whispers my name. I scramble back to his side.

"I'm here, Nick."

Gently, I move his hand from the wound and place mine on the bloody jacket. He wheezes and grabs at my free hand. I hold onto him as best I can.

"Cat, Cat, I'm so sorry."

I force my voice to be calm as I murmur, "It's okay, Nick. Save your breath. Help is on the way."

"Cat, listen. I'm not going to make it. I'm sure of that. There isn't much time. I need you to know how I got mixed up in this mess. I'm not evil, Cat. I never wanted to hurt you or those girls. I'm so sorry."

"Nick, please don't try to talk. There'll be time later. You'll pull through this."

He lets go of my hand and touches my face.

"Don't cry, Cat. Save your tears for someone who deserves them. Don't argue with me. Listen to me. Please hear my story. Perhaps then you can forgive me."

"Nick, stop. Save your energy."

But he continues to talk until his voice gives out.

His story begins after he left high school. He was in university and struggling with both money and grades when his baby brother was born. One of those mid-life surprise births. Nick's alcoholic father wandered off and never returned. A few weeks later, his mother committed suicide. Nick asked for a leave of compassion from school until he could find a way to take care of his brother Ted.

When his fraternity brothers saw his struggles, they banded together and appealed to their alumni to pitch in. That's when Nick first met the senator. Jim was still in private practice but was testing the waters for political office. He was collecting an entourage of eager young men to be on his team. Nick's fervor to take care of his baby brother made him an easy target to groom for anything the senator might need doing down the road.

The senator invested thousands of dollars in childcare for Ted and in Nick's education in criminal justice and computer science with an emphasis on cyber security. His large donations plus tutors got Nick into law school. After graduating from Columbia with a degree in criminal justice, the senator saw to it that Nick landed at the FBI Academy in Quantico, Virginia.

As Nick's career soared, Ted found his niche with a group of young activists. Nick was proud of Ted and encouraged his activities. The peaceful demonstrations at the state capitol subtlety changed. The placards changed from benign to dangerous.

The city fathers became nervous, and extra police were hired. The FBI was asked to set up a task force to ensure the demonstrations stayed peaceful. Because Nick's brother was involved, he couldn't participate, but he was present as an interested citizen during the Saturday demonstrations.

One bright Saturday morning, an object was thrown at a law enforcement officer. In a single moment, one shot rang out. Nick watched in horror as a black hole with a trickle of blood appeared on Ted's forehead. As he fell to the ground, the placard he was holding toppled with him. As Nick rushed toward him, an officer ripped the placard, but not before Nick saw the words: SENATOR JAMES MADISON = ORGANIZED CRIME.

The drugs, alcohol, loss of job and being rescued once again by the senator poured out of Nick with each painful breath.

Without shifting, I hold him in my arms and tell him he is safe. I thank him for saving my life. I whisper how brave he is and how I forgive him with my whole heart. When he hears the word forgive, he sighs mightily and drifts away.

60

Sporadic drops of rain hit the roof of the van. Without windows, there's no indication of what time it is. I try to calculate how many hours have passed. The brooding darkness inside the van provides no hint. We could have been here for an hour or twenty-four. Nick is either unconscious or lost in thought as he hasn't spoken for a while. He's exhausted from the loss of blood and his confession of sorts. Without a jacket or shirt, I shiver in the black silence.

The van swerves abruptly off the paved road. It bumps and sways as the tires dig into sandy soil. Without anything to hold onto, our bodies are tossed about. Al's moan is low and soft, but a blood-curdling scream leaves Nick's mouth. I check my jacket. He's bled through. The worst thoughts enter my mind.

He grabs my hand and whispers. I lean in to hear him, "I'm so sorry, Cat. I didn't mean to hurt you. You were always my best pal."

His hand falls away. I cradle his head and sob.

The van stops. I'm petrified, but this may be my only chance. I slide along the wall until I'm crouched next to the doors. The Krav Maga lessons command me to *Breathe! Focus! Act!*

The doors swing open. I lunge squarely into George's chest. He doesn't even lose balance. He simply grabs my hair and rams his fist into my face. He keeps me in a chokehold as he slams the door to the van and drags me through the sand and weeds toward the water. He pauses a second to adjust his hold. I let loose with every trick Chuck has ever taught me. The final one is to ram my fist in his most vulnerable spot. For a second, he releases me. During that second, I scuttle a short distance away. He pulls out his gun and takes aim. I close my eyes. A single shot shatters the silence.

George gasps and clutches his shoulder. Men clad from head to toe in black point sub-machine guns at us. Two of them drag George off.

All I can manage to squeeze out between heaving sobs is, "Please help us! We need a doctor!"

"Yes, ma'am."

The others stand down, although the guns stay trained on me. Someone yells for an ambulance.

"Sorry, ma'am. Do you know the condition of the two men in the van?"

Through heaving sobs, I whimper, "One's shot in the leg. The other is shot in the chest. He's critical."

He asks who I am and who are the men in the van.

My voice is hollow and shrill, "Who are you? Put down your damn guns and get medical help now."

"Yes, ma'am," he says and backs off, pulling the others with him.

A voice I recognize booms through the early morning light. "What's going on? Cat, is that you? Are you okay?"

Sobs wrack my body as Sheriff Blackwell gathers me in his arms and holds me tight. His big hand pats my hair.

"It's okay. It's okay. The ambulance is almost here. You just hold tight. Let me get you an ice pack from that shiner."

I gently push him away. "Please help the others. I'm afraid Nick might be dead, and Al—I don't know."

The wail of the ambulance stops. Doors open and close. Sheriff Blackwell pulls me away so I can't see what's going on. The assessments go quickly. Nick and Al are transferred to stretchers. Before the door to the ambulance closes, I break loose from the sheriff's hold and watch in horror as the sheet is pulled over Nick's head.

While I'm waiting, I'm checked out by a paramedic and told I'll live but will have a lot of discomfort for a few days. A blanket has been placed around my shoulders, an ice pack pressed to my face, and a cup of coffee placed in my hands. The ambulance pulls away—no siren to announce its departure.

"He's dead, isn't he?"

"Unless they can resuscitate him on the drive back that'll likely be the result. I'm sorry, Cat. He was a bad guy, but I know he was an old friend of yours. I'm sure when you knew him he was a good man. It's tough when someone you care about messes up so bad it can't be fixed."

"But sheriff, he tried to fix it. If he hadn't jumped in front of me, I'd have been the one with the sheet over my head. But there's a lot more to his story you need to know."

"Tomorrow, Cat. There's time tomorrow. You come down to the office in the morning, and I'll take your statement. Right now, I'm sending you home. Cassie's already there waiting for you."

"But what about Stephanie? Has she been found? And the senator? You have to arrest him right away as he's behind this entire operation. And George, he's the guy who shot Al and Nick and tried to shoot me. Did that shot kill him?"

"Cat, you're exhausted and in shock, so I'm not going to give you a lot of details. You'll have to trust me that we've got everything under control. Stephanie is safe. She's in the hospital. Her sister and mother are with her. I'll tell you about the senator and Alice later. George isn't dead. Once he's patched up, he'll be behind bars. Okay? Once you've rested, we'll talk."

For once, I don't protest. The only feeble remark I make is, "Will you drive me home, please?"

He pats me on the back and says, "No, Cat. I have to stay. This is a crime scene. Since it's my turf, I'm the lead. That means I have a few more hours to put in. I've arranged a car and driver to take you home. Come on. I'll walk you to the car. You'll be in good hands."

He keeps his arms around me as my feet sink in the soft, warm sand. I lean into him as we move to the waiting car. He opens the passenger door of an unmarked vehicle and settles me in the front seat. He leans across me and says to the driver, "Take good care of her. Keep her safe. Stay with her and bring her to my office tomorrow. Okay?"

I mutter, "I don't need a babysitter."

The sheriff pats my hand and says, "Sure you do."

The driver's cap is pulled down over his eyes. He offers a curt nod. I cling to Sheriff Blackwell, not wanting to let go. After a bear of a hug, he unclenches my hands, tucks the blanket around me, and closes the door. There's total silence in the car. I don't look at the driver. I don't want to see another unfriendly face for a very long time.

When he places his hand on my arm and says *Cat* the entire world spins crazily. I collapse against him and sob. It's hard to say how much time passes while Lorenzo holds me in his arms—a minute or a year—it's the same. He gently lifts my face and wipes my eyes, nose, and the drool dangling from my mouth.

"Let's go home."

I nod. He starts the engine. The bright headlights show the way out of the densely populated forest. The car bounces and bucks before the sandy soil turns to pavement. We glide into the night with the windows down and a Lowcountry breeze rushing through my hair.

The miracle of life encompasses me. I'm alive.

61

I reach across and pat the space next to me. It's empty. My eyes remain shut while I listen for familiar sounds like water running in the shower or filling the coffee pot. I sniff the air for the aroma of coffee or warm pastries. I stretch and moan as every muscle in my body screams.

But I'm alive, more than alive, as I remember how gentle Lorenzo was as he treated my wounds. The thoughts of his tenderness keep the pain at bay as well as the horror of what occurred.

The bed jiggles as he sits next to me. He holds me in his arms being oh so careful not to touch the battered and bruised parts of my body.

It's after ten before I can force my body to move. Lorenzo has coffee and pastries waiting. When I think about arriving home last night, I vaguely remember Cassie hugging the crap out of me until I begged her to stop. She moved from me to Lorenzo and kept thanking him. Before she left, she held me again, but not as tight.

She whispered, "If you need me for anything, call. But I think you're going to be well taken care of. No wonder you can't get over this guy."

This morning, we smile endlessly across the table at each other. Lorenzo finally gets up and stands behind my chair. He leans down and nuzzles my neck.

"We're late. Sheriff Blackwell will be in a stew if I don't show up with you this morning."

"I know, but what a shame we have to spend our whole day with the sheriff."

We laugh—happy in our belief that all of this mess will somehow end well.

As we pull up to the stately white building, a lump lodges in my throat, along with images of Cassie sitting on the bench while she considered killing herself or the senator. Thankfully, she didn't do either. Why, oh why, didn't I understand how close she was to the edge?

We park in the same lot as the sheriff's car. As I glance across the way, another lump rises in my throat when my eyes land on the Witness Tree. So much history has paraded under this magnificent oak. So many stories told about those who have left an imprint on this land under this tree—This Tree of Life. Across from the Witness Tree is The Pat Conroy Literary Center. I wonder what this incredible Southern writer would make of this sordid tale?

Lorenzo senses my sadness and gently turns me toward the front door. We're led to the back conference room. There's coffee, more pastries, and a quiche from Herban Market just across the street.

"Thought y'all might be hungry this morning. Particularly since you look like you just rolled out of bed. That shiner looks nasty, Cat. How're you feeling?"

A scarlet blush spreads across my face. I mumble that I'm fine. The sheriff grins a big ol' smile, "Okay, you two, we need to get down to business. Cat, a lot has happened—some you know about and some you don't. Before I shed light on all the activities that have occurred over the past few days, I need to get your statement."

Lorenzo pulls out a chair for me and hands me a cup of coffee and a slice of quiche. He plants a kiss on top of my head and flops in the chair next to me.

"I'm ready, Sheriff Blackwell, but my mind needs prodding after everything that's happened. Without a prompt or two, I might not remember anything."

Two hours later, I sign the statement for my story and for Nick's.

"Why don't y'all go ahead and take a lunch break? We can reconvene at two. Or, if you want to keep on going, we can plow through. It probably won't take more than an hour to fill you in."

"Then go ahead. I need to know what happened. Is George dead or alive? And the senator? What role did he play in all this? And."

"Whoa, whoa! One thing at a time. This is an intricate story. It started many years ago, as most stories do. According to Alice, it seems our less-than-esteemed state senator had been abusing her since they were children. When that wasn't enough to satisfy him, he livened up his life by taking a liking to underaged girls. He was crafty and careful how he went about it. He created an entire backstory about the mission of his project. Told the whole world it was to rescue druggies and prostitutes. Even asked for donations, and all the do-gooders in his district opened their purses. Initially, he and his buddies—the ones he easily lured into supporting and partaking of what they called *the product*—were satisfied with the young prostitutes.

"All this time, Nick was on the payroll—had been trapped in the senator's clutches when he was a very young man and in a desperate situation. But you know that part of the story, don't you?"

Lorenzo tightens his arm around me as tears trickle from my eyes, "Yes, Nick told me everything."

The sheriff waits until I stop sniffling, then says, "After reviewing his FBI file, I understand better what happened and how it happened. He certainly benefited from the senator's mentorship, and I can understand how he might have thought he was a good man. The sad part was he believed he was indebted to the senator. Once he felt that way he wasn't able to extricate himself from the evil and corruption.

"What about Alice? What did she know?"

"Well, I'm getting to that, so don't get ahead of my story. Let's see

—at some point, the senator got married and had a couple of kids until his wife caught on. She, with Alice's help, hired a private detective and blackmailed James into letting her take the children and leave the country. Alice was deeply involved as she paid for the private investigator and used the pornographic photographs of James with a multitude of underaged girls to blackmail him."

"Wow! Did either George or Nick know about the abuse?"

"I'm coming to that part, Cat. Lordy, girl, give me a chance. Now settle back. Lorenzo, get her some water."

Sheriff Blackwell stood up and stretched while Lorenzo left the room.

"Cat, this is a messy business. It'll take days to fill you in, so you're getting the condensed version. After you leave here, you can ask Lorenzo to provide whatever other details you'd like to know. He's been the driving force behind the scenes. We wouldn't have captured these people or have been able to rescue you if he hadn't coordinated everything through the FBI. Your guy has some clout. He put the wheels in motion right after you contacted him that first time. Lord, he loves telling the story of you Zooming with him in a party dress with that expensive necklace around your neck."

"Not so funny," I mutter.

"Cat, don't you want to take a break? You and Lorenzo need to get away. How long has it been since you last saw him? That man is crazy about you. You're wasting time here listening to me."

"No, sheriff. I want to keep going. A million questions will pop into my head later, and I'll pick Lorenzo's brain for answers. But right now, I want to hear what happened from you. You were there. First, tell me how Al is."

He sighs, hitches up his trousers, twists his torso in some attempt to stretch, and sinks in the chair. Lorenzo pops in with water and says he's needed in the interrogation room. I nod for the sheriff to continue.

"That man's gonna be okay. His leg is busted up pretty bad. Once the doctors got him stabilized, they sent him up the road to MUSC.

He'll need surgery and will be out of commission for a few weeks, but he's lucky to be alive. That was a damn stupid thing y'all did going out to Carrington. I'm not gonna even ask you how that happened."

I squirm and mumble that I'm sorry, but the sheriff ignores me.

"And you already know or have guessed that your friend Nick didn't make it. I'm sorry, Cat. That's a hard thing to deal with."

I stifle a sob and nod.

"Senator Madison was an evil man. Don't know how that happened. I'm not in that line of work where I have to analyze the why's of a situation. Any man who defiles his own sister is either crazy or doesn't have a moral compass. Who knows what creates that kind of monster, but his childhood behavior charted this man's course. His brain was warped early on. How the man got to be a state senator is beyond me. Just shows you how corrupt the world is. He even called his perverse activities Operation Save the Children. He fooled anybody who wanted to be fooled. Of course, that's what our illustrious politicians do. His ultimate scheme was to kidnap underage girls—clean and pure—not the street variety he'd been using."

I gasp. "So the senator purposely went after Diana and her sister?"

"Not so much him, but his henchman George. But it was all done at the senator's direction. Now, that's a man to ask Lorenzo about. That guy is way beyond me and this small town. He's part of an international mafia-related gang—Russian-based with ties to Albania, Italy, and the US. Lorenzo mentioned that when we were on that Zoom meeting. He knows far more about George than I do. All I can tell you is some of the surface stuff that occurred recently."

Involuntarily, I shudder and say, "Lorenzo told me there was a connection between George and the SCU. Now I have to wonder if he wasn't sent here by Riccardo to kill me as well."

"Now, don't go down that road, Cat. Everything is okay, and it's only going to get better. This here story I'm telling you has a happy ending. There are reasons the senator's little side operation didn't go well. Two people made extraordinary efforts to stop the evil.

"Diana was one of those people. She was feisty and ready to give her life to save her little sister. She didn't care how that happened. She was the one person able to reach Nick's broken spirit. She was young and vulnerable like his brother had been. That's what I believe changed his direction—that and dragging you into the situation. That was something he really regretted. Once he realized that both of you could be killed, he regrouped and got on the right side of things."

Tears well up as I say, "Nick finally found his conscience. Deep down, he was a good man."

"Maybe, Cat. He did save your life, the count's, and by default Diana and Stephanie's. But he'd have gone to prison for a long time for his role in this operation. If I have any say, George will never see daylight again. It was his job to kill all of you. Y'all are real lucky to be alive. But what I haven't told you is the senator is dead."

"Dead? Who killed him? When? Nick told me when he left the senator's house, he was alive. The thing that worried him the most was George telling him to get out but to leave his gun behind."

"Nick was right to be worried. It'll take a while to work everything out, but we have our suspicions. The gun left next to the senator's body had Nick's fingerprints on it. But they were smudged as if someone with gloves actually used Nick's gun. It was either Alice or George. Since Alice was shot, I'm guessing it was George. The bullets are in the lab now, and ballistics will hopefully give us the rest of the story. My guess is the senator shot Alice, and George shot the senator."

"Is Alice alive? Nick said she was when he left the senator's house."

"Yes. She's in the hospital. She'll recover. I questioned her some, but there's still a lot more to learn."

He pauses and says, "So we have sort of a loose story about what happened. According to Alice, George brought Stephanie to the house at the senator's request. Then he left. The house, which belongs to both Alice and James, was supposed to be off-limits for the senator's dalliances. Alice arrived home from her evening of bridge and found the senator with Stephanie. She claims he was raping the girl. When Alice tried to stop him, he shot her. The bullet removed from her shoulder matches up with the gun that has the senator's finger prints on it. Alice said this man she'd never seen before came crashing through the door. He and the senator struggled. She said the senator fell, and the man shot him in the back. She's identified the man as Nick. Now George, for some unknown reason, returned just as Nick shot the senator. George tackled Nick, and according to Alice, Nick dropped his gun and ran. George was afraid he'd be implicated, so he ran too."

"You can't believe that. Not after my statement and Nick's story."

"Of course, I don't believe her story. I don't believe any of the stories. Particularly after the doctor told me that while traumatized, Stephanie wasn't raped."

"Oh, my gosh. What a relief."

Sheriff Blackwell sighs, "There's more. In George's version he says he returned to the senator's house because he forgot to leave the girl's belongings. He interrupted Nick shooting the senator, and tackled him like Alice said. When Nick ran off, George figured he'd be in a heap of trouble. He said his conscience required that he go after Nick and turn him in."

"Oh sure, that's just crazy. A normal person would have called an ambulance for Alice and then called the police. He could have easily told law enforcement that Nick shot the senator. George's story makes zero sense. Nick knew he was dying when he talked to me. He had no reason to lie. I believe him when he said the senator was still alive when he left. George is the one who shot the senator."

"I suspect you're right, but it's going to take a while to untangle this mess."

"What is George's explanation for having Al, Nick, and me in his van?"

"Well, he said he drove to the plantation because he thought that's where Nick would go. When he got there, he said Nick had already shot Al. He thought he'd also shot you, because you were lying in a pool of blood. George admits to shooting Nick in self-defense. He said with his record, he knew he'd be blamed. In a panic, he decided to dispose of the evidence—meaning the bodies."

"You know none of that is true."

"Oh lordy, Cat. I don't know anything right now. Except I do think Alice and George are in cahoots. Alice wanted the senator dead for years because of the sexual abuse he inflicted on her. She pretty much gave up her life for James. And what does he do? He brings these girls into their home. Alice was the one paying to keep the ex-wife out of the country. That's all messed up with the two family businesses—JMM and A. Aldridge Properties. Lorenzo said you figured out the JMM and pointed him to ask the FBI about Alice's full name. You were right. Her name is Alice Aldridge Madison."

"Well, that explains a lot, doesn't it?"

"It sure does. Things were going along pretty well until Cassie entered the picture. Alice was sick and tired of putting up with James' dalliances. She figured if he married Cassie, then she'd be stuck paying another wife off. My guess is she approached George and asked him to kill James. He was more than agreeable to help her for a very large sum of cash. He told her he wanted to take over the operation, so it worked with his plans. What she didn't know was that sooner or later, George would have killed her, too. He may or may not have wanted to take over the operation, but he did want the money. Alice played right into his plans as we found a huge stash of cash in the van."

"Wow! So Alice paid him to kill the senator. Can you prove that? If you did, she'd go to jail for quite a while, wouldn't she?"

"Yes, but they both lawyered up. The conversations dried up. We do know George thought all three of you were dead. From both Al and Nick's wounds, you were covered in blood. But he didn't much care if you were dead or alive when he threw you in the van. His goal was to dump y'all in the marshes and head to the border. We also discovered he's got a criminal record a mile long back in South Africa. That's another story that'll make your skin crawl about how he escaped jail and landed in the US."

"Okay, so either George or Alice killed the senator. My bet is on George. How strong is the case?"

"Lordy, Cat, this all just happened. We don't have a case yet, much less know how strong it will be. But the one thing that's on the top of the list is to extradite George to South Africa. That would solve most of our problems. If he's gone, I think Alice will cooperate with the FBI."

"Well, the only story I believe is Nick's. You have both Al and me to back up that story about the shooting at the plantation. Do you think Alice will be cleared for actually killing the senator? Although she probably hired George to kill James, she didn't pull the trigger. While I think she's despicable, I feel sorry for her. Her life was ruined at such an early age. She's been subjugated to this monster for years. Maybe this is an opportunity for her to put her life back together."

"Could be, but again, it's too soon to tell. All I can say right now is I'm so grateful that Cassie didn't get herself involved."

"Me too! That's the best part of Nick's story. When he told me Cassie was headed for the senator's house with a gun, I thought the worst. But he said she changed her mind and left. She could have been the one that killed the senator, but she didn't. It gives me the creeps to think how close she was to destroying her life all because of this depraved individual. Is Cassie in any trouble?"

"Nah, not anything I can't fix unless you're going to bring charges against her for stealing your gun."

"Of course, I'm not. You know I wouldn't."

"I'm just picking at you, Cat. Don't go getting all huffy."

I sputter for a few seconds before asking, "What happened to Stephanie? Was she hurt? Was she still at the senator's house? Who rescued her? Did she see the shooting?"

"Shucks, my heart aches for that kid. We can only hope she's resilient. She's seen way too much for a fourteen-year-old. She was found wandering around at Carrington. I guess George just dumped her out. Not sure why he didn't kill her. She's in the hospital. They're checking her out. Your Dr. Ginny is already there. She'll be under her care for a long while."

"What do you mean, my Dr. Ginny?"

"Ah, don't be getting all snappy. Cassie recommended Dr. Ginny. When I asked about her credentials, she said you'd vouch for her. So I figured you must have spent some time with her too. But I have a question for her. Okay? You ask her for me what makes you keep jumping into situations that aren't yours to jump into. Lorenzo told me all about what happened to you in Italy."

I have the decency to duck my head to avoid eye contact with the sheriff, but he keeps on talking.

"So here's the deal. If we extradite George, there won't be a need for Stephanie to testify. I wouldn't let that happen anyway. In fact, I'm willing to go on record before the court and tell them she's too traumatized to be a witness. She's got a long road to recovery, but she's young. Her mom and Diana are going to be right by her side. The whole family needs counseling after what happened."

"I'm so thankful Stephanie wasn't killed. I'd say that's a miracle, wouldn't you?"

"Sure would and her sister, Diana, is one brave young woman. Do you know she was able to identify the previous girl that washed up at the marina? I asked her if she'd look at some photos of missing girls. I thought she might recognize some of them that were picked up the same night she and Stephanie were. When she saw the red hair clip, she started crying. Said it was hers and that the girl's name was Hannah."

"That must have been heartbreaking for Diana."

"It was. These girls are so young and innocent. A stupid mistake almost got them messed up for life and, even worse, could have killed them like it did Hannah. It's a sorry world."

"Hmmm, it's not going to be easy to sort through all of this. I am glad to hear the entire family is in counseling."

"Yeah, me too. Well, before we wrap up, is there anything else you want to know?"

"What about the van? How did you find us?"

"Surely you've seen enough detective shows to know about tracking devices. The FBI placed one on the limo that George used to drive the count around. That led them to the plantation. They discovered the cotton sheds and the vans and decided to put trackers on both of the vans. The big problem occurred when George called Al and said Nick had Stephanie. When he insisted you two come out and try to persuade Nick not to kill her, Al borrowed a car from the inn. That meant there was no tracking device. What were ya'll thinking by driving out there? Where was your brain?"

I squirm in my chair but keep quiet.

"George thought he'd shot all of you, so he dumped you in one of the vans. Then, he started a fire to destroy any evidence that he might have been left behind and to create a diversion. He knew the sheriff's department, the police and other rescue units would be on the scene, and that would allow him time to get rid of the bodies and get on the road. Thank goodness he decided not to roast all of you in the fire, or the whole bunch of you would be dead instead of just Nick."

"So how did you find us?"

"It was a huge problem for us when Al picked you up in a borrowed car. Without the tracking device, we had no clue that you and he were on your way to the plantation. That little bit of missing information almost got you killed. If George hadn't used one of those vans, you would have been in the those marshes off of Tybee 'cause that's where he was headed. Your bodies may or may not have ever turned up. But the van George was driving had the tracking device. Once it started moving, the FBI took up the chase. Of course, no one knew y'all were in the van. You're lucky, damn lucky, Cat."

I nod and change the subject. "Are you absolutely sure Cassie isn't going to be in any trouble over this?"

"Hmmm, Cassandra had a bit of explaining to do before I let her off the hook. She made a really bad decision, but haven't we all when our emotions are involved? I've known her all my life. I love her like my own daughters. She'll be okay. But you two need to keep your noses in your party planning and catering business. You're not cut out for sleuthing, although Cassie did tell me you're becoming a Krav Maga expert."

He laughs a good hearty laugh. The muscles in my neck and shoulders release as I join him. Lorenzo opens the door and sticks his head in.

"You two have gone over the hour limit. I'm buying lunch now. *Andiamo.*"

"Naw, you two kids go have some fun. I need to check on ballistics. I want to get George charged, and I need to stop by the hospital to check on Alice before I go home. We've got a lot of work to do. If I'm right, George and his slick lawyer will fight the extradition. Our best bet is to turn him over to police in South Africa. They are already rattling the cage to get him extradited. Boy, am I glad most of this is going to fall under FBI jurisdiction. It's complicated, and those crafty lawyers are gonna pull out all their tricks."

"Thanks, Sheriff Blackwell. Oh, I just thought of another question."

Both men grin—one's exhausted and thankful I'm leaving. The other exhausted but happy we'll have the afternoon together.

"Cat, get out of here with your fella. I'm not answering anymore of your questions today."

62

C arrington Point Plantation sizzles with excitement. The grounds have been whipped into a fairyland of sparkle and shine. Tables groan from the weight of Spanish pottery piled high with delectable tapas. Champagne and wine glasses are filled and then refilled. Twinkling white lights hang from the grand angel oaks. The six-count, eight-step pattern of the Carolina shag storms across the polished dance floor illuminated by a crystal chandelier dangling like Spanish moss from the limb of a giant oak. The music is laid-back—easy and slow-paced, reminiscent of Fat Harold's Beach Club in Myrtle Beach and warm summer nights with the ocean lapping at my toes as I softly kiss the boy I once thought was my true love.

It's a glorious night. Al never lets me out of his sight. It's not like I saved his life, although, in his mind, that's exactly what he thinks. I can't convince him otherwise. The more Al hovers, the more Lorenzo snarls and mutters. It's delightful to watch two grown men spar.

Yet, deep inside, memories curl and distort. Does Lorenzo really care? When he asked me to stay in Italy with him, was it because he loved me or felt he owed me? In the cruel aftermath of Stella's death, were our emotions misplaced? Have we drifted apart? Is my memory playing tricks? Have I've imagined our relationship is more than it really is? As time and distance keep us apart, has the reality of what we might have had melted away into faded memories? I sigh deeply as there are no answers.

Lorenzo is here. Nothing has been said. Neither of us brings up the subject. Thoughts of a life with him drift in and out of my mind. He does nothing to encourage them.

Little by little, Al has become a part of my life. His enthusiasm for the Moringa Project draws me in, as do his courtly manners. He approaches me with the utmost respect, all the while carrying his heart in his hand. He is much like the Tree of Life—his roots are deep, his branches strong. He exudes strength and calmness—attributes that feel safe, comfortable, and warm.

There are no quick decisions to be made. Neither Lorenzo nor Al has completely won my heart. Numerous roadblocks of my own creation require attention before I'm ready to make a commitment. Maybe I'll never be ready. Life is so much simpler without the complexities and complications of another soul attached to mine.

As the last notes of *I Love Beach Music* fade into the breezy night, Al takes the microphone from the lead singer and calls for everyone to gather. The crowd jostles for position. The dress code for the event is casual. Al is dressed like the Spanish count he is—black chinos, a crisp white shirt, and polished-to-perfection Gucci loafers. He's graduated from a hard cast to a soft one. He's thrilled to be walking with an almost natural gait. He signals me to join him. My white skirt swirled with black geometric shapes flares around my knees. I let go of my dance partner and move toward Al.

Lorenzo grabs my hand and whispers, "Remember who you're going home with tonight."

His smile fills my heart with joy.

Al sees the exchange. When I reach the stage, he pulls me into a close embrace, and the crowd applauds. I push back and search for Lorenzo. He's wandered away from the dance floor to stand by Cassie and Chuck.

My entire being smiles when I see those two together. While Cassie continues to hold him at arm's length, Chuck is a patient man. He doesn't hover, but his love for Cassie is evident. Every time he sees her, he lights up like a fireworks display.

The crowd murmurs restlessly. Al holds up his hands and leans into the microphone.

"Thank you for coming tonight. This occasion is far more than a celebration of a new endeavor. Without Cat."

His voice trails off. He shudders and pulls me back into his embrace.

"Without Cat and her friend Lorenzo and, of course, the FBI and Sheriff Blackwell, this project would have died before it began. Most of you have seen the news, read about it, or heard the story from someone. It's been the only topic of conversation for weeks. But that's all behind us. Carrington Point Plantation is free and clear of all liens. The human trafficking trade that was discovered on the premises is no longer in existence. And I am now the owner of this magnificent place."

Applause bounces through the trees surrounding the dance floor. It's a hollow echo. It belies the fear—the fear of the big names who were caught up in the trafficking of minors and drugs. Al leans into the mike.

"The best part of the story is one most of you haven't heard. Several of the young girls were found and returned home or to places that will protect them. We are fortunate that one of those young women was brave enough to risk her life to escape. To find her little sister alive was her only goal. On her journey, she was fortunate to be noticed by Cat and rescued by Sheriff Blackwell. Her information helped to put these nasty people out of business. And, yes, in the process, her sister was found and is recovering. We are so fortunate tonight to have this young heroine with us, Diana Abbot."

He gestures. The crowd parts as Diana makes her way toward us. She's radiant in a short white skirt that pairs with a pale sage v-necked pullover stitched with silver threads. Her abundant blonde curls bounce with every step, and her smile spreads like spilled milk. My eyes overflow with tears as I see a young Stella in this vibrant girl. Her arm with two compound fractures is still in a cast that's now covered with signatures and stickers. She throws herself at me and sobs.

"Hush, it's okay. It's over. You're safe. Stephanie is safe."

Diana wipes her eyes and nestles in between us.

Strangely, she has gravitated toward Al and me as if we're her long-lost parents. She is, with her mother's consent, in my care for her final year of high school. Her mom and sister will be close by, but she will actually live in my guest house. Al has hired her mom, Gloria, to be in charge of housekeeping once his resort is up and running. A small bungalow is already being built for her and Stephanie on the property, with a room for Diana when she needs to be with her family.

Diana has secured a spot in the freshman class of culinary sciences at Johnson and Wales University in Charlotte. We couldn't be happier since Sam, Cassie's daughter, is in her final year at JWU. During summers and spring breaks, both Diana and Sam will live in my guest house and learn the catering business. When it's time for their internships, Al has offered them spots at Carrington Estates Boutique Hotel, Day Spa, and the Southern Cuisine Restaurant. He's assured them they'll have jobs waiting when they graduate. Who knows, maybe one day they'll put Cassie and me out of business.

I tune back in as Al describes the hotel, restaurant, and spa and mentions that both Cassie and I have been offered partnerships, which we are considering. Cass and I haven't had time to talk about it yet. In a few days, we leave for a girls' retreat at the Cloisters. Sam and Diana begged to come with us, but Cass and I need to regroup— only the two of us. I'm in a wounded state of mind, as is Cass. We've been through too much and need time to process and restore our relationship. While we're away, Al, Gloria, and Sam are going to show Diana around campus.

The crowd quiets when Al holds up his hands for silence. "There are two reasons we're here tonight. The most important reason is standing with us. Diana wants to say a few words about the fundraiser we are holding tonight. The proceeds will go to non-profit organizations working to eliminate human trafficking. There are brochures at the entrance and on all the tables. Please make your donations large."

Al turns the mike over to Diana. She bravely tells her story, only losing her composure once. We hug her fiercely as the applause thunders loud and long. After she's finished, she slips away and joins Sam, Cassie, and Chuck.

Next on the agenda is Al's beloved Moringa Project. His face glows as he speaks about experimenting with this crop in South Carolina. My eyes peruse the crowd. I'm surprised to see Mrs. Harrington here. Instead of paying attention to Al, her daughter leans in and listens intently to whatever her mother is saying. John Ashley is slumped in his chair, his face crumpled in boredom. How thankful I am that our relationship went south.

I glance at Mrs. Harrington and wish I could read lips, but it's easy for me to imagine how the conversation will go as she leans toward her daughter and whispers,

"Well, I didn't realize Cat was involved in this project. But, of course, I'm behind her continued success. If I hadn't fired her, she wouldn't have accepted work from the likes of Sarah Fitzhugh, and she would have never met the count. Her success is my doing. I might even ask her to cater an event for me. Of course, she'd have to apologize first."

I chuckle to myself as I imagine this heart-to-heart conversation the two of them are having. They're still chatting when Mary Elizabeth Cunningham Berkley struts into their midst. I don't have to be a lipreader to understand what Mary Elizabeth is revealing to the Harrington's. She's telling them that her wedding reception will be the very first ever event to be held at Carrington Point Plantation since its revival. She's joyfully thumbing her nose at them in her Mary Elizabeth fashion. For once, I want to applaud her. My approval won't last long as I'll be the one putting up with her demands for an absolutely perfect event. From the shocked look I see spreading across Mrs. Harrington's face, I'm going to do my best to make it the event of the year.

I don't waste any more time on them. My gaze sweeps over the crowd until I find Cassie. Our eyes meet, accompanied by big smiles. Chuck has his arm protectively around her shoulders. The look on his face is fierce. It dares anyone to mess with her.

Next to them is Gloria Abbot. She clings to Diana. Even from this distance, I see her body tremble. I'm actually shocked she's allowing Diana to stay with me. We had a long talk well into the night as she poured out her soul about her life as a single parent. Her fears, real and imagined, had all come true with the kidnapping of her two girls. Another mother might have used the incident as a way to keep the girls under lock and key, but Gloria said it made her realize how strong and resourceful Diana is.

"She's ready to make her own way. I couldn't ask for anyone better than you to be there to guide her. If you hadn't given her your card, I don't know if she would have made it. You gave her hope."

With that, she handed Diana into my care—me, someone who knows nothing about kids. But Cassie, Chuck, and Sam have already circled the wagons. Al jumped right in and offered his support. We've all been through a lot. We are all survivors. This year with Diana will be an adventure for both of us.

Turning back to Al, I listen as he invites those attending to join in the venture to feed the world. I try not to speculate about what the next year will bring. I'm hopeful for Al and this Moringa Project. Only time will determine its success or failure. But if anyone asks my opinion, I will say, "Yes, he will succeed. How can he fail when he's growing Moringa: The Tree of Life?"

Tonight, in this place surrounded by friends who have become my family, I believe in the power of goodness. This small town on the South Carolina coast is my home—the land, the water, and the sky all come together. They whisper that I belong. Stella's voice still resides in my heart, but it's no longer the driving force in my life. Tonight in this place, I believe in the magic of the Lowcountry and the love of my friends—past and present.

It's close to midnight as we stack plates, cups, and glasses into busing trays and haul load after load to the waiting vans. Thankfully, Al rented several along with drivers to haul the dirty dishes and linens back to the rental company for their clean-up service. Al, as promised, has done everything to make my job as easy as possible. The flowers and leftover goodies go in another van headed to Beaufort Memorial Hospital to thank the staff for the exceptional care they provided to both Diana and Stephanie.

The night hangs without movement. Creature sounds float on the still air: the hoot of an owl, the chirp of a cricket, the croak of a frog. Fireflies dance to some unheard music. My heart slows from the manic pace of the past few days to the sweet rhythm of night music.

Italy is but a faint image in my thoughts. This is my home, my place, my time. I shiver as the breeze drapes its damp tentacles around my body. I lean into the table where I've been folding and stacking tablecloths and napkins and realize I'm alone. Panic rises in my throat as I stare at my surroundings—the vans with doors open still parked on the lawn, the port-a-potties casting giant shadows, and the grand oaks whose arms reach toward me with malice. Where is everyone?

Out of the dark night, a tiny glow emerges. Large dark beings in a massive lump move with the light. The closer it comes, the stronger my urge to scream and run like hell.

"Happy Birthday to you, Happy Birthday to you, Happy Birthday dear Cat, Happy Birthday to you."

The dark bungling group untangles and spreads apart. Cassie's face beams with joy and love. In her hands is a monster chocolate cake and enough candles to brighten the faces of Chuck, Lorenzo, Al, Diana and Sheriff Blackwell.

Stella's face swells into my vision. Tears leak as I whisper I love her and wish her *buon compleanno*. Does she know I'm happy? Does she know I'm truly home? I believe she does.

63

T he marsh sun inches softly into the lush glow of morning. Turning from the window, I force my eyes to acknowledge his suitcase already by the door. Last night, we talked for hours. We listened to each other's reasoning. There were no resolutions. My emotions are fragile, as delicate as butterfly wings. One thing I know is I'm not cut out for a long-distance relationship. If I have a partner, I want him by my side. I've loved Lorenzo since I was a child. My love for him has grown just as my love for Italy has. With Stella leaving me her villa, the pull is strong to return. But is a life with Lorenzo a reality, or is it simply a fantasy —a dream that will never come true? I could pursue the dream. I could make it my reality, but some dreams are better left as dreams —better suited to our "what if" imaginations. That is what I still have to determine.

Movement in the hallway alerts me to his presence. I hit the button on the espresso machine and let the comforting whoosh lull me into believing he won't leave. My heart weeps in anticipation of the moment the airport shuttle whisks him away.

He walks into the kitchen, his hair still damp from the shower and his smile full of hope. I hand him a cup, pick up mine, and silently move to the screened porch. I sink into the cushions on the swing bed and adjust the pillows behind my back. He sits at the far end. I stretch my legs and let my bare feet rest against the warmth of his thigh. His fingers massage my toes. Little shivers of pleasure dance up and down my spine.

"Come back with me, Cat."

"Lorenzo, we've had this conversation too many times. Neither of us is ready to make the necessary concessions for us to be together."

His fingers continue to knead my feet. He knows just how much pressure to apply to the pad and arch until I'm almost hypnotized.

"What if I become a consultant for the FBI?"

"Is that a possibility? Do they need a mafia expert?"

He chuckles and says, "I could check it out."

"Lorenzo, both of us have to be happy wherever we are and with whatever we're doing. We're not inexperienced kids. Loving each other isn't all it takes to keep a relationship strong. Your work with the Guardia is all-consuming. In a few years, you'll be recalled to Rome and join the ranks of the higher echelon. If I move to Castello to be with you and then you move to Rome, the relationship will fall apart."

"I've already told you I won't move to Rome. I'd resign first."

"Really, you'd give up a job you love? Would you retire? You're too young! What would you do?"

He doesn't answer, so I continue, "Sure, I could close my business, particularly since Al wants to buy me out—or at least he wants me to merge my business with his."

"Cat, he wants you to do more than merge your business with his. He's thinking in terms of merging your lives. Is that what you want?"

"Lorenzo, this conversation is about you and me, or am I wrong?"

He flushes and says, "You're right. I interrupted."

Morning sounds of gurgling marsh, rushing river, swaying trees, buzzing insects, and chirping birdsong surround us. It's such a peaceful scene—conflicting with the turmoil in my heart.

"I could sell my business to Cassie and move to Castello. But what would I do? After all these years, I've finally found my passion. I've created a niche for myself in this area. I love what I do. I love this place. We both know that an American caterer in Italy would be a joke. Ninety-five percent of Italians are weaned on making pasta."

His hands massage my ankles, "What about Giorgione's restaurant? You know he'd offer you a job."

"I've thought about it, but after working in a restaurant under someone else's tutelage, I want to be my own boss, and catering is what I love. Now, I have Diana to consider. She's in my charge until she finishes high school. I can't let her down. Plus, I have events on my calendar scheduled well into next year. It would take a lot of thought and planning for me even to consider a move. Lorenzo, why does it have to be me who gives up everything?"

"Why do you say that?"

"Well, one of us has to make a sacrifice. Right now, I have the best of both worlds. I have a job and a wonderful group of friends. Yes, I love Italy. It's been my second home for as long as I can remember. But my love for the Lowcountry is just as strong. Anytime I want, I can hop on a plane to Italy and be in Castello del Mare with you."

"But that's not a permanent solution. You've already said you don't want a part-time arrangement. So where does that leave us?"

"Nowhere," I respond. "But that's not all I have to think about."

"What are you talking about?"

"Riccardo."

"Cat, you can't live your life in fear."

"What do you expect me to do? Sooner or later, he's going to be released from prison or extradited to Albania. Do you really think he won't come after me? You were at the trial. I read the transcript. He spent a lot of time blaming me for Carlo's death. He's a vengeful man. He's alive, Lorenzo. As long as he is, I'm not safe in Italy—maybe I'm not safe here either."

"You are safe. It's my business to make sure you're safe. He received the maximum sentence and will be in prison for at least ten years. He's in my sights. I'm fully aware of everything that's going on with him. You'll be the first to know if anything changes."

"What about his friends on the outside? Don't you think they know exactly where I am and what I'm doing?"

"I don't, Cat. Carlo was *il padrone* not Riccardo. If Carlo had survived, you'd have reason to be frightened. Riccardo doesn't have the contacts or the power that Carlo did."

He shifts toward me, moves my feet into his lap, and roughly rubs my calves.

"Ouch!"

"Sorry. You have to believe me when I say you're safe. Plus, Cassie tells me your friend Chuck has been teaching you Krav Maga. I'd say Riccardo doesn't stand a chance."

I arch an eyebrow. Lorenzo chuckles.

"Cat, I want us to be together. Don't you think it's time?"

"Yes, it's what I want too, but so far, we haven't come up with a solution that works for both of us. Let's see what else we can think of during our separation. I'll be in Castello in September. We'll discuss it then. Maybe some miracle will occur, and the solution will be clear-cut for us."

He leans toward me and says so softly I almost don't hear, "Come to Italy in August. You know August is when I spend time in Leuca. We could be together for two months instead of one."

My heartbeat accelerates. August won't happen. Two years ago in New York, I made a promise to Stella—a promise I plan to keep. She had given me the packet with all our plans. It was supposed to have been the grand celebration of our lives, our friendship, and our fortieth birthdays. She booked a villa at Casali di Casole Resort near Lajatico for a week-long stay. Included in the packet are two executive tickets for the once-a-year event. It's the only time Andrea Bocelli holds a concert on his farm in Tuscany. Stella had said so breezily, "There's a limo picking us up for the executive cocktail hour before the concert, and we have backstage tickets for after the concert. We'll meet the maestro."

That's so like Stella to keep on giving even after her death.

My flight is booked. Would Lorenzo understand why I have to make this journey? I don't think so. I already know he would try to talk me out of going, or even worse, he'd want to go with me. This is a personal pilgrimage. It's one I have to make alone before I can let go of Stella. Even now, the memories of her are vague and fuzzy. They hover somewhere out in the universe. One day, I fear they will be lost to me. This is the last journey Stella and I will make. I will fulfill her last wish.

"Sorry, Lorenzo," I say, turning my hopefully innocent face toward him. "I can't. My schedule is already overbooked for August. I simply can't get away."

He shakes his head in disappointment.

"You could change your plans."

"No, Lorenzo. I've made commitments. I have to keep them."

His hands release my ankles and slide up my legs. With a gentle jerk, he pulls me toward him.

"You'll be late," I say.

"There's always another flight," he responds as the swing bed rocks in the early morning glow. Sunlight streams across the marshes and marches through the massive oaks. But we are oblivious. We are lost in our own magic.

Yes, there's always another flight.

Acknowledgments

W hen I started writing the Cat Gabbiano Mystery Series, I had no idea what shape they would take or what stories would be told. All I knew was the idea for a mystery originated before I wrote my first book, *Solo in Salento*.

It was during a stay in the region of Puglia (Italy) that I experienced a mysterious connection to the place, and the seed for writing a mystery came to life. However, thinking about what I might write and what I actually did were two different things. Instead of a mystery, my first book was a memoir. But as soon as I wrote The End on the memoir I begin writing the mystery.

Book #1 in the Cat Gabbiano Mystery Series, *The Red Starfish,* was released in October 2023. In *Solo in Salento,* I write about the red starfish necklace I bought in Otranto, Italy. That necklace became the storyline. It danced around in my head and landed on paper along with the secondary theme of the ocean's ecology and how badly we humans are trashing it. I wanted to introduce readers to the beautiful and brutal coast of the Adriatic Sea.

Book #2 *Moringa ~ The Tree of Life* came to me because of the Tree of Life mosaic floor in the Basilica Cattedrale Santa Maria d'Annunziata in Otranto, Italy—also found in *Solo in Salento*. The idea of the Moringa Project came from a *New York Times* article I read. The underlying purpose of Moringa focuses on abuse, incest, and human trafficking. We cannot be silent on these issues. There is no reason for human trafficking or world hunger—yet it is an ongoing problem.

Book #3, *One Note Murders* (working title), is in its incubation stage. It will have something to do with music, which also originates from *Solo in Salento* from a chapter called Night Music. I don't have a secondary theme yet, but eventually, it will be revealed to me.

Donna Keel Armer

There is no rhyme or reason to my writing. The stories are just there, pouring out as my fingers hover over the keyboard. The words were always there, but they could not be freed until the day I found my voice. That solo time in Otranto, Italy, unleashed the magical world of words that had languished in my heart for years. Now, they dance across each page I write, and they fill my life with great joy.

This is my life now. I thank the people of both Southern Italy and the South Carolina Lowcountry for granting me a peek into their secrets—the *chiaroscuro*—both the light and the shadowy parts of life.

Perhaps the biggest change for me in 2022 came when I met Stephanie Larkin of Red Penguin Books. The publishing part of writing became magical and sweet instead of something I dreaded. Stephanie, thank you and your team (particularly Denise Reichert) for the amazing support you offered me. Working with you has been such a positive experience.

As always, it's the generous spirits of my writing community who make all of this possible. *The Sea Island Spirit Writers* are acknowledged in every book because they always have my back. They are my "writerly" sisters and the strong women in my life. I've been part of the group since 2016. Thank you, Katherine, Ginny, Ellen, Susan, and Jackie—you were there that first evening and have guided me through all of my writing angst. Over the years, the group has changed and flowed with other amazing women who offered their words of wisdom: Karen, Kim, Carolyn, June, Emily and those newly added: Erin, Cookie, Michelle, and Beth. Each of you stepped into the circle with me and gave me the gift of friendship, encouragement and support.

My Beta Readers are a huge part of my writing community: Alexis Bomar, Gail Greene, Jeff Baker, and Mary Flynn—thank you for pushing me to be better, go deeper, see more, and write as my heart dictates—*grazie mille.*

The Pat Conroy Literary Center, with Jonathan Haupt at the helm, is a safe haven for all writers, students, readers, teachers, librarians, citizens against book bans, tourists and locals, DAYLO, and all who seek to understand and support the necessity for the written word to continue generation after generation. Pat's far-reaching philosophy about the wretchedness and goodness of life offers us hope. I am so fortunate to be part of this inclusive community.

And it was through my role as docent at the Literary Center that I met Tracey Tannenbaum and Peter Woolrich. Several years ago they were visiting from England and I was their tour guide. We have remained friends and Tracey is now my editor. She's the best one I've ever had. I was floundering with *Moringa* until her suggestions turned me in the right direction.

Crucial to any book is the final, final proofing. BrendaGael Beasley-Forrest and Susan Dickey did the fine-tooth comb on Moringa. Thank you my friends for the huge amount of time you invested so that Book #2 is as error-free as possible.

This year, we lost a dear friend, Mihai Radulescu, in our Pat Conroy Literary community. Mihai, along with his wife, Marly Rusoff and Pat's wife, Cassandra King, created the Pat Conroy Literary Center. Although Mihai wasn't well, he attended my book launch for *The Red Starfish*. I am grateful for this gift he gave me. He was everyone's best friend. He made us question the obvious and appreciate our freedoms. And one night, when we were gathered around the table, he shared one of his favorite tunes—Seven Spanish Angels. It hums in my mind every day. Mihai, the last king of Romania, you are well-loved and missed.

And to all my friends, American and Italian, thank you for your love and support and for your patience in answering questions and listening endlessly to my "book/write" conversations.

To readers everywhere who read to escape to unknown lands, venues, and adventures through imagination, words, music, movies, art, and all forms of creativity—thank you for joining me on this journey with Cat and these characters who live in the Lowcountry of South Carolina and the small coastal villages of Puglia, Italy. Thank you for reading and supporting writers and other artists.

And Ray, you are the one steadfast person in my life—always

supporting, encouraging, and loving me every step of the way. Forty-one years—we are still renewing our annual contract. *Sei mio cuore....*

You Have Become A Forest

One day, when you wake up, you will find that you've
   become a forest.
You've grown roots and found strength in them that no
   one thought you had.
You have become stronger and more beautiful, full of
   life-giving qualities.
You have learned to take all the negativity around you
   and turn it into oxygen for easy breathing.
A host of wild creatures live inside you, and you call them
   stories.
A variety of beautiful birds nest inside your mind, and
   you call them memories.
You have become an incredible self-sustaining thing of
   epic proportions.
And you should be so proud of yourself, of how far you
   have come from the seeds of who you used to be.

—Nikita Gill

Author Notes

This is a work of fiction. While I use some real names for places, most are figments of my imagination or a conglomerate of places. The FBI and the Guardia di Finanza have international connections; however, the scenes I created are pure fiction, as are all the characters. They are loosely based on a variety of personalities that have crossed paths with me, along with a collage of places I've lived or experienced.

The Moringa tree is miraculous and surely is the Tree of Life. We must continue to fight poverty and hunger and search for and develop unique ways of feeding the world.

https://www.phgmag.com/grow-miraculous-moringa-in-the-desert/ - https://desertmoringa.com

http://www.epitomejournals.com/VolumeArticles/FullText PDF/230_Research_Paper.pdf

In 5000-year-old Vedic records from India, Moringa Oleifera and its healing properties are documented for the first time. The plant obtained a high significance and was included in the traditional Indian medicine, the Ayurveda. The different parts of the tree...are said to alleviate and cure 300 diseases. Even nowadays, Moringa is still utilized in holistic pathology and dietetics teachings and steadily gains recognition from modern, academic medicine.

https://www.ncbi.nlm.nih.gov/pmc/articles/PMC5958191/

Human trafficking, also known as modern-day slavery, is alive and well in the United States. Every year, millions of people in the world, including in the U.S., are bought and sold for forced labor or sexual exploitation. It can happen to any demographic, gender, race or nationality.

https://deliverfund.org/

https://www.archives.gov/research/investigations/fbi/classifica tions/031-white-slave-traffic.html

https://sclchttf.wixsite.com/website ～ Lowcountry Human Trafficking Task Force

https://www.scag.gov/human-trafficking/

The marshes of the Lowcountry are crucial to our ecosystem. For those of us who make our homes in the low-lying areas on the East Coast, it is our job to become stewards of these beautiful coastal areas, to preserve and protect them so that they will always be here for every generation to enjoy. www.saltmarshguide.org

I had never heard of Krav Maga until my writerly friend Karen Warner Schueler wrote about it in one of her wonderful stories. Since I didn't have a clue what it was about, I contacted Chuck Elias one of our local entre-preneurs who patiently explained Krav Maga. I am and will always be a

complete novice. Chuck owns and operates Club Karate. He received his 1st Degree Chuck Norris System Black Belt in 1983. In 1988, he opened Club Karate in Port Royal, SC. In 1998, he quit his day job to pursue his passion for teaching martial arts full-time. Master Elias, currently a 9th-degree blackbelt, serves on the Region 7 Board and is the Tournament Director. He is also a coach for Chuck Norris's *Team Chun Kuk Do*.

http://www.clubkaratellc.com and

http://www.clubkaratellc.com/karv-maga-force

Preview

One Note Murders

Cat

A younger face of Caterina Maria Lucia Gabbiano stares back from my Italian passport. I check the expiration dates on both of passports—American and Italian. All those years ago, Stella and I were the only kids in our class with dual citizenship. Even at that young age Stella fed off the celebrity.

Now Stella is gone from my life. More than two years have passed since that last fateful time in New York. We never knew it would be our last time together. I haven't returned to Italy since Stella was murdered. I want to, but it isn't that easy.

All I have left now are the images of us as kids splashing in the Adriatic Sea and even those have grown dim. Since I returned to the Lowcountry, her face only comes to me from a watery grave. My heart and my fears have grown heavier.

I lift the flaming red Dolce & Gabbana gown from the box that just arrived from Italy. With tenderness, I touch the elaborately twisted waist and godet hem. The neckline plunges even lower than the black silk Versace dress Stella bought me for that astounding gala at the Metropolitan Museum of Art. The event honored Stella's work as an international actress. I was so proud to be there, to celebrate her accomplishments. Now, my beautiful friend Stella is only a fading memory. Closing my eyes, I monitor my breathing—in, out, in, out. It steadies me. The internal trembling stops.

I press the dress against my body and stand in front of the full length mirror. The silky material flares revealing the center-front slit. Sequins twinkle in the gathering twilight and once more she and I are standing arm in arm. The magic of that moment surrounds us. Stella strikingly gorgeous in red with the magnificent starfish necklace at her throat and me, looking like a proper starlet in the sleek black designer gown. I remember the exact moment Stella removed the starfish necklace and clasped it around my throat. She had leaned toward me and whispered, "One day it will be yours."

She smiled, as only Stella can smile and gave me a hug and said, "When that day comes, I hope you'll wear it and remember me. Promise me you will."

Tears for Stella leak from the corners of my eyes. They no longer flow or bring on shudders or painful sobs so deep they rack my body. My sorrows, like my memories, have softened into the haziness of long ago summers spent together, shared secrets, open wounds, and a friendship bordering between love and hate. While Stella will never stray too far from my thoughts, the hard edges have been tempered by time and replaced with a sweet bitterness that comes with ambiguous loss.

The red dress in all its glitz and glitter is carefully folded. I tuck it into the last empty space in my already packed-to-capacity luggage. Next to my suitcase is the last letter Stella wrote to me. There's hardly a need for me to read the creased and tear-stained words, as they are forever embedded in my mind...

I was a fool. I'm so sorry for all the times I let you down. I never meant to hurt you. I hope you'll stay and fight in my place. But if you believe your life is in danger, then Go Home Now! Whether you stay or go, live your life fully and beautifully for both of us.

I love you, my forever friend,
Stella

The packing is finished. I close luggage. I'm returning to Italy. But am I ready? Can I honor Stella's last request?

Chapter 1

Every one of her days hums with the possibility
that she might be doing it wrong ～
Karen Thompson Walker, *The Dreamers*

For the tenth time I check my purse. The packet containing the tickets to the concert is still there along with the itinerary and the reservation at Casale Santa Lucia. As I've done many times since Stella handed me the large envelope, I examine each item of the trip she planned for us, this once-in-a-lifetime trip to Lajatico, Italy to attend an Andrea Bocelli concert. There are plane tickets and reservations at a plush resort and multiple sets of tickets for the executive cocktail party, the concert, and the backstage event to meet the Maestro. It's all there in the packet—those plans of Stella's and mine. But Stella isn't here. These plans mean nothing.

After she presented me with the packet, my curiosity won out and I Googled the accommodations and discovered that Casali di Casole is an over-the-top luxurious resort. Scrolling through the photos, I was in awe of the views over the Tuscany hills, the private infinity pool, the cool greens and creams of the decor. A slow tear had journeyed down my cheek when I realized Stella had booked the villa named Santa Lucia. My given name Caterina Maria Lucia Gabbiano has a long history in my family DNA. Stella must have remembered, or at least I like to believe she had.

I've sorted through the folder so many times that the edges are frayed. Stella's assistant or used-to-be assistant covered every detail with me numerous times. Still I question myself. Why do this? Why put myself through the agony, the reminder that Stella is gone. The

345

ʤwer is always the same—-Stella would want me to follow through with our plans. She would do this for me.

Shoving the packet back in my purse, I check to make sure the blue velvet jewelry boxes are still there before I browse the menu and check out the crowded restaurant and lounge at the Hilton Airport in Rome. It's packed with Americans—shorts, flip-flops, baseball caps, and captioned T-shirts—all smack American. Throw in the loud "I'm from the USA" attitude, and you'd think you were in the middle of Times Square.

I'm not hungry so I opt to sit in the raised cocktail lounge that overlooks the restaurant. At eight in the evening every table is occupied in both areas. Several men have filed by the vacant chair at my table with questioning eyes. One being so crass as to place his hand on the chair and start to sit down. Each time I made it clear there's no room for a table mate.

The chips, peanuts and pretzel mixture in a souvenir container are so American. I tell myself I booked here because it's an old habit and a hard one to break. This is the hotel where Stella and I often met to reconnect and together fly on to Brindisi where her chauffeur would be waiting at the airport to whisk us to Castello del Mare.

Somehow with Stella by my side this place seemed okay. Now I find myself sneering at the boisterous voices and overly contrived outfits that scream a desire to look 20-30 years younger than the wearer actually is—along with the face lifts, botox injections, and heavy eye makeup that rob women of their natural beauty. The men are no better with their hair transplants or combovers, loafers without socks or sneakers without laces, and the ever present aviator sunglasses.

A bleached blonde sips a martini and clings to her decades younger escort. A table of five young women are intent on a game of Balderdash. Their boisterous laughter fosters attention, apparently something they're seeking. A guy seated at the bar jiggles his right leg to some known-only-to-him tune. Flight crews weary and ladened with luggage make their way to the back room where a round-the-clock buffet nourishes their bodies if not their souls.

The crisp Rosato I'm sipping is crisp with hints of strawberries and earth. Absently, I nibble on a pretzel while surveying the unruly crowd. For a brief moment my view of the restaurant is blocked when the waitress leans in to ask if I would like another glass of wine or something to eat. As she reaches across the table for my empty glass, a slight movement behind her catches my attention. For a second my eyes connect with the beady black eyes of a man seated in the restaurant.

There is instant recognition for both of us. His eyes intentionally stay locked with mine. I half rise from my chair as the waitress straightens up blocking the view. The eye contact is broken.

"Madame do you wish anything else?"

"No," I murmur as I crane my head to look around. But it's too late.

She sights and frowns before moving. I stare at the empty table where the man had been seated.

Grabbing my purse, I race out of the restaurant with the waitress trailing behind calling, "Madame, madame, you haven't paid your bill."

The lobby is empty except for the reception desk. I rush from corridor to corridor as people curiously glance my way. The poor waitress with flushed face catches up with me and waves a ticket in my face. "Madame, please sign. I will lose my job."

Leaning against the wall to stop the spinning, I focus on her trembling lips and a single tear winding its way slowly down her face.

"*Mi dispiace*—I'm so sorry."

I scribble my room number, signature and hand her a ten euro bill.

"Oh madame, it is too much."

"No," I respond. "It's not enough."

She nods rapidly and bolts away from me. The wall supports me as I allow the evil, sullen face of Riccardo to reenter my mind. He was at that table. I'm sure. It means only one thing. He's out of prison. Yet I hesitate. My mind has let me down before. Although a few months have passed since the last flashback, being here could resurrect old fears. It could be jet lag or simply that I'm in Italy again and the old images are surfacing. Or, maybe it wasn't him.

Two years ago the nightmare began. Two years since Stella was murdered. Two years since I was kidnapped and nearly killed. Two lousy years. Carlo was dead. I saw Gino shoot him. Riccardo had been sentenced to a minimum of ten years.

It had been a while since Lorenzo and I last spoke, but he assured me Riccardo was still in prison and that no court order had been filed to extradite him to Albania. Had something changed? But Lorenzo would call me. He'd promised.

Only Cassie and Dr. Ginny know I'm here, and they were sworn to secrecy. If I call Lorenzo and tell him I saw Riccardo, he'll want to know why I'm in Italy, and why I didn't let him know. He'll be furious and insist on coming to my aid and providing security whether or not I want it. And he'll do his best to stop me from attending the concert. Or, even worse, he'll insist on going with me.

Even my trusted friend Maria doesn't know I'm here. I asked her to ship Stella's gown to me in South Carolina so I could pack it and bring it with me. It would have been less of a hassle to stop by the villa and pick it up along with my car, but Maria would have joined Lorenzo in insisting I not attend the concert. This pilgrimage was difficult enough without all these people trying to put roadblocks in tmyway.

Dr. Ginny declared me fit to travel. The nightmares and blackouts rarely occur. She encouraged me to attend the concert that Stella and I had planned before her death. She said it would be an opportunity for me to honor Stella as well as let go of painful memories. She said I was ready. But am I?

Pushing away from the wall, I trudge back to the lounge. The bartender sneers and turns away. It's clear the waitress reported my attempt to leave without paying the bill. He chats with every person sitting at the bar before arriving to take my order.

"I'd like a Rosato to take to my room, *per favore.*"

He shrugs and takes his sweet time pouring a simple glass of wine. I glare at each person in the restaurant and lounge. My eyes linger on each face as I search for anyone who has the slightest resemblance to Riccardo. It's destructive for me to keep thinking that every shadow is a potential murderer, and I'm a potential victim.

Did I really see Riccardo is the question I have to address. My imagination continues to conjure up ominous figures threatening to kill me. They turn up no matter where I am. Perhaps returning to Italy isn't the best thing for my health? Maybe I'm not ready.

The table where I thought I saw Riccardo is now occupied by a couple. The man's arm is in a sling. The woman's scrunched up expression indicate he's in big trouble. Red splotches appear on his face as she ratchets up the decibel level of her voice. The conversation drifts across the restaurant and lounge.

"You idiot. You've spoiled our vacation. A trip of a lifetime you said. Humph!"

He hangs his head and doesn't respond.

I turn back as the bartender slides the bill across the bar. He holds onto the glass of wine until after I sign the tab. The wine slushes over the rim when my shaking hand grabs the stem. I turn away and rush to the bank of elevators and the safety of my room.

About the Author

Donna Keel Armer is the author of *Solo in Salento: A Memoir* which has been translated into Italian as *Un'americana in Salento*. She recently completed a book tour of Southern Italy. She's a photojournalist and has published magazine and anthology articles with accompanying photographs on travel, food and wine, home and garden and various other topics. When she's on the road, she writes a private travelogue. Contact her at donnakeelarmer@gmail.com to be added to the list. She graduated with honors from Mississippi University for Women with a double major in psychology and social sciences and graduate studies in theology. Her first job during high school was a gofer for a furniture company and her last position before turning to writing was president of the hospitality business owned by Donna and her husband Ray. She's a former board member of Friends of the Library, a member of Sea Island Spirit Writers, and a docent at the Pat Conroy Literary Center. Donna and Ray split their time between their forever home in the South Carolina Lowcountry and their beloved Italy. Follow Donna on https://www.facebook.com/donna.k.armer/ or www.donnaarmer.com.

Printed in the USA
CPSIA information can be obtained
at www.ICGtesting.com
JSHW021941030624
64165JS00001B/4